HOPES AND DREAMS, FORTUNES AND FUTURES HANG IN THE BALANCE AS THE CLOUDS OF WAR FIX THE FATE OF THE LONE STAR REPUBLIC . . .

Montrose Daventry is the young, violet-eyed beauty whose tomboy spirit fuels her hatred for Mason Regrett's traitorous mission—even as she yearns for his lessons in loving . . .

Mason Regrett is the arrogant rancher who is as determined to see Texas become part of the United States as he is to see the lovely Montrose become his willing partner in bed.

Richard Daventry is the aristocratic plantation lord who vows that the Republic will stand—*especially* if it means the ruin of the Regretts.

Louise Warren Lynchley is a scheming vision of spun sugar whose venomous plan to snare Richard as her husband could prove disastrous to both of these feuding Texas families.

NO GREATER LOVE

"Rich in Texas lore, rich in Texas love, *NO GREATER LOVE* is a lusty, spellbinding read."—Parris Afton Bonds, author of *SNOW AND ICE*

No Greater Love

Alison Irving

ST. MARTIN'S PAPERBACKS

NO GREATER LOVE

Copyright © 1991 by Alison Irving.

Cover art by Leslie Pellegrino.

ISBN: 0-312-92463-1

Printed in the United States of America

St. Martin's Paperbacks edition/April 1991

10 9 8 7 6 5 4 3 2 1

For Mother and Dad with love.

Chapter 1

It was a bitterly cold day in February 1845 in Washington. The weather made itself felt in the small, poorly constructed Senate Chamber. There were only four tiers of seats for the sixty members, who sat clothed in their heavy coats. Some even had blankets pinned at their throats. All wore their hats despite two smoky Franklin stoves that were fed with hickory wood.

Richard Daventry and his daughter, Montrose, stood on the circular gallery for spectators that extended all around the room and over the presiding officer's chair. The air in the room was stale and fetid as always in winter. Montrose Daventry's small, pert nose wrinkled briefly in distaste and she drew her fur-lined, hooded cape close against the chill. Richard Daventry, in his black greatcoat, lifted his straight patrician nose a little higher. His gray eyes, intense with dislike, fastened on Mason Regrett as he strode to the podium after being welcomed by Senator Winslow of South Carolina.

Regrett was an arresting figure in a tailored black broadcloth suit and snowy cravat. He stood six feet three and his nose, arched like a hawk's, gave his face a predatory but attractive arrogance.

Monty, as Montrose Daventry preferred to be called, felt a familiar unsettled sensation as she observed the lean, broad-shouldered man step up on the podium. She could feel her father's visceral animosity toward Regrett. Both her father and their neighbor beside them, George Huntleigh Cavenal, had attended for the sole purpose of hearing what this man would say to the Senate of the United States. Reluctantly, she acknowledged her own mixed feelings of curiosity and attraction to Regrett. A slight murmur arose around the silent three as Regrett began to speak.

"My friends—and I would like to call you my fellow countrymen—I appreciate Senator Winslow's arranging for me to speak to you once more before the vote on annexation comes up again. I know you are well briefed on the Republic of Texas, but I hope to refresh your memory." He smiled then, the completely disarming and winning smile that was so much a part of him.

It carried Monty back to the day she had first laid eyes on him, when he rode up to the front of the big, redbrick house on the Daventry farm and plantation. He and his brother, Julien, had just begun to make their ranch pay. He had dismounted and swept off his old, curled brimmed hat in a deep bow to her, as he held the lead on two fat longhorn cattle and a fine gelding her father had bought from him.

That had been over six years ago and she had been but eleven. Still, looking into his darkly tanned face and seeing his endearing white smile that day, she had felt something deep within her quiver, turn over slowly, and settle warmly deep within. Her father and the Regretts had been friends then—before this miserable question of annexation reared its head so demandingly.

". . . and I wish to reassure you regarding the slavery question. I know the Anti-Slavery Society has said 'All who would sympathize with that pseudo-republic hate liberty and would dethrone God!' My friends, ninety percent of

Texans are neither slaves nor slave owners and you know our former President Sam Houston is no friend of that peculiar institution." Regrett's deep resonant voice was persuasive. "I, like most Texans, own no slaves and what little slavery there is in the republic is in the deep south. Sympathy for it throughout the land is fading. It is only a matter of time until those who are slaves will be freed—the trend is set."

His black eyes swept the gallery, lingering for a moment on Monty. Her pulse quickened. To her annoyance, her color rose hotly and his next words slipped by her.

Daventry scowled. He was passionately dedicated to seeing that the republic would eventually spread to the Californias and the Pacific Ocean. He had worked tirelessly to forestall annexation during the last two years. He and George Cavenal had powerful friends in Congress who had vowed to stand against it. Now Mason Regrett's deep baritone rang out over the cold room with warmth and conviction. Grudgingly, Daventry conceded to himself that the man was a persuasive scoundrel.

"There are those men in Texas now who would see the republic expand—as far as the Pacific Ocean. I am well acquainted with some of them." Regrett's black eyes were challenging now and they went once more to the gallery where Daventry, his daughter, and George Cavenal stood.

"By God," Daventry said in a husky whisper, "I think the bastard's going to *name* us!"

Monty sucked in her breath and her heart bumped alarmingly against her ribs.

"These men have influential friends," Regrett went on. "No, they have more. They have *relations* in Great Britain who are more than anxious to see Texas expand far beyond her present boundaries. These men maintain close ties—dangerous ties—to Britain. They and others are working even now to see that the United States does not secure the vast lands of the Republic of Texas, with all its riches in forests, game, and minerals."

"Damned blackguard!" Daventry swore under his breath and exchanged glances with George Cavenal, whose heavy golden brows were drawn over his imperious nose. Daventry made no pretense of guarding his language in his daughter's presence. He treated her as an equal most of the time, chastised her infrequently and spoiled her all of the time.

"These men and their friends are plotting against the interests of the United States as assiduously as traitors," Regrett continued. "And, as you know, the British claim the Oregon country. It is rumored they will aid the Republic of Texas in acquiring the land between it and the Californias. Further, it is rumored that England will be willing to negotiate Oregon, which, with the western lands, would make the Republic of Texas a nation larger than the United States. We cannot allow that to happen!"

Monty slanted a glance at her father. His face was white with fury, his features coldly controlled. He clenched his hand on the beautiful gold-headed cane that had been his great-grandfather's. As Regrett continued, Monty's mind slipped back to the Daventry farm and plantation and to that of George Huntleigh Cavenal as well as the Regrett ranch. Roughly, they were great triangles of land, each one abutting the other where the apex of the triangles met at Three Points Lake. It touched all three properties and each property contained thousands of acres.

When had bad blood come between them? It had really started with that unfortunate incident of the mare the Regrett brothers had sold her father. The mare had broken an ankle while her father rode her and had to be put down. Julien Regrett, Mason's younger brother, had been furious, and had accused Richard Daventry of criminal carelessness in the way he rode a horse. That had been the start of it.

Then over dinner at the Daventrys' one night, the question of annexation had come up, and before the meal was over, the men were shouting at each other. After that, the Regretts had come no more to dinner at the Daventry place.

Still, Richard Daventry continued to buy his beef and his horses from them, fuming as he did so, but knowing he must have them. He had quarreled with Monty as well, over her riding, with an escort as always, to the Regrett ranch to look at horses. Horses were a passion with Monty. She worked with them, rode them like a Valkyrie, loved each one in the Daventry stables. She loved the colts, mares, and stallions in the Regrett stables as well. It was one of the unhappy things about her Washington visit. She achingly missed her horses, and she missed wearing the comfortable, tightly fitted pants she loved for the freedom they gave her.

Her eyes went to George Cavenal, he who had never given up his British title. He leaned negligently against the gallery rail, tall and fair, his slender, superbly muscled body at ease. His hazel eyes met hers. He had been watching her. He did not often see Monty Daventry in women's clothes and her body was sensuously beautiful in royal-blue silk under the open fur-lined cloak. He smiled slowly and Monty, who had known him for years, returned the smile, unaware of the heat in his eyes.

"Some of you have doubts about annexation," Regrett was saying reasonably, "because you fear it would mean war with Mexico. My friends, I submit to you that Mexico is, in effect, still at war with the Republic of Texas and that eventually war with them is inevitable for you—as well as for us. We cannot allow that to stand in the way of the United States in its inexorable western expansion. To be territorially safe, the United States of America *must* extend from the Atlantic coast to the Pacific coast."

There was a sustained burst of applause in the chill, smoky room at these words. Richard Daventry's jaw was rigid with rage. Monty knew her father's quick hot temper, for she had inherited it. Now she glanced over at the young lord she had long ago nicknamed Cav when he had settled in Texas at the same time as the Daventrys. He turned on his booted heel. In passing, he brushed Monty's arm and murmured, "I don't have to listen to these insults," then strode from the gallery.

"Papa, let's leave," Monty whispered to her father. "You don't want to listen to any more of Mase's foolishness."

"No. I want to hear it all." His voice held barely leashed violence.

"But you know the American Congress isn't going to risk war with Mexico. They'll turn down annexation, just as they always have."

"Not with this smooth-talking blackguard oiling the wheels. Not with James Polk running for President and shouting for annexation—he's getting all the states up in arms about it."

"But Cav's already left. That shows you how little he thinks of this speech." She glanced at the men and women near them who were spectators. All were obviously caught up in Regrett's ringing words.

"Cav has estates in England. He hasn't the motives I have for seeing our republic become a great nation. I'll be as landed and powerful as my father someday."

Monty fell silent. Her father was the third son of Lord Arthur Milford Daventry in England and born to his second wife at that. Primogeniture had kept Richard from inheriting any land in England, but Lord Daventry had been more than generous with his youngest son and his second wife at his death. Her father now had a healthy income from the estates owned by his older brothers. Monty's mother, Elizabeth Montrose, who died of a fever when Monty was not quite three, had been of noble birth. Monty herself had been born in her grandfather's great manor house in England, but she felt no loyalty to England. She loved the land she lived in. Even now, she felt the restlessness to return home.

Her father had promised to let her return home by steamer after the ball at the British Embassy this weekend of the fifteenth of February. She turned her mind once more to the man on the podium who disturbed and confused her.

"In closing," he was saying, "I would point out the potential wealth the United States would be gaining. There are riches in the republic that are undreamed of now, but future generations will realize their fruits. More than one hundred thousand Americans *long* to join with you once more. I urge you to consider all these things when the question of annexation of the Republic of Texas is put before you one last time." Regrett bowed gracefully and stepped down.

The applause following his speech was spontaneous and it was apparent that Regrett had made telling points, stirred the Senators, and more, he had fueled the fear of Great Britain moving with Texas to settle the rest of the western portion of the continent. This was certain to be a deciding factor in the upcoming presidential election.

As Mason Regrett left the podium, his gaze went once more to the gallery and fastened on Richard Daventry and his daughter. His eyes were twinkling with malicious humor and his sudden smile at them was mocking before he walked among the Senators and began shaking hands.

Monty had heard enough of the speech, despite her efforts to ignore it, to know that his words carried the ring of truth. She also knew that her father's hope for the future was gravely threatened and she felt a quick dart of hot anger at Regrett.

She took her father's arm, feeling the heavy muscles rigid with suppressed rage as both of them smiled at friends and acquaintances.

Captain Charles Elliot, the British chargé d'affaires in the Republic of Texas, did not smile as he shook Richard

Daventry's hand on the steps to the Senate Chamber. He was older than her father. Forty, at least. But they had been good friends for a long time, their friendship having begun at least twenty years ago in London when her father had been no more than sixteen or seventeen.

"Your neighbor in the republic is a real menace to our plans for the future, Richard," Elliot said dryly.

"He's a fool!"

"But a persuasive fool. I've heard talk about him—fought beside Sam Houston at San Jacinto—received most of the big grant of land next to yours and Cavenal's for it." Elliot fell into step beside them as they set forth on the frozen muddy path from the building. "Miss Monty, let me take your arm."

Monty smiled at him. She had always liked this man with the kindly and twinkling brown eyes and dark hair. He had been in the big Daventry home in Texas twice since he came from England, and her grandmother, Lady Abigail Daventry, always enjoyed talking to him.

Richard Daventry's mother, at fifty-eight, was statuesque and regal, but with a heart so kind, a nature so thoughtful of others that everyone on the place called her Miss Abby. Monty had missed her during the two months she had been gone.

Even the prospect of attending the British Embassy ball failed to stem her impatience. And it would take another month to make the long steamer trip to Galveston.

The afternoon sky was overcast and it was snowing heavily. The wind was rising and it struck them sharply as they merged with others leaving the Senate building.

"We're all well acquainted with Regrett's participation in the fight to free Texas," Daventry was saying impatiently. "It's his friendship with Houston that's brought him here now."

"Is there no way we can persuade him to take our side?"

Elliot asked, moving to take Monty's arm and brace her against the wind as they walked.

"I have tried," Daventry said grimly. "Told him he'd have more land, more cattle—the best of English stock shipped over here for breeding purposes with his horses and cattle." His voice grew bitter. "Like Houston, he works for it openly as well as deviously. And now—something I never suspected—I find the bloody Frenchman's an orator!"

"Papa!" Monty spoke without thought. "You know he's not a Frenchman!"

"His father and mother were French. He's from Louisiana, and with that name, he has to be French."

"His people came to New Orleans nearly two hundred years ago. Grandpa Daventry's mother was Irish—does that make you an Irishman?"

"Are you defending the man, my dear? Are you so interested in him?"

"I'm not interested at all! I dislike him as much as you do!"

"Well," Elliot said easily, "whatever the man's antecedents, he's a damned good speaker." Then halting, he added, "I'll have to leave you here, as I'm going to the White House. Our ambassador's arranged a talk with President Tyler for me—not that it will do any good. The Americans always expect the worst of us. A pity you threw in your lot over here, Richard," he finished, laughter in the words. They paused, the snow swirling about them.

"Good afternoon, Captain Elliot," Monty said, her soft red mouth curving in a smile. "I'll see you at the ball this weekend."

"Incidentally, there's a young widow visiting Washington from Charleston and she's coming to the ball. I want you to meet her, Richard," Elliot said mischievously.

"My God, Charles," Daventry said, groaning, "my mother's been trying to marry me off for years. I hope you aren't going to begin."

"No, no! I only want to bring a little cheer into this celibate life of yours, Richard!"

"You forget Rebecca's house in Victoria, Charles." Richard laughed dryly. Monty looked at him sharply. *She had heard about Rebecca's house!*

"Ah, but this lady's almost as beautiful as your daughter, and there's an intriguing amount of scandal about her."

"Scandal?"

"Just enough to make you want to protect her!" Lifting his tall beaver hat, he bowed to them. "Good afternoon, Miss Monty. I'll see you both at the ball, if not before."

He was soon lost to sight among the thinning crowd. Monty drew her cloak close about her full skirts, her little boots crunching in the dirty frozen path beside her father's.

"Now, my little lady, what's this about Regrett not being a Frenchman?" When she made no answer, he took her hand from his arm and caught her elbow. "Answer me, Monty! Have you been seeing the man?"

"Of course!" she blazed. "You know well enough that I go with Big Miguel to the Regrett ranch to see his new horses and to see *my* horses being trained there—why, you take me there, Pa!"

"And I'm with you every minute of the time—or Big Miguel is. You haven't time for any personal talk with the likes of him!"

"You know yourself he was orphaned years ago when the fever was so bad in New Orleans—and he left his little brother with relatives when he came to Texas in 1835! He's told you all about himself!" She looked rebelliously at her father in the half-light. Snow stuck to his dark winged brows under the tall hat and to the dark lashes around his stormy gray eyes. She thought him very old at thirty-six. Still, the anger in his eyes was as young as her own.

"I'll not have you defending him, by God! If I have to stop your going to the Regrett ranch—"

"Pa!" She was stricken. "You wouldn't do *that!* You know it's my Warlock I'm interested in! And the new mare Mase is raising for me—the one you promised me!" She added desperately, "All right—he's a Frenchman if you say so. Only please don't make me stop going to see the horses—"

"Ah, Monty—you needn't beg," Daventry said tiredly. "I've a quick temper." He wouldn't apologize, but he added more gently, "You can go see the horses with either me or Big Miguel—or even Young Miguel. God knows, I have to buy our beef and milk cows from him and he does raise the best horses this side of the Atlantic Ocean."

They made their way silently toward the hotel. Wind pushed harder at them and particles of snow stung Monty's smooth, fair face, whipping loose bright tendrils of hair from her fur hood. Her hands were growing cold despite the matching fur muff they snuggled in for warmth. They were still nearly half a mile from the hotel.

"Come, Monty, we'll stop in at the Indian Maid Tavern. I'll have a brandy and you can have hot chocolate. I know you must be freezing."

She looked up at the sign swinging in gusts of snow. There was an Indian girl painted beside the printed words. Through the small square panes of glass that formed a broad window, the delicious warmth of lighted lanterns glowed. People sat drinking, talking, and laughing.

Daventry pushed open the heavy wooden door and they were immediately enticed by the fragrance of steaming coffee threaded with the scent of roasting meats.

When they stepped out of the tavern an hour later, the wind was still blowing but the snow had ceased. Underfoot, the frozen ground crunched, but the sky was clearing. It was late afternoon, however, and despite the brightening sky, it would soon be dark. Washington would be its usual quagmire when the freezing weather broke.

The last person Daventry expected—or wanted to see—was the one approaching them as they stepped out. Mason Regrett. His greatcoat flared as he strode toward them. His quick smile was full of mockery.

"Good afternoon, neighbors. I saw you two with Cavenal in the gallery. You enjoyed my speech, I trust?"

"We *heard* it." Monty was succinct and cold.

"And you are a damned fool, Regrett," Daventry said. "The men who visualize the republic expanding to the Pacific are farseeing and you could be part of it!"

"They're the fools." Regrett's mouth tightened. "This continent should be one nation. It's the only way we'll ever be safe from European incursions and wars."

"You as good as called me and my friends traitors—"

"Aren't you traitors to the vast majority of our republic, Daventry?"

"I'm not the traitor—you are! I'm working to see that the republic is preserved—strengthened and expanded. You, sir, are betraying it far more than I by suggesting we give away our sovereignty!"

"You'd relinquish sovereignty fast enough if we were petitioning to become part of the British Empire." Regrett's eyes narrowed.

"That's another lie!" Daventry's voice roughened, and his face turned whiter with mounting fury. "You've been a guest in my house often enough—and you know that I gave up my English citizenship long ago. I am Texan."

"Ninety percent British. Ten percent Texan," Regrett drawled, his smile as cutting as the words. "And Cavenal's still every inch the British lord."

Speechless with rage, Daventry raised his gold-headed hickory cane and, with swift accuracy, brought it down on Regrett's head. It knocked his high-crowned beaver hat to the ground. Regrett ducked aside as the cane came down hard again on his shoulder.

Monty's hand had fallen from her father's arm as he first raised the stick. Her cape flew open now and her full skirts swirled as she reached up to pull him back.

"Papa! Don't—"

Blind with anger, Daventry brought the hickory cane high, throwing off her hand, and she slipped on the ice, falling to the ground in a small heap of fur and royal-blue silk.

Regrett caught the cane as it descended a fourth time, jerking Daventry forward as he wrenched it from his grasp. The younger man's tanned face darkened as he seized the stick and broke it fiercely over his upraised knee. Throwing the pieces aside, he bent over the fallen Monty.

A hoarse curse escaped Richard Daventry as he leaned to retrieve the pieces of the fine cane, unaware that his daughter had fallen.

Regrett slipped hard, strong hands under the cape and beneath her arms. The feel of them, warm against her flesh through the thin silk dress, was like a shot of raw whiskey, and she caught her breath. *That's the first time he's touched me since he hoisted me into the saddle when I was thirteen,* she thought.

Richard Daventry turned then and saw that Regrett had lifted his daughter to her feet and was brushing off bits of dirty snow that clung to the woolen fabric of her cloak.

"Monty! I didn't know you'd fallen! You—here! I'll help my daughter!" He dropped the broken cane and swept forward.

"I—I'm quite all right, Papa. It was only a little fall," she murmured as her father took her arm.

"You're a ruffian, Regrett, and yet you play the gallant to my daughter! That cane was my great-grandfather's and you've destroyed it!"

Brushing the snow from his beaver hat, Regrett warned, "If you ever try to cane me again, I can promise you I'll break more than the cane, Daventry."

"If you insult me again, Regrett, I'll use my fists."

"And I'll meet you halfway."

"Oh, please! If you fight I'll scream!" Monty cried. "This is a political matter—the United States Congress will decide it! Let them do it!"

Both men were still breathing hard, faces flushed, eyes bright with anger. Suddenly Regrett laughed aloud and clapped his beaver hat on his dark unruly hair.

"She's right, Daventry. I know you have powerful friends in the Senate and the House—and here in Washington. So have I. Neither of us will ever convince the other."

With that parting remark, he turned and went into the Indian Maid Tavern.

"Oh, Pa! All that was so unnecessary!"

"You weren't hurt by your fall, were you, Monty?" he asked, ignoring her comment.

"No, Papa."

She could not tell him that Mason Regrett had affected her so strangely. Warmth still surged in her veins as she remembered his hands under her arms, lifting her roughly at first, then more gently as he became aware of her soft, yielding flesh. It had been a fleeting moment, but it had fired her blood.

Loyalty to her father seeped into her. She disliked Mason Regrett as much as he did, no matter the unsettling weakness she knew at his touch. Her chin lifted and she drew in a deep breath of the cold, clean air.

And as they walked to the hotel, she silently recounted all the reasons why she shared her father's passionate desire to see the Republic of Texas grow into a mighty nation.

Chapter 2

On Saturday evening, Richard Daventry and his daughter rolled up before the British Embassy in a rented carriage. Built on the Virginia side of the land ceded by Maryland and Virginia for the capital, the embassy was a fine structure. It was made of red brick, imported from England, as was the exquisite furniture that filled it. The brick and most of the furnishings in Daventry's own house had been shipped into Texas from England, and he looked at the building before him with renewed appreciation.

Joseph, the tall, thin English butler, opened the door and greeted them by name, taking their wraps and ushering them into the salon. It was crowded with people, gaily clad, their finely designed and tailored clothes a paradox in the roughly built City of Washington in the Territory of Columbia.

Captain Charles Elliot, resplendent in his uniform, hastened to greet them. Henry Jameson, the ambassador from Britain, followed, and both men greeted the father and daughter warmly.

"You're as lovely as a Reynolds painting, Miss Monty!" Elliot exclaimed, taking her hand.

Monty wore a pale blue satin dress, with revealing décolletage. It set off her alluring little breasts, their arching white curves demurely revealed. The scent of fine French perfume her father had bought her on their arrival in Washington drifted on the air about her.

"You're very kind, Captain Elliot." Her quick smile was sunny.

"Richard, I'm so glad to see you both!" Jameson was saying cordially. "I glimpsed you and Lord Cavenal in the gallery as that bounder Regrett made his speech decrying you as traitors to the republic." He paused and added regretfully, "Lord Cavenal was so disgusted he set off for home the next day."

"I know," Daventry said somberly. "He called on me before he left."

"It's hard to believe, but Regrett is coming tonight with Senator Winslow of South Carolina who, as you know, is his sponsor here in Washington. In fact, there are two or three here I suspect who do not fancy the republic as a sovereign nation." He laughed dryly, adding, "But that's diplomacy."

Richard Daventry shrugged. "If Regrett and his ilk are here, I'll endure it, but there are times our English diplomacy tires me."

"Miss Monty," Elliot put in quickly, "a visitor from England, Anthony Pembroke, saw you in the Indian Maid Tavern with your father a few days ago and I've promised him an introduction." Elliot gestured to a smiling group of men and women.

Joseph, the butler, drew up before them with a glass of wine and snifter of brandy for Richard and his daughter, followed by a tall, smiling Englishman with a thatch of sandy hair.

"Miss Monty, I want to introduce Anthony Pembroke, the son of my good friend, Sir Thomas Pembroke of Westchester, England."

Laughter and conversation flowed about them as they moved to join the others in the room, but Monty's eyes followed her father, Jameson, and Elliot as they joined a circle of attentive men gathered about a lovely blond woman.

As Monty exchanged pleasantries with the admiring Pembroke, her attention was held by the exquisitely coifed woman with hair the color of gleaming wheat. She was small boned, a good two inches shorter than the tall, slender Monty, and her bare arms were delicately rounded. She was perhaps ten years older than Monty, but she was a beauty, and her smile at Richard Daventry as Elliot introduced him revealed small, perfect white teeth. Monty was struck by her father's stance.

Richard Daventry stood shocked into momentary silence as Elliot added, "And this is the delightful young widow from Charleston, South Carolina, I told you about, Richard —Mrs. Louise Warren Lynchley."

The beautiful woman before him bore a stunning resemblance to the wife Richard had loved so well and lost, so long ago—Lady Elizabeth Montrose of Montrose Manor in England.

"Captain Elliot has told me so much about you, Mr. Daventry, and your lovely home—so far away from Charleston." Mrs. Lynchley's voice was light as a silver bell as she put her hand on Richard's arm, subtly withdrawing from the admiring men around her, all her charm focused on the man so obviously struck by her.

Richard reached to place his empty brandy glass on a nearby table as a trio of musicians at the end of the salon began to play. He placed a suddenly possessive arm about her narrow waist and his voice was husky when he asked her to dance.

"I would adore dancing with you, Mr. Daventry." The bell-like voice was almost a whisper and thick gold lashes fluttered as blue eyes rose to meet his gray ones. Her small white hand tucked itself into his with appealing helplessness and Richard knew a surge of protectiveness he had not experienced since Monty was an orphaned baby of three.

Monty smiled mechanically at Pembroke but her eyes were still on her father as he swung the widow into the crowd of dancers. She had never seen such intense fascination reflected on Richard Daventry's countenance. A sharp, intuitive foreboding sent gooseflesh along the backs of her arms and she was suddenly half-frightened. It made her respond with undue fervor to Anthony Pembroke's extravagant gallantry.

"I would *love* to dance with you, Mr. Pembroke!" She smiled as he took her half-finished glass of wine and gave it to the ubiquitous Joseph. The two mingled with the dancers.

An hour and a half later, she had danced with half a dozen young men and exchanged merry conversation with even more. And her father had introduced her to Louise Warren Lynchley briefly, between dances. The widow was even more beautiful at closer range, but every nerve in Monty's body quivered with distrust. She could not rationalize the instant dislike she felt on meeting the exquisite little blonde.

Two huge sideboards in the large salon were laden with platters of thinly sliced turkey, ham, and roast beef, complemented by side dishes of legumes and condiments. There was a wide assortment of breads, tarts, and small cakes covered with sweet, smooth icings. The dancers stopped often to sample this feast on small china plates, which Joseph, supervising eight maids, replenished regularly.

Glasses of champagne, wines, brisk whiskies, and brandies were refilled as soon as they were consumed by the guests and merriment increased accordingly as the evening progressed.

Monty sat on one of the damask-covered rosewood sofas, half-finished plate in hand, listening to talk of politics from a senator from Maine on one side of her, and Pembroke on the other. As they talked, the orchestra, consisting of a cello, a violin, and a pianoforte, ended a selection.

Monty's apprehension increased. She could not reconcile herself to her father's attentions on the widow. She still followed the two from under lowered lashes. They stood close together and the widow's fan fluttered as she smiled up into Richard Daventry's eager eyes. Her father suddenly looked disturbingly younger than his thirty-six years and Monty's dislike of the widow deepened.

Charles Elliot approached, smiling, drink in hand. "You're alone! I can't understand that! Ah, I see Pembroke is getting you a glass of wine."

Monty turned vivid blue eyes on him and spoke abruptly. "Captain, you told my father there was an intriguing bit of scandal about Mrs. Lynchley. What is it?"

"It has to do with the death of her husband—supposedly a hunting accident. He was shot, but details about it are conflicting—and you know how ladies talk!" He spread his hands deprecatingly. "She has a younger orphaned cousin, her uncle's child, who was taken by her father to raise—that's she"—he gestured casually—"over there in that chair by herself."

Monty glanced swiftly at the girl sitting alone, a glass of wine in her hand. She was soberly clad in unattractive gray bombazine and her hair, which was as blond as her cousin's, was closely netted. Monty realized that she had not seen her dancing and had been only peripherally aware of her presence. Now her glance held unexpectedly, for the girl's pensive features were beautiful and her skin flawless, but she was so unattractively dressed that a careless glance would not reveal her astonishing beauty. She did not look much older than Monty herself.

"What's *her* name?"

"Faith Warren—I'll introduce you— Ah, Anthony! I see you are here to claim Monty's attention."

As Pembroke joined them, Monty asked one last question. "I suppose Mrs. Lynchley's husband left her well fixed?"

"According to the ladies, no." Elliot shrugged. "Mrs. Jameson says that Mr. Lynchley left most of his estate to his mother and sister." He laughed suddenly. "That's part of the intrigue. She has a small inheritance from her father. Barely enough to keep up a front. Mrs. Lynchley is executrix of her father's will and of her uncle's legacy to his daughter, Faith." He spread his hands once more, smiling. "That's really all I know about the two ladies." He bowed slightly and turned away.

The brass knocker at the front door sounded dimly among the guests as Monty smiled up at Pembroke. He handed her the small filled wine glass.

A sudden silence fell over the guests in the salon and Monty put the untouched glass on a side table, rising to her feet beside Pembroke. A man who towered over the shorter, pear-shaped man beside him stood in the entrance to the salon. Joseph took the greatcoat from Mason Regrett and turned to assist Senator Winslow as well. Regrett's eyes met Monty's across the room. His look was challenging and he appeared to be acutely aware of the disapproval of those who regarded him silently before the hum of conversation resumed.

"Who is that man?" Pembroke asked with sudden hostility. "He looks as though he knows you well—the impudent upstart."

"He does, but not well. He's our neighbor at home. His land borders my father's estate. His name is Mason Regrett."

"Regrett! The bounder who made the speech to the Senate earlier this week? If I'd been there, I'd have challenged him! Ambassador Jameson said he called those who didn't agree with him traitors." His angry eyes were on the newcomers.

Monty was grateful for this because her face was hot and she was unable to look away from Regrett, who strode toward her now, Senator Winslow following. There was astonishment in his narrowed eyes, something akin to disbelief.

"Why, the rascal's coming—" Pembroke began. Then low-voiced, he said, "I *will* challenge the man if he says a word amiss to you, Miss Monty!"

Senator Winslow and Regrett continued past her to their host, Henry Jameson. The sound of his voice carried easily to Monty and her companion as he, Jameson, and Winslow exchanged greetings.

"I apologize for our lateness in arriving, Ambassador Jameson, but the senator and I had two meetings that demanded our attention."

"Quite all right, Mr. Regrett, Senator. We are glad that you found time to come at all."

"Gracious of you, Henry," the senator replied with a touch of irony. "I see that all of our—friends?—are here."

"Not all," Jameson replied with irony of his own. "But almost."

"Enough anyway," Regrett drawled. "And the senator has cautioned me not to take issue with any of them—physically, at any rate."

"I hope you'll abide by the senator's suggestion, Mr. Regrett." Jameson was austere.

"I wouldn't think of taking such rude advantage of your kind hospitality, Ambassador." Regrett turned slightly and once again his eyes touched Monty's, for both she and her companion were openly eavesdropping. Derision colored Regrett's sudden laugh.

Both Pembroke and Monty turned away abruptly, and when she looked at Pembroke, she saw the sandy-haired Englishman's face was ruddy with anger.

"Bloody bounder," he muttered, then swiftly added, "I beg your pardon, Miss Monty. He appears to be a very offensive man."

Monty said nothing and Pembroke began hastily, "I don't imagine he's a friend of your father's—or yours—or perhaps I'm mistaken?"

"No, he's no longer friendly with my father—we merely buy our horses and beef from him." Monty was cool.

"Then he and your father were friends at one time?"

"When I was a little girl they were. But when the question of annexation grew pressing . . ." She trailed off, looking at the glass of wine still on the side table. "I'm . . . not hungry, but I *would* like a small slice of cake with the wine."

He said eagerly, "I'll fetch it for you. I'll be right back—" He moved quickly to one of the sideboards and spoke to one of the white-aproned maids.

"Hello, Monty." It was Regrett, bowing slightly as she whirled to face him. His smile turned down at one corner abruptly and he added, "Or must I say 'Miss Monty'? You've been such a—surprise to me this past week. Even more so tonight." His black eyes touched the bare white bosom, then swept upward to linger on her rosy mouth and suddenly pinker face.

"It most certainly is 'Miss Monty' to you, Mr. Regrett! Though it wouldn't surprise me to see you presuming on our previous acquaintance."

"My, my! Miss Abby has done a fine job of educating you in the language, Monty—Miss Monty. You know how to put words together that slap a man right in the face."

"I'd like to slap you right in the face, Mason Regrett!"

"What in the world for?" His pretended amazement was infuriating.

"Just the way you look—at me!"

"And how do I look at you, Monty—Miss Monty?" He appeared genuinely curious.

"You know very well how— Oh, Mr. Pembroke! Thank you *so much*!" She took the glass of wine. "Have you met Mr. Regrett? No? Let me introduce you. Mr. Anthony Pembroke of England, Mr. Mason Regrett of the Republic of Texas."

Pembroke bowed stiffly, but Regrett spoke cordially. "Mr. Pembroke, is this your first trip to the States?"

"I visited here with my father in 1836—"

"The year Texas won her independence!" Regrett's pleasure was undeniable.

"And it will remain that way." Pembroke scowled.

"What way?" Regrett asked with pretended innocence.

"Independent," Pembroke said, reddening once more.

"And if annexation is chosen?" The question was genial but Regrett's smile was sardonic.

"It won't be," Pembroke replied confidently.

"Actually, the United States hasn't made the offer of annexation officially yet." Regrett laughed.

"And they won't, despite your speech, Mr. Regrett."

"You may be right, Mr. Pembroke. Ah, the music is starting again. May I have this dance, Miss Monty?"

The request was made with such impersonal courtesy, there was no way she could refuse without being rude. With his hand firmly at her waist, they swung out among the dancers.

"I think you're a fraud, Mason Regrett," Monty said at last.

"A fraud?"

"That's a polite way to say I think you lied, when you agreed with Mr. Pembroke."

His jaw tightened. "I swore to Senator Winslow I wouldn't start trouble at this social gathering, Monty. And I didn't agree with Pembroke."

"You said he might be right."

"That's a polite way to say he's dead wrong."

"How can you be sure?"

"I know there've been a number of consultations between President Tyler and the Congress, and I'll lay money on the line that there'll be a very liberal bill passed offering annexation before this month is over."

"You are the most disgustingly biased man in the world! What makes you think our country will choose to accept such an offer?"

"Monty, don't talk. Just dance. You're so beautiful—such a change from the rude little tomboy I've known for years— let me enjoy it."

Unexpectedly mortified, she was speechless. She did not even protest when he whirled her around through the foyer and into the big empty library, where all the guests' wraps had been placed by Joseph and the maids. Burning logs in the broad fireplace cast a warm glow into the room, which was lit by only two lamps. There were deep shadows in the corners and around the big wing chairs and divans. He stopped before the fire and it cast burnished light on her bright hair. His arms were still about her.

A vibrant silence hung between them. Both were achingly conscious of their nearness and the powerful urge to touch one another. Their eyes held and unconsciously Monty swayed toward him. He met her with an urgency that would not be denied, as her head tilted and the full lips were turned up to his.

Louise Warren Lynchley was heady with excitement and triumph.

"Your home in that wild country sounds fascinating, Mr.

Daventry! Oh, I would love to see it!" Her blue eyes sparkled and she swung gracefully to the music under his strong, sure hands. *He's serious about me!* she thought. *He's attractive too and his home is far away from all the old cats in Charleston and their wagging tongues. They've shut me out of their respectable society and gossiped about me until my reputation's in shreds.*

"My dear Louise, I would so enjoy showing it to you. Of course, as I told you, Regrett's house is not far from mine—we've all built at the apex of the triangles of our land. But Cavenal's is equally close and he's a man of integrity and wisdom."

"Oh, I've heard of Lord Cavenal—just as I've heard of you—only not so many wonderful things as they say about you, Richard." She fluttered her thick gold lashes, and as she smiled, Richard thought he had never seen such a beautiful mouth. Not even Elizabeth Montrose had had a smile like that of this totally feminine and entrancing woman.

"Regrett is the one neighbor in the whole of the territory who is a hard-headed believer in annexation." Richard's voice roughened as he spoke Regrett's name. "We used to be friends, but now we're civil only because I buy my horses and beef from him. I'm sorry to say we are the bitterest of enemies regarding the destiny of the republic." He looked down into her eyes, his gaze taking in the red, shining lips, the dimple in her rounded chin, and thought how it would be to crush those curved lips with his own, to kiss the shadow at the base of her slender throat.

"You sound very . . . harsh, Richard." The way she spoke his name was a caress. He felt himself hardening involuntarily, and drew back as their thighs touched through her full skirts.

"The Regrett brothers are a bad lot. Julien, the younger, is a hotheaded fool. Because I had to put down one of the mares he sold me when she broke an ankle in a prairie-dog hole, he's absolutely insulting when we meet. And both of them are full of practical jokes—though Julien's the worst." He smiled at her, his heart in his gleaming gray eyes, and added, "But enough of an unpleasant pair—you would love the south-central country. We're close enough to Galveston to have luxuries imported from the East Coast and England and far enough inland to miss the worst of the spring and fall storms that blow in from the sea."

"It sounds like a paradise when you talk of it," she said, with just the right touch of reserved longing in the words. "Perhaps someday I'll get to see it all—as it grows more settled, of course." She must not seem too eager. If she played her cards right, this man would propose to her. She knew it, from long and varied experience. He was very handsome, she thought once more, and she felt the physical pull of him strongly in her loins. She allowed it to show in her half-lidded look up at him and was rewarded by his quick, indrawn breath.

Yet from the corner of her eye, she saw Mason Regrett dance Montrose Daventry into the foyer and disappear. Her every sense was alert to all around her as well as the man who held her. She knew the women were gossiping cruelly about her while the men were secretly admiring. Most interesting was the fact that the man Richard Daventry hated so deeply had just led his spoiled young daughter off into an empty room. Curiosity and an intuitive sense told her it would be worth her while to investigate—for Regrett's eyes on Montrose had held the same intensity that Richard's held on her.

Under her breathless and fascinated gaze, Richard had confided his whole background to her, and she knew that Montrose was his greatest joy. What could Regrett have in mind, taking her away from the crowd? Richard was so engrossed in watching every nuance of Louise's expression that he was totally unaware of anyone else in the room, and she knew it.

When the music stopped, she drew away, flaring open the fan at her wrist and fanning her beautiful, flushed face.

"My dear Richard," she said demurely over the fan, "you are such a divine dancer, you've left me quite breathless! Will you forgive me if I go get a handkerchief from my reticule? It will take me but a moment. And don't you let any of these pretty ladies take my place while I'm gone! I want you all to myself!" This last was bold, she knew, but she had found boldness was often an aphrodisiac to men. She was rewarded by sudden bright heat in Richard's eyes.

"My dear Louise, nothing and no one could deprive me of the pleasure you bring me. I'll have a glass of wine for you when you return."

Yes, she thought with satisfaction as she walked toward the foyer with skirts swaying gracefully, she intended to marry Richard and leave the ugly rumors behind her. During his visit, she would see him often, and each time she saw him, she would be more pliable, more engaging—ah, she knew a thousand ways to snare a man!—and he would ask her to marry him before he left Washington. She swept silently through the foyer. At the entrance to the library she halted.

Ah, she had been right! Mason Regrett's mouth was fastened to Montrose's and their bodies melded together. It was such an intense and passionate embrace that Louise felt its echo in her own thighs as an involuntary and piercing thrill shot through her. Ah, passion was a sharp, cutting pleasure and Regrett was one of the most attractive men she had ever seen! For a moment she merely stood, savoring their embrace, which grew hotly closer as the girl's arms slipped up about Regrett's wide shoulders.

"Oh!" Louise gave a little cry of simulated surprise. Then as the two broke apart violently, she said in a low voice,

"I'm so sorry! I came only to get a handkerchief from my reticule . . ." She trailed off, her thick lashes sweeping upward as she looked into Montrose's shocked face, which whitened slowly under Louise's knowing scrutiny.

"Do come in, Mrs. Lynchley," Regrett said, unperturbed. "It seems we meet again and under different circumstances this time."

"Oh, I know," Louise said. "Very different from sitting across from you at the Pierces' luncheon. And I do apologize for interrupting such a—an intimate moment."

Regrett bowed. "I'm sure it was accidental, Mrs. Lynchley, and we can count on your discretion."

"Indeed you can," she replied with a radiant smile, her eyes sliding to the still, pale Montrose. What was the matter with the girl? Her eyes were dilated and there was passion, fear, and fury in their wide violet depths. She said nothing. She did not move. She merely stared at Louise.

"May I escort you back to the salon, Monty?" he asked.

"No," she said with repressed violence. "Go on back. I don't want to see you again this whole evening!"

He smiled tightly. "I won't apologize because you enjoyed it as much as I." He turned and left them.

Louise went swiftly to the girl. "Dear Montrose, don't worry! I know how your father feels about Mr. Regrett and I saw how you returned his—ah—ardor. But that will be *our* little secret, won't it, dear? I would never tell your darling father anything that would hurt him."

Monty looked at her with undisguised loathing, but she feared what this woman would say to her father. "I would appreciate it if you say nothing to my father."

"You can count on my silence," Louise said unctuously. Then with a sly smile, "Your father is still a young man himself. No doubt he would understand—if it were anyone but Mr. Regrett."

"You know about my father and Mr. Regrett?" Monty's surprise was sharp.

"Oh, yes. Your father and I have become . . . very well acquainted this evening. Actually, I'd heard a great deal—many nice things about your father—and *you,* dear, before I met the two of you." Her smile was so artfully ingenuous that Monty's distrust became as great as her dislike of the lovely woman.

"Come, darling," Louise said comfortingly. "Your father will miss us both—we must return." Her bell-like laughter sounded before she added, "How smart it was of you to arrange that you shouldn't be seen returning to the salon in Mr. Regrett's company!"

As the two stepped into the broad foyer, Faith Warren rose from a shadowy chair in a corner of the library and looked after the two slim figures.

The tears of hurt and frustration she had come into the library to hide had long since dried on her smooth cheeks. She had been an unwilling witness to the entire exchange between Monty, Mason Regrett, and Louise. Faith knew Louise well, though she was scarcely a year older than Monty. Familiar hurt and quiet humiliation deepened and mingled with apprehension as Faith moved slowly across the broad foyer and into the salon beyond. *As Louise says so often,* Faith thought bitterly, *no one will notice or care.*

She was wrong.

Mason Regrett noticed her enter the room so soon after Monty and the smiling Louise, but his black eyes were expressionless and his tanned face did not reveal his intuitive knowledge that this quiet girl had witnessed it all.

Chapter 3

Monty *looked out the window* of the Maryland Hotel at the lowering gray sky over the City of Washington. Mud would be ankle-deep in the rutted road if the weather were to break and the hard crusty snow and ice were to melt. People leaned into the cold wind as they passed each other on the weathered planks that served as a walkway in front of the building across from the hotel.

She tapped her small slippered foot impatiently. She was completely dressed and her father had left to get the carriage over an hour ago. He was to take Monty to the Chesapeake Bay Landing where she could board the steamer for Galveston. Other carriages, coaches, and barouches mingled and passed men on horseback, chopping up the muddy slush in the street below, but she recognized none of them.

Her small trunk and portmanteau had long ago been packed with all her clothes and the many small gifts she had bought for those at home.

As she watched, the carriage drew up before the hotel and she saw her father debark. Her impatience increased as she waited for him to ascend the stairs and come for her, but in minutes he appeared with two porters, who went immediately to the small trunk and portmanteau.

"Pa, I thought you'd never get here!" Then, suddenly ashamed of her eagerness to leave, she added, "I do hate to leave you in this cold, busy place—I'll feel guilty when I get home, knowing you're still here."

"Don't, Monty—feel guilty, I mean. You know the vote on the bill offering annexation is coming up before the week's out. I'll leave for home—in high spirits, I hope— immediately after that."

"No matter whether it passes or not?"

"No matter the outcome, my pet!"

The porters shouldered her luggage and disappeared into the hall. Monty made her second brief sortie through the bedroom she had occupied on the far side of the sitting room to see that she had forgotten nothing.

"I'm betting our friends among the northern senators will finish that bill—and there'll be no more efforts to end our republic for a long while after that!" Her father's voice was light and held a new vibrancy.

Monty looked at him sharply. He had that young, boyish look about him again, which for some reason sat poorly with her. He had left her alone much of the past week and she had been hard put to entertain herself.

"You certainly are sure about it," she replied, trying not to sound glum. "And mighty lighthearted too, Pa, considering that powerful speech Mason Regrett made to the senators." At the mere mention of his name her breath shortened. Damn Mase and that kiss! His were the first male lips to ever claim hers and it was as if he had somehow put a brand on her.

Her father laughed with pleasure. "I am lighthearted, Monty. I never felt better or more hopeful, despite Regrett's accusations!"

"I hope you're right."

"And if I'm not, Cav and I and the Arterburys and Bedfords will continue our efforts to see that the republic becomes a western empire in America," he said confidently. "You'll see, Monty!"

They stepped out of the hotel and stopped before the carriage. It was driven by a man her father had hired. Daventry opened the door for her. Drawing her fur-lined cape close, muff and reticule in one hand, she caught at the side of the coach and stepped into it, her father's hand at her elbow. Immediately she realized there was another passenger in the carriage.

"Monty, you remember Mrs. Lynchley? You met her at the ball." Then, as he seated himself, he called out, "Esau, we can leave now. We have two hours to reach the boat, so you needn't hurry." The carriage lurched forward and the plumes on Mrs. Lynchley's pale blue hat bobbed gracefully. The color exactly matched her wide, thick-lashed eyes.

Her laugh tinkled. "Oh, Montrose, you look lovely in your furs. Here, sit beside me, darling, for the long ride!"

Startled and dismayed, Monty murmured an indistinguishable greeting, but seated herself by her father across from the woman. Louise, undeterred by her cool greeting, continued gaily.

"Richard, it's no wonder you're so proud of her! She's a lovely child! She's going to be a beautiful woman when she grows up."

Monty was silent. This woman's remarks were calculated to make Monty appear a child, and they met with success for she suddenly felt twelve years old and very gauche.

"Are you excited to be taking such a long voyage? All around the Florida peninsula, Richard tells me, and into the Gulf of Mexico, with many stops along the way, before you reach Galveston."

"Yes," Monty said briefly; her eyes on her father were accusing. Why had he brought this odious woman along to spoil their last hours together before the long voyage began?

"Richard tells me you two came to Washington by land and most of the way by coach. Did you find it tiring?"

"No."

"But he said he didn't want you returning that way, because of the dangers—Indians"—she gave a little shudder—"and other things."

"I think she'll be safer going by boat—and I know Captain Rogers of the steamer, *Fulton,* very well. He'll look after Monty until she reaches Galveston, where Big Miguel and his son and our LeRoy will meet her," Richard said, smiling.

"And they'll escort you all the way to Richard's beautiful home," Louise put in, her beaming warmth directed at Richard. "Your father is a most remarkable man, Montrose. I've never met anyone in my life who is so wise and knowledgeable." Her laughter rang out as she added, "And he's so handsome, too! It isn't fair for one man to be so gifted!" She cast Daventry a reproachful glance, with a trace of alluring wickedness in it.

Monty realized with sudden clarity that this was a woman of powerful expertise with men and for one brief moment she was smothered by fear.

By the time they reached Chesapeake Landing, where she was escorted by her father and a charmingly purposeful Louise onto the steam packet, she was heartily sick of the woman. During the long ride, she had repeatedly sent exasperated glances at her father, only to catch him watching Louise with fascination. She had given up and subsided into angry silence.

When the whistle on the steamer sounded cheerfully, they said their good-byes.

"Since I won't be seeing you again, Mrs. Lynchley," Monty said firmly and with forced politeness, "I'll say how much I enjoyed meeting you."

She watched them go down the gangplank, Mrs. Lynchley's hand possessively on her father's arm. Indignation burned in her, but she was comforted by the thought that she really would never see the beautiful woman again—and that her father would be home in a few more weeks. She had enjoyed most of her stay in the City of Washington and she had schooled herself to avoid thinking of Mason Regrett and that sweet, shocking moment when their lips fused in the embassy library. Even now, as the boat pulled away from the quay and she waved to her father and Mrs. Lynchley, she willed her heart to slow its acceleration. But the dark face of Regrett burned bright behind her eyes.

Thirty-three days and several stops later, Monty stepped off the packet to be greeted by the two Miguels and black, beaming LeRoy, his face wreathed in smiles. It was nine in the morning when the boat docked. Two hours later they were on their horses, her baggage lashed to a sturdy, broad-backed packhorse, and on their way home.

Big Miguel was a tall, thickset man with a rugged face, and his curling black hair was shot with gray. His tall son, Young Miguel, had the face of an aristocrat, clean even-cut features that might have graced a Roman coin. His blue-black hair was swept back from his classic face in an easy wave. Like black LeRoy, he was an expert with horses, possessing as well the many talents required of a man working on a farm that produced hundreds of acres of cotton and had a good-sized orchard of plums, peaches, and oranges. There was not much, from shoeing and caring for horses, carpentering, riding patrol against the Indians and roving Mexican soldiers, that the two Miguels and LeRoy could not do. In this, they were like Richard Daventry's other employees, Texans of Spanish heritage.

Daventry had blacks on his place, all free. He was against slavery in principle, but he did not quarrel with his friend George Cavenal, who had over fifty slaves on his place. He had expressed his disapproval to Cavenal, who had laughingly said he would free them "all in good time." After that, the two men did not discuss the matter.

"We all sure missed you, Monty," LeRoy said, grinning broadly as they reached the road heading northwest from Galveston. "Miss Abby most of all, I reckon."

"I'm so glad to be back," she replied, patting Warlock's gleaming black neck. She had chosen him when he was a spirited colt cavorting in the Regrett corrals last year. He had a hard mouth and a mind of his own, but he was beautiful. And it was so good to be once more astride her favorite horse, clad in the heavy twill pants that clung to her slender thighs like a second skin.

March would last six more days, but already a heady spring wind was stirring the countryside; on either side of the narrow wagon trail, the earth was ablaze with wildflowers. They cast such a snare of perfume into the air that Monty was caught up in it, and an unbridled glee swept her. She dug her heels abruptly into the young stallion's sides and, startled, he sprang forward.

The men watched her burst of joy with smiles, but they stepped up their pace to keep her in sight until the horse slowed and she reined him in to wait for them.

They drew near the big Daventry house two days later and well before the supper hour. Big Miguel's other two sons, Carlos and Joseph Puente, had spotted them a mile from home and had joined them on their mustang ponies. Joseph, who would soon be thirteen, had dashed ahead to alert the household.

As they drew up before the two-story, oak-shaded redbrick house, Monty drank in the sight of it. Her heart swelled with pride as she looked at the flag bearing its lone star on the red, white, and blue background fluttering above the second story. Abby had made that flag for her son. Richard had had the tall, slender pine flagpole shipped in from east Texas. It was the symbol of all he held dear in the republic, and it was a source of great excitement among the children of the workers, who vied with each other to raise it each morning. Looking at it, Monty drew a deep breath. She was *home!*

Then she saw Lady Abigail Daventry out under the trees, waving. With her stood Josey Beane and Feenie, LeRoy's wife and sixteen-year-old daughter. Dorita Puente, Big Miguel's wife, could be seen running around the corner of the house, followed by a stream of small Puente girls, all sisters to Young Miguel and his two brothers. Another troop of golden-skinned children and their mothers rounded the corner and stood on the broad graveled drive that formed a half-circle in front of the Georgian colonial house.

In minutes LeRoy had unlatched a wide gate in the broad-planked, white-painted fence that protected the sweeping lawns around Daventry's house. The welcoming crowd spilled around the travelers when they entered on horseback. LeRoy closed the gate behind them as Monty flung herself off Warlock and into Lady Abigail's arms. There was a babble of voices until Monty's rose above them.

"I've goodies from Washington and New York for everyone—just wait until the Miguels and LeRoy get my baggage off that horse and into the parlor!"

Later, with much laughter and a flow of merry chatter in both English and Spanish, Monty passed sweets around to the children and gave silk scarves to their mothers.

When they had all left the big parlor and only Monty and her grandmother were left, Abby said severely, "Monty, your nose is sunburned. Didn't you wear your hat at all on the way from Galveston?"

"I forgot," Monty said ruefully, putting an enquiring finger to her pert nose. "Besides, the sun and wind felt so good after that freezing snow and ice in Washington."

"When is your father coming home?"

"He *said* as soon as they voted on the new annexation bill. He was sure the northern senators would kill it."

"When was the vote taken?"

"Toward the last of February. If I'd stayed another week, I'd have known which way it went—but the week after the ball at the British Embassy, Pa was so busy I scarcely saw him and I was so *bored* by then."

"Did you meet any young men—any you liked?"

"Not that I *really* liked!" She made a face. Then with a sudden flush, she added, "Mase Regrett made a speech for annexation to the Senate. Pa and I were there and heard it all. He as good as called Pa and Cav—the Arterburys and Bedfords, too—traitors!"

Abby read her granddaughter's pink face and her little smile was kind. "Maybe Mase thinks what Richard and the others want for us is rather traitorous—to the wishes of the majority of Texans."

"Abby, I know you think Mase is right about this annexation business even if you won't come right out and say it!"

"Not about everything," Abby temporized.

"Ah, just because he and Julien have always brought you seeds and bulbs and rose cuttings from Galveston and New Orleans for your garden, you're partial—even to their politics!"

Abby laughed. "That—and the fact that both boys were orphaned and had to make their own way in a hostile world. And they did it so well and honorably, too."

"That doesn't make them right." Monty's rounded chin lifted and her smooth jaw hardened. "Mase was at the embassy ball and he was insufferable!"

"How?" Abby asked mildly.

"He was so *sure* the United States would admit our country to the Union." Monty averted her eyes. Abby knew her too well and Monty did not want her grandmother to see any echo of the newly awakened passions that made her heart thunder when she remembered—and she remembered so often!—Mason Regrett's mouth on hers.

"You haven't forgotten that nine out of ten Texans have already voted to join the Union?"

"No, I haven't, but they aren't as farseeing and wise as Pa, Cav, and the others. Why, Texas will be a bigger, stronger nation than—"

"Well," Abby cut her off tactfully, "we won't argue the point. Did you buy any pretty new dresses?"

"Yes, and some new riding pants—better material than the boys' pants I've had to buy in Galveston. Now! The best for last, Abby. I hope you like them." Her father had helped her choose Abby's gift when they made a marvelous trip by train to New York one cold weekend.

Abby took the exquisite pearl earrings out of their velvet box. Carefully she removed her gold studs and replaced them with the new earrings. A small pearl drop at the bottom of each one bobbed entrancingly when she tossed her head for her granddaughter.

"You look beautiful, Abby," Monty said admiringly. Abby was still as slender as Monty and, despite her fifty-eight years, rode like a centaur. Further, she would not permit anyone to work in her English garden on the east side of the house, preferring to do it all herself.

"Thank you, my dear. Now come along. I know you want a nice bath before supper, and Josey and Feenie have been keeping water hot in the kitchen since this morning."

April came and with it the further greening of the orchards and fields. Everyone on the Daventry plantation-farm began to relax, even the men who rode patrol over the many acres of the three big properties that met at Three Points Lake. This was because food was becoming plentiful over the broad countryside and Indians did not come prowling to the two Georgian colonial homes of Daventry and Cavenal.

The Indians and Mexican soldiers were always careful of the rambling adobe brick Regrett ranch, spring, summer, and winter. This was because the two brothers and their many Mexican workers were crack shots and did not hesitate to pursue any predators who attacked them. But more than this, if he approached in a friendly manner, an Indian might be rewarded with a whole beef by either or both brothers during the short but cold winter months.

Monty had been home a little over two weeks in April when she announced her determination to ride the two short miles to the Regretts' ranch. Lady Abigail agreed to go with her.

"I want to see the mare I picked out last fall that Pa's buying for me," Monty told her. "Julien and Mase were going to break her to the saddle this spring."

Big Miguel, with his long rifle, and Young Miguel, with his prized pistol, accompanied them. Because of roving Mexican soldiers and Indians who were even better at concealment until they attacked, Daventry never allowed any woman to ride more than a mile alone.

When the small entourage arrived at the Regrett ranch mid-morning, they were met by the Regretts' housekeeper, Twyla Salazar, wife of Andrew Salazar, the Regrett foreman.

Twyla was fat and jolly with dimples in her pretty brown face and everyone called her Mamacita.

"Come in, come in, ladies!" she cried, opening the broad, hand-hewn front door. "I go fetch lemonade. Is so hot outside already!"

"Wait, Mamacita." Monty's smile was sunny as she dismounted. "First, I want to see the mare Pa let me pick out last fall." She tethered Warlock to the hitching rail. The two Miguels had already gone to the stables to visit with Salazar and Renaldo.

* * *

Later, walking back to the house with her grandmother, Monty said restively, "She's beautiful, but not as beautiful as Warlock, even if she'll be easier to handle—as Mase says every chance he gets."

"And as Renaldo and Joe have just said," Abby replied, looking at Monty's flushed face and her coppery hair gleaming in the sunlight.

They approached the house. Thick, hand-cut shingles on the roof had weathered a silvery gray, giving the place a lean, masculine look, strong and dependable.

"I seem to remember Warlock threw you once, down by the lake," Abby continued.

"He was scared! I told you there was a rattlesnake—"

"And you know very well they go to the lake for water."

"Does that mean I can't stop there for Warlock to drink? Or take a swim on hot days?"

Abby said firmly, "We all use it. And you know very well I've never approved of your swimming in it."

"I've only done it a few times since I—I grew up," Monty said shortly as she opened the broad door to the house. "And always in my clothes, more's the misery, even as a child!"

"Sit, ladies," Mamacita said, beaming as they entered. "Here is lemonade. Ver' cool—water from the well."

"Mmm. It's delicious, Mamacita!"

"Plenty more, Monty, Miss Abby." Twyla Salazar had known Monty since she was barely eleven and had come to the Regrett ranch with her father to buy cattle and horses. In fact, all the people who worked on the Regrett ranch knew and loved Monty and Abby. They had expressed sorrow, vocally and often, that the Daventrys and Regretts were no longer friends. "Is too long between visits now," Twyla added mournfully.

"We'll come more often," Abby said quickly, to forestall

the usual laments that went with Mamacita's disapproval of the enmity between the men.

"I think Señor Julien come home to eat soon. He go this morning long before the sun is up. He been to Victoria with some cows two days ago an' come back with a letter from Señor Mase." Twyla's good humor was restored.

"And we must go," Abby said, extending her empty glass with Monty's. "We'll miss lunch as it is. Josey will dress us down properly."

They were ready to leave when Julien came in the back door.

Chapter 4

Returning Twyla's greeting, Julien slung his worn hat on a nearby chair, his eyes on the two visitors. He strode into the parlor where they were just rising from the largest sofa in that portion of the big stone floor Mase had lowered to insure coolness.

The furniture was handmade, with some woven pieces brought in from Mexico. Mamacita and her friends had added bright splashes of color with woven rugs, pillows on couches, and touches of Spain in the curtains.

"It's the Daventry ladies." He grinned. "What brings you into the enemy camp?"

"My mare," Monty said, unable to restrain a return grin as she and Abby sat back down on the sofa.

"Ah, I saw Slyboots was in the corral—so you've seen her? Grown a bit, hasn't she? Better under a saddle, too."

"Slyboots?" Monty cried indignantly. "You've named her? But I wanted to name her!"

"You can name her," Julien said, laughing. "Mase only calls her Slyboots for *you*."

"For *me?*" Monty's indignation mounted. "I'm no Slyboots!"

"Oh, but you are, miss." Julien's amusement grew. "You

wind Daventry around your finger. You always wangle things your way. Only you could get your father to pay such a price for a mare—even a blooded mare like Slyboots. And who else could persuade Mase and me to train her personally? She's got Mase and me eating out of her little hoof." Still smiling, he added, "What do you want to name her?"

"Glory," Monty said, maintaining her air of wounded dignity.

"Don't you think," Abby put in dryly, "that Glory's a little pretentious for such a spirited little Slyboots?"

"Pa won't think so! He won't like the name Slyboots— especially for *me!*"

Julien's handsome face darkened and a little vein in his forehead pulsed strongly. "We're selling you Slyboots *only* if you ride her yourself. Your father's not to sit her—even once!"

Stung, Monty lashed back. "Julien Regrett, you know well enough it broke Pa's heart to have to put Lady down after she broke her ankle. You're cruel to hold it against him."

"Neither Mase nor I would ever ride a horse through a prairie-dog village. Daventry's been here long enough to know about them."

"I don't know why you keep selling Pa horses, feeling as you do about it!" Monty's anger was rising. Looking into Julien's tanned face, she was reminded sharply of his brother. She had been a fool with Mase and could not forgive herself.

"I wouldn't sell him another horse if his life depended on it." Julien's voice was hard and cold. "It's Mase who maintains the relationship between us—if you call it that. Daventry, like Cavenal and the rest of you transplanted Britishers, is a menace to this country."

"I won't sit here and listen to you insult my father and his friends! This is *our* country just as much as it is yours and Mase's—and we'll keep it that way!"

"My dears," Abby said firmly, "we came in friendship and we remain in friendship. Monty loves the mare, Julien, and I'm sure Richard wouldn't think of riding any of Monty's special pets. He never rides Warlock." She paused, looking from the quick-tempered Julien to her equally hot-headed granddaughter. Then she said smoothly, "Mamacita tells us you had a letter from Mase recently, saying he'd be home soon. Tell us, did the bill of annexation pass?"

"With flying colors, Miss Abby," Julien replied, a broad smile replacing his frown. "Now it's our turn to delay for the best terms possible for statehood. All we have to do is write a state constitution, pass it and the resolution to join. Then we'll be part of the United States."

"We're not part of it yet!" Monty said, disappointment sharp in her reply. She was reluctant to end the quarrel between them.

"Did Mase mention if he knew when Richard was leaving for home, by chance?" Abby interrupted.

"Mase is coming home early next month. He's coming by land on Coffee." Coffee was Mason Regrett's prized stallion, bred and trained on his ranch and of impeccable English and Arabic stock. Regrett credited him with almost human intelligence. "He did mention that Daventry's still working with his friends to get the bill rescinded, but it's hopeless." Julien's dark brows drew together again as he added, "I suppose he'll be home, Miss Abby, when he finds out that it is."

"If I know my father, it's not hopeless!" Monty burst out. "And I'll bet you something happens between now and the proposed annexation that blows the whole thing sky-high!"

"Stubborn little firebrand, isn't she, Miss Abby?" His smile at Monty was sarcastic. "When Mase gets home, Monty, we'll finish training Slyboots. She'll be ready about the end of summer, I figure. She has a fine, smooth gait and is much easier to handle than you are, miss."

"Let's go, Abby," Monty said coolly. "Thanks for the lemonade, Mamacita."

As Abby and the two Miguels reached Three Points Lake on their way home half an hour later, they were surprised to see George Cavenal approaching with two of his riders who patrolled the Cavenal acres against Indian and Mexican intruders. Trees grew thickly around the lake and beyond it as well.

The three men from the Cavenal place trotted down the narrow, shaded road, and as they drew near, Cavenal swept off his hat and bowed deeply to the ladies.

"How pleasant to see you both!" His accent was flawlessly British and his courtesy equally so.

"What brings you out here in the middle of the day, Cav?" Abby asked, smiling.

"My man Josiah told me there were a great many quail in my north acres, and I've been hunting. We just put three brace of birds in the game shed on the Guadalupe—would you like one of the Miguels to get several for your table?"

"That would be lovely, Cav." Abby smiled. "It's been quite a while since we've had any."

"Now I'm on my way to the Regretts'. He may be an insulting beggar, but his horses are better than those from Virginia. I promised Georgina and Mother I'd buy them two new mounts, and Abraham, my foreman, heard from Renaldo Flores that Regrett had some fine young mares this spring." All the while he was talking, his clear, golden eyes were admiring Monty's piquant face, observing the narrow nose and full, red lips.

"I know your sister loves to ride." Abby smiled warmly. "And she does it so well."

"That's true, my dear Miss Abby. You know, ladies"—his ready laughter revealed even, white teeth—"Mother and Georgina have never really reconciled themselves to Texas, even after seven years. They still want to return to England, but I imagine when we become a great nation, they'll feel differently about it."

"We've been to see my mare, and Julien just told us the annexation bill passed," Monty said glumly.

George Cavenal swore softly under his breath and apologized for it to the two women before he added angrily, "I'll wager that speech Regrett made in the Senate was partly responsible! By God, something ought to be done about those Regrett brothers, horses and cattle notwithstanding. They need a good lesson in minding their own business and letting their superiors take the necessary action."

"By superiors, you mean yourself and Richard?" Abby's gray eyes were veiled but the question was ingenuous.

"Of course," Cavenal replied arrogantly. "A pair of uneducated, quick-tempered fools like Mason and Julien Regrett can cause a great deal of trouble. I wouldn't be surprised if they didn't bring some down on themselves. They richly deserve to be taught a lesson!" Then he added admiringly, "Monty, you look exceptionally beautiful—and anger becomes you!"

"I've just had a set-to with Julien over the annexation," Monty said. "And Mase is coming home early next month, crowing over his victory, I'm sure."

"Well, I'll avoid talk about the annexation—after all, I want to buy horses, not a quarrel." Then tipping his hat, he said, "You ladies must come have tea soon with Mother and Georgina."

"We will," Abby said equably and they moved away.

Monty's eyes followed Cavenal briefly. He was almost as old as her father, but he was a handsome man with that fair, curling hair and those hypnotic golden eyes. His legs were long and muscled and his shoulders broad. Since she had grown up, he had been punctilliously polite and complimentary to her, and she had a sudden and entirely new and adult thought. It intruded on the residue of her anger and banished it. She had a strong sense that George Cavenal would like their relationship to be more intimate. She shrugged as they rode down the shadow-dappled trail—she had known Cav too long, and while she liked and respected him, she had never entertained the thought of a warmer relationship.

It was near the middle of May when Feenie, Josey Beane's sixteen-year-old, galloped into the parlor where Lady Abigail and Monty were taking afternoon tea.

"Miss Abby—Monty!" she cried breathlessly. "They's a carriage—a coach an' four—an' a man on horseback comin' down the road to the house!" She ran out toward the kitchen to alert her mother and the Mexican workers who might be in their cabins. Visitors were too few and far between to be missed.

When Abby and her granddaughter went out on the graveled drive that circled spacious lawns, others began coming around the corner of the big house. The flag atop the pine pole snapped in a stiff south breeze that ruffled live oaks and murmured through pines that surrounded the house.

"Your father may be on that horse by the coach," Abby said, her gray eyes twinkling with anticipation. "I see he's got all his gear on a packhorse."

"That's not Pa," Monty said slowly, narrowing her eyes. Sunlight, filtering through the trees, struck fire in the long loose braids of her copper hair. She never put it up when she was home.

"No," Abby replied thoughtfully in her cultured, still faintly British voice. "That looks very much like Mason Regrett. Perhaps your father's in the carriage—though I can't believe they'd travel together."

"It *is* Mase Regrett," Monty said, and unbidden excitement streaked through her. Jamming her fists into the pockets of the fitted pants she wore, she willed resentment to rise up. Mase would be gloating over his triumph.

It's not final. Texas hasn't agreed to it yet and maybe it wouldn't ever agree to it. Her faith in her father's influence and Captain Charles Elliot's diplomacy was unshaken. She meant it when she told the mocking Julien that something could blow the whole thing sky-high.

As the coach and horses beside it drew near, Abby and Monty could see the hard-faced man astride Coffee. His eyes held a wisdom beyond his twenty-seven years. As an ambitious, hard-driven seventeen-year-old in 1835, he had been close to Sam Houston.

Abby was reflecting on the fact that he and his brother had made the Regrett ranch the largest cattle and horse-raising piece of land in the fertile lower section of Texas. Monty, watching the approaching coach and horses, with dust clouds behind it, was remembering Mase's wintry smile when he told her, "You might say our differences with England's proposals go back to the American Revolution." And her resentment grew.

By now there was a group of women and children around Monty and Abby, eagerly awaiting the arrival of the coach. Suddenly Regrett put his coffee-colored horse into a gallop, coming ahead of the coach and the packhorse tied to it, and he reached the wide drive arching before the house ahead of them. Sweeping his worn hat off crisp black hair, eyes gleaming, he bowed to the group.

"I've had the honor of escorting what I'm sure will be your father's happy surprise to you, Monty, Miss Abby. Fresh from South Carolina, via Washington—his new bride." His eyes narrowed as he registered their expressions. Monty's was what he expected, shock and disbelief first, then hot anger. Abby, in a manner unusual for her, let her surprise show, and with it an interested hopefulness, which meant that Monty had not told her grandmother of the woman her father met in Washington. She said nothing now.

Regrett knew Miss Abby had long hoped her son would remarry and find new happiness, and now he thought with sudden cynicism that most likely the coach did not contain happiness for Richard Daventry. He had made the long trip with the coach and its passengers, and having come to read people well, he read Louise Lynchley—Daventry now—very clearly.

"You and Richard must have parted friends," Abby said quickly, even more hopefully, "for him to ask you to ride escort for his wife."

Regrett slid from Coffee and bowed again to the smiling woman. "Sorry, Miss Abby, but no. Mrs. Daventry and I met quite by chance at an inn in Nashville and the bride asked me if we could journey together for safety's sake. I rode escort at her request. I expect Daventry will be very annoyed to learn of it." His ready laughter made light of the situation. "Despite your son's wish to keep our republic, in effect, a part of the British Empire, riding guard for his wife was my gesture of goodwill."

"Didn't she have protection?" Monty asked sharply.

"Ezekiel, one of her slaves, is on the box and he is very good with the Kentucky rifle—and pistols as well. The road from Washington to Texas has become much safer in the last ten years. Still, the more guns you have en route, the better."

"Slaves?" Abby said, frowning. Like her son, Lady Abigail did not approve of slavery.

"She has two young blacks with her—her personal maids —and her driver. And of course, her orphaned cousin, Faith Warren," Regrett told Abby.

The coach was rattling nearer and all eyes were on it, but Monty's stormy gaze still focused on Regrett. He was filled with enjoyment at her shocked dismay.

As the coach rolled to a halt, Monty thought furiously how jaunty and uncaring Regrett was. He was as light-hearted as if statehood were practically a fact. Before she had left Washington, her father had told her that Texas itself seemed to be dragging its heels under the new President, Anson Jones. Elliot had added that Jones seemed hopeful of keeping the republic as it was.

But now she was faced with this horrible news. When Regrett had said the name of Faith Warren, Monty knew at once it was Louise Warren Lynchley in this coach. Her thoughts were boiling. She refused to accept it. How could her father do such a thing? As she attempted to control her feelings, Regrett stepped forward and opened the coach door, before Ezekiel could dismount from the box.

A white-gloved hand placed itself in his big tanned one and the new Mrs. Daventry put her small foot gracefully on the coach step, then to the pebbled drive before the stunned group.

She was a spun-sugar vision in pale green muslin. A small green bonnet topped her golden curls. Even her slippers, which peeped out demurely as she stepped forward to meet the women, were a matching green. Monty knew her dress, with its many flounces, tight bodice, and modestly high neck framed with a collar of white lace, was the latest fashion. Many petticoats made her dress stand out piquantly and they rustled richly as she stepped forward to take Abby's extended hand.

"I'm Louise Warren Lynchly—Daventry, now. Darling Richard and I were married the end of February and he didn't write because he wanted to surprise all of you—happily, I hope!" Her high little voice was filled with pleasure. "He was coming with me, but at the last minute some meeting or other—about these politics, you know—kept him—and I was so *anxious* to meet you, I persuaded him to let me come ahead. But he did say to tell you he'd follow me as soon as possible." She tilted her head coquettishly. "You *must* be his mother, dear Lady Abigail."

"Indeed I am, Louise. I bid you welcome." She made a gesture to the big Georgian brick house. "Richard's been single too long—nearly fifteen years." Her sincere smile revealed white teeth, remarkable in a woman her age.

"You still have your marvelous English accent," Louise trilled. "How lovely! When Richard told me you were the widow of Lord Daventry—I was so impressed!"

"I was his second wife and bore him one son, Richard, but he had three others by his first wife—"

"Primogeniture! And that's why Richard came to the New World to make his own way," Louise finished happily. "How lovely though, that Lord Daventry settled a legacy on you both. It's so nice to be independent."

"Richard takes his cotton crops very seriously, despite our income," Abigail Daventry said dryly. "We ship cotton to England from Galveston regularly. This is a working plantation, as you will find, my dear."

"It's charming. I know I'll love it here!" She exuded confidence.

"You're quite beautiful, Louise, and so fashionable," Abby said sincerely.

Monty stood silently by and stared, keeping her face carefully blank as these pleasantries were exchanged. If Louise wanted to ignore her, two could play that game.

"This year promises to be a good one for change, Lady Abigail. Eighteen forty-five has already ushered in more petticoats. Oh, heavens, I've forgotten Faith and my maids!" she cried prettily. "And poor Zeke—he's been on the box driving all day, pushing the horses to get here."

Standing beside the coach was Faith, tall, slender, and dressed somberly in dark gray despite it being the month of May. Her smooth, delicate features were half concealed by a gray bonnet. At her side were two light-skinned blacks.

They were pretty women in their early twenties and slim as reeds. They were obviously sisters, but the younger one had a luxuriant mass of silky, mahogany-red hair tied back with a black ribbon. It tumbled down her back in rich profusion.

"Do come here, Faith." Louise's tone was patronizing. "Don't stand there like one of the servants."

The girl, perhaps a year older than Monty, walked the short distance and took Abby's outstretched hand. Then in a low voice, she said, "It's good to see you again, Monty."

"Monty!" Louise cried in astonishment. "But it *is*! Montrose! I can't believe it—I simply didn't know you in those dreadful—those tight pants and boots, my dear!"

Monty said nothing; nor did she smile.

Chapter 5

There was an awkward pause before Louise went on blithely. "My cousin Faith is Uncle Tom Warren's daughter. Her whole family is gone—died in that awful plague of typhoid in Charleston ten years ago. She was destitute and Father took her in. When he died, I knew my duty. I let her stay with me as my companion."

Monty said shortly, "I was introduced to Faith at the embassy ball in Washington. How are you, Faith?" She bent a warm, welcoming smile on the young girl. Faith had no opportunity to answer, for Louise interrupted.

"Oh? I didn't know—and these two darkies are Merzella and Tina Moses. They've been my maids for years. And Zeke, on the box, is a legacy from Father as well. You *do* have slave quarters here, don't you?"

"No." Monty's answer was abrupt and flat. "My father doesn't believe in slavery. But we have cabins in back for extra help during picking season." She was filled with disbelief that her father—who loved her so—had taken this odious woman as his wife.

"Ah, Montrose"—Louise turned guileless blue eyes on her—"you're such a sweet child." Her quick laughter was spontaneous. "You know, I mistook you for a boy. Those—

um—breeches and that man's shirt you're wearing are deceiving." Her eyes swept up and down Monty. "But I see there's no doubt about your being female."

"Mason," Abby cut in smoothly, "would you show Zeke to our stables and get your own mount and packhorse served there as well? You must stay and rest a bit before riding on to your place. LeRoy will be at the stables and he'll show Tina and Merzella to one of the empty cabins." Her voice was clipped, but her eyes on Regrett were warm. She *liked* the tough, vital man, no matter his politics.

"Glad to, Miss Abby."

"Then come back and join us inside for a glass of cold lemonade or brandy, if you prefer—before you ride home."

"My pleasure, Miss Abby."

He strode to the coach and loosened his packhorse. As he remounted, the two black maids scrambled back into the coach and slammed the door.

"These are our people, Louise"—Abby gestured to those clustered nearby—"our friends who work with us to make crops pay each year."

The men, women, and children bowed and smiled shyly at Louise, whose return smile was brilliant. But she wheeled about suddenly with an angry frown as the carriage began to rumble down the drive after Regrett.

"Tina! Merzella!" Her voice lifted imperiously. Both girls' heads appeared in the coach window.

"Yes, ma'am?"

"You two and Zeke bring in all my baggage at once—the trunks strapped to the top as well as the portmanteaus in the boot—before you do anything else!"

The crowd around Abby began to melt.

"And I want a hot bath this evening," Louise shouted peremptorily after the carriage.

"Yes, ma'am," the maids chorused as the coach disappeared around the house.

Louise turned back to Abby, her scowl smoothing magically.

The workers had moved silently down the graveled pathway toward the rear, leaving the three young women and Abby, whose smile had become mechanical.

"Come, my dears." Abby led the way to the big house. She looked at her granddaughter's closed face, beginning to understand why Monty had not mentioned meeting this woman and her cousin in Washington.

"Incidentally, Mrs. Lynchley—Louise—I find these pants very handy on the farm." Monty's voice was hard as they entered the house. "I could never handle my horses in skirts like yours. In fact, you may come to that conclusion yourself."

Louise looked at her and thought, *There must be some way I can drive a wedge between Richard and this headstrong daughter of his.* Of course Montrose had been gowned beautifully at the ball in Washington, but dressed like this— Perhaps she could use these clothes as an issue to begin a gradual, but necessary, alienation of daughter from father. Louise had no intention of being second to anyone.

"Oh, dear me, no! No breeches for me! They just aren't worn by *ladies.*" She swept past Monty and Faith followed like a small gray shadow.

"I'll send for Josey," Abigail said, taking a small silver bell from a foyer table and ringing it. In an instant, Josey's dark, attractive face showed in the door.

In England, Abby would have referred to the room they had entered as the salon, but now she said, "Josey, please bring a large pitcher of lemonade to the parlor. And you might bring the decanter of brandy for Mr. Regrett later."

"I love this house!" Louise was pulling off her white gloves. "So *different* from the other houses I've seen since coming to Texas. It's really like those in Virginia."

By now, the four women had seated themselves comfortably, Monty and her grandmother on a sofa, the other two in large wing chairs. Feenie came in with a handful of wide palmetto fans.

"Ma say you ladies might like these. It's so hot for May." She gave them to Abby and disappeared.

Abby distributed the fans, which Richard had brought back from a trip to Galveston, and spoke to Louise once more.

"Richard had brick sent from England for this house. It was designed by Charles Graves, an English architect. However, we have our Spanish Texans to thank for the building of it."

"And it's so cool inside." Louise fanned herself idly.

"That's because of brick construction," Abby said. "This part of the republic is often referred to as a fertile belt. It's very warm and everything grows lushly and quickly, grasses, cotton, fruit—even cattle fatten quickly and are being shipped east more often than you might think."

"Darling Richard told me." Louise savored the name and the endearment. "He said the Spanish discovered this country's attributes first." She grew pensive. "And he said when his wife died in Charleston, he was so unhappy he wrote to the new Republic of Texas and bought over thirty-six thousand acres from the government."

Abby's smile was distant. "Tell me, how did you meet my son?"

"Didn't Montrose tell you?"

"No, I didn't," Monty said shortly.

"I surely thought she would." Louise's tone was wounded. She continued more brightly, "Oh, dear Lady Abigail, it was love at first sight! We met at the English Embassy ball about the middle of February. It was a whirlwind courtship."

"It must have been," Abby said dryly. "Do tell me about yourself."

"Since Montrose didn't see fit to tell you, I suppose you don't know that I am—was a widow?"

"No," Abby said, with a touch of sympathy. "I know personally how sad that can be— Ah, here we are!"

Josey entered, bearing a silver tray with crystal glasses, a tall pitcher of lemonade, and a decanter of liquor.

"That looks so delicious!" Louise said, pleased. "I thought Montrose said you had no slaves?"

"We haven't!" Monty's temper flared. "Josey's no slave! We pay her wages, and her husband's, LeRoy's, and Feenie's, too!"

"Don't become so agitated, Montrose. Anyone would think you were an abolitionist," Louise said coldly. "You may pour for me, Josey," she added haughtily.

Josey put the tray down on a low table, poured a glass of lemonade, and handed it to her. Louise took it without comment. Josey then served Faith, whose face beneath the bonnet she still wore was pale. Faith murmured, "Thank you, Josey."

Monty rose and went to the girl. "Faith, I'll be happy to take your bonnet. You'll be much cooler without it."

"Thank you," she said. Her eyes seeking Monty's were suddenly bright with a plea for understanding. "You're very kind, Monty." When Monty took the bonnet, she saw that Faith's thick, gold hair was dulled by a heavy gray net, as it had been the night of the ball.

"I'm very glad you came with Louise, Faith," Monty said quietly. "Pa said you're near my age. I know you'll enjoy it here."

The girl swallowed and nodded wordlessly.

"You were saying that you are—were a widow, Louise?" Abby resumed her conversation.

Louise sighed. She put down her glass on the small mahogany table beside her chair. As the moment drew out, and all eyes turned to her, she slowly took a lace handkerchief from her reticule and pressed it to the corners of her eyes.

"Ah," Abby said softly. "Perhaps you'd rather not speak of it."

"I don't mind talking to *you* about it, dear Lady Abigail, for you must know how I felt. Only Randolph's death was so unnecessary. It was a hunting accident. He kissed me good-bye and he never came back."

"Never came back?"

"I mean he didn't return—alive."

"What kind of hunting accident?" Monty asked bluntly.

Louise's light eyes flicked over Monty, then shuttered.

"You see, Montrose, Randy loved hunting and his gun collection. He went out early one summer morning to hunt game birds—on our estate outside of Charleston—and when he didn't return by supper, I, his mother and sister— we all sent out a search party. It didn't take long to discover him. He—he apparently had been carrying his gun improperly—or something. He had tripped over a log and the gun went off. It—it struck him in the head." Her voice broke. Then smiling bravely, she added, "It was terrible. Faith and I stayed on with his mother and sister in the big house for months. But when Mrs. Gilbert Tucker invited me—and of course, Faith—"

At the mention of the girl's name, Abby and Monty looked over at her. For one so young, Faith's face was remarkably controlled. Her clear hazel eyes were unreadable.

"—to Washington for a visit with her and Senator Tucker, I thought it would be very good for me—for us. A diversion from my grief, you know." She looked appealingly at Abigail and added under her breath, "You can't imagine, Lady Abigail, how dreadfully old Mrs. Lynchley and her old-maid daughter treated me—us!"

Faith's thick gold lashes swept downward, covering eyes that had flashed nakedly for an instant.

A little smile crept along Louise's red lips. "And of course, it was wonderful in Washington. I met my darling Richard there. And the minute he mentioned that he had lived in Charleston, I knew we would have a great deal in common." She bent a dazzling smile on Monty. "You see, Montrose, fate works in strange ways to bring two people together. I had thought I would *never* love anyone as much as I loved Randy." Her eyes narrowed to gilt-lashed glitter. "But I love Richard more—and he loves me *more.*"

"More?" Monty blurted out.

"Why, my dear young Montrose, isn't a husband supposed to love his wife more than *anyone* else?" Her eyes added, *Certainly more than a daughter.*

Mason Regrett chose that moment to enter the room. "Miss Abby, the horses are being curried and fed by Carlos Puente and LeRoy. Now where's that drink you promised?" A dead silence greeted him. Slowly, his black eyes registered Monty's white, shocked face and he added, "Am I interrupting?"

"Of course not," Abigail said, her voice more British than usual. "Do sit down, Mason, and help yourself to some brandy—"

"Miss Abby." It was Josey Beane in the parlor doorway. "Ain't none of Mister Richard's brandy left. That's ol' man Watkins's corn likker from down on the Colorado, what LeRoy brung this week. Reckon you an' Mr. Julien used to that, ain't you, Mister Mase?"

"Sure am, Josey," Mase drawled, reaching for a glass.

"No, Mase," Louise said swiftly, rising. "You sit down and let me serve you. After all, this is my home too now and I must make you welcome. You've done me such a service, riding all those long dusty roads from Nashville—protecting us from heaven knows what!" She had taken the glass before Mason Regrett could seat himself and was pouring a good stiff drink for him. He was still standing as she extended it.

Abby smiled, but her eyes on Louise were speculative. She looked from her new daughter-in-law to Josey, who was still standing in the foyer doorway. How long Josey had been there, listening, could not be guessed from the dark mask of her face. Feenie's round eyes could be seen behind her mother's shoulder and there was no mistaking what she thought of the exchange that had just taken place.

After his first swallow, Mase Regrett's grin was sardonic. "You are too gracious, Mrs. Daventry." Then, his smile broadening, he announced, "Now I'm *home,* Josey. If I'd had some of Richard Daventry's fine imported English brandy, I'd think I was still in Washington."

"Josey, please show Tina and Merzella where Mister Richard's room is," Abby interjected.

"Yes, Miss Abby."

Louise still stood beside Regrett. Her hand came out and stroked his broad shoulder, her face young and ingenuous. "You dear, dear man! I shudder to think of what might have happened on the trip without you."

"You make too much of my service, Mrs. Daventry." His smile was cynical and he did not seat himself. "I was coming home anyway and Zeke had his musket and pistols—and the roads are fairly well traveled now, if you take the right ones."

"You can say that, now that we're safely here." She shivered delicately. She had apparently recovered from her confession of grief. "Now, do sit down, Mr. Regrett. You need to rest."

Over his glass, Regrett observed the women in the room. Louise was taking off her hat, putting it on the chair beside her. Faith Warren was motionless, but her hazel eyes were alive with hidden emotion. Miss Abby's features were totally unreadable, but Monty Daventry's open face was a study in barely controlled fury. Regrett hid a smile.

"Miss Abby"—he grinned amiably at her—"LeRoy has asked me to take a look at a couple of Richard's horses that seem to be ailing." He downed the last of the liquor and added, "I can't hope to regain his friendship—but I'd like to keep his respect—and my knowledge of horses is one way to do it."

"Mason, you know I don't hold with politics making enemies of good neighbors!" She looked into his darkly tanned face, with the strong, hawklike nose. Little lines fanned out from black eyes, as much from frequent laughter as from squinting at distances. Unknown to the others, her sympathies lay with the wily Sam Houston as he sought to pit England against the United States in the matter of annexation. Houston knew perfectly well, and so did Abigail, that the more England sought to prevent it, the more likely the United States would be to take in the Texas Republic.

"Miss Abby, you confirm my intent to marry you," Regrett said, his eyes twinkling. "But for now, I'll bid you ladies good afternoon." As he turned to leave, he winked audaciously at Monty, who blushed.

Louise saw it and laughed delightedly. "Ah, Mr. Regrett, you are indeed a rascal and I'm going to patch up this foolish quarrel between you and my darling Richard." She added archly, "And I assure you, the little secret you, Montrose, and I share will be safe with me."

Monty's breath went out of her and she paled, but Mason Regrett turned a grim smile on Louise.

"Mrs. Daventry, I can see you're an astute woman," was all he said, before disappearing into the shadowy foyer.

Louise rose, her skirts swirling gracefully, and picked up the pitcher of lemonade to refill her glass. She sent Monty a roguish glance. "I can see you need my influence, Montrose, in the matter of dress and education. Don't you agree, Lady Abigail?"

"Everyone calls me Abby, Louise. And as for Monty, I think you'll find her hard to influence." The words were frosty.

"As a matter of fact," Monty said abruptly, "Abby has educated me very well and I would prefer you call me Monty—or I'll not know you're speaking to me." Her grandmother was convent-educated, and fresh fuel was added to Monty's anger that this superficial woman should fault her education at Abby's hand.

"But Montrose, darling! Monty is such a *man's* name—I knew a Montague we called Monty." She pursed her lips. "No, I can never call you Monty—and Lady Abigail, I *must* accord you the respect of your title!"

Abby laughed wryly. "Only the Cavenals have retained their titles, for they have also retained their estates and citizenship in England."

"Montrose was my mother's maiden name," Monty persisted angrily, "and my father chose it with the understanding that I could shorten it as I liked. He told me so himself."

"I can see your father has indulged you too much, Montrose. You're a young lady and must be addressed—and clothed—as such. As your new stepmother, I insist upon it."

"Louise," Monty said hotly, "life's not easy on this plantation. And I'm interested in horses—*my* horses—"

"Don't worry, Montrose," Louise cut in, laugh tinkling. "I'm quite good on a horse—sidesaddle, as any lady should be. But I intend to do my duty. You'll learn to be a lady, and I'll personally instruct you."

Monty's face grew paler under her crown of bright hair and she put her glass of unfinished lemonade on the table beside Abigail. Across from her, Faith Warren sat straight and stiff, her face as white as Monty's, her full lower lip caught between her teeth.

"Abby," Monty said with barely controlled fury, "I am going to ride Warlock to the Cavenals'—"

"Not alone—" Abby said swiftly.

"You know well and good the patrols are still riding this early! I'll have supper with Georgina and maybe stay the night as well." She strode out of the parlor, her small booted heels sounding on the polished foyer floor. Louise turned wide, innocent blue eyes on Abby.

"Did I say something—to send her off in such an ungracious manner, Lady Abigail?"

"It's possible. Excuse me a moment, Louise—and Faith. I must see that Monty is escorted. I'll return in a moment."

Louise sipped modestly at her glass as Abby made her way to the kitchen where Josey and Feenie were busily preparing food. A large roast was on the spit in the big kitchen fireplace and the air was filled with the fragrance of baking bread.

"Feenie, run out to the stable and tell Mason Regrett that Monty is going to ride Warlock to the Cavenal place. I don't trust that young stallion, despite Monty's love of the animal, and she's angry enough to go alone. Tell Mr. Regrett to bring her back—if he can."

"Yes, ma'am." Feenie started for the door.

"And if he can't—tell him to stay with her until she reaches Cav's place in one piece."

Feenie's eyes were wide. Monty had lost her temper again. She could tell by the way Miss Abby looked—and it was over an hour's ride to Lord Cavenal's. Alone! That was forbidden by Mister Richard himself!

Abby turned to leave, then turned back. "And if Mr. Regrett's already gone, see if you can find Miguel and his father to go instead—hurry!"

Mason Regrett saw Monty as she ran past him to Warlock's stall. With LeRoy Beane, he had finished examining a deep cut on a big gray gelding's fetlock. He had just recommended that LeRoy use some of his wife's strong lye soap to bathe it twice daily.

Monty did not speak to either of them or to Young Miguel where he was currying Regrett's big stallion in an adjacent stall. She had saddled her stallion and was out of the stable before Feenie came flying out the back door and across the broad sweep of yard between stable and house. The lean hunting hounds around the cabins barked at her swift exit.

"Mister Mase, Miss Abby done told me to ask you to take after Monty an' bring her back here! She say she's on her way to the Cavenal place alone an' she say if you can't persuade her to come back, to stay with her so's she gets there in one piece." Feenie paused to catch her breath. "I think her new stepmama done said somethin' to tetch off that gunpowder temper of hers."

Regrett rose to his feet and went to the stable door, looking toward the south. He was just in time to see the stallion lift Monty gracefully but wildly over the fence and onto the road beyond the wide area that housed the cabins, stables, and other outbuildings.

Monty never opened the gate to the road past the south pasture and cotton fields beyond. She always took the fence with practiced ease. Warlock was accustomed to lifting his narrow ankles high and sailing over that fence with his willful rider. She did not look back.

Regrett swore softly under his breath. He wasn't tired, but he was looking forward to getting home. He hadn't seen his brother, Julien, in over seven months. He turned to the stall where he had left Coffee with Young Miguel Puente.

"Thanks, Miguel," he said to the young Mexican who had just finished currying the horse's mane. "I've got to catch that wildcat."

"I'll saddle him, señor," Young Miguel offered, but

Regrett shook his head and slung the saddle himself over the horse's broad back.

"Monty get speed out of that big black horse when she's mad," Young Miguel said, grinning, as Regrett tightened the cinches under Coffee's belly. "At leas' Coffee's have a little rest."

Young Miguel's voice was deep and musical and he was extraordinarily tall. His Spanish accent was noticeable, and he had the classic features of his conquistador forebears.

Feenie stared at him admiringly before she turned at her mother's call from the kitchen door.

Regrett swung his lean body into the saddle and took off at a gallop, fluttering chickens and setting the dogs to barking once more. Like Monty, he did not stop to open the gate, but leaned into Coffee and soared cleanly over the high fence with two feet to spare.

He could see her far down the tree-shadowed road, where she had Warlock in an easy lope. This was the road around the apex of the triangle. It led to both the Regrett and Cavenal properties. On one side, beyond a heavy stand of oaks, were the Daventry cotton fields. On the opposite side, to the west, were the orchards—Richard Daventry's pride and joy. The deep green leaves of the trees glistened over new young fruit in the late afternoon sunlight.

That girl needed a good spanking, Regrett thought angrily, as he put spurs lightly to Coffee's sides. The big horse had glimpsed the girl and other horse and sensed its rider's goal. Now Coffee stretched out his long, powerful legs and moved steadily up on the two. Coffee was a bigger horse than Warlock. He was older, stronger, and better trained. He gained rapidly on the two ahead.

Monty, hearing pursuit, looked back and recognized the horse and its rider. She bent low over her mount and urged him on.

The sun was closer to the horizon now and soon dusk

would fall over this whole fertile region of south-central Texas. To the west lay the more than fifty thousand acres belonging to the Regrett brothers, and several thousand head of mixed-breed cattle grazed the richest of lush grasses that grew for miles and miles.

To the south lay the plantation belonging to Lord Cavenal. He had built a house every bit as fine as Richard Daventry's and he had brought slaves from New Orleans to work his own acres and acres of cotton.

Monty knew they were nearing Three Points Lake, and Warlock was tiring. She had not expected pursuit. She had expected to slow her mount and trot at a leisurely pace to Cav's house, allowing her rage to cool in the balmy spring air.

Instead, she found herself in a race with a man who disturbed her deeply and whom she disliked intensely. She surmised correctly that Abby had sent him after her because she had disobeyed the cardinal rule of never riding more than a mile without an escort. Newfound, active hatred for Louise merged with the unsettled feeling Mason Regrett stirred in her and her body hummed with rage. She rose slightly in the stirrups, giving Warlock his head and heard Regrett, behind her, give vent to his own anger.

"Rein in!" His deep voice was carried strongly by the wind. "Rein in before that buck stallion throws you and breaks your neck!"

She flailed the horse about the neck with her reins, goading him forward with her heels. Ahead she saw the lake among thick green-leaved trees. It was fed by several natural springs, and all three of the men whose property met there used the clear cold water for their stock by mutual agreement, though the lake was actually on Regrett land. The road split here, the west one to Regrett's, the south to Cavenal's.

"If you don't rein in, I swear I'll pull you out of the saddle!" Regrett drew up beside her.

She turned a furious face to him. "You have no right to stop me!"

"Miss Abby sent me after you. Now rein in, goddammit!" He moved Coffee in close and she refused to look at him, bending low over Warlock and urging him on.

As he had threatened, Regrett dropped his reins, reached over with both hands and pulled her from the saddle. Coffee, trained for years by the man astride him, slowed immediately.

Monty fought him with all her strength, writhing in his powerful grasp. Her heavy copper braids, already loosened by the wind on her wild ride, were loose now. As she fought with Regrett, they loosened further until her hair was free of all restraint. Holding her in the saddle before him with one arm, Regrett reached up and caught a handful of it, forcing her upper body against his. Still she lashed out with her feet. She was aware only of her hoarse breath and Regrett's hard, unyielding body wrenching submission from her.

When finally she subsided and was still for a moment, he spoke soothingly to Coffee, slowing him to a complete stop. Holding Monty tightly, he slipped to the ground. As she felt her feet touch the grass, she twisted violently and he released her. They stood facing each other, breathing hard, faces flushed and eyes flashing in the dusky light.

"You have a hell of a nerve!" Monty shouted. "Acting as escort for that—that witch—then chasing me down when I had to get away from her—her and her 'our little secret is safe with me'!" She dragged in a breath. "I hate you both, Mason Regrett! I've always—"

"Shut up!" he said harshly. "I didn't want to chase you down! I did it for Miss Abby. You don't think I give a damn whether Indians get you, or you break your neck over your new stepmother, do you?"

"Stepmother!" she yelled, flinging back the long, burnished hair. "She'll *never* be stepmother to *me*—"

"Yes she will," he said grimly. Having found a nerve, he prodded it again. "You're mad as hell because your father's found a beautiful woman he loves—maybe better than his spoiled brat of a daughter. And you might as well get over it."

Her eyes darkened with new rage. Her arm flew up and her hand cracked against his flat, hard cheek. She put all her strength behind it, and it sounded like a pistol shot in the wind.

He drew a quick breath. Reaching out, he caught her arm before it could fall back to her side.

"You little devil," he said, "I've always thought you needed a good strapping with a leather belt—" He caught her to him by the belt around her narrow waist. Then switching sides, his hand went inside her pants at the back. He lifted her by the pants and belt like a sack of cornmeal and strode toward the trees that surrounded the lake.

Chapter 6

Hanging ignominiously by her belt, Monty yelled, "You let go of me this minute, Mason Regrett!"

"I will, when I get where I can lay into you proper."

"What do you mean?" she cried.

"I mean to give you the licking your father has failed to give you all these years."

"What?"

By then he had reached the narrow beach of the spring-fed lake and seated himself on a fallen hackberry tree trunk. He turned her forcibly across his knees, and holding her down with his left hand, began smacking her firm, round little bottom with his right.

Mason Regrett was a strong man and he did not spare his strength as he brought his big hand hard and flat to Monty's rear. The blows rang loud and clear, and they brought tears of pain as well as fury to Monty's eyes. The indignity she was suffering made her cry in earnest. She ceased to struggle and put her hands to her face.

Her bottom was stinging hotly when he put his hands about her waist and set her down on the log beside him.

"There," he said, "that ought to teach you to be a little more respectful of your elders."

"What elders?" she asked stormily.

"Me, for one. And your new stepmother for another."

"You *like* that awful woman?"

"Well," he said evasively, "she's very beautiful and obviously your father loves her. That fact alone should make you try to get along with her."

Monty was silent, turning to look back at the horses. They were cropping the rich grass that grew in such luxurious abundance around the lake. Both of them stallions, they kept a respectful distance between them.

Then she dropped her head to her hands and began sobbing again The worst had happened to her. Her father had married a horrible woman, she had been chased by this terrible man who affected her deeply, caught by him and beaten by him. She'd been shamed and humiliated by both Louise and Regrett.

Looking down at the slender shoulders shaking beside him, compassion stirred in Regrett. Maybe he had struck her a little harder than he should have. And after all, that beautiful Louise Daventry was a chancy woman. Experience had taught him long ago to recognize that kind of trouble and avoid it.

He put a casual arm around Monty and, with his other hand, lifted up the tear-stained face. God, she was beautiful.

"Monty, don't take it to heart. You can get used to most things you can't change, even a new stepmother."

"She's no kin of mine, not even by law! Nor will she ever be—"

He hugged her against his lean, hard waist and chest and his hand slipped, brushing one of her firm, challenging little breasts. The shocking awareness he had known in Washington, when he saw her for the first time dressed as a woman, shot through his veins and he felt himself growing hard.

He drew away. He'd admired Monty Daventry even when

she was a tempting little eleven-year-old. He admired her spunk and determination, her love and appreciation of horses. Now, hot desire for her flooded through him. The damage was done.

In the dusky light, she turned gentian eyes on his, moist lips full and trembling, and drew a hand across her wet cheeks.

"Mase, she says she's going to change me. She calls me Montrose and says she's going to put me in dresses all the time—teach me ladylike airs." She leaned toward him with innocent provocation, her breast against his arm.

He turned on her with sudden fierceness. "You need a few ladylike airs, Monty—"

Then with abrupt surrender to forces that were shaking both of them, he swept her into his arms, his lips feeling for her warm, tear-wet mouth. He found it, soft and parting to him. Crushing her against him, he felt her nipples through the light shirt already hard against his chest. This was not like the flash of passionate desire that had seized him that night at the British Embassy in Washington. That had been but an ember compared to the flame that burned in him now.

His kiss was long and thirsty. He felt he could never get enough of the taste of her. One coherent thought flashed through the smoky desire in his mind. Had he always wanted her so, even as he watched her grow up before him?

It was her innocent response that made him abandon all restraint. He slipped his tongue between her lips, gently at first, only to find it met by hers as the two tangled together in a mating of the senses.

He lifted her off the log, holding her in both arms, their mouths still joined, and laid her on the narrow beach of the lake. A warm, scented wind blew off it, mingling with the distant fragrances of the orchards and all young, growing things, tender and new, fresh and tingling.

He began to unfasten her shirt and was met by her helping hands. In an instant, the piquant breasts were bare beneath him and he bent his head to caress them with his lips. The scent of her flesh was a powerful stimulant to his desire.

"My God, Monty," he groaned, "you're so young—and I can't stop—"

"Don't stop," she breathed. Monty had never known such uncontrollable sensations and all of them delicious. She had never been kissed by anyone, before this man had kissed her in the warm gloom of the library at the embassy. She found herself helping Mase Regrett pull off her boots, her fitted pants, her thin silk chemise. After that, her nakedness to the evening breeze, to the silty damp sand beneath her back, merged with the tide of desire sweeping her.

She watched through heavy lids as Regrett removed his clothing, and for the first time, she saw him naked before her. A thrill as sharp as pain coursed through her, and because it seemed so natural and so right, she wondered if she had dreamed it before.

When their bodies touched and she felt the hard erectness of him, her head was light, and she clung to him as the only solid thing in a swimming world about her. His hands caressed her, their roughened palms evoking a shivering anticipation. Then one of them played itself into the warm, tender, and furry moistness between her legs, stroking, probing, promising newer and more frenzied delights.

Little gasping cries of pleasure escaped her, and she whispered against his mouth, "Oh, don't stop, Mase. Don't stop!" and her legs shifted, widening beneath him, under the wooing movements of his fingers. She marveled at his gentleness when the wildness in her craved wildness in return. But his teeth were easy on the tips of her breasts, and his finger exploring inside her warmness increased with every kiss, every sensual caress, every touch of their warm naked bodies in the summer fragrance of the evening air.

When at last he entered her, she flung her arms about him, pulling him down to her, placing little kisses all about his mouth before fastening on it hungrily.

Mason Regrett, experienced though he was, had never known a delirium of passion such as the one that shook him when he mounted Monty. Her frantic, unbridled movements told him she had never known, never dreamed of what had seized them both. She was caught up in the mindless joy of mating with a man who knew exactly how to evoke such passion from her.

As their fusion grew more turbulent, more reckless, their pleasure increased accordingly. Regrett's skilled movements were met by Monty's upward thrust of her hips, until their mating became uncontrolled and savage, until their breaths mingled in gasps and the world was blotted out in a brutal, untamed gust of passion. Their bodies coalesced in a primal absorption, bursting at last into an explosion that was shattering, blinding, and wholly devastating.

Regrett lay spent across her and she clung to him. He was still the only solid thing in a world that had vanished around her. Her breath came quick and shallow. She looked up beyond the dark head on her breast at a sky brilliant with stars.

"God, Monty," he murmured deeply, "you're sweet. The sweetest thing this side of heaven."

"Am I?" she whispered, still shaken and trembling. "I never knew anything—anyone could be so—wonderful."

He lifted his head. A touch of the old mockery was in his next words. "I wonder if you'll feel that way in the morning, my sweet."

"Nothing can change what we . . . shared—the wonder of it. I never knew it would be like that." Growing up on her father's land, she had seen animals mate often enough, but had registered it only as a fact of farm life. The vague stirrings she had felt within her she had discounted. Except for that moment of sweet madness she had known in Washington, when Regrett's lips had claimed hers. But she had even discounted those feelings. How could she have known the furious passions that were banked like raging fires inside her slender body? Now she was swept clean of the miserable emotions that had gnawed at her as she had fled her home earlier. And as they sat upon the cool, damp sand, she looked toward the east and saw the old moon rising slowly.

"We'd better dress," Regrett said quietly. "I must get you home safely, or Miss Abby will send out a search party."

"Can't we sit here by the lake . . . longer?"

"No, we can't. I'm already out of favor with your father. You know, don't you, that he'd shoot me on sight if he knew what we've done."

"But it was so . . . glorious. I—I've never known anything like it."

"I've put a burden on you, Monty," he said grimly.

"What kind of burden?"

"You've been raised on a farm. You know how horses, cows, pigs, even dogs mate," he said brutally. "And you know the results, don't you?"

"Oh."

"Jesus, Monty, I didn't know you were such an innocent!"

She looked away from him, feeling rejection, and the old emotions surfaced once more. Why, damn him, he was telling her she might be pregnant! With that realization, a thousand recollections flooded her mind. All of Regrett's visits to the Daventry house and hers to the Regretts' rose up. With them came a sharply renewed awareness of his long, lean body beside her. From under her thick black lashes, she scrutinized his profile, all the more attractive with the hump where his nose had been broken in a long-ago fight. *She could smell him!* He smelled of sun and wind, of good horses, and there was a male odor that was neither sweat nor dirt, but of his own muscled flesh.

She shivered. Desire lingered, reluctant to leave before a rising anger.

"And now that you've had me, you're through with me," she said, flinging back her long, bright hair. "Well, I've learned something else today." Her voice was sharp and sarcastic. "Pa's right about you. You're a light-minded man who doesn't know what's good for him or his country."

She started to rise and he reached a rough hand out to catch her arm. Dragging her down beside him again, he pushed her to the ground and loomed over her.

"Damn you, Monty Daventry! You know that's a lie!" He was over her and his body covered hers. Their bare skin touching had the same effect as before on Monty. The uncontrollable fire rose in her, blotting out reason or resistance and leaving only the blind drive for union between them.

She kissed his mouth as he bent his head and her arms twined about his neck and shoulders, pulling him tight against her. But as before, he held her off, drawing out the pleasure of their melding bodies. He explored with his lips and tongue the delicate sensitive places on her, letting his fingers play with her breast and along her legs, fondling the place that ached for all of him.

Mason Regrett had known many women, but he had never known one with the passion and fire of Monty Daventry. Unable to control his desire for the warm, tender body beneath him, he took her with driving force. She arched to meet him, crying out with pleasure, meeting him again and again in surging waves of heated sensation. It culminated at last in the blinding roar that filled his ears with the pounding of his own blood.

They lay, spent with the final glory of their shared emotions. He stayed with his bare flesh covering hers and felt her quickened breathing, her sweet breath against his lips.

"It's getting late," he murmured, lifting himself to lie beside her on the sand that had been their bed. Stars winked down from the dark blue arch above them.

"I don't want to go."

"Monty, you're wonderful! But tomorrow you'll remember tonight. You may even remember it before tomorrow and you might even hate me again." His laugh was knowing.

It fired her with a new and completely unexpected fury. She did not realize her emotion was jealousy—jealousy of the women he might have known before her. She only knew she was angry. She rolled away from him and in the pale light of the old, waning moon, she snatched up her clothes and began hurriedly to put them on.

"Now what's set you off?" he asked lazily, beginning to draw on his own breeches and boots. His broad chest with the dark curling hair, darker for the night around them, was still bare.

"Nothing," she said between her teeth.

"Lying again, eh? You're mad as hell. What's done it, Monty?" Reaching out, he caught her again as she was buttoning her shirt over uptilted breasts. She twisted in his grasp, but his fingers were steel prongs. "Not until you tell me what's wrong."

"What's wrong?" She looked up into the dark, lean face, a lump forming in her throat. By heaven, she swore silently to herself, she would *not* cry before him again! "You told me clearly enough what's wrong! What we've done is wrong—and it means no more to you than a barnyard mating!"

"Another lie—"

"You said yourself it was," she broke in perversely.

"I did not! I was trying to tell you—to protect you from—"

"From what? Yourself, of course! You've done this to girls God knows how many times—what a fool I've been!" With her free hand she pulled at his strong fingers on her arm. "Let me go, Mason Regrett. I hate you for what you've done to me!"

"By God, it's happened sooner than I thought it would," he swore, releasing her and turning to pick his shirt off the ground. "I knew you'd have second thoughts, this being your first time—"

"And second time, thanks to you! Oh, you've taught me something, Mase. You're a *good* teacher!"

"Thanks, Monty. I'm glad you enjoyed it." His voice was deep and there was laughter hidden in it.

"I'll never do it again!"

"I hope you won't—with anyone but me."

Speechless with rage, she ran toward Warlock, who was grazing among the trees only a short distance from the lake. Her sudden approach startled him, and he threw up his head, nickering, and shied away from her.

"You come here to me, Warlock," she said, low and sharp. "Come on."

Warlock lifted his head and looked across the moonlit spaces between the trees. A wind had risen and was rustling among them coolly. Regrett's horse did not move as his owner approached.

"Want me to help?" Regrett called to her.

"No!" She was trying to coax the horse to stillness, but each time she drew near, the young stallion threw up his head, loose reins flapping, and backed farther away.

"Come now, Monty—we may have to ride double on Coffee to get you home before midnight!"

"We'll do no such thing! I'll walk first."

"Like hell you will. Miss Abby sent me out to fetch you, miss, and fetch you I will." His voice was cold, and Monty knew he meant it.

Again she approached the nervous stallion and again he flung up his head and shied away.

"Let me try to get him," Regrett said.

She didn't want that, she thought swiftly. With sudden determination, she ran after the stallion and he took off at a gallop. Regrett put his heels to Coffee's flanks and urged him forward. Warlock, looking back and observing that his pursuers were now three, let his legs stretch in mile-eating leaps.

"Damn!" Monty whispered in frustration. A walk back to the Daventry house *would* get her home after midnight. She wasn't afraid, despite her father's edict that no woman venture alone out of sight of the house. Abby would surely have the whole place searching for her, having already gone so far as to send Regrett after her.

Out in the moonlit meadow, she saw Regrett rein in his horse and turn back. Warlock was out of sight. He would no doubt head for the Regrett ranch anyway, for her father had bought him for Monty from Mason Regrett the year before.

Dejected, Monty turned and went back to the lake, where she dipped up water and bathed her hot face.

"Get aboard, Monty," Regrett said evenly as he trotted up beside her. "I've got to get you back to Miss Abby and pick up my packhorse. And I'd like to get home before midnight myself." He extended a hand down to her.

Monty caught it and swung herself effortlessly onto Coffee's rump, then sat stiffly upright as Regrett put the big stallion into an easy lope.

"Montrose has certainly been gone a long time," Louise remarked pensively as she put her second glass of cool tea down on the long Daventry dinner table. "I thought surely Mr. Regrett would bring her back in time for dinner."

Faith began timidly, "But—isn't it a long way to—to—"

"The Cavenals'," Abby supplied swiftly. "Yes, it is, Faith, and I'm sure that's why they aren't here yet."

"Still—I'm really worried." Louise sighed. "I simply can't go up and take my bath until we know she's safe."

Abby's gray eyes on her were bland. "I know you must be tired, Louise. Why not go up and have your bath? Mase is very dependable. I'll wait in the parlor for their return."

"I couldn't do that, dear Lady Abigail." Louise was injured. "I'd be remiss in my duty as her stepmother."

Abby contemplated the beautiful face before her, lips almost too ripe. Louise's eyes, on the other hand, were rather small, but she kept them so widely open, and the gold lashes were so thick a frame, that the illusion of wide-eyed innocence and sincerity was undeniable. It would not be wise, Abby reflected, to dislike this young woman on such short acquaintance. Still, her voice was cold when she spoke.

"My dear Louise, it's admirable to take one's duty seriously. But considering that it's been no more than two hours —and it's just now dark—I think your rest and refreshment would be Richard's wish."

Faith rose from the supper table immediately at the command in Abby's cultured voice, but Louise was slower.

"You may be right, Lady Abigail," she said, pursing her lips judiciously, "I *am* very tired . . ." She let the words trail off in a sigh.

"I'm sure Tina and Merzella have unpacked for both of you by now"—Abby's voice had not changed—"and will be happy to bring hot water for your baths."

"You're very kind, Miss Abby." Faith spoke softly.

"You must call her Lady Abigail, Faith!" Louise was sharp and critical.

"I think not, Louise," Abby said, growing colder. "I prefer that Faith call me Miss Abby. If you insist on my former title for yourself, I will not object." She rose and the two young women followed her to the foyer. "Richard's bed was built for him in London, Louise, and is half again wider than the customary double bed." Abby's voice softened imperceptibly. "And Faith, I'm sure you'll like that bedroom next to Richard's—and Louise's. It was Monty's before she decided on the one at the south end of the hall."

"I think it's beautiful," Faith said quietly.

"Yes," Louise put in. "When you took us up to wash before supper, both of us were impressed—by the real magnificence of such a home in the—ah—wilderness."

"And it is a wilderness, Louise," Abby replied firmly. "As for the patrols, there are only two men from each estate—six in all—and sometimes they range as far as fifteen miles from the houses."

"So far?"

"This is a broad land and there are thousands upon thousands of acres in each of our places—Cavenals', Regretts' and Daventrys'." At the foot of the stairs, Abby stopped. "Good night, then. Sleep well."

She went into the kitchen after the two girls had climbed the stairs to the landing. Feenie had finished the dishes and was preparing to put them back in the china cabinet in the dining room. Josey was putting away the remainder of the food.

"You want another glass of tea, Miss Abby?" she asked.

"I'd like that, Josey."

She seated herself at the broad kitchen table in the center of the room. Her glass of tea was only half finished when she heard Mason Regrett's deep baritone outside the kitchen door.

"You can call me gloating if you want to, Monty, but it's a statement of fact."

The door burst open and a flushed Monty stormed into the kitchen. Josey and Feenie stopped to watch as the two squared off before Miss Abby.

"Abby, Mase says because the Congress voted to take us in, it's settled—he thinks Texas will vote to join—and that'll be the end of it!" She turned angry eyes on her grandmother.

"I didn't say that would be the end of it," Regrett said swiftly. "Mexico'll never let Texas go without a fight. I'll bet you a five-dollar gold piece there'll be a hot little war between the United States and Mexico after Texas becomes a state."

"But Mexico agreed—we've been a republic for ten years!"

"No, they didn't agree. Santa Anna agreed, but they threw him out and his agreement with him. And you know how regularly Mexican soldiers raid in Texas." He shrugged and added, "Monty, Spain conquered Mexico in 1521. Then finally Mexico rose up—and threw out Spain. Mexico's been throwing out governments ever since. They won't balk at trying to throw out the United States."

"But a war!"

Abby watched them with interest and sipped her tea. Monty was disheveled and her lips appeared full, almost bruised. She looked like a girl who had just had her emotions in a turmoil more far-reaching than this political quarrel.

Regrett's smile was ironic. "Don't you know that land always belongs to those who can hold it? And sometimes by war?"

"But Pa says England will protect Texas from Mexico!"

"I'm sure they would. But who will protect us from England?"

There was a small silence, then Abby asked mildly, "Aren't you two hungry?"

Monty whirled on her. "Abby, how could you have sent *him* to fetch me, when you know how Pa and I—I hate him?" At the sound of her angry voice, Josey and Feenie moved to the back door, closing it quietly behind them.

"What took you so long to get back?" Abby ignored Monty's question.

"Warlock ran off. I reckon you'll have to send Big Miguel and some of the boys to chase him down," Regrett drawled. "Monty and I did our best to catch him, but he's not very accommodating—or grateful. He's like some people I know."

"Hmm." Abby's eyes on Monty were reflective. "Last time he ran off, he wound up back in your stables, Mase. I expect we'll find him there in the morning."

"That's likely," Regrett said ruefully. "Monty made us give him to her before Julien and I were through training him—"

"You'd trained him long enough!"

"Nope, Monty. We should've kept him three months longer. I hope you don't rush the mare you and your father picked out." Then, without hesitating, he put his old hat on his head and added, "Thanks, Miss Abby, but I'll pass on your offer to feed me—I want to get home. I've a feeling Julien could use another hand around the place."

He nodded to Monty, who turned her back on him. Then he went out the back door, closing it with quiet finality.

Chapter 7

Abby rose and took the remains of the roast beef from a cupboard, along with a loaf of bread.

"I'm surprised," she said, as she began making a sandwich for her granddaughter, "that Mase can get such a rise out of you, Monty."

"Ah—he doesn't," she replied with an heroic effort to sound indifferent. "It's just that he's so *sure* of himself."

"That's a good characteristic, if it's not carried to an extreme," Abby said, sending her granddaughter an amused glance. Monty wasn't going to tell her what had preceded their quarrel over politics, Abby thought, and tried to push away the picture that was growing in her mind. She had made a mistake in sending Mason Regrett for Monty, and she knew it now.

"He carries it to an extreme—I'll go out to the springhouse and get a glass of milk."

Later, as she sat eating, Monty asked, "And was Louise as domineering with you the rest of the evening as she was with me?"

Abby's smile was wintry. "Now there's one who carries her self-confidence to an extreme."

"So," Monty replied triumphantly, "you see it, too! She's a perfect witch! What did she do after I left?"

"Talked. She plans to rearrange your father's house."

"What! How?"

"For one thing, she says the buffet ought to be where we have the china cabinet. She spoke of getting the servants to move all the furniture tomorrow. She wants to surprise Richard with her tasteful arrangements."

"My God!" Monty burst out. "What a nerve!"

"That's not all, my dear. She wants all the silver and brass polished by Feenie and Josey tomorrow, and they were just polished a week ago. She informed me in no uncertain terms that she had always had them polished every four days at her previous home." She paused, then added, "Merzella and Tina carried up hot water for baths—they're still up there."

"Bathing her, I'll bet! Abby, you've run this house for years! What did you say to her?"

"I was polite to her. She's your father's wife and is officially mistress of this house now," Abby replied somberly. "And maybe she'll get it all out of her system before Richard returns."

"I hate her!"

"Reserve judgment, Monty. Wait until your father returns."

"Her and her 'Montrose this' and 'Montrose that'!"

"You must be polite. You don't want your father coming back to a house full of ugly quarrels! Doesn't his happiness mean something to you?"

"Yes," Monty said slowly, realizing her grandmother had touched a vulnerable point. She would put up with a great deal to make her father happy. Realizing this, she felt a yoke settling about her slender shoulders. "But Abby, don't you think she's brazen?" she appealed. "And self-centered?"

"I do. But I'll bear with her until Richard arrives—and so

will you. He may . . . gentle her abrasive ways with us. If she wants to take over managing the entire house, let her. She may find it not to her liking after all—later."

"Not Louise," Monty said bitterly. "Abby, you know that woman will be selfish to the end of her life. Oh," she finished distractedly, "I don't know what came over Pa when he met her in Washington!"

"You wouldn't remember, Monty, but Louise resembles your mother remarkably—but only physically. Her character is—totally alien to Elizabeth's."

"I know that little painting of Mother in Pa's room, and I don't think she looks anything like Louise. My mother's eyes were much bigger and bluer!"

"But her smile, her hair, and her pretty figure were much like Louise's. Promise me you'll hold your tongue, Monty. Please, for your father's sake—and mine."

Monty pushed away the plate holding her half-finished sandwich, for suddenly Regrett's words rang like a knell in her mind. *You've been raised in the country. You know how horses, cows, pigs, even dogs, mate. And you know the results, don't you?* That was what she had done with Mase. Would there be a baby?

"Finish your sandwich, Monty."

"I'm not hungry, Abby. I—I lose my appetite just thinking about that woman." A faint pink color climbed into her cheeks. Perspiration broke over her upper lip and the back of her neck. She was a fool to have succumbed so quickly and fiercely to Regrett. What had driven her to such wild abandon? *I should never have done it,* she thought guiltily.

"Abby," she said, looking into the affectionate eyes across from her, "do you suppose this woman and Pa could have a baby?"

In the golden lamplight, Abby's smooth face tightened.

"It's very possible. They're both well and she seems healthy. Your father's only thirty-six."

"What if she doesn't want to spoil that pretty shape of hers? Are there ways to keep from having a baby?" The color slowly receded from Monty's face under her grandmother's keen eyes. "Well, are there, Abby? I've heard about Rebecca's house in Victoria— What do those women do?"

"Who would tell you about that—brothel?" Abby asked sharply.

"Feenie. She says they don't have babies."

"I'm ashamed of you—and Feenie, too."

"Well, isn't there *some* way?"

"I know of one way," she replied slowly, "but men don't like to do it. I haven't taught you yet about marriage, Monty. Seventeen is so young, and I supposed life on this estate had educated you about mating."

"Oh, I know about *that*," Monty retorted, with a labored effort to be airy. "But it's Louise and Pa I don't know about." Her eyes lifted to Abby's. "How could Louise keep from having a baby?"

"She could ask your father to withdraw—just before his seed is planted—and avoid pregnancy. But it puts a strain on a man and your father's not a patient man. Furthermore, it's not foolproof. There's always a chance."

Monty looked away from the penetrating gray eyes.

"Cheer up, Monty." Abby laughed suddenly with a touch of cynicism. "She didn't have any children from her first marriage—and she was married to Randolph Lynchley for four years. It's possible she's barren."

Monty eyed the sandwich with distaste. What Abby had told her didn't help now. She got to her feet slowly, said good night and left the room.

Abby sat at the kitchen table, looking after her departing granddaughter, and thinking. She had been aware of the electricity that sparked between Mason Regrett and Monty through the years when he had come to the house. Even when he brought stick candy to the eleven-year-old tomboy, ruffled her hair and called her Red. She had been aware of Monty's half-angry, half-laughing responses to the man. Further, she had sensed the tight rein Regrett held on himself as he teased Monty and pulled her braids.

Last year, when he had brought Warlock to Richard for his daughter, Regrett's glances at the sixteen-year-old Monty were veiled. But Abby had recognized tension between the two of them—and she knew that even Mason Regrett had not been fully aware of his reaction to Monty.

Yes, Abby reflected, sending Regrett to bring Monty back or see her safely to the Cavenals' had been a mistake. She had asked him hastily and without thought. They had been gone a long time and Warlock had run off.

Monty had not deceived her grandmother with her questions about Louise, and now Abby hoped there would be no consequences following this time Monty had spent with Regrett.

Mason Regrett took the same route back toward the spring-fed lake that he and Monty had just ridden. It was the shortest route between the vast cotton and corn fields of the Cavenal and Daventry ranches, and the endless acres of the Regrett ranch.

He opened the gate this time for Coffee and his packhorse, closing it carefully after them. He spoke softly to the horses under the pale night sky and swung back up on his stallion.

Monty's fiery abandon to him had been a shocking and pleasurable surprise. He realized now that it had been in his mind since he first laid eyes on her, standing with her wide blue gaze on him as he rode up to the Daventry place over six years ago with two longhorns Daventry had bought earlier that day.

Their passion had been so much greater than any he had

ever experienced in his life that he was still shaken by it. Monty was seventeen, and for all her fevered responses to him, he realized marriage had not been in her mind. She was like an untamed colt, always used to taking her own headlong way in life, and it troubled him.

He looked up at the starry sky above him and drew a long, hard breath. Every muscle in his body was loose and relaxed. He felt better than if he'd slept for twelve hours. Only his mind was troubled.

He swung his thoughts with abrupt determination to the City of Washington. He'd have plenty to tell his brother. Washington boasted some twenty-five thousand inhabitants and those who visited or worked there called it the Mudhole. Those more literate referred to it as the Quagmire, for in those winter months, when not frozen, the mud was ankle-deep in most streets.

He smiled suddenly and stroked Coffee's neck. The animal's ears twitched appreciatively. It hadn't been unpleasant in Washington. There'd been parties and balls given by those who favored statehood for Texas—of special pleasure was the English Embassy ball, where practically no one favored annexation but Monty Daventry had certainly favored him. He had wakened what slept deep in her eyes that night, he thought with satisfaction. And tonight that fervor had come to life with breathtaking suddenness. Exasperation filled him. He couldn't get her out of his mind.

He circled Three Points Lake with its fringed silver pattern of moonlight, and in little less than thirty minutes, he crested the slight rise at the rear of his long adobe ranch house. Pride and affection swelled in him, as he drank in its sweeping lines.

Andrew Salazar, the first man he had hired on a permanent basis—before he ever sent for his younger brother, Julien—had supervised the building of the first and center section. And as he hired them, through the years, each of his men had worked with him and Salazar to build more. Now it sprawled out, its graceful lines showing it to be nearly two hundred feet north and south, with cabins and big stables within the circling cross fences.

He halted his horses, looking at it through the moon-dappled trees. It represented nine years of hard work and was a source of great satisfaction to him. Lamps were twinkling now. Good! His brother was still up.

He opened the back gate of the fence that enclosed the hub of the ranch buildings and outbuildings. Coffee and the packhorse followed him in, and he closed it once more. At the long row of stables, he saw a lantern and came upon Joe Herrera and Renaldo Flores, still in the stables rubbing down two big geldings.

They broke into excited Spanish when they saw him, one taking the lead to the packhorse, the other, Coffee's bridle. All three men spoke Spanish for a few moments, then in heavily accented English, Renaldo added, "Señor Mase, we welcome you back. This place are not the same without you—"

"Though Señor Julien, he work very hard to keep this place just right," Joe cut in.

"Your brother," Renaldo added, "he ride out all day with the vaqueros to see about the herds an' he stay late. We just now rub down his horses, what he use."

"It won't take long to rub down and feed my packhorse, Renaldo. He's had a good rest and food at the Daventry place, but Coffee's hot and hungry. He had an extra trip to make. And so did I—so I'm hungry, too."

"I go tell Mamacita to hurry, that you home an' hungry. She coming to heat your brother's supper anyway," Joe said, beginning to take the saddle from Coffee.

"Good. Renaldo, just bring the packhorse baggage to the kitchen for me. I'll put it up."

In long strides, Mase covered the distance between the

stables and house and entered through the kitchen, which was still fragrant with bread baked earlier. His steps grew light as he entered the kitchen. He wanted to surprise Julien.

He stood quietly in the doorway to the main room. The twenty-two-year-old Julien was seated at a large desk on the upper level of the two-tiered room, poring over a stack of ledgers and making entries. The big room was cool because of the heavy adobe-brick walls and flagstone floor. Regrett breathed deeply as he silently took off his hat and dropped it on a nearby chair.

Julien had a large pewter mug beside him, from which he steadily took sips, and Regrett knew it was some of old man Watkins's best corn liquor. As Josey had remarked earlier at Daventry's, the Regrett men chose to drink the liquor of the territory.

Back in 1834, when the two Regrett brothers had lost mother and father to fever in New Orleans, Mase had sent his younger brother to relatives in Natchitoches while he went to Texas to seek his fortune. He reached it in 1835, just in time to get in on the infancy of the revolution, fight in it with tenacity, and become good friends with Sam Houston.

In fact, it was Houston who fired Mase's imagination when he told Mase that he himself intended to enter the cattle business. So Mase, after the war, had taken for his services a portion of the fertile south-central part of Texas. He'd picked his spot and struggled with collecting wild cows in the mesquite thickets. He hired his Mexican-Texan help one by one after acquiring the land. And when the first part of the house had been finished, he sent for Julien.

Now he looked at his brother with affection and pride. Julien was nearly as tall as he, lean and muscular, and he had adapted smoothly to the uneasy but rewarding business of raising horses and cattle. As time went by and Mase sent to England and Spain for blooded stock to breed with his wild cows and horses, Julien proved himself astute and ambitious. He was as enthusiastic as Mase regarding his breeding plans. There was a deep unspoken bond between the two brothers.

But unlike his older brother, Julien remained impulsive and impatient, even as he proved himself time and again in the saddle. He had an endearing sense of humor, but he had not yet learned to control the legendary hot French temper of the Regretts.

"Ho!" Mase said from the doorway and Julien looked up in startled disbelief. Then he pushed aside the ledgers and his mug and came to hug and pound on his older brother.

"By God, it's good to see you, Mase! I've missed you. And if I have to go over another tally, or pedigree, I think I'll throw 'em out." Laughing, he added, "Can I fix you a drink? It's old Watkins's best four-year-old. Then you can tell me the latest from Washington. The two letters you wrote that got through were pretty sketchy."

"I'll have a little of the four-year-old. I saw Renaldo and Joe at the stables and Mamacita's coming in to fix us a hot supper in a minute."

Mase ran his hand through his thick, unruly black hair. It felt so much cooler in here. The soothing comfort of it washed through him. As the brothers flung themselves on one of the huge wicker couches in the lower level of the room, Julien handed his brother a pewter mug of liquor and water and drew a deep breath.

"I know they've passed a resolution to annex—but you said in your last letter that Texas seems to be dragging her heels now that it's come at last. I don't understand that, Mase."

"There was a rumor in Washington when I left that England had proposed what they called a Diplomatic Act, which would arrange for peace with Mexico in exchange for

Texas remaining independent. Mexico would formally recognize our independence and the act would settle Texas's boundary limits."

"Good God! That'll be the day hell freezes over—damn the Daventrys and Cavenals for the meddlers they are!"

"Julien," Mase said suddenly, with a chuckle, "waiting now can only make the United States more anxious to have us join. Besides, you're just sore as a boil because we have to sweat for our money and the Daventrys and Cavenals don't."

"I don't mind sweating for it," Julien replied defensively, "if we could just be sure we were going to keep it. With the damned Bosquezes raiding constantly now and the Texas treasury empty—"

"The Bosquez brothers are operating around here again?"

"They raided Tom Arterbury's place two months ago. Felipe Bosquez shot Jim Arterbury dead when he protested the so-called Mexican Army 'requisitioning' half the Arterbury cattle and all their chickens."

The brothers fell silent. Felipe Bosquez, the older of the three Bosquezes, called himself a captain in the loosely organized Mexican army. His two younger brothers, Lorenz and Hernando, were lieutenants in Felipe's troop. Mase Regrett reflected silently on his run-in with them over his own cattle only last year, when the small army that worked for the Regretts had run them off empty-handed. Regrett thought he had discouraged the Bosquez brothers from raiding the south-central area, when three of their men had been killed in the skirmish.

"So they killed Jim." Jim was Tom Arterbury's oldest son. "He and I were the same age," Mase said, turning his mug slowly around in his big, tanned hands.

"All our political quarreling has made them cocky, Mase. Tom Arterbury told me at Jim's funeral that Bosquez said he'd been given authority by General Ampudia himself, in

Mexico City, to raid into Texas and do what he could to run us off—*until and if* some agreement between Texas and Mexico could be reached."

"So he shot Jim in cold blood?"

"He claimed he was defending himself—that Jim was drawing a bead on him. And maybe he was. Anyway, Tom told me Bosquez and his band were all decked out in new uniforms, with plenty of gold braid and medals on their chests."

"And you went to Jim's funeral—"

"I thought I ought to—even though we don't agree politically," Julien replied gloomily, then added, "Monty and Miss Abby were there. Monty cried." He paused, then added, "I didn't think that horse-crazy kid could cry."

"Why not?"

"She's not the type." Julien shrugged. "She's a beautiful cockleburr in tight pants. More beautiful since her trip to Washington with her father—and meaner, too. We damn near came to blows over her father when she and Miss Abby came here to see Slyboots a while back." He laughed suddenly, adding, "She's mad as hops at us because you named the mare after her—Slyboots."

Mase said nothing.

Julien looked at his brother with sudden sharpness and said, "She wants to name that mare Glory."

"Good Lord! What a name for a feisty little piece of horseflesh like Slyboots."

"Mase"—Julien's black eyes narrowed on his brother's face—"you don't fancy that mean-tempered little baggage, do you?"

"I sure do," Mase drawled, putting his drink down on the long low table before them and rising to his feet. The air seemed close and warm suddenly. He stripped off his shirt, exposing his broad, muscled chest with its thick, wiry covering of black hair to the cool air of the room.

"Since when?" Julien asked finally.

"Since I delivered her new stepmother to the Daventry house—on the way here."

"New stepmother!"

"Yes. Beautiful and young. And Monty hates her like poison."

"Naturally."

"For what it's worth, Julien, it's mutual."

"So Daventry's caught himself a young mare and a beauty." Julien's laugh was hard. "I'll wager it won't soften the bastard up and it won't do *you* any good with Monty. He fancies our horses and cattle, but not us."

"Just the same, I fancy Monty Daventry."

"As a wife—or just a fancy?"

"I haven't gotten that far yet," Mase temporized.

"You'd better watch yourself with that one. She's trouble—"

"Ah, Señor Mase! It's so good you are home again!" cried Twyla Salazar, who had come in from the kitchen. She stood on the upper level of the room, her plump face beaming, hands on generous hips.

"Mamacita! You look mighty good to me, lady. And I'm hungry, as usual—"

"Renaldo tell me you are hungry—an' your brother come in so late he miss the supper I fix." She gave Julien a reproachful glance.

"I couldn't help it, Mamacita," Julien said with his disarming grin. "I had to chase down two old cows with calves, who'd gone into the brush. Wolves would've made a good supper off those calves."

"Sí." She sighed. "I know." She started back to the kitchen, then wheeled about. "Ah. Señor Mase, Andrew say tell you that big black stallion Warlock, the one you sell to Señor Daventry for Monty, is come back here by hisself again. He got on a saddle but no rider." Her brows drew

together. "You think maybe Monty is fall off—he throw her an' hurt her?"

"No, Mamacita. He didn't throw her. She dismounted and the stud ran off and left her. I took Monty back to the house on Coffee. That's why I'm so late getting home."

Satisfied, she nodded and went back into the kitchen. Julien turned wary, gleaming eyes on his older brother.

"So? And how'd you get that choice piece home? In front on your saddle, or behind you on Coffee's rump?"

"Behind me," Mase said coolly. "And very pleasant it was, too. She had to hold me around my waist."

"I can see it all now," Julien said with cynicism that held a curbed bitterness. Julien was a good hater and he hated Richard Daventry. "Hell, I'd give a hundred in gold to have seen it *all.*"

"I wouldn't sell at any price." Mase's eyes were cold and he put his empty pewter mug on the long, low wicker table in front of them.

"What are you going to do about her horse?"

"Let her come and get him," Mase said briefly.

Chapter 8

Monty awakened after a fitful sleep. She knew she had slept no more than three or four hours. After bathing her face in the basin on the washstand, she stood before the big, oval mirror her father had ordered from England especially for her. Clad in close-fitting pants and tailored shirt, her body appeared as piquant and slender as ever—the face above it smooth and fresh, except for faint blue shadows beneath bluer eyes.

How could she look so calm, when a tight knot of anxiety would give her no peace? How many days? Five? No, four, after today. Then she would know if she carried Mason Regrett's child.

As she brushed and braided her gleaming hair, she spoke a silent prayer. *Oh, God, if I can come through this without having a baby, I'll be so good!*

A skeptical little laugh escaped her as she looked into the mirror. How stupid to pray now—*now* when it was too late.

She paused at her door, listening. There was a great deal going on below. Her stepmother's sugary voice floated up to her.

"No, no, Josephine! That piece of china should be on the top shelf. Change it—carefully."

"By damn," Monty said to the quiet on the stairs, "she's at it already."

"Monty." The whispered word startled Monty. She whirled about and saw that it was Faith. The girl's fine hazel eyes were enormous in the gloom of the hall. Drawn by their urgency, Monty moved toward her.

"What is it, Faith?"

Below them, Louise's voice lifted with asperity and Abby's quiet tones, etched with ice, could be heard.

"Monty, I—I just wanted to tell you how much I appreciate your—your taking me in, letting me come with Louise. Your father is so very *kind* and so are you and your grandmother."

Touched by the girl's pleading, gold-flecked eyes, Monty reached out and caught her outstretched hand. "Faith, you're ever so nice! It's our pleasure to have you here— surely you know that?"

"I—I'm a poor relation, Monty, and I know I must live on charity. But it's so wonderful to meet people like you and your father and grandmother." She swallowed hard and withdrew her cold small hand from Monty's warm one. "People who don't make me *feel* like it's charity."

"It isn't charity, Faith. We're *glad* you came! In fact," she said, her voice cool, "if your cousin were more like you, we'd feel the same way about her. But—" She let the word hang as her eyes swung back to the stairs and Louise's voice came up clearly.

"We're simply going to have to get another worker— someone big enough to help LeRoy with that large buffet. There are other pieces in the parlor that I want changed, too. Josephine, run out and get one of the other male servants."

"I—I'd rather you didn't tell Louise I said anything— about charity, I mean." Faith spoke quietly, but hastily. "I didn't mean to give the impression that she's—"

"I know what you mean, Faith," Monty said gently, her eyes narrowing. "I won't say a word to Louise about any-thing—*not anything* that you and I talk about—ever." Her heart went out to the frightened girl.

"That's—I—You don't look like him, but you're very like your father. So very kind!" She finished the words in a rush, and in a flurry of skirts disappeared into her room once more.

Monty thoughtfully pressed her full lower lip with a fingertip. Faith had not given her a chance to ask if she would like to visit the stables after breakfast or take a ride with her. Well, there would be time for that later. She turned once more to the stairs.

"Dear Lady Abigail," the sweet tones floated upward as Monty took the first step, "why don't you let young Jose-phine get you a pot of tea and rest in the sitting room? Young Josephine!"

"Ever'body call me Feenie—"

"Don't be impudent with me, you little snip! You're named for your mother. Now you fetch Lady Abigail a fresh pot of hot tea. Right now!"

"Never mind, Feenie." Abby's voice carried authority as Monty took the last step down. "I don't wish any tea now. But if you'll go wake Monty and fix her a bit of breakfast in the kitchen, I'd appreciate it."

"The child shouldn't be allowed to oversleep like this, Lady Abigail," Louise said as Monty stepped out of the foyer into the dining room to find all the furniture except the china cabinet and buffet shoved into the middle. The fine Turkish carpet was rolled up against a wall.

"Good morning, Abby," Monty said cheerfully, ignoring Louise. "I'm sorry I missed breakfast. Feenie, you needn't worry about it. I'll fix myself a snack." She noted that Josey was no longer there. She had evidently gone to get another man to help LeRoy, who stood awkwardly beside the big buffet. Monty's temper flared anew as her grandmother turned and silently left the room.

"Don't you think, Louise," she said with biting coldness, "you should wait for my father to return before you completely rearrange our house?"

"It's *my* house now, my dear Montrose. And for your information, Richard will be delighted with any changes I see fit to make." The sharp voice sweetened. "Poor little Montrose! Darling, I know you've always been the favorite with your father—he told me so—but you'll just have to get used to the fact that you aren't any longer."

In the silence that followed, Louise added with honeyed understanding, "I know it will be hard on you, Montrose, but I'll help you. You must go right back upstairs and put on one of your dresses. Your father told me you have trunks full of them. I simply will not tolerate you in those skin-tight breeches and shirts another day."

"You go to blazes!" Monty shouted and flung out of the room.

Louise hid a secret smile.

Josey returned to the dining room where Louise sat drumming her buffered nails on the mahogany dining table.

"Big Miguel say he'll send his son to help us in a few minutes, ma'am," she said, her tone carefully neutral.

"He'd better do it soon! You two and LeRoy can't move that heavy buffet by yourselves." Louise was completely exasperated with Josey, Feenie, and LeRoy. Then, as they tried to push the big piece of furniture, she cried, "Stop! You'll ruin the floor! I want that piece of furniture *lifted*. Do you understand me, you thick-headed fools?"

Josey drew herself up and said with cold flatness, "Miz Daventry, we ain't slaves. We *works* for Mister Richard an' Miss Abby."

"You'll do as I say, Josephine—just like Tina and Merzella—and Ezekiel."

Abby stepped back into the room. "You haven't finished?" The question was chill.

"I will as soon as these stupid darkies get someone to help with the larger pieces."

"Josey, did you ask for help?"

"Yes, Miss Abby, an' Big Miguel goin' to send Young Miguel in, soon's he finishes curryin' his hoss. Feenie, go back out and see he do come."

"Do you intend to change the entire house today?" Abby asked her daughter-in-law, as Feenie left the room.

"No, I'll do more each day until I have it looking lovely. When I've finished, you'll see, Lady Abigail, how good I am at decorating."

"I'm sure you are," Abby replied blandly. "Josey, when you're through we'll discuss the supper menu." She paused, then added, "Unless, of course, you want to do that yourself, Louise."

"Not today." Louise waved a slender hand. "I'll look into that when I've arranged all the furniture properly."

Abby turned and left the room once more and Louise thought, *High-nosed old hen!* She looked at the two black faces before her. They were set in lines of implacable dislike. Well, she'd show them too who was mistress of this house before the day was over.

She took up drumming long, well-tended nails on the table once more. How unutterably stupid and boring life was going to be in this place! From what he had said, it might be two or three more weeks before Richard arrived. How in God's name would she entertain herself 'til then? He had indicated there were neighbors—English neighbors and some of them *young* and attractive. His stone-faced mother had corroborated it.

In less than five minutes, Feenie returned with a tall,

muscular young man. Louise sent a sharp, surprised glance at his aristocratic features. Why, the boy was more beautiful than a Greek statue! A delicious and familiar heat sprang up in her loins.

"This is Young Miguel Puente. His pa, Big Miguel, is overseer an' foreman, an' Young Miguel helps LeRoy with th' horses an' livestock. Miguel, this here is Miz Daventry," Josey said grudgingly, "Mister Richard's new wife."

Louise's pale blue eyes lingered on the young man's face momentarily, then moved swiftly to the mutinous faces of LeRoy Beane and his women.

"I have heard that Señor Richard's mos' beautiful wife is arrived," Young Miguel said with a small dignified bow. His quick, white smile at Louise was completely winning.

"I have arrived and am making a few changes, Miguel," Louise said lightly, sending him a swift, seductive smile. "Now if you will take one side of the buffet, LeRoy and Josey will take the other. I believe you can lift it across the room and put it against this wall."

In minutes, the piece of furniture had been moved. Josey and LeRoy worked in silent anger and Feenie simply stood and watched.

"Now the china cabinet—"

"Oh, Miz Daventry," Josey cried, "you ain't goin' to have us move that! It's full of all Mister Richard's finest pieces of china."

"Nevertheless, with Miguel, you three can move it quite easily— Oh, look! That must be the figurine my darling Richard said looked exactly like me!" Opening the cabinet's glass door, Louise lifted out the exquisitely wrought Dresden figure of a fifteenth-century French aristocrat. "This is far too lovely to remain hidden in this cabinet. I'll place it on one of those mahogany tables in the parlor where everyone can admire it."

"Miz Daventry, that's Mister Richard's most favorite piece

outa all his Dresden china he an' Miss Abby brung clear from England." Josey made one last despairing protest.

"Then he'd certainly want me to put it where it would make me happy," Louise retorted. "Especially since he has so many fine pieces of Dresden." And with a swirl of blue silk skirts and petticoats, she went through the hall to the parlor and reappeared shortly without the figurine.

"There!" she said triumphantly. "Now let's move that cabinet over here."

"I'll take all th' china outa it first, Miz Daventry," Josey said firmly.

"We can set it on th' dinin' table, ma'am," Feenie said placatingly as she saw the small, perfect red mouth set in angry lines.

"No, Josephine. You will move it as it is. Miguel is so expert"—she flashed the boy another smile—"I'll even help." She came to stand near Young Miguel, taking hold of the protruding edge of the tall cabinet.

Miraculously, the cabinet was moved with no breakage. Feenie, who had held her breath the entire time, let it out with a gusty sigh and a silent prayer of thanks.

Louise was smiling up at Miguel, her face angelic and grateful. "You're so strong, Miguel," she said softly, running a small hand over his bronze forearm and on up past his rolled-up sleeve. Her touch was intimate on his bare flesh under the coarse white shirt. "And you are quite a *man!* How old are you, Miguel?" She let her hand trail down his arm and away, slowly.

"Nineteen—an' a half, Señora Daventry."

"Nineteen? Your choice of help was a good one, Josephine. In fact, I need some furniture changed about in Richard's and my room, Miguel. You'll do that for me next, won't you?" She looked up appealingly at him. Then with a careless gesture to the others, she said, "I'll need only one for that. You three can stop for the day now. We'll do the parlor tomorrow."

Feenie, Josey, and LeRoy silently left the room, glancing back at Louise and Miguel, their black eyes unreadable.

Pale blue skirts swishing alluringly, Louise led the way upstairs, with Miguel following. As she motioned the young man into the big bedroom, Faith stepped out of her room next door. She halted when she saw the two in the hall.

"Miguel's going to move some things in my bedroom for me, Faith. Miguel, this is my cousin, Faith Warren."

Miguel bowed and murmured, *"Buenas dias,* Señorita Faith."

Faith acknowledged the introduction with a nod before turning abruptly and closing the door quietly behind her.

"Don't mind her, Miguel." Louise laughed. "She's such a rabbit. A legacy from my father—his brother's child and penniless. Come on in." Miguel entered the room and Louise closed the door. "Now first, Miguel, I want you to move that empty trunk from beside the washstand and put it by the door. When we've finished, you can take it to that storage room Josephine told me Richard had at the back of the —the big barn? Yes, she said the big barn."

"Yes, señora."

As he moved to do what she requested, Louise opened the door swiftly and peered into the hall. Ah, Faith had not come out again. Not that it mattered what the girl did!

In the bedroom, Miguel went immediately to the trunk and hoisted it onto his shoulder, moving it easily to the wall beside the door.

"Now move the armoire to the end of the same wall it's presently against."

With his back to her, he heaved the heavy armoire with its mirrored doors of beveled-glass.

Swiftly Louise unbuttoned her basque and let her pale blue silk dress slip to the floor. With smooth, easy speed, her matching petticoats fell in a heap over the dress, the chemise and camisole following in quick order. Her creamy white body was nude, revealing perfect cup-shaped breasts with their rose-pink nipples already firm and distended. The vee of curling blond hair between her slightly parted legs made a tantalizing picture and she knew exactly the vision she created as Miguel turned to ask for her next command.

His dark eyes widened. Shock, embarrassment, and disbelief registered in quick succession across his face. Louise counted each emotion. Desire would be the last to show, she thought, and a throaty warm laugh broke from her.

"Madre de Dios, señora!"

Louise stepped from her heap of pale blue silk, kicking off her blue slippers, and went to him where he stood rooted to the floor. She pressed her naked breasts against his chest, moving her hands to his face, then his neck, where she felt his racing pulse.

"Kiss me, Miguel," she murmured as she began unbuttoning his clean, coarse white shirt.

"No, señora."

"No? But why? You want to, don't you?"

"Yes—no—you're Señor Richard's new wife!"

"Yes, but I haven't seen the Señor in over a month—and I wanted you the moment I saw you, darling. Don't worry, Richard will never know!" She removed his shirt, running her fingers along his smooth sinewy chest. Miguel trembled violently, still making no attempt to do her bidding.

"Which is it, Miguel—no or yes?"

He could not move, but remained motionless before her as she unbuckled his belt, helping his breeches slide to the floor, looking up into his stunned face as she did so. Then stooping, she lifted each foot and cast the breeches to one side. She unfastened the ties on both his sandals, aware that her honey-colored hair swung down her back and along her face, where it brushed against his bare legs.

Once Miguel's body was exposed, he was powerless to control his reaction. Louise, rising now, took his hands, cupping one under a breast and the other low to the blond curling vee between her legs, rubbing it against the moist warmth.

He was caught in the web she had so expertly spun. Laughter bubbled deep in her throat as she gently stroked his sensitive parts with her slender fingers. He groaned deeply.

"But the good Señor!" he said, as she leaned her body against him once more, slipping her fingers gently down the sides of his bare body, then up, letting her nails run smoothly along his shoulders until she saw gooseflesh rise on his skin.

She pressed her mouth rapaciously to his chest, then withdrew it to drop small kisses on it, and gazed with lazy eyes into his tortured face.

"Do not think of the Señor, Miguel! Think only of me. Am I not beautiful? Are you afraid?" Turning, she ran lightly on bare feet to the door, turned the lock and put the key on a nearby table.

She stood by the table for a moment, allowing herself to drink in the sight of the tall, brown-skinned young man before her while permitting him to gaze, fascinated, at her beautifully proportioned bare body. Intuition worked best for Louise when dealing with lust—for lust was the overpowering necessity in her life. "You've never been with a woman, have you, Miguel?" She knew the answer before he said it.

"No, señora."

She eliminated the distance between them and, taking him by the hand, led him to the bed. "Then I shall teach you, Miguel. You couldn't have a better teacher than I."

She spread herself on the big four-poster bed, never letting go of his hand or taking her silver-blue eyes from his face.

"Come lie with me, dear one. Yes, that's it. Now, kiss me, Miguel."

Miguel moved in complete compliance with her suggestions, which were husky with passion. His arms circled her small body and his mouth met hers. It was a kiss unlike any Miguel had experienced and his senses swam. Embarrassment fell away, along with his fear of hurting the good Señor he and his family had known and loved all his life.

When the insatiable woman beneath him groaned and praised him for his prowess, his heart swelled with a sense of power and ecstasy unknown to him before this moment.

At last they broke apart, and Louise sat up on the edge of the bed. Her face was flushed with satisfaction and she stretched her slender arms above her head.

"You are the mos' beautiful—no, the sweetest and mos' beautiful woman that ever lived, señora!" Miguel spoke with new confidence, smoothing his hand along the curve of her back.

"You're sweet yourself, Miguel—very sweet. I like you very much. We'll have fun—lots of it. But you must go now. Hurry and get dressed. We'll have to be careful when the— Señor comes home."

Louise rose from the bed and crossed the long room to stand behind a screen where a blue china basin and matching water pitcher waited. When she had finished cleaning herself, she stepped from behind the screen, still naked, to see Miguel fully dressed, his worshipful eyes on her.

She went to the pool of blue silk she had let slip to the floor and began slowly to dress. Miguel watched her every move; she was sinuous and graceful as she pulled the garments on, one by one.

A wise smile curved her lips. When they were as young

as Miguel, they could be troublesome pets. Clothed, she went to him and looped her arms about his neck, pulling his mouth down to meet hers.

As he responded with instant passion to her embrace, she ran her small tongue inside his mouth once more, then pulled back, laughing.

"You must go now—" She went to the door, and unlocked it and turned the brass knob silently. Just as silently, he stepped out into the hall.

"Wait a moment, Miguel—don't forget my empty trunk!" she whispered.

"I did forget," he murmured, smiling. Then in a whisper, "When will—how soon—will you see me again, señora?"

"Soon, Miguel, dear—soon. I'll send Tina for you. Not a word to a soul—remember!"

"Never! Never, señora. Adiós."

As Miguel hefted the trunk onto his back and slowly descended the stairs, Louise stood watching. When he had vanished below, Faith stepped from her open door. Her freshly washed hair gleamed in the faint light and her face was paler still, but her eyes burned brightly.

"Oh, Louise," she whispered, "you told me it was different this time! You told me you loved Richard! And we haven't been here but two days and already you—"

"Shut up! You didn't *see* me do anything, in spite of spying on me."

"I wasn't spying—it's only that I don't want what happened to Randolph happening to Richard—" The girl shrank back as Louise approached her. Faith was taller, more slender, but Louise leaned toward her with menace.

"Now"—she punctuated the word with a hard slap on Faith's left cheek—"you"—she slapped the right cheek—"keep your mouth shut!" This last was said with a shove that sent the girl off balance. "I won't have you passing judgment on me, Faith—and I *do* love Richard." Her voice fell and thickened. "If you dare mention one word about me, I'll do worse than kill you. *I'll tell!*"

Tears filled Faith's eyes and Louise's palm prints were red against the white cheeks as she backed away from her cousin.

"I've never said anything to anyone—ever—Louise. You know I haven't—"

"And you'd better not, unless you want to be shipped back to Charleston in disgrace!" She added, with contempt, "They'd never believe anything you said anyway, if they knew the truth about you."

Faith retreated farther, her throat working as she swallowed hard. Her eyes glistened with tears. Her heart beat fast as it always did when Louise was angry. Sometimes, Faith thought with despair, she felt as if she were still six years old and had just come to live with the Warrens. The sixteen-year-old Louise had terrified her, threatened her, and had even beaten her then. Louise was a violent woman. Faith knew it and feared her accordingly.

Chapter 9

Five days dragged by, with sparks flying each time Monty met with her stepmother. Louise was alternately sweet, then cajoling, always maneuvering the conversation to make herself appear misunderstood, while earnestly trying to reason with Monty. Her constant carping on Monty's apparel was the hardest to bear.

Monty was relieved only briefly when it developed she was not carrying Mase Regrett's child. She still felt guilty when her eyes met Abby's. But she rejoiced when she saw Abby become remote and aloof with her new daughter-in-law.

Abby was the fount of wisdom, kindness, and gentleness. But she indeed became Lady Abigail with Louise, and Monty enjoyed her stepmother's baffled face each time she confronted Abby's cold, appraising eyes. The two women had reached an unspoken agreement; each avoided the other as much as possible.

Faith kept mostly to her room. Monty had persuaded her to come to the stables twice, but Faith haltingly admitted that she did not know how to ride. This astonished Monty and she offered to teach her.

"I couldn't put you to so much trouble—" Faith protested.

"Pa will see that you learn if he has to put you on his horse before him and ride off with you!" Monty insisted.

To her surprise, color dyed the girl's fair face to the roots of her netted golden hair, and she shook her head at Monty wordlessly.

The morning of the fifth day, Louise was still engaged in moving the furniture. She had almost arranged the lower floor to her taste, when Monty told Abby she was going to ride over to the Cavenals' for lunch.

"Monty, you must take Big Miguel as escort today," Abby said.

Monty sighed. "All right, Abby, and Cav's Abraham can see me home."

Later, in the stables, Monty passed Warlock's empty stall for what seemed to be the hundredth time, and once more she silently cursed the big stallion. He had gone back to his birthplace before—this made the fourth time! Each day she thought perhaps Joe Herrera or Renaldo Flores would bring him back. Mase Regrett certainly wouldn't.

Well, she would go get him herself. And soon, she vowed, as she greeted Carlos Puente, Big Miguel's second son.

"You take Dolly this morning, Monty?" Carlos grinned. "Mi padre, he take ol' Johnsy." He turned his grin on his father, who was saddling the gelding, Johnsy.

"Yes, I'll ride Dolly," Monty said restlessly, looking at the young mare with disfavor. She was a shining bay with an easy, even temper, and she was quiet as Carlos saddled her. Still, it would be good when the new mare was ready to be picked up. Slyboots, indeed! She'd wager a five-dollar gold piece the Regrett brothers were teaching Slyboots to obey by that name.

She and Big Miguel rode past the houses of Daventry

workers, some adobe, some frame. Big Miguel's house at the end of the row and nearest the fence was the most spacious, because he had the biggest family. He and Dorita had seven children, the oldest being Young Miguel. They were a close-knit, loving family.

It was little more than an hour's ride to the Cavenals'. Monty and Big Miguel rode in companionable silence. About halfway, they saw through the trees the Daventry patrol, Juan Dominguez and Santiago Espinosa on horseback. They were too far away to wave a greeting to them.

When at last they came within sight of the Cavenal house, Big Miguel said, "I leave you at the gate, Monty. From here I see many men in Lord Cavenal's fields."

At the gate he dismounted and opened it for Monty to ride through. He closed it behind her and mounted his big gelding.

"Adios, Monty. You get Abraham to ride you back home —don't forget!" the big man admonished.

"I won't." She turned Dolly's head toward the buildings, large and small, that were enclosed within the sweeping fences made of crossed, slender saplings. She rode around the side of the house and took the graveled drive that curved to the front, which faced south.

The Cavenal house was built on a small hill, just slightly higher than the fields of cotton surrounding its broad lawns. To Monty, it was as beautiful as the home her father had built, and in some ways, even more so. Both houses, defiantly English Georgian, were a paradox in a land of long, low log, frame, or adobe houses.

Cavenal had been twenty-four when he built the big house, and acquired a retinue of over fifty servants in the New Orleans slave markets. After that, he sent for his mother and sister. They had come reluctantly, bringing servants from England with them, and stayed despite Lady Marguerite's many complaints. Monty knew Lady Marguerite Cavenal lived in anticipation of the time when her son would tire of this raw land and return them to the civilized world of London.

Their aristocratic ways and manners had stayed with the Cavenals and their English help in the supposedly classless society of the land. Further, income from Cavenal estates in England allowed them many luxuries and indulgences.

Still, Lord George's reputation among neighbors was not one of amiability. The Cavenals held themselves aloof, but for their close friendship with the Daventrys, Arterburys, and Bedfords. And it was rumored his treatment of slaves was suspect. Even so, Cavenal wielded influence and power in the region. He was not only astute, but exceedingly efficient.

Now Monty passed the turn where the drive led to the house. It cut through towering cottonwoods, and the big redbrick house itself was surrounded by oaks, giving it a cool and gracious appearance. Sophie Jones, a beautiful mulatto, was sweeping the broad granite front steps. Her five-year-old son, Sammie, her constant shadow, was by her side.

He was a beautiful child, more white than black, with aquiline features. Lady Marguerite had let blond Olen Jensen, their overseer, go over her son's protests. Jensen was rumored to have fathered the child, though he had protested his innocence up until the day he departed. As a result, Cavenal had made a big, intelligent black, Abraham Johnson, his foreman. Abraham had been purchased in Galveston five years ago, and he had long ago proved himself invaluable. Further, he always obeyed Cavenal without questioning him.

Now Monty raised her hand and called, "Hello, Sophie— hello, Sammie!"

The two looked up and waved, smiling broadly. The

cheerful, impulsive Monty was always welcomed by everyone at the Cavenal place.

"Howdy, Miss Monty." Sophie beamed as Monty dismounted before the hitching post. Sophie grasped the reins, adding, "I'll get my Ephraim to come fetch your horse an' feed an' curry her. She do look hot!"

Monty reached into her shirt pocket and pulled out a wrapped stick of candy. "I was hoping I'd see you, Sammie —so I could give you this."

The child clutched the candy, smiling shyly, then retreated behind his mother's skirts.

"Is the family all at home now, Sophie?"

"All 'cept'n Lord George, an' he be out lookin' over th' east fields. He due back 'bout now for tea with his'n sister an' Lady Marguerite—" She broke off at the sound of fast-approaching hooves. Both she and Monty looked back down through the arching cottonwoods to see a dusty horseman on a dustier horse. He had glimpsed them and put spurs to the animal. Horse and rider turned off the road into the shade of the long graveled approach to the front of the house.

Monty tensed with excitement. "Sophie, who is that? He looks like—he looks like—"

"Looks like Cap'n Charles Elliot—we ain't seen him in over two years!"

"It *is* the captain!" Monty cried. "And he must have important news, the way he's riding!"

Captain Charles Elliot's horse scattered gravel as he hurriedly dismounted and pulled off his dusty white hat.

"Why, Captain Elliot!" Monty greeted him excitedly. "What are you doing way down here? I thought you were in Washington!"

"And I hardly recognized you, my dear, in those pants and that shirt! The last time I saw you, you were in blue satin that just matched your eyes." He struck his hat against his thigh, trying to clean it. He looked as if he had traveled many miles and was exhausted. "As for why I'm here, I can tell you I'm a cross between a messenger, a mediator, and an ambassador. I've just come from Mexico City."

"I hope it's good news!"

"It is, my dear. Let's go inside, and I'll tell young George and all of you about it, though it's to be kept quiet until announced by President Anson Jones."

"You all come in out'a this here heat," Sophie said, opening the broad, square-paneled door. "I'll go get Ephraim to take care of your horses. An' I'm sure Mister Jarrett'll be right— Here he is now!"

Sophie, with the child following, disappeared behind Lloyd Jarrett. A tall, spare man with a kindly face, Jarrett had been butler and valet to the Cavenals for thirty years. He smiled warmly at the visitors.

"Do come in! Good morning, Miss Monty and Captain Elliot—it's good to see you after these two years." He held the door wide and Monty and Elliot entered the cool, gracious foyer.

"By heaven, Jarrett! It's good to know some things don't change. I remember so well when you were butler and valet to old Lord Cavenal all those years before his death."

"Yes, God rest his soul. We all thought you still in Washington City, Captain Elliot."

"I'm on my way to Washington-on-the-Brazos, Jarrett, and I think young George will be exceedingly glad to see me when I tell him the news I'm bringing." He patted the leather pouch that hung from his shoulder. "Knowing the Cavenal place was on the way, I hoped to stop and rest my animal and myself—see George and all of you."

"Come into the salon, Captain, Miss Monty. I'll fetch you a cool whiskey with a sprig of mint and a dash of sugar, Captain, and tell the ladies you both are here."

"You remembered my favorite drink." Captain Elliot

sighed, seating himself in one of the big, luxurious chairs in the salon. "Jarrett, you are a marvel."

"I'm sure Lord Cavenal will be back in less than half an hour now." He bowed and left.

Monty seated herself decorously in a cushioned chair despite her tight pants. She looked at Captain Elliot with interest and affection.

"So it's more politics that brings you to Texas, Captain." She smiled, her eyes twinkling. "I won't ask what your news is—I know you want to tell it to Cav first. But can we ladies listen?"

"Of course, of course! But I know you will say nothing of it until you hear that President Jones has signed this treaty and put it before the people of Texas."

"Of course we won't. We want to see Texas as free and independent as it's been for ten years."

"Charles Elliot!" Lady Marguerite swept into the room. Her entrances were always impressive, and as always, a touch of awe followed her warm greeting. "How good to see you. What brings you so far from the seats of government?"

"I'm on my way to see the President of Texas, Anson Jones, with a very important document from those in power in Mexico. I've ridden steadily for days, and I knew your hospitality would give me and my horse a day's rest."

"I have sent Abraham after George. He has been riding in the fields since early morning." Marguerite Cavenal was not only a composed, efficient woman, she was handsome, with her thick, pale hair pulled back smoothly into a heavy chignon. Today she wore a pale orchid dress Monty knew was the latest style from England. The scent of lavender followed her as she greeted Monty and bent gracefully to kiss her cheek.

Georgina came quietly into the room as her mother seated herself on the large, velvet-covered sofa. The aura of lavender clung to her, as it did to her mother, but her dress was a crisp blue and the neck was scooped with a trim of darker blue velvet ribbon, which set off her honey-colored silky hair and pale, clear eyes. She was a pretty young woman, who bore a remarkable resemblance to her brother, but there was a look of intensity about her that sometimes put off strangers. Monty often wondered about it. The whites of her eyes were pure as milk, making them appear larger than they actually were. Right now, they were focused intently on Charles Elliot.

"It's so good to see you again, Captain," she said in her high voice. "It's been much too long since you paid us a visit. And I still remember those bonbons you used to bring me when you came to visit my father in London."

"You were so little!"

"But I remember."

Jarrett came in bearing a gleaming silver tray. The silver pot of tea was steaming, and alongside it stood the tall glass containing Elliot's whiskey. Anticipating the arrival of George Cavenal, Jarrett had brought four cups and saucers.

"Will you pour, Lady Marguerite?" Jarrett asked, and at her murmured assent, he placed the tray and its contents on the low marble table before the divan.

The salon was sumptuously furnished, as was the entire Cavenal house, which was one of the reasons Monty loved to visit them.

As Lady Marguerite was pouring tea, there was a hubbub in the back of the long foyer hall and suddenly Lord George Huntleigh Cavenal came through the doorway.

Cavenal was a man of immaculate appearance. He could ride over his entire estate and still look as though he had just stepped from a tailor's shop. He wore the same kind of brown breeches Monty's father and Mason Regrett wore, but Cavenal's always had a crease to the point where they were tucked inside high, carefully polished English riding boots. His white shirt was unbuttoned at the throat, where a scarf was tied. His hair was a gold helmet on his well-shaped head and he exuded a powerful physical magnetism. Cav looked deceptively cultured, but he was a man of lustful sexual hungers.

Monty, looking at him now, through eyes opened by Mason Regrett, saw him for the first time as a *man,* and not the easy friend she had known since she was ten. For the first time, she felt uncomfortable under his quick, appraising glance.

"By God, Charles Elliot, when Jarrett told me it was you, I didn't believe him. I had to see for myself!"

Elliot put down his drink and rose to clasp hands with his young friend. He drew a deep breath, and sank back onto the couch beside Lady Marguerite, as the two men began to talk of their last meeting in Washington.

"Please pour me a cup of tea, lady mother," Cavenal said courteously. Lady Marguerite complied, handing it to her tall, slender son. He took it and remained standing as Elliot spoke of his mission. Excitement was back in Elliot's voice and fatigue fell away from him.

"And I can tell you, it's good news for us, George," he continued. "You remember we had persuaded President Jones to give us ninety days to work something out—to give both Britain and France a chance to pressure Mexico into signing a treaty of recognition and peace."

"Yes. Richard wrote me a letter from Washington about that."

"And fortunately for us, Santa Anna has been replaced with General Herrera. As England's emissary, I managed to convince Herrera that Mexican indecisiveness was producing the worst of all worlds. Annexation would mean the final loss of Texas, and the planting of the United States flag on the Rio Grande."

"And did Herrera agree with you?"

"He did." Again Elliot patted the leather pouch beside

him. "He gave me a signed treaty that recognizes Texas's full independence, provided the republic does not join the United States. And President Jones will have it in another two days. Jones has said he'll sign it—that Texas is better off right now than it has been at any time since the revolution. He'll put the question to the Texas Congress, and we'll turn this movement around."

"It sounds good, Charles!" Cavenal smiled. "And Jones is ready to go with it?" At Elliot's nod, he added, "That'll put an end to this annexation furor."

Captain Elliot looked at the ladies and said, "I know you ladies will say nothing of this until I've had a chance to put the document into President Jones's hands."

"There's really no one we can tell," Lady Marguerite said with a cool smile. "And I'm sure Monty will say nothing. Will you, Monty?"

"Can't I tell Abby?"

"Your father ought to be home soon," Charles Elliot said slowly. "He will tell her. I'd just as soon the Regretts didn't hear of this until it's an accomplished fact."

"Abby wouldn't tell them!" Monty said indignantly.

"That would be fatal, Monty," George Cavenal said. The pale golden eyes on her narrowed. "You know your grandmother's never given up her friendship with those two worthless men, despite your father having fallen out with them long ago. And if the Regretts learn of it, they could stir up enough trouble to forestall any good that might come of it."

"Abby goes weeks without seeing the Regretts, Cav! You talk as if she'd ride over there just to—"

"No. But I think the Regretts—or more likely, that loud-mouthed, loose-tongued Mason Regrett—might ride over to see her, and she'd let it slip." Cavenal's words carried deep anger.

"Not if I told her it was a secret!"

"How does the Lady Abigail put it?" George Cavenal's chiseled lip went down at one corner. " 'You know I never let politics interfere with friendship.' And she considers the Regretts old friends. You'll grant me that, won't you, Monty?"

"I *admire* Abby for not falling out with old friends!" Monty said mutinously.

Elliot sighed. "Monty, I'll have it in President Jones's hands day after tomorrow—then you can tell anyone you like."

"I'm sorry!" Monty was crestfallen. "You were kind enough to include me in the good news and I'm like an excited ten-year-old—I wanted to shout it, I'm so glad! Forgive me, Captain—I swear not to tell anyone—not even Abby!"

"I was sure I could trust you." Elliot smiled as Lady Marguerite rang the small silver bell on the table at her elbow.

"Bring Captain Elliot another whiskey and mint, please, Jarrett," she said, as the butler appeared silently in the doorway. Then, as Jarrett took the captain's empty glass, she added, "Charles, surely you'll stay long enough to fully rest yourself and your horse?"

"I'll stay the night, Lady Marguerite—for I am extremely tired. But I must leave in the morning before dawn."

"I'll have Mavis tell Nonny and Emma to start heating water for your bath right now. You can rest after that."

"Then," George Cavenal inserted smoothly, "you'll be ready for a fine dinner."

"And I won't bore you ladies with any further talk about politics. I know you must be tired of it."

"George speaks of little else," Georgina put in. "And it does become tiring." She turned a sweet smile on Monty, adding, "And Monty, when Jarrett told us you'd come, I was hoping you'd spend the night with us, too. I'd love to have your company on an afternoon ride today."

"That sounds wonderful, Gina," Monty replied, pleased at the prospect. She had no desire to return to the house where the new Mrs. Daventry was wreaking such havoc.

Monty and Gina had an enjoyable ride, though they went no farther than the game shed on the Guadalupe River. Then, after dinner, Cavenal and Elliot sat at the long linen-covered table still talking Washington politics.

Monty wore her casual pants and shirt for dinner. The Cavenals knew her carefree ways and accepted them indulgently.

"If you gentlemen will excuse us," Lady Marguerite said, laying aside her napkin, "the girls and I will go out to the orangerie while you have your after-dinner coffee and brandy."

Both men rose with the three women, and Captain Elliot said, smiling, "The dinner was delicious, Lady Marguerite —and I might add, the company superb."

As the three women made their way to the orangerie, Georgina said, "Monty, I'm working a piece of needlepoint —I hope you won't be bored and wish you were home."

"I won't wish I were home," Monty said as they entered the big-windowed room, lined with greenery. There were potted palms, dwarf orange and lemon trees, vines and ivies, hibiscus and oleander plants among them. Monty loved the place, for the air was always filled with perfume. Tonight it was lemon blossoms—the small trees were in full bloom.

"As a matter of fact," Monty continued, seating herself in one of the cushioned chairs beside a lemon tree, "I'm glad to be away from home right now." She felt she might as well tell the two women what she had refrained from mentioning all day.

"Why?" Georgina asked alertly, aware of tension in Monty's voice.

"Because my father has sent his bride home, and she's turning the house upside down."

Both Cavenal women were too well schooled to show astonishment, but Monty was comforted by the fact that they widened their eyes.

"His *bride?* " Gina murmured, her voice faintly disbelieving.

"A wretched woman named Louise Warren Lynchley." The words tumbled out of Monty now. "She's changing all the furniture around in the house. She's got poor Josey, Feenie, LeRoy, and Young Miguel—and God only knows who else by now—pushing and pulling it from wall to wall."

"And all day you didn't say a word, Monty! Surely she can't be that bad—" Georgina exchanged glances with her mother. "How old is she?"

"She's about twenty-seven, and she brought her cousin, Faith Warren, with her. Faith is a nice person who'd be very pretty if Louise didn't treat her like a poor relation. Honestly, Gina, you'd find it hard to believe how awful Louise is. She calls my father 'my darling Richard' in the most sickening voice, all the while acting so sweet that sugar'd be sour beside her." Monty paused, then added bitterly, "And she hates *me.* "

"Oh, Monty," Lady Marguerite exclaimed, "that can't be true—"

"It is true," Monty said in a low voice.

"How do you know?" Georgina asked.

"Gina, can't you tell when someone doesn't like you? You *feel* it."

"Then you only *feel* she doesn't like you?"

"For one thing, she knows that everyone calls me Monty. I've told her more than once. And she calls me Montrose constantly and says she's going to teach me how to be a lady —that I must not wear my pants and shirts anymore." In the silence, she added, "It's the *way* she says these things that makes me know she hates me."

"Well," Lady Marguerite murmured finally, "it appears you two have gotten off to a bad start. Moving all the furniture immediately on arrival was a most inappropriate start for her."

"She says it's *her* house now. You never saw anyone so obnoxious."

"In a way, it is her house now," Georgina said reflectively, "but it was most unmannerly of her to say so."

"It is *not* her house," Monty retorted. "It's my father's house."

"When she married Richard, dear, his house became hers too, of course—just as everything she owns became his," Lady Marguerite said gently. "How is Lady Abigail responding to her?"

"Very politely," Monty said despondently. "Abby says to wait until Pa gets home. Oh, I wish I could camp out until then!"

"Staying the night and the morning with us will keep you away from her a bit longer, Monty. And then, Georgina and I would enjoy driving over to meet your new stepmother. I'd like to see all these changes she's making." Lady Marguerite spoke kindly. She was fond of the outspoken, headstrong Monty. There wasn't an ounce of deception in the child, Marguerite reflected. But slyness, deception, and silence were characteristics her own daughter possessed in plenty. That she lived vicariously through her brother, Lady Marguerite knew, and it worried her considerably. Georgina's emotional makeup was too fragile to sustain itself alone, and she depended on George's strength as much as her own. This, Lady Marguerite accepted reluctantly.

"All right," Monty replied. "And you'll see how she talks to me."

"I'll ride my new mare over," Georgina replied, taking up her needlepoint. "She comes of Irish stock, Julien Regrett told George—and her gaits are perfection, as you saw this afternoon, Monty."

"She's beautiful," Monty said, her face clearing at the mention of horses. "I can hardly wait for my own mare! She's a bay and Pa helped me choose her when she was just a long-legged colt. Now Julien and Mase are training her for me." Monty suddenly remembered, "I didn't tell Abby I was going to stay the night—"

"I'll send Abraham to Lady Abigail right away. And I'll tell her we're coming to call tomorrow afternoon. I'm sure George will go with us, for he'll want to meet Richard's bride as much as we do."

It was nearly dark when Abraham Johnson rode up to the back door of the Daventry house. He was a beautifully proportioned man, his shoulders wide and his chest broad, tapering to unusually narrow hips. There was an inborn dignity in his bearing, and he was dependable as a clock. Now he faced Tina at the back door.

"I got a message from Lady Marguerite to Lady Abigail," he said in his deep baritone. "I got ter deliver it to her personal, she say."

Tina, her thick curling hair gleaming reddish-black in the lamplight, stared at him in silent admiration. She could find no words to answer him, so taken was she by the sight of him.

"Who are you?" Abraham asked at last.

"I'm Tina Moses—I belonged to ol' Mister Warren before he died," she blurted out. "Now I'm his daughter's, Miss Louise." Tina stood rooted to the spot, for he was the most handsome man she had ever seen.

"Would you tell Lady Abigail—or take me to her?"

"They're at table—havin' after-dinner coffee, but I'll take you. Follow me." She turned to find that Josey and Feenie had stopped in the middle of their chores and were interested observers.

"I'm takin' this gentleman to Miss Abby," Tina said shyly.

"So you say," Josey said, but Feenie's eyes were round and admiring. She had seen Abraham often, but he wasn't interested in a girl as young as she. He was twenty-eight. Feenie had found that out by asking Sophie Jones, when the Cavenals and Daventrys had a joint picnic back in April a year ago and all the servants had their own down by the Guadalupe River.

Abigail put down her coffee cup and greeted Abraham warmly. "It's good to see you, Abe. Have you taken one of those comely girls of Cav's as a wife yet?"

"No, ma'am." He smiled slightly. "I ain't in a marryin' mood, Miss Abby. Just an ol' bachelor, I expect. Lady Marguerite done sent me over with this message." He handed her the envelope. "I'll wait, 'case you want ter answer."

Louise was scrutinizing him closely, and Tina stood by, mesmerized by the handsome black, until Louise spoke to her angrily.

"I told you to help in the kitchen, you lazy wench! Get back in there and help Josephine," she said sharply.

Abraham turned and looked at Louise fully. There was no expression on his face that Louise could find offensive, but she felt a strong wave of animosity from the black man as Tina hurried back to the kitchen.

"Ah, I thought as much," Abby said, laughing softly. "My granddaughter's going to spend the night with the Cavenals." She looked up, still smiling, and met Faith's timid smile. "And tomorrow, they are all coming to visit and meet you and your cousin, Louise, Faith! All of them."

There was undisguised pleasure in Abby's voice as she added enthusiastically, "I'll have a high tea served when they arrive."

"I've never had a high tea, Miss Abby," Faith murmured. "What is it?"

"Don't be a dolt, Faith," Louise said acidly. "It's something the nobility have in England. They serve all manner of good things with it. It's almost like a luncheon, isn't it, Lady Abigail?" She was annoyed because Abby had managed to ignore her all evening without being openly rude, something the cultured and aristocratic Abby could do with ease.

"Yes, Louise. It might be compared to an American light luncheon." She smiled faintly, then added, "Marguerite mentions having a social when Richard returns, to introduce you and Faith to our neighbors, the Arterburys and Bedfords who emigrated from England—along with others in the region."

Louise's eyes sparkled. A social at the Cavenals'! Richard had told her about them. The Cavenals were *real* nobility and lived very elegantly, he had said.

"A social for us!" she cried with unconcealed pleasure. "How lovely! Something wonderful to look forward to now —besides my darling Richard's homecoming." The last was added hastily.

"Wait, Abraham, I'll pen her an answer." Abby rose and went to the gleaming Governor Winthrop desk, and took up her quill and paper.

"You belong to Lord Cavenal?" Louise asked Abraham arrogantly.

"Yes, ma'am. I works for him."

"You mean you're his slave."

"Yes, ma'am. I works for Mister Cav."

"Don't you call him Lord Cavenal?"

"Most peoples call him Lord Cavenal, 'ceptin' us workers. He likes us ter call him Mister Cav."

"Hmm," Louise murmured. "The title is his in England and here when he chooses to use it."

"I suppose so, ma'am. But he likes the nickname little Miss Monty give him 'way back."

"How very democratic of him." Louise's eyes were avid with curiosity. She would enjoy tomorrow!

Abby folded her note and put it in an envelope, handing it to Abraham. "Abe, you must have a bite to eat before you start back. I'll wager you didn't eat before you left."

"No, ma'am, I didn't, an' I'd sure appreciate a bite an' a col' drink of water." He bowed to Abigail as he took the envelope from her hand.

When he had disappeared into the foyer on his way to the kitchen, Abby remarked, "He's Cav's second in command. A very smart man and very trustworthy. I never worry about Monty when I know he'll escort her home from the Cavenals'."

In the kitchen, Tina was helping Josey and Feenie serve Abraham, and she sat with him and talked while he ate. By the time he unhitched his horse from the rail at the rear of the big house and prepared to depart, Tina's eyes were shining and her delicate coffee-colored features were glowing. She had fallen wholeheartedly in love for the first time in her life, and with a man she could only hope to see occasionally.

Chapter 10

The following dawn saw Captain Charles Elliot on his way to Washington-on-the-Brazos, and four hours later, the three Cavenals and Monty set out for the Daventry estate.

Lady Marguerite, ever vigilant against the hot Texas sun, rode in a closed carriage with Abraham on the box. Georgina rode her new mare beside her brother, on his big Appaloosa. Monty on Dolly was at Cav's left. Expert horsewoman that she was, Georgina rode sidesaddle. Her riding habit trailed gracefully along the horse's flank. The habit was light green, which enhanced her extraordinarily wide white eyes, centered with pale, clear blue. The mass of silky blond hair was caught atop her head under a dashing hat that allowed a few provocative curls to hang down the slender column of her white neck.

Monty scorned riding sidesaddle. She had long ago decided it was another of the foolish distinctions inflicted on women by men, to keep them hobbled—except for household and kitchen duties. *Louise says she's expert at riding sidesaddle.* The deep visceral anger the woman instilled in her stirred afresh and Monty's dark winged brows drew together.

"Not remembering something too unpleasant, I hope, Monty?" Cavenal asked lightly.

She looked at him and smiled, but she knew a twinge of that strange new uneasiness at the intensity in his eyes. Why should she suddenly mistrust him after all these years?

"It's only that I—I dread seeing Louise again," she said too hastily.

Cav, misreading her flushed face, smiled with lazy satisfaction.

His sister gave him a sharp look, but she said easily, "She won't dare scold you about clothes or manners in front of guests, Monty, dear."

"You don't know Louise," Monty replied glumly, refusing to look into Cav's eyes where desire lay so thinly veiled.

"Gina, can't you see Monty's determined to worry about the woman?" he teased.

Since Monty had been awakened to desire, she could see it now in Cavenal's eyes—and she was repelled. But she must refrain from showing her distaste. She knew she must keep a tight rein on her impulsive nature. It had propelled her into enough trouble as it was.

"I think she's a little prejudiced against the new Mrs. Daventry." Georgina smiled. The eyes she turned on her brother were rich with sympathy, yet in their pale blue depths lay some darker emotion, as if in some way she fed on the man's vitality.

Monty thought, *What is it about Gina that is as unsettling to me as Cav?* So Monty said nothing and Cav shot her a mischievous glance as they rode on in silence.

It had rained the night before and there was hardly any dust, for which Lady Marguerite had been outspokenly grateful. As they drew nearer to the Daventry house, they could see the big two-story building looming up among the trees. The outbuildings consisted of the huge stables, two large barns, a slaughtering shed, and the inevitable smokehouse, wellhouse, and living quarters for those who worked there.

Monty's eyes narrowed and darkened suddenly. What—who was that in the central section of land around the house and buildings surrounding it? Could it be Mexican soldiers dismounting!

"Look, Cav! It's that bunch of Mexican soldiers who raided us over two months ago—and the Arterburys just before that! And you know what happened to Jim Arterbury when he tried to stop them! I'm going ahead right now!" Bending low over the mare, she urged Dolly forward.

"I'll ride with you!" Cav called, putting the Appaloosa into a gallop. Cavenal knew it would take too long to send for help from his place. The soldiers would finish their depredations and have left long before his blacks could arrive.

Lady Marguerite was leaning out of the carriage, calling to Georgina to ask what was happening, as Monty and Cav raced past.

The back gate was open when they reached it, and they bolted through at a hard gallop. All the women in the house had been herded out into the area back of the house. One soldier stood guard over them with a rifle in one hand and a pistol in the other.

The Puente family and other Mexican workers were gathered in another group near the stables, and they were also guarded by two soldiers with their weapons ready.

The soldiers were gaudily dressed in scarlet coats and breeches of varying shades of royal blue. Their constant riding had covered them in a thin layer of dust. Monty recognized their leader, who wore a glittering array of medals on his chest. He was their visitor of two months ago, Captain Felipe Bosquez. He wheeled his beautiful Andalusian stallion around to face them as they approached. Other soldiers were coming and going into the smokehouse, wellhouse, and raiding the chicken pens.

Monty reined Dolly in so sharply her forefeet lifted, hooves pawing the air, before the horse slid on her haunches. She recognized the two nearest Bosquez men as Felipe's younger brothers, Lorenz and Hernando.

"Wasn't what you and your brothers took from us two months ago—and the Arterburys before that—enough for you?" Under her wide-brimmed hat, Monty's face was suffused with fury.

Bosquez pulled off his sombrero and bowed in the saddle. "So—it's the pretty señorita who always wears the clothes of a boy." His eyes roved over Monty's body. Then his smile faded and he replaced his hat. "The señorita is aware that we are authorized to requisition supplies for the army of Mexico by General Avrillago, Mexico's leader?"

"I call it stealing." Monty was curt. She could hear the carriage containing Lady Marguerite rattling up. Glancing around, she saw Georgina's pale face.

"The señorita is wrong. Our government has given us orders. And you know well enough, Texas is still officially a province of Mexico. These supplies we take belong to Mexico." Bosquez was cold, his black brows drawn.

"You're taking *our* food," Monty said angrily. "What about the farms in Laredo or Falfurrias? Why don't you requisition *them?*"

Bosquez's laugh was short. "But we have, señorita. We have all the vegetables and fruit we can use. It's your fine beef and ham, and chickens, we need."

Monty's mouth trembled with rage, and George Cavenal pushed his mount past hers. "Bosquez," he said sharply, "are you aware of the treaty between Texas and your country, wherein Texas has agreed to reject any offer of annexation to another country—and in exchange, you have recognized us as an independent nation?"

Monty shot him a quick glance. They had promised Captain Elliot—but if Cav could convince Bosquez, the thievery might cease.

"If you speak of the old Diplomatic Act of last year, yes, I am aware. We no longer regard that as worthy!" Bosquez spat on the ground contemptuously.

"No, Captain. I'm referring to the new Protocol for ninety days' peace between Texas and Mexico, which your General Avrillago has just signed. It is sponsored and defended by Great Britain and France. President Jones will announce it any day now. I know this is true, for my old friend Captain Charles Elliot, who was carrying it to President Jones, stopped off at my house only yesterday. He will reach Washington-on-the-Brazos any hour, and it will be official."

The soldiers surrounding Bosquez moved restlessly, their gleaming black eyes filled with distrust. Bosquez pushed his sombrero back from his swarthy forehead, eyeing Cavenal with suspicion.

"I know of no such treaty or protocol. We have been on the trail for several days—"

"When you return to your country," Cavenal cut in, "you will find that we are at peace with Mexico for three months —there will be no annexation."

Bosquez laughed and spat again. "There will be annexation, señor—and Mexico will go to war with the gringos— take this country back from them. And until I hear from my friend, General Ampudia himself, that we are at peace with this Texas, I will continue to make requisitions as we need them."

The women standing in the hot sunlight were white-faced. Only Abigail Daventry appeared in total command of herself. Monty saw Louise's pale, sick face as the woman looked at the guns and the dark-skinned men who let their eyes roam freely over her and the other women.

Bosquez glanced with even greater contempt at the group of Mexicans who stood a little distance from their dwellings.

"And these traitors to their country, who work for the gringo Daventry—they will be shot when we take Texas—shot as traitors!"

Only Young Miguel spoke up. "I am not a traitor! I am proud of Spanish heritage, but I am prouder I am Texan—and if it is to be, I will be proud to be American—"

Lorenz, the youngest Bosquez brother, spurred his horse forward and struck the boy with his quirt, leaving a long red welt on Miguel's bronze cheek, but the boy did not flinch.

"Come back here, Lorenz," Bosquez ordered curtly. "Can't you see he is but a boy?" Lorenz acquiesced to his brother in Spanish, but his eyes on Young Miguel smoldered. Bosquez turned again to Cavenal. "Until I hear from my government, Señor Cavenal, we believe Texas will choose to annex—and when she does, it means a greater war with Mexico."

Cavenal was unable to let it go, and, made more furious by Bosquez's obstinacy, he shouted, "Why don't you raid the Regretts? They're your real enemies! They *want* annexation! They're *working for it!*"

"Their workers are my countrymen, also turned traitor" —Bosquez's shrug was eloquent—"just as these have. They say, like this young fool, they are Texans—but they are worse. The Regretts have trained them to be killers and keep them heavily armed. No, we do not go to the Regretts ranchero for supplies."

Soldiers sent to plunder the Daventry larder were returning now, bringing two packhorses loaded with sides of beef, hams, and a large number of chickens tied squawking in bunches of three to be hung from saddle pommels.

Dolly whickered nervously, sensing her rider's agitation. Monty backed her away as the four soldiers joined the others. Bosquez signaled those guarding the women as well as those threatening the Mexican workers. They thrust rifles into saddle holsters, shoved pistols in their belts, and hastily mounted their waiting animals to link up with their comrades.

Putting spurs to their mounts, they passed Monty, Cavenal, and his sister. Lady Marguerite had not stepped from the carriage, though she craned her head out several times to see and hear what was taking place.

The armed men were laughing now and speaking rapidly in Spanish. Bosquez and his younger brothers were the last to go. They stood guard, guns raised, as their companions galloped through the open compound gate.

"Come, Hernando, Lorenz, we go." Bosquez rode close to Monty in passing. Dolly reared nervously, backing away. "Such a pretty señorita, wearing your too-tight boy clothes!" He grinned.

"Be glad we take only food—this time." The youngest brother, Lorenz, laughed, showing tobacco-stained teeth. "Next time—more."

Felipe Bosquez laughed then, stretching his neatly trimmed mustache, and with loud cries, the brothers joined their hard-riding comrades beyond the open gate. They disappeared down the long, shaded road beyond. Those around Monty broke up into smaller groups, the men muttering angrily, the women's voices a low, murmurous hum.

"That bloody blackguard!" Cavenal swore. "It would almost be worth annexation to see him whipped!"

"Monty"—Georgina rode up beside her, eyes wide— "you really shouldn't say a word to them. If you talk or fight back like James Arterbury did—who knows what they might do?"

Abby, who had never lost her composure, said to Josey, "Make two pitchers of cold tea, Josey. Feenie, you may help serve it when our guests come into the parlor." She paused, then added, "We will have our high tea in an hour—after we've all settled down."

She moved swiftly then, toward the Cavenals. Louise

lifted her head like a dog scenting the wind. Her imperious attitude returned magically with the departure of the soldiers.

"LeRoy," Abby called, "will you unhitch Lady Marguerite's horse and see to him and the carriage? Carlos, please take care of the other animals."

Abraham handed the carriage reins to LeRoy. His eyes were on Tina, who was smiling shyly as she came forward to greet him. Abby did not miss the small byplay, and added, "Tina and Merzella, see that Abraham has some cold tea. The sun is very hot on that box." She took Lady Marguerite's hand. "My dear Marguerite, and Cav and Gina —do forgive this dreadful welcome!" Louise was at her elbow, smiling expectantly.

"Abigail, you know they have requisitioned provisions from us, too. Only those dreadful Regrett brothers seem able to stand them off," Lady Marguerite responded.

"Do come in—all of you—into the house. We'll have a chance to compose ourselves before high tea." She said firmly, "Monty, child, go wash your face and comb your untidy hair while I introduce my new daughter-in-law and her cousin."

Faith was standing back a little, but Louise was close to Abby as she made introductions immediately. Monty did not stay for the amenities but put Dolly's reins into Carlos's hands. Though only sixteen, he was nearly as big as his brother, Young Miguel.

"Did anyone from the Regrett ranch bring Warlock home today?" Monty asked the boy quietly.

"No, señorita. Miguelito and I both thought they would —it's been a week since he ran away from you."

"I'll go get him myself soon enough."

"Señorita, I'll be glad to go get—"

"Never mind. I want to see Mase Regrett myself about

that horse. Warlock should know after nearly a year where he belongs." She made her way to the house rapidly.

Louise took Lady Marguerite's white, smooth hand with a little curtsy and a murmured compliment on the woman's beautiful skin. But her eyes had been caught by Cavenal, with the sunlight gilding his golden hair as he stood, hat in hand, before the ladies. She was astounded by the man's handsomeness, his impeccable clothing and polished English boots. The large bulge revealed by his close-fitting twill pants was unexpected, and it excited her unbearably. Her pulse pounded as he turned, caught by her expression, and his sleepy lids lowered.

He came forward at Abigail's mention of his name. "Monty nicknamed him Cav years ago, and he's been Cav to us ever since," Abigail said, smiling.

He bowed low over her hand, his lips just brushing the skin. Gooseflesh crawled between Louise's thighs, and she lowered brilliant eyes.

"How nice to meet you, Lord Cavenal," she said huskily.

"Ah, but I must be Cav to you too, Mrs. Daventry. I had no idea Richard's bride would be so exquisite."

"You are very kind . . . Cav," she murmured, fluttering thick gold lashes.

"And I would say Richard is an extremely lucky man," he added.

"Do let's get in out of this broiling afternoon sun," Lady Marguerite said impatiently.

Abby, observing Louise and Cav, frowned faintly as she replied, "Indeed we will, Marguerite."

"I'm really too terrified to notice the weather," Louise said as she followed Abigail. "Those villainous-looking men —I thought surely they were going to kill us all!" Her little laugh caught in her throat with just the right amount of remaining fear.

Faith looked at her cousin, her expression neutral, but her eyes anguished. She had lived with and learned much—too much—during her twelve years in Louise's shadow. She had noted Cavenal's expression as he looked at Louise. Young as she was, Faith recognized in their tawny depths the same wild insatiability that drove Louise.

Now Lady Marguerite spoke to her as they took the broad granite steps up to the wide, cool hall. "You're quiet, Faith. Are you happy here in Texas with your cousin?"

"Yes, Lady Marguerite."

"We're going to make both of you so welcome, you'll be very happy you came," Lady Marguerite proclaimed in her royal manner. "Even though Georgina and I long terribly for our lovely London, we too have learned to make the best of it. And we'll help you do the same."

"That is so kind of you, Lady Marguerite," Faith replied, her eyes still on Cavenal and Louise as they walked side by side conversing. Cavenal was speaking.

"You must not be alarmed by those soldiers, Miss Louise. We are often raided by soldiers from the Mexican army. You see, they've never given up claim to Texas."

"But I heard you say Captain Elliot was carrying a treaty to the President of Texas—Anson Jones. I met Captain Elliot in Washington."

"Yes. We learned of it only yesterday and were to keep it secret, but I thought I could prevent Bosquez's raid with the news. It seems I was wrong." With that he launched into a dissertation on the terms of the treaty.

Tall, cool glasses of tea were served in the parlor immediately. Louise had seated herself as near to Cavenal as she felt would be considered proper, but every fiber of her slender body was crying out to touch him.

"Tell me, Cav, what you have on your estate. Is it the same as . . . as ours?" Louise's pale blue eyes were intense, her full lips red and shining.

"Yes. I think Richard has more cattle than I. The Regretts keep him supplied, of course. But I have more horses, much to Monty's dismay. She would like three stables full."

"I worry about Montrose," Louise said pensively. "She's such a hoyden. Those clothes!" She gave a little shudder. "I'm hoping when Richard gets home I can persuade him to curb her boyish ways."

"I think Monty does very well." Cav's smile was cynical. So there was jealousy in both women, he thought, amused, wondering if there was a way he could turn it to his own advantage. He added a touch of fuel to the fire: "Her figure in those clothes is very, well, attractive."

Louise's eyes flashed, but she dropped her lids quickly, and said, "That's just it. She doesn't realize it, the dear young thing, but she invites attentions—the kind she wouldn't know how to handle. Like those ruffians that just robbed us."

"Don't sell Monty short, Mrs. Daventry," Cavenal laughed, in no way deceived by Louise's solicitude and demure ways. He felt the hot desire in her, for his own had risen to meet it. He had even grown hard, just sitting this near to her, and he knew full well that they would come together and soon. From long experience with women, he knew Louise's hungers. They were like his own—ungovernable.

Louise batted her lashes swiftly. "I would so enjoy seeing your home and plantation," she murmured. "Lady Abigail has told me how beautiful it is."

Lady Marguerite, Abigail, and Georgina were talking interestedly with each other. Faith was a quiet listener. Thus, Cavenal and Louise spoke in comparative privacy.

"But you will see them, Mrs. Daventry, and soon. My lady mother and I, as well as Georgina, are planning a welcoming social for all the Daventrys as soon as Richard returns."

"How divine! I adore parties. And I do love taking the air

in the mornings, so perhaps I can call on you and your mother and sister before Richard returns. In Charleston, I always went out in my carriage for an hour or two." There was a faint note of regret in her voice, but she brightened, adding, "Still, I've been enjoying morning rides around here equally—even though I must always have an escort with gun in hand."

"That's very necessary, my dear Mrs. Daventry," he said gravely. "Of course, there is the so-called Mexican army. Very infrequently Indians show up. In fact, the only good thing that coarse, headstrong Sam Houston ever did was to make peace treaties with the Cherokees, Wacos, and Tonkawas. They form a good buffer between his southern area and the bloodthirsty Apaches and Comanches who roam the western and northern plains."

"Dear me, I didn't realize that!"

"As for Mexican soldiers," Cavenal continued, "sometimes they kidnap our people and hold them in Mexico City for ransom and bargaining purposes. And you've seen their depredations for yourself today."

"They were dreadful!"

"You must remember those things and always have a good, reliable escort, Mrs. Daventry."

"Oh," she said, breaking into an ingenuous smile. "I have already. Young Miguel Puente. Lady Abigail says he's remarkably good with a rifle and pistol as well as expert with horses. Beside"—she looked at him archly—"I never go anywhere without my reticule, and I always carry a small pistol ready to fire. I'm really quite accurate with it."

Abigail and Lady Marguerite had grown quiet and Louise's remark caught their attention.

Abby said softly, "A small pistol wouldn't avail much against Bosquez." At that moment, Josey and Feenie came into the parlor with large pitchers, ready to replenish their glasses. They were followed by Monty, in fresh pants and shirt. She had tied her mass of copper hair back with a strip of deerskin. Louise noted this and was offended anew at the girl's attire. She leaned closer to Cavenal and spoke.

"Would you like something stronger, Lord Caven—I mean Cav?"

"No," Cav replied, taking in her face, his eyes slowly sliding from her inviting eyes to her mouth, then to the alluring cleavage that exposed the high curves of her breasts. "It's a bit early for that. Besides, I'm looking forward to tea."

Monty took a glass of cold tea and watched this exchange. She flung herself into a large cushioned chair, her stormy eyes still on Louise. Monty was not so young and inexperienced that she did not know Louise was throwing herself at Cav. She marveled anew at her father's choice of this woman as his wife.

She had been seated but a moment when she rose abruptly, glass in hand, and without a word, left the room.

Two hours later, after they finished the hot tea, pastries, and other delicacies, Lady Marguerite announced, "I'm going to have to travel to Gonzales in five days. Next Monday to be exact, to see my doctor. Georgina will be going with me and, of course, Ephraim and Abraham will drive us. Would any of you ladies care to come and stay a day or two in town with us?"

Abby demurred and Faith smiled, shaking her head. Louise was the one who put down her empty cup and spoke regretfully. "I'd love to go with you, Lady Marguerite, Georgina, but you know, any day now my darling Richard could arrive, and I couldn't bear to be gone when he does."

Lady Marguerite looked at her approvingly. Then her eyes went to her son fondly, and she said, "I wouldn't go if I didn't have to. It's George—he won't let me go a year without an examination. It's a wonder he doesn't go with me just to make sure I do it!"

"I'll demand a note from the doctor for that remark, my lady mother. And make sure you've done as you should."

Unnoticed, Abigail's clear gray eyes rested thoughtfully on Louise Daventry's little smile as Cavenal made his affectionate remark to his mother.

Monday, Louise was thinking. *That means George will be in his fine home alone.*

Chapter 11

The days slipped by, and Monty, nerves drawn tight, endured her stepmother's presence silently. Her room and Abby's were the only two in the house that escaped Louise's changes, and only because Abby had put her foot down.

Now that she was almost satisfied with the house, Louise's morning rides with Young Miguel as her escort were regular. She always returned looking rosy and refreshed. Even Young Miguel wore a look of satisfaction that indicated they'd had a pleasant ride.

When Louise returned from these sorties, Monty escaped to the stables where she stayed most of the afternoons, currying Dolly and her father's favorite gelding, Nate, and working in the corrals with her other favorite mounts. Carlos asked twice about Warlock in as many days.

"I'll go get him—"

"I told you, Carlos," she replied with annoyance, "I want to talk to Mase Regrett about my Warlock—about the fact that he's still going back to the Regrett place even after a year here."

"Only four times, Monty," Carlos reminded her.

"That's four times too many."

Over coffee Monday morning, Monty remarked, "When

Velma Flores came over to see Dorita yesterday, she said Warlock was getting fat on Regrett bran mash. If Mase keeps feeding him like that, Abby, he'll break down our stable doors to get back there. I'm going to get him today."

"I'm surprised you haven't gone before," Abby replied. She had relinquished her place at the head of the table at Louise's request.

"Warlock?" Louise looked at Monty sharply.

"The horse Pa bought for me last year from the Regretts." Monty's tone was just short of being rude.

"You should send some slave after him."

"I told you, we have no slaves." This time the retort *was* rude, and Louise knew it.

"Then you should send a worker." Louise was frowning now. Her mouth had thinned with anger as it always did in an exchange with Monty.

"Why? I'm perfectly capable of riding over there with Big Miguel or Miguelito as escort. It's not as far as the Cavenals'." Monty finished her coffee and rose. "If you will excuse me, Faith and Abby?" She ignored Louise.

"I haven't said you could go, Montrose!" Louise's pale blue eyes were dark with rage.

"And I haven't asked your permission," Monty said evenly. Her eyes went to Faith. The two young women exchanged glances. Faith was an ally, Monty knew, for all that Louise had intimidated the girl for years.

"Oh! You just wait until your father gets home, Montrose. There'll be some changes made—"

"That's what I'm counting on," Monty replied, and she left the dining room, her boot heels clicking firmly on the pecanwood floor where the rug ended. There was a small silence, then Louise, her composure restored, broke it.

"I think I'll have Young Miguel escort me to the Cavenals' this morning myself." She smiled brightly at Abby.

"But today's Monday, Louise," Abby replied, "and you

recall Lady Marguerite said she and Gina would be leaving for Gonzales early this morning."

"Oh, that's so . . ." Louise said slowly, looking disappointed. "I had completely forgotten." Then with a shrug, she said, "It doesn't matter, Lady Abigail. I only want to see the plantation—house and grounds. I'm sure a servant can show me around." She put her cup down and smiled again at her companions. "Dear Lady Abigail, I won't leave as rudely as Montrose. Faith and I will stay until you are finished with your coffee."

"You are too kind, Louise," Abby said dryly. But her eyes on Faith were twinkling, and her smile at the young girl genuinely affectionate.

Dorita and Big Miguel had accepted their son's promotion to escort for Señor Daventry's new wife with pride at first. But by the third morning, Dorita had begun to notice how absentminded her son had become, how anxious he was to perform his chores for Señora Daventry. And she had seen the boy's face and eyes when Señora Daventry was mentioned. She had talked about it with her husband only the night before, but he laughed and told her the boy probably worshiped the woman from afar.

This had not satisfied Dorita, for she had noticed the looks her friends Josey and Feenie gave Señora Daventry, when she and Young Miguel set off on their long morning rides.

As for Young Miguel, he rejoiced when he accompanied his new mistress out to take the morning air. They usually rode as far as Three Points Lake. After they arrived at the lake, Louise always dismounted and beckoned to Miguel.

The place they had found by the lake was thickly wooded with willows, their drooping branches making a very private trysting place. They were almost hidden by them. There they took their pleasure in each other completely free of anxiety. By their third coupling, Young Miguel had learned much, and was becoming an expert lover.

Now, after several assignations, on this summer Monday morning Louise sat on a fine sorrel mare wearing an ivory lightweight riding habit. She had chosen her clothes with care for her first visit to the man who had occupied her mind since the day she laid eyes on him, surrounded by the swarthy Mexican soldiers.

Her beauty was not lost on the adoring Miguel. He could scarcely keep his eyes off her, and he was deeply disturbed as his father approached from the stables when the two were about to leave.

"Monty is go to the Regrett ranch after Warlock in a few minutes, Miguelito, an' Miss Abby says you to escort her— you know Warlock best. LeRoy can take Señora Daventry to the Cavenals."

Young Miguel swallowed hard, and his disappointment was evident. Big Miguel's eyes on his son were sharp. Maybe Dorita was right.

Louise smiled warmly at both Miguels. She was relieved, for it would be an irritation to manipulate Young Miguel when her mind was obsessed with Cavenal.

"You need worry no longer with me, Miguel. I know you're anxious to get back to your regular chores anyway," she said lightly. She had begun to discourage Young Miguel two days earlier. Now she was ready to dismiss him entirely. The boy was bewildered, his fear of losing her evident.

Later, when she and LeRoy rode around to the front of the big Cavenal house, Louise sighed with pleasure at the sight of it. It was bigger than Richard's house, though built in the same Georgian style. But then she had sensed that Cavenal was a much wealthier man than Richard Daventry.

The long row of arching cottonwoods that led up to the front and around the side from the back afforded cool shade for them. For the first time she spoke to her silent companion.

"It's a lovely house, isn't it, LeRoy?"

"Yes, ma'am."

As they trotted around the curved drive, the wind through the trees was cooling despite the summer heat.

"It's really much grander than ours," she added, envy in the words.

"I don't think so, ma'am. Ain't no place as fine as Mister Richard's." LeRoy drew his horse to a stop in front of the wide granite entry. Unlike the Daventry house, there were two tall chimneys at each end. Cavenal had been unable to resist English fireplaces, despite the almost tropical climate.

"You can take the horses to the stables—water them. Do you know anyone here to visit with?"

"Yes, ma'am," he said, giving her an odd look. "I know lots—Ephraim Jones, the blacksmith for Mister Cav. I knows him an' his wife, Sophie, too. She has a little boy—" He broke off, his eyes veiled as he assisted Louise to dismount.

Then, remounting his horse and taking the bridle to Louise's horse, he cantered back to the rear of the big house, as Louise took the steps. Reaching the brightly polished brass knocker, she rapped smartly on the door.

Almost immediately, Jarrett opened it, betraying no surprise at seeing the beautifully dressed young woman before him.

"Good morning," Louise said with a twinkling smile. "I'm Mrs. Richard Daventry. I am returning the visit Lady Marguerite and her family paid me last week."

"Good morning, madam. I am Jarrett, Lord Cavenal's man. Please come in." As she entered the big, cool dark foyer, he added, "I regret to tell you, m'lady and Miss Georgina left very early this morning for Gonzales."

"Oh, dear! She *did* mention something about a trip—I

completely forgot!" Louise followed him, picking up the train of her creamy riding habit.

"M'lord is riding his fields, but I'll send for him immediately. He wouldn't want Mr. Daventry's wife to go unwelcomed by a member of the family."

Louise hesitated briefly, putting a finger to her pink lips as though gravely disappointed. Then she lifted a sparkling smile to the butler. "That would be very kind of you, Jarrett."

"Please come and have a chair in the salon. I will bring you tea after I send for m'lord."

After he had shown her to a seat in a velvet-cushioned chair, he disappeared down the hall, leaving Louise to inspect the room to her pleasure.

It was a gracious room. The furniture was of infinitely fine quality and placed tastefully. It was as she had expected, a room reflecting the heritage of an English nobleman. How marvelous it would be to preside as mistress over this beautiful room!

When Jarrett served her tea in the thinnest of fine china, she sat sipping daintily and anticipating George Cavenal's entrance. She was so lost in admiration of the room and her thoughts of the man himself, his appearance almost startled her.

"Louise!" Cavenal said with genuine pleasure. He was, as always, immaculate in a white shirt with the hint of a ruffle at the throat. A thick strand of shining blond hair had fallen over his forehead. "How good of you to return our visit so soon. I do regret that my lady mother and Gina are not here to share my pleasure in seeing you."

"I completely forgot about Lady Marguerite and Georgina and their errand in Gonzales until Jarrett reminded me!" She rose and swept forward to meet him.

He took her extended hands. As they met, a sharp thrill

coursed through her. His lips touched the back of one hand and lingered.

Then he said over his shoulder, "Jarrett, do refill the teapot and bring some pastries. I'll have a cup with our guest."

Jarrett bowed, his face impassive as he left the room.

"I hope I'm not interfering with your work, Lord—I mean, Cav." She didn't like to use Monty's irreverent diminutive, but she felt it pleased the man.

"Certainly not. I would have been coming in for a cup of tea around this time anyway. How are you adjusting to your new home and relations, Louise?"

"Well enough, I suppose. Though Montrose is a—well, the only word is 'vixen.' The Lady Abigail is a wonderful—though, ah, cold person. But I'm sure I'll win both of them in the end." Her musical voice made light of the problem.

"Yes," he replied, "Monty is an unbroken colt, and very used to having her own way. But I know that anyone as beautiful"—his voice dropped lower—"and, I might add, as desirable as you are, will always win through."

"What a lovely thing to say," she murmured, her lashes little gold crescents against her cheeks.

Jarrett returned with the steaming silver teapot and asked courteously, "Madam Daventry will serve?"

"Indeed I will, Jarrett," she replied quickly, imagining briefly once more how delightful it would be to preside over this rich English household.

As they sipped their tea, Cavenal and Louise discussed everything except what was uppermost in the minds of each. They spoke of the political situation in Washington and in Texas, the raising of cotton and the exporting of it to England. At her request, he told her of the great gray stone manor and sumptuous town house he had left in England.

"We brought some of our servants, those who wouldn't be left behind actually." He laughed. "There's Emma Watson, Cook as we call her—been with us for years. But there's Nonny Jenkins, our fairly new maid, who came over two years ago and served her two-year indenture. She's only twenty-three and wanted the adventure of the New World, just as I did, so she's stayed. Mavis Bryan, our head housekeeper now, had been my lady mother's maid for years. And of course, there's Jarrett, who was my father's valet and butler and is most loyal to me now."

"What a wonderful household. Don't you have slaves, too?"

"Indeed we do—over fifty of them, and brilliant and clever as you are, you wouldn't remember their names if I told them to you," he said, smiling.

Her laugh was merry, but her mind was fastened on the strong male body of the man seated before her. Cavenal, in their conversation, had injected subtle compliments, conveying the promise of physical pleasures.

She drained her cup, and over the rim, her blue eyes, darker with anticipation, echoed that promise as she spoke.

"I really should tour your house as you suggested when you visited us, Cav," she murmured, "and then I must return. After all, Richard should be coming home at any time."

There was a powerful current of sensuality between them as he took her arm. She left her riding hat with its provocative feather in a chair, and they went from the big, cool salon into the spacious library.

After the dining hall, he showed her two large bedrooms for guests. In the kitchen, she met the cook, Emma Watson, Nonny Jenkins, and Mavis Bryan, whose brown hair was graying at the temples. Louise estimated that both Mavis and Emma must be in their late forties.

Louise put a hand to the back of her upswept curls as they took the stairs, and sent Cavenal a seductive glance. He moved so close to her their arms touched, and she felt heat between her thighs. She felt herself helplessly growing moist in anticipation. Though the sensation was a familiar one, it was of greater intensity than anything she had known before. It was all she could do to control herself.

As he showed her Lady Marguerite's room, Georgina's room, and the additional rooms for guests, Louise ached with desire. He came to one last tall paneled door and, opening it, spoke huskily.

"This is my bedroom, Louise." He put a hand out and took her elbow, pulling her gently toward him. Even expecting it, she was not prepared for the violent emotion that swept her into his arms.

He did not kiss her at first, but instead held her body against his as he examined her chiseled features, which were indeed like those of Richard Daventry's porcelain French aristocrat now gracing a small mahogany table in the Daventry parlor.

"I wondered," he said, relishing the feel of her, "how long it would be until you came." His heavy-lidded gaze moved leisurely over her lips, parted now, breath short between them. "It's sooner than I thought—and that's good."

Moving away from her, he turned the key in the door, locking it against intruders—he knew there would be none for his servants knew him only too well. But Louise Lynchley Daventry did not know that, and he locked the door to assure her response.

He bent his head then and put his mouth on hers, gently at first. Then in a rising crescendo of passion that flared white-hot, he flung her on his broad bed and together they began frantically removing their clothing.

When Louise came out through George Cavenal's bedroom door, she was not the same woman who had entered. She moved as one in a dream. For the first time in her hungry, empty life, she was filled and brimming over, seared by flames as rapacious and devouring as her own. But more than that, she told herself, *I have found the one man who can satisfy me.*

When Cavenal helped her onto her waiting horse beside LeRoy, Louise still drifted in the afterglow of their consummation. But even then came the thought, *When can I see him again?*

"Thank you for tea, Cav—and the lovely visit."

LeRoy looked at her, puzzled by the white beauty of her face and the brilliant blue eyes.

The sun on Cavenal's hair was pure shining gold. He appeared to her as one of the long-ago gods of Greek civilization that she had studied during her brief schooling in Charleston.

"It was my pleasure, Louise. You must come again—and soon."

LeRoy looked at him with sudden sharpness, then at Mister Richard's wife. Her face was flushed now and she looked —she looked as if a fire burned within her. She was radiant. He set his horse moving restlessly, and turned his face away.

Cavenal's appetites were well known among the workers at all the homesteads in the area, but he would never dare touch Richard Daventry's wife, LeRoy assured himself. They rode the curving drive around to the back in silence.

Louise's was the silence of deep satisfaction. Never had she known such strange and frenzied delights as Cavenal had shown her. How long had so many ways to bring such aching delight existed? How many times in that too-brief two hours they shared had she tossed in that lashing sea of passion he knew so well to bring on her?

She adjusted the small, feather-tipped hat, urging the mare to a trot. LeRoy followed, his dark eyes filled with uncertainty. Under the leafy shade that covered most of the long trip, the breeze was hot, and Louise pressed her lace handkerchief to her damp brow. She was conscious of disapproval emanating from LeRoy. She finally resolved to erase it.

"I was gone so long because it's a very big house, LeRoy. Too, Lord Cavenal insisted that I have tea and cakes with him." She laughed disarmingly, adding, "And you know how the men love to talk of annexation. I thought he'd never stop, and I hated to be rude!" She laughed again.

"Yes, ma'am."

"Wouldn't it be wonderful if my darling Richard had come home while I was gone? Oh, I'll be so *happy* when he arrives."

"Yes, ma'am."

She gave up and let her mind roam freely over the two hours spent in George Cavenal's arms. As she did so, her first doubt assailed her. Had she been as marvelously satisfactory to him as he had been to her?

The thought rocked her and some of the iron-laced confidence that was an armor about her seeped away. A small touch of panic shook her, for Louise knew she *must* have Cavenal again and again, no matter the cost. She would have to be very careful with Richard—he was not a man to be handled as she had handled young Randolph Lynchley. Daventry was a man of pride and steadfast honor.

Confidence rushed back into her and she laughed aloud. She would manage Richard! She'd keep him eating out of her hand. It would be a pleasure to deceive him, and she began planning her course of action at that moment.

Ah, there would be further pleasure in making that little slut Montrose pay and pay for her impudence—her hatred. Louise, a creature of the senses, had become aware of Montrose's dislike for her long ago. How sweet would be the pleasure of maneuvering Richard against his spoiled daughter, while she planned to rid herself of both of them—and become the Lady Louise Cavenal! The thought of presiding over Cavenal's mansions in England dangled like a misty dream before her. Richard could meet with a convenient accident, she thought vaguely, after Cavenal confessed he could not live without her. Even divorce was a possibility, if all else failed, scandalous though it might be.

As for Miguel, she could finish disposing of him in the next few days. She would simply be cool and remote—let him know she had lost interest. He might mope for a while, but she would ignore that. After all, he was but a child.

Anything was possible for Louise. She always won. And now she would win Lord George Huntleigh Cavenal—no matter what obstacles stood in the way.

Chapter 12

The sun was warm on Monty's back as she and Young Miguel left the road and cut around the lake toward the Regrett ranch. Spring roundup was over. She hoped to find Mase at the house.

How pleasurable it was to have such information as Captain Charles Elliot had brought to the Cavenals a week ago —and to be free of her bond of silence! By now, President Anson Jones had the treaty and would present it to the Texas legislature. It was news by now in Washington-on-the-Brazos. The fact that Mase had no way of knowing this latest development made it an even greater triumph. How important this ninety-day truce would be to her father's plans—and what a blow it would be to the plans Mase had worked on so long.

Young Miguel had been very silent on this ride. Usually they talked about the Daventry horses. Monty glanced at him. He looked dejected. No doubt it was having to ride escort so often for her unpleasant stepmother.

"How do you like riding guard, Miguelito, for that monster?" she asked, laughing.

"What?"

"How do you like it, being at her beck and call? Does she give you as hard a time as she does me?"

Dark blood suddenly mottled Young Miguel's face, and he stammered an answer.

"I—it is a great honor to escort Señor Richard's so beautiful wife, Monty." He swallowed convulsively and added, "She is very kind." He did not meet her astonished eyes.

Monty stared in silent surprise. His voice was filled with passionate gratitude, and she said no more. As they rode with silence between them, suspicion slowly grew. Had that woman deliberately set out to enamor Young Miguel? Remembering Louise's movements, her smiles and alluring glances at Cav, she didn't need to ask. It was obvious that the boy worshiped her.

Monty's lips tightened. She ached suddenly for her childhood playmate. One more mark against Louise Daventry, she thought angrily as she and Young Miguel rode uncomfortably, without speaking, until they circled Three Points Lake.

As they entered the gate to the main Regrett compound, Monty said, "I guess you'll want to visit with Renaldo and Joe?"

"Yes. I haven't seen them in over a week." He closed the gate behind them and spurred his horse toward the nearest stable, where Renaldo Flores could be seen forking hay just inside the barn. All the Mexican employees on the Regrett ranch and Daventry's place were good friends. They were impervious to the quarrel between the two families.

Monty trotted Dolly up to the long, adobe-brick house, dismounted, and looped her reins over a peeled cedar hitching rail before the front of the house.

The sound of women's voices chattering in Spanish could be heard, and suddenly Twyla Salazar and Velma Flores came out the door with large woven baskets of soiled linens and clothing.

"Ah, buenos días, Monty!" Then glancing over her shoulder to see Young Miguel dismounting at the first barn, she added, "So glad to see you an' Miguelito have come—for Warlock."

"Where is everybody, Mamacita? I only see Renaldo."

"Señor Julien an' four of the men have gone with many horses to Galveston—Andrew is with them," Twyla Salazar said, laughing. "The horses, they goin' to be ship to some buyer 'way up in Virginia who Señor Mase met in Washington last winter."

"The rest of the men is out with the cattle, Monty," Velma added. "My Renaldo, he work feedin' the horses in the barn—an' breakin' some of 'em, later on."

Monty hid her disappointment. Now she'd have to get Warlock and head home. "I did come after Warlock. I guess Mase is with the men and the herd?"

"No. He's in the last horse barn. He work on his saddle an' lariat. He have to go one day soon with reports he write, to find General Sam at Washington-on-the-Brazos." Mamacita's smile broadened. "Your Warlock, he have an easy life this week. No one ride him, he just eat like a pig."

"So Velma told Dorita," Monty said, smiling at Velma. "That's why I'm here. But I thought sure someone on the ranch would bring him back to me."

"The men—they have been so busy!" Velma said defensively.

"An' Señor Mase," Mamacita added, "he write these many papers to take to General Sam. He leave in a week— or maybe two now."

"Well, I'll just walk down to the last barn—since I'm sure both Warlock and Mase are there." With a wave, she struck out across the wide grassed patch of land that surrounded the house and headed toward the outbuildings.

Twyla and Velma followed, for they had the big three-legged black iron washpot boiling over a fire under a spreading oak. They would boil the linen and clothes, poking them with a long pole kept for just that purpose. It was also used to lift the clothes into the rinsing pots.

Monty entered the cool, dark stable, her eyes adjusting slowly from brilliant sunlight. There was a high, sharp whinny. Warlock had recognized her. She moved forward, eyes searching for Mason Regrett. She did not see him. She realized he was in the tack room, where the saddles were kept and all leather goods repaired, when the soft sound of a whistled tune came to her ears.

She went to the door and, without knocking, opened it. His dark head was bent over the rifle holster on a fine leather saddle. His crisp, curling hair had fallen over his forehead, softening the strong rugged features of the man. Sleeves of his blue denim shirt were rolled up past the elbows, revealing muscular lower arms and black curly hair.

Monty was powerless to stem the tide of warmth that flooded through her at the sight of him. She took refuge in ready temper as he looked up quickly, eyes sharpening in recognition. She had worn a bright blue shirt that accented her eyes and sunny hair.

"It does seem to me you could have spared *someone* to bring Warlock home."

"It does seem to me you could've spared someone to come after him," he parried, his smile white in the light from two windows in the tack room. "Instead, I'm favored with a personal call from the fiery Miss Daventry herself. I like that."

He stepped down from the tall stool he had been seated on, putting aside his awl and the strip of rawhide with which he was working. Stretching his arms above his head in relaxation, he looked a foot taller than his six feet three inches. He came toward her.

Monty backed against the door, which she had thoughtlessly closed behind her. He leaned over, putting both hands on the door, and brought his face down close to hers.

"Don't you owe me something for his room and board?"

"I don't owe you anything! I sometimes think you trained that stallion to come here anytime he gets the bit in his teeth."

"I did." He laughed. "I wanted him to bring you here."

Monty looked up at him from under her hat. No one rode out under the Texas sun without a hat, but Mase reached a quick hand up and flipped it off.

"I'm not going to stay," she said quickly. "I just wanted to get Warlock—and to tell you some important news. I can tell it now, because Anson Jones has presented it to the Texas legislature by now!"

"News," he said alertly, his hands back on either side of her against the door. "From your smug expression, I can guess it's bad news for me and the annexation."

"Then someone's already been by and told you—" She was deflated.

He laughed aloud. "No one's been by with any news. Go on and enjoy your little triumph. It's not going to matter in the end."

"It will matter! You're so know-it-all—and you could be wrong! I was at Cav's when Captain Charles Elliot stopped there last week. He took President Jones a treaty signed by Avrillago, the head of the Mexican government, giving us a ninety-day truce with them that's backed by England and France!" She paused to catch her breath as she saw a flicker of dismay cross the sun-browned features. "And during those three months, we're pledged not to become annexed to *any* country! Cav knows for a fact that Anson Jones is in favor of Texas expansion, so you can bet he'll honor the truce!"

"Damn Cavenal for the liar he is! Another delay—" he muttered. Then his eyes narrowed on her blue ones. "It means I'll have something else to tell General Sam—and Jones, too—if he'll listen." He laughed at her hopeful face. "Go on. Enjoy yourself, Monty. As I said, it won't matter in the end. Texas is going to be part of the United States."

"Not if my father and others like him can stop it!" she retorted fiercely.

"They can't. Britain and France *and* Mexico have merely fallen into the trap Sam Houston set for them long ago. This will have to go before all the people of Texas, and it'll be voted down."

"You don't know that!"

"Yes I do. And it'll add fuel to the fire General Sam has built under the United States. They'll be so eager to have Texas come into the Union, they'll fall over themselves in coming to terms with us to get it."

"After ten years of begging to be let in? I don't believe it!"

"Believe it, Monty. This truce or treaty or whatever will probably make it possible for Texas to enter the Union with more privileges granted her, because of her independence, than have been granted any state before." He began laughing aloud.

"You're a fool, Mason Regrett! I never heard such a pack of half-baked dreams!"

"If you could see your face!" He laughed harder, then dropping his hands swiftly, caught her to him. "It's irresistible."

Suddenly his warm, strong mouth was over hers, and the old familiar weakness spread a pervasive warmth along her limbs. She stiffened. She had promised herself this wouldn't happen again. Pulling away, she opened the door behind her.

"I came for Warlock—" She stepped quickly into the cool gloom of the stables. "I heard him as I came in."

"He's in the last stall—down there where we keep the feed and hay piled at the end of the stable. And you don't think you owe me at least a couple of kisses for Warlock's keep?"

"Pa paid you plenty for this horse," she said, approaching the last stall. "Enough to cover his keep for a few days."

As they reached the stall, his arms came out and caught her again, tipping her face to his. In the pale light from the small openings in the wall of each stall, she could see the heat in his eyes, and her lips parted as he put his mouth over hers once more.

Of their own volition, her arms went around his shoulders. She could feel their hard, coiled strength beneath her hands as she clung to him, unable to pull away.

"Mase, you aren't playing fair with me," she whispered against his seeking lips.

"What's fair?"

"You know what happened last time—"

"I know, and I liked it. So did you."

"But I can't—we mustn't!"

"You can and we must."

His hands ran over her tight little buttocks, lingering as they sought the pants buttons in front. Then, without opening them, he picked her up and carried her to the sweet, fragrant fresh hay, spread for easy filling of the stall troughs.

He laid her down upon it, and the clean smells of the stable filled her lungs. Bran and mash, hay and good horseflesh. As he bent over her, he pressed her half-resisting body deep in the hay, and once more began to unbutton her pants. But as he did so, he brought his mouth to hers again.

Excitement rose higher and hotter within her as reason fled and instinct took her. Her eyes widened looking into his. There was a flame in Mase Regrett that Monty was powerless to resist. She felt the hard length of him over her and blindly began to help him undress himself and her.

"Don't fight it, Monty—kiss me."

His hard tongue played with hers until she was filled with

the smell of clean, scrubbed male flesh, tobacco and saddle leather. Her legs parted under him as he kissed her body in every sensitive part. Her breath became shorter and shorter.

He entered her smoothly. The thrill of penetration caught her breath. She gave a little moan of delight. Then suddenly her eyes flew wide and she stiffened.

"Mase—oh, Mase, would you do something for me?"

"What, love?"

"Would you withdraw—before—before you—just so I—I won't get pregnant? Oh, Mase, I worried so before—"

"What did you say?" All his movements had stopped, and he lifted his mouth from her piquant breast.

She repeated her request, with more emphasis, for fear swept her.

He withdrew with difficulty and, breathing deeply, moved to a sitting position beside her. She looked up to find the black eyes glittering in quiet fury.

"Where did you learn of a whore's trick?" he demanded. "I know I was the first with you—who's told you a man could do that since then?"

Frightened by his barely curbed rage, she hastened to explain. "Abby—Abby told me, Mase!"

"Miss Abby? What the hell were you doing talking to Miss Abby about a thing like that? I suppose you told her all about us—about that evening by the lake!"

"No! Of course, I didn't. Mase, I was careful talking to her. I was talking about Louise. I said how I'd hate to have a sister or brother from that—that woman Pa's married. And I just asked her if it was possible for Louise not to . . . have a baby if she didn't want one! Abby thought I was asking about Louise—I swear, Mase!"

Mase began putting on clothes swiftly, anger killing the emotion he had felt. Jerking on his breeches and shirt under her startled eyes, he muttered between his teeth, "I suppose that's the truth, but don't think for one minute you fooled

Miss Abby! The whole thing sounds like it's straight out of Rebecca's house in Victoria. You underestimate your grandmother, Monty. I'll wager she's put two and two together—your coming home late on Coffee with me, Warlock gone. Hell, I'll bet she knows all about us!"

"But it's such a little thing! Mase, why are you dressing—why—why don't we make love?"

Monty's own blood was coursing hot through her still. The ache in her loins, unsatisfied, traveled to her chest, and she felt tears burn her eyes. She fought them angrily. Her own disappointment was making itself felt in all sorts of unpleasant ways. She felt terribly uncomfortable sitting naked on the hay and reached for her own clothes.

"Why, Mase?" she asked stiffly, pulling on her chemise first, then her shirt.

"I shouldn't be taking advantage of you, Monty. I got carried away again by—by what you do to me. You'd be better off to stay away from me, because I can't guarantee you'll ever be safe when we're alone together."

"It's partly my fault," she said dully, disappointment like iron fingers in her throat.

"As you say, we don't want you getting pregnant at seventeen, Monty. It won't happen again—we'll get Warlock and you can ride home—safe. No fear of pregnancy."

Tears would not be denied, and Monty angrily dashed her hands across her eyes. She felt awful—unfulfilled, hurt, frustrated, and most of all, sorry. She shouldn't have said anything. She had wanted him with such hunger. She shouldn't have worried about being careful! She had escaped pregnancy those two times by the lake. There was no reason to think she couldn't get by again.

He had left her, and she could hear him putting on Warlock the same saddle that he had worn when he ran away from her at the lake.

Stamping into her boots, she went to join him.

As they both started out with Mase leading Warlock, she stopped by the tack room and picked up her hat. Then together they went into the blinding sunlight of the open area around the stable and corral. Twyla and Velma could be seen lifting the boiled linen from one big black pot to the other under the spreading live oaks.

"We'll tie Warlock alongside your other mount and you can come in for a mug of cold tea. I know the ride over here was hot," he said, with conversational politeness. "Who came with you—Young Miguel? That must be his gelding down yonder."

"Yes," she said coldly. "And no tea, thank you. I'm sure you have better things to do."

"Now, Monty," he said with a dry laugh, "don't get on your high horse with me. Charge it off to mutual misunderstanding and forget it."

Monty said nothing. When they reached the rail, Dolly nickered a welcome, and Warlock snorted his interest in her.

"Uh-oh." Regrett chuckled. "Better tie him pretty far upwind of your mare. He's young and eager."

And so were you, Monty thought dolefully, *until I let Abby's suggestion slip. What a fool I am!* Still, she followed him into the house. He stopped in the big cool kitchen, where he poured two metal mugs of cold tea from a pitcher.

Monty took the mugs as Mase put his hand on her elbow and steered her into the living room. She looked at the two-tiered room and the easy, casual furniture, all bought in Mexico and brought in by freight wagons. She loved this spacious, low-slung house that rambled nearly two hundred feet long, with its fitted flagstone floor.

"I don't guess there's any use in me telling you not to ride Warlock for any long distance from your home, is there?" Mase asked as he stepped down into the couch area with her. Each sat on a separate sofa.

"No. I'll ride him when and where I please."

"I'd feel a lot better about you on Slyboots than on that hard-mouthed stallion. He's no girl's mount. In another three months Slyboots will be the finest, best-trained mare I've ever turned loose from the Regrett stables."

"A mare!" Monty said contemptuously. "Oh, she's beautiful, and I love her, but anyone can ride a mare. It takes a horseman to ride Warlock!"

"Then you ought to leave him here at least a week or so more, and let one of the vaqueros ride him hard—get some of the devil out of him."

"Thanks, but I can do that myself."

"Like you did at the lake that evening?"

"He was skittish because of Coffee, and you know it!"

"He's full of hell, and you know it."

She put down her empty pewter tea mug and rose. "I didn't come for a lecture on how to handle *my* horses. I'll take Warlock and go now." She wouldn't look at him. She still burned to touch him. "I'll ride Warlock home, and Miguel can lead Dolly."

"Listen to me, Monty, that mare's just about to come in season, and Warlock is aware of it. I'll go with you two. I'll lead Dolly and ride Coffee, if you're determined to ride Warlock."

"You will not! I'm perfectly capable of handling both of those horses."

"No girl can handle a full-grown stallion when he's coming onto a mare. I'm going with you and Miguel. As far as the gate to your ranch—when I can see LeRoy get a hand on Warlock."

"I'm sorry, but I'm leaving *now*. Besides, your saddle needs mending."

"The rifle holster on my saddle needs mending and it can wait, since you're so damned obstinate. And you'll wait for me to saddle up or I'll blister your bottom again." His black brows were drawn in a furious scowl, and his mouth was set.

Monty knew he meant what he said. So she stood uncomfortably at the back of the house while he told Velma and Twyla where he was going; then he went down to the third barn and saddled Coffee. When he rode out of the corral, he went to the first barn to get Miguel. The two men were talking together as they rode toward her. Miguel laughed hard at something Mase said, and Monty felt she was being joked about.

As they drew up before her, she mounted Warlock hastily. "I suppose Mase is telling you how stubborn I am," she said to Miguel, frowning.

"Why, no, Monty. We talk about Slyboots an' how she throw Señor Julien yesterday." Young Miguel looked bewildered at her angry tone, and she was chagrined.

"I didn't know the mare had that much spirit," she said grudgingly as Mase took Dolly's bridle, and the three riders set off.

After they passed through the gate, and followed the little road to Three Points Lake, Monty had to admit secretly that she was glad Mase had come with them. Warlock was extremely fractious, and pulled so hard on the reins her arms ached. Dolly's scent was on the wind, and twice he would have bolted, but Coffee, responding perfectly to his rider, headed the younger stallion off.

Monty was thankful too for the long stretches when they reached the main road, where heavy stands of oak provided shade, for the day was very hot. They rode in silence. Young Miguel was a sensitive boy. He sensed the strain between Monty and Mase. And unknown to the two he rode with, he nursed a hurt of his own. Louise Daventry had seemed happy that he did not escort her today, and he had recognized it. Worse, she had been cool and withdrawn the last two days.

Halfway home, after Warlock almost got away from Monty, Mase finally spoke up.

"Don't you think you'd better mount Dolly, and finish our trip on her—let me lead Warlock?"

"No." She shook her head stubbornly, hoping the young stallion didn't pull her arms from their sockets before they reached home.

She was exhausted by the time they drew up before the gate to the Daventry compound. She dismounted swiftly before Regrett could, and opened the gate. Removing her hat momentarily, she wiped her damp face and forehead on her sleeve.

Looking up, she saw Regrett smiling down at her sardonically as Warlock made a sudden dance at Dolly, which Coffee intercepted smoothly. For a terrible moment, Monty thought the two stallions would fight, for both reared high before Warlock backed down. Regrett kept his seat easily. He spoke low and reassuringly to Coffee.

Monty clenched Warlock's reins and Miguel dismounted to take them from her. He said persuasively, "I take him, Monty. He's tired now an' here comes LeRoy." LeRoy was walking fast and smiling broadly.

By now, Regrett had dismounted, and he carefully closed the gate, replacing the steel bar that held it in place.

"I'll be going now, Monty," he said, looking at her through the boards of the gate. "And I'll have to compliment you on your ride." He swept off his hat and made a bow. "You're some horsewoman!"

With a grin, he remounted Coffee and took off, as LeRoy reached Miguel with the horses. Monty stood watching a moment, thinking Regrett might look back, but he didn't. She turned angrily, following Miguel and LeRoy who were leading the nervous mare and stallion away.

It won't happen again. His voice echoed in her heart and it sank heavily. He was going away soon, to see Sam Houston in Washington-on-the-Brazos. It would be a long time before she saw him again and even then— Well, Mase Regrett was a hard man. He would stick to his vow.

She turned to see that several of the Mexican workers were in the open area of the yard. Dorita and Big Miguel were smiling as happily as LeRoy, talking swiftly to each other as well as to those around them.

Something was happening, Monty thought dully, her mind and heart still aching with the memory of those sweet but unfulfilled moments in Regrett's stable. The hay had been so soft and his body so clean and hard—

"Miss Monty," LeRoy said over his shoulder, "hurry on! Your pa come home about a hour ago. Miz Daventry come in from her visit to the Cavenals' just in time to greet him. There's a happy homecomin' goin' on!"

Chapter 13

"Señor Richard's home!" Dorita sang out, and Big Miguel beamed at Monty as she ran toward the house.

"LeRoy told me!" Monty's voice lifted with joy. "Oh, I can't wait to see him!"

Young Miguel asked quietly, "Have you all greet him yet?"

"Yes, yes!" several workers chorused.

Then Dorita said, "He'll come back out an' see you, Miguelito, when he's settled in—like as not he send for you."

Miguel turned his face away to hide his dismay. He felt a mixture of shame and betrayal. He was not anxious to see the man he had looked up to and loved like a father. Guilt gnawed at him as he took his horse toward the stable.

Monty burst into the house through the kitchen door. *Now Louise would be set back! Richard Daventry would hate all his furniture in strange places.*

Rushing through the kitchen, she cried to those in it, "Tina—Merzella—Feenie, I know he's here! Where—"

"In the little office, Monty," Josey answered with a wide smile.

Monty ran to the small office and burst in. There was a

vitality in the air, as if a clean west wind had blown through the house, clearing out all the irritation of the past weeks. An atmosphere of joyousness pervaded the room.

Monty flew into her father's outstretched arms, not even noticing Faith, Louise, and Abby seated about the room.

Richard lifted her easily off the floor, and swung her in a tight circle before setting her on her feet.

"Let me look at my little girl! You're as beautiful as ever, and you had a birthday in March, didn't you?"

Like Cavenal, Daventry wore only the finest English leather boots on his long, hard legs. His hair was brown, thick and curly without a trace of gray for all his thirty-six years. He was young and vital, and he dominated the room completely.

Louise was sitting in a comfortable old rocker near the door to the office, while Abby and Faith were on the horsehair sofa. Louise spoke up, her voice rich with warmth. "Yes, Richard darling, your young daughter is quite old enough to be a *lady* now." She smiled at her husband.

She was going to break that young snip, she thought silently. She had never met a woman, young or old, she hadn't been able to make second to her. *And Montrose Daventry will be no exception.* Her smile widened, and she continued, "I was quite distressed to find her dressed in this manner. But we plan to do away with those masculine clothes, don't we, Montrose?"

Monty turned from her father and looked with concealed loathing at his wife. The woman was still wearing the creamy riding habit she had worn on her morning visit to the Cavenals'. The jacket was open and full, piquant breasts were tantalizingly revealed.

Monty ignored her question, and bubbled to her father, "How did it go in Washington, Pa, after I left? We're all so anxious to know. And have you heard of the ninety-day truce with Mexico? They promise to recognize our independence as a nation, if we don't annex. I was at Cav's when Captain Elliot came through from Mexico with the treaty in hand! It was so exciting!"

"Yes, Monty," he said, seating himself on the edge of the heavy mahogany desk and swinging his booted leg casually. "I stopped by and saw President Jones before coming on home. He's sent out the announcement of the treaty, but I have grave doubts the Texas legislature will vote aye on it. The rumors are, it'll be rejected. I'm not admitting defeat—" He broke off and there was a long pause before he added, "When Cav told me he knew Anson Jones favored independence, I think he was misled. But at least Jones is willing to put it before the legislature, even if they reject it."

"Don't say that, Pa! When it's passed—we have ninety days!—Texas can be a great nation!"

Daventry's laugh was dry. "We've got to be prepared either way, minx. I won't lower my Lone Star flag, even if I must fly the Union flag above it."

Abby spoke up suddenly. "Even if Texas becomes a state, it won't mean the end of our good fortune. It's possible that it means an even better life for us."

"Abby! How can you say that? All our strong ties with England will be broken!" Monty cried.

"Not necessarily, Monty," Abby replied. "As you know, we English have a rare talent for adjusting. We do a great deal of business with the Union despite the fact that the states won their independence some years ago."

All this talk bored Louise, and she was seething. Faith, though she said nothing, looked at Monty with such open admiration and affection that Louise was further infuriated. She had exercised iron control to stem the cutting remarks that boiled within her. Now she spoke in loving tones and with a ready laugh. "It will soon be time for supper, Richard darling. Let's go upstairs and wash up." Then with an arch look, "And we can have our first moments *alone.*"

"Of course, my dear." He gazed at her ardently. "But I do want to give each of you my gifts first." He smiled, winking at Monty with love and pride. "Especially for you, my little girl, since I wasn't here for your birthday."

"Pa, I can hardly wait!" Monty cried excitedly. She was so happy to see him, the loving look he gave Louise didn't trouble her.

Louise paused in the doorway, observing Richard's backward glance at his daughter. Pleasure was in it, and deep paternal love. She was going to change *that* and soon!

Richard put a possessive and protective arm about Louise's shoulders, and together they left to get the gifts he had left in the foyer. Monty looked after them a moment, a certain uneasiness stealing into her. She turned swiftly to Abby.

"What did he say when he saw all the furniture changed around?"

Abby spread her hands. "He said it was an improvement. Then he kissed Louise for her enterprise and excellent taste."

With an explosive breath, Monty sat down in the chair Louise had left. "I can't believe it!"

"Your father loves her, Monty. You must accept that."

Monty looked up, meeting Faith's compassionate hazel eyes, and she burst out, "Faith, I don't see how you stand her!"

"I must." Faith's voice was low and bitter. "I have no income, no talent for making my own way. I'm her one charity, and that only because her father put my upkeep in his will. I find my escape in the wonderful books in your father's library."

"You read too late at night, my dear. You should try to sleep more. And you, Monty, *must* stand Louise," Abby said with finality.

"Never!"

"You'll alienate your father," Abby warned.

"No I won't!"

"Please, Monty." It was a pleading half-whisper from Faith. "You don't know how—how Louise can twist things. If you love your father, try to please her!"

"What did he say about his favorite piece of Dresden, sitting precariously on that table in the parlor?" Monty demanded.

"He liked that too, for he thinks it's a miniature of Louise. In fact, she pointed out all her changes and he said it was a pity she hadn't rearranged your room and mine," Abby replied.

Tears stung Monty's eyes suddenly with her first realization that her father had changed. She hadn't allowed herself to fully believe this woman could change him.

With his wife preceding him, Richard reentered the office, his hands full of packages.

Louise cried, "Look at these gorgeous ear bobs my darling Richard brought me! Aren't they just too beautiful for words?" She tossed her head so the earrings flashed and sparkled, bright as her happy laughter.

Monty looked silently at the diamond and sapphire droplets suspended from Louise's ears.

"They're lovely," Faith said in a strained voice.

Richard smiled indulgently as he passed his packages to Monty, Faith, and Abby.

Monty tore into her package to find a pair of exquisite, handmade English leather boots.

"Oh, Pa! They're the most beautiful boots I've ever had— and I *need* them!" She immediately pulled off her worn, dusty boots, and stamped into the new ones. "And they're a perfect fit!" Then quickly, "Thanks, Pa!" and she flung her arms around him once more, planting a kiss on his cheek.

"I slipped a pair of your old boots into my luggage—so they would be a perfect fit," Richard smiled.

Abby's gift was a white Madeira lace shawl, which she draped about her shoulders with pleasure.

Faith sat holding her package, her face pink. "You shouldn't have, Mr. Daventry—"

"But I should! You're Louise's own cousin, and you're a very deserving young lady." Richard spoke swiftly, looking at the girl's face, where pleasure struggled with humility. "And if I remember correctly, you promised to call me Richard before you left Washington."

Faith's blush deepened. Slowly she opened her package with reverent fingers. Her hands trembled as she held aloft two tortoise-shell combs encrusted with pearls. "Oh," she breathed, "they're beautiful, just beautiful, Mr.—Richard." Then thickly, "I've never had such a fine gift in all my life." There were tears of gratitude hidden in her muffled voice.

"Then stop wearing those dull gray nets on your lovely hair, and put the combs on instead," he said.

There was a momentary silence following his suggestion, broken by Louise's irrepressible laughter. "That's what I've told her, darling, but she's such a little rabbit. She *likes* those nets, and won't do without them."

Faith did not look up, but her full lower lip trembled perilously. Monty, observing her narrowly, saw her catch it between her teeth to steady it.

"I'm glad everyone is pleased," Richard said, smiling.

Monty, who had had nothing but a glass of cold tea since breakfast, was hungry. Because her father told them about his activities in Washington, and kept the conversation full of wit and laughter, she was able to eat heartily of the bounteous supper.

Louise, expert that she was, kept her twinkling blue eyes adoringly on her husband. To any observer, it would appear that she couldn't keep from touching him with love.

* * *

For four days, Louise said no more about Monty's dress or her manners. Instead, she went for her morning rides with Richard in tow. As for Monty, she avoided Louise as much as she could. When she couldn't, she was painstakingly polite to her.

Big Miguel and Dorita saw how their oldest son drooped as these days went by, and they were deeply troubled. On the fifth day, he told them he was going to ask Richard Daventry if he objected to his going to work for the Regretts. They were silent with shock, and disapproving. Richard was dumbfounded.

"Why the Regretts, Miguelito?" he asked when Miguel approached him in the stables. Richard and Monty were examining Dolly for a rock in her shoe, which was causing her to limp. "Why not the Arterburys or the Bedfords? Or even the Cavenals?"

"I do not like Lord Cavenal, Señor Richard—he has slaves. An' I do not know the workers at the Bedfords' an' Arterburys', but I am good friends with all the people at Señor Mase's."

"That's true," Richard said, pulling at his chin. "But why this sudden decision to leave me? I thought you were happy here."

Young Miguel's face reddened under the dark tan. "I have been, Señor Richard," he said hastily. "And I am. It's that I think I should strike out on my own—I've been under my madre and padre's wings too long."

"You know I have no use for the Regretts," Richard said shortly. "I hate to lose a good man to them—and you are a good man, Miguelito."

"Thank you, señor. I admire you very much—but I mus' be my own man now. Señor Mase say he give me many horses to care for—to help him breed. I will earn my way."

As the boy walked away, Monty burst out, "Pa, I'll bet I know why he's leaving!"

"Why?"

Suddenly doubt assailed her. She could not tell her father what she suspected—that Louise had seduced Young Miguel.

"I—he—he wants to be on his own," she said lamely.

"So he said."

Richard looked at her keenly. He was not deceived by her response. What did his daughter suspect? Something she was afraid to tell him. He filed it away in his mind. He would not forget it.

And so Miguel packed his belongings that night. Daybreak found him gone. Richard remarked on his absence at breakfast that morning. Big Miguel and Dorita, and all Young Miguel's brothers and sisters mourned his departure for two days after that.

The sixth day, Louise remarked pensively that she would love to pay Lady Marguerite and her daughter another visit.

"I missed them the first time I went, Richard darling—can you ride with me?"

"No, my dear. I told you I have to go to the Arterburys'—it's a two-day trip. I won't be home for the next three nights. Arterbury has some new seed for corn. And I want to take him some of the Egyptian cottonseed I brought home from Washington."

"I'll be lost without you," Louise said, pouting prettily. "When did you say you were leaving? I guess I just didn't want to hear—"

"About ten this morning." His smile was loving.

"Then I shall surely go to see the Lady Marguerite, to keep from missing you so dreadfully!"

"Be sure and take Ezekiel with you. No matter how familiar you become with the terrain hereabouts, never go without protection."

So Richard set off for the Arterburys', some forty-five miles away, and Louise for the Cavenals'. She was feverish with anticipation. It had been days—how many? Too many! And how would George arrange for them to escape his mother and sister? She put it from her mind. He was a resourceful man. He would find a way.

She did not carry the heavy pistol Richard had given her, when she and Ezekiel left. Instead, she carried her reticule containing the small derringer with which she was very familiar. No fears beset her as the two riders passed the Daventry patrols, then the Cavenals'. And as they approached the rear of the Cavenal fields, she saw the rolling land studded with green cotton bushes. There was a horseman among the workers, and though he wore a hat on his gold head, she recognized the slim, taut body of George Cavenal. He was there! She'd visit with Lady Marguerite and Georgina, have tea with them. Then George would make an excuse for them to be alone!

When Ezekiel had taken the horses around to the stables and Jarrett had admitted Louise through the broad front door, Lady Marguerite swept forward to greet her, followed by Georgina.

"Good morning, my dear Louise! How lovely to see you." Her voice was cool, but welcoming, and Georgina echoed her words. Georgina held a piece of handwork, needle and yarn in the other hand.

"I forgot about your journey that Monday, and made the trip over here, missing you both, when I returned your call," Louise said, smiling.

"Jarrett told us. Such a pity, my dear! We will make up for it today! You're just in time for late morning tea. Jarrett and Cook are preparing it now."

"And my ride has given me a good appetite!" Louise laughed as she removed her perky riding hat.

Lady Marguerite took it, saying, "Do come into the

orangerie. The south breeze is so refreshing. I will give your hat to Jarrett—I'm sure he's told Cook we have a welcome guest."

As she left, Louise took one of the light reed-woven chairs in the center of the blooming fruit trees and blossoming hibiscus.

"How are you today, Gina?" she asked, using Cavenal's pet name for her.

"Very well, thank you, Mrs. Daventry."

"Do please call me Louise. 'Mrs. Daventry' makes me sound so old, and I'm sure we're not that far apart. I'm twenty-eight. How old are you?"

Georgina gave her a strange sliding glance, and Louise was impressed by the milky whiteness around her pale blue irises. It made her eyes appear enormous. They were trimmed with thick black lashes, despite her blond hair.

"I'm twenty-six."

"I think two years' difference is hardly enough to matter," Louise responded, still smiling.

There was something about George's beautiful and quiet sister that was unsettling. Georgina's clear pale eyes were still on her. It made Louise conscious of the artfully applied kohl about her own eyes. It was scarcely visible, she knew, but she had the feeling that Georgina saw the faint kohl and fainter rouge, and looked beyond them. Her slow answer was even more unnerving.

"No. In earth years, two is not a great difference. In other records of time, it could encompass a whole life."

She picked up her needle, and resumed work on her needlepoint. An odd chill ran through Louise, but shaking it off, she made another effort.

"I love the needlepoint you're working—such lovely, vivid colors!" She came to stand beside Georgina, to see her work better. "What is it, Gina? I've never seen one like it."

"This is one of my own design," Georgina replied with

sudden intensity. "I made the pattern—drew it all myself before I began to work it."

To Louise's unschooled eyes, nothing about it looked familiar. The oddly stiff figures were barely clothed, and the headdresses were totally alien.

"What is it, Gina?"

"It's the story of the younger brother of Cleopatra, and of their life and love together."

"I see. And what's this right here?"

"That's a basket of snakes. It represents all those who were so against their love for each other."

"Where is Cleopatra?"

"Here. Lying on her bed, waiting for her brother to come to her. See? Here he is, walking with all his devoted servants."

Louise feigned interest. But the figures looked grotesque to her—too tall, stiff, and thin to be beautiful. She was relieved when Lady Marguerite returned to the orangerie.

"Now tell us, dear, how things are at the Daventry estate. We heard, of course, that Richard has returned." Lady Marguerite smiled.

"Yes, and it's wonderful to have him home with me! He would have come with me today, but he had brought some new kind of cottonseed back from the East for the Arterburys, and has gone to deliver it to them."

"He is always so thoughtful of others. Such a gentleman —a man of great honor."

"I wish his daughter had inherited a bit of that."

"Is Monty giving you trouble, my dear?" Lady Marguerite's smooth face held a look of concern, and Georgina looked up from her needlepoint.

"Oh, yes." Louise sighed prettily. "She seems to resent me—to have taken a great dislike to me."

"Monty's been a bit spoiled by her father," Lady Marguerite said, her voice kind. "But I'm sure it will all work out, and you two will have a very pleasant relationship."

"Who'll have a pleasant relationship?" It was George Cavenal entering the orangerie, smiling.

To Louise, he appeared more charming, more handsome than he had in her dreams of him. As always, he was impeccably attired in a white shirt, open at the throat. Dark blue breeches fitted muscular legs tightly, and his feet were encased in knee boots of the finest leather. They gleamed in the diffused light of the cool green orangerie.

"Monty and Louise." Lady Marguerite smiled indulgently at her son.

"Of course they will!" he said heartily. Then, taking her hand, he murmured, "Louise—the beautiful and enchanting Mrs. Daventry!"

A quicksilver thrill ran through Louise as he pressed his lips slowly to the back of her hand, as if he were savoring the taste of her flesh. At once the ache began deep in her thighs.

"I wanted to come and see Richard when word reached us that he was home," Cavenal said lazily, "but there are so many things to see after on an estate this size. I'm sure you are learning that with Richard."

"We'd be delighted to have you come, all of you, to stay for dinner and the night!" Louise kept her voice light.

"And we plan to have a social honoring the two of you soon. The Bedfords and Arterburys would be delighted to come." Lady Marguerite added casually, "They're the only other ones with good bloodlines hereabouts in this benighted land."

"My lady mother and Gina have never reconciled themselves to living here, despite my efforts to make it as English as possible," Cavenal said, laughing. "I suppose after I get my estates here set up, I'll have to take the two of them back to London."

"There are so many lawless people here." Lady Marguerite shivered. "The Mexicans—the Indians—even renegades from the States, such as those rough Regrett men who raise such beautiful horses."

"Yes." Georgina spoke up. "George told us how Mason Regrett insulted all of his English neighbors—from the podium of the United States Senate in Washington."

Cavenal's face darkened. "He'll pay for that," he said quietly. "No one insults a Cavenal and escapes punishment."

"I wish we were all out of this terrible, uncivilized country!" Georgina said with unexpected venom.

"Now, Gina," her brother warned, "don't start that again. You know I don't want to go back to London yet."

There was a moment of awkward silence, for Lady Marguerite's eyes on her daughter were soft with sympathy. Then she said, "Let's all go into the salon for tea."

Cavenal's eyes found Louise's, and the heat and promise in them filled her with excitement.

Later, she only toyed with the elegant and elaborate tea Lady Marguerite served. Her dainty sips and half-finished scones were all she could manage. An attentive "Really?" and "Do tell!" were enough from her to keep the conversation going. But she realized from what Lady Marguerite and Georgina were saying that it was only their love for and loyalty to George Cavenal that kept them in the Republic of Texas.

"And if this country should become a state—" Georgina began angrily.

"We shall certainly prevail upon George to return to our estates in England," her mother finished.

"My lady mother, let us talk about the social you are planning to honor Richard and Louise," her son said smoothly.

It seemed to Louise they talked interminably before

Cavenal put down his teacup and said, "My dears, I want to show Louise about the place. She's not seen much of it. I must show it all to her before she returns home."

At last! Louise's heart began to beat heavily. She had feared she would have to make her adieux and leave with Ezekiel. She shot Cavenal a quick glance to find he was looking at her with undisguised desire under his sleepy lids.

She said her good-byes to the two women, and she and Cavenal told Ezekiel they would return after she had toured the estate. Cavenal was mounted on a fine, reddish-brown stallion, and he reined it in tightly to keep step with Louise's dainty mare.

"We'll go to the game shed, my love," he said, as soon as they were away from the stables. "We can be alone together there. It's the perfect trysting place."

"Game shed?"

"It's a log house very close to the Guadalupe River about a mile and a half from here—well out of sight. It's where we take game we've shot. Deer, antelope, pheasant, partridge— any game we hunt. We skin them or clean and pluck them there. I have the slaves put fresh hay on the floor each week."

"That sounds wonderful!"

"Yes, we'll meet there as often as we can. I'll send Abraham with notes—and you can send your man Ezekiel to me."

"Oh, Cav, it's perfect! We have all summer before us. I know I can handle Richard easily."

"Ah, Louise, if you were only free!"

She made no answer. *If she were only free.* Well, she could think about that possibility later. Right now, the fever in her rose higher and hotter. She could scarcely wait.

When they reached the game shed, it proved to be as Cavenal said, a small log house nestled in among trees and scrub. The murmur of rushing water in the Guadalupe River a few yards away could be heard. Thick willows and brush obscured it, but the sounds were soothing.

Inside, one half of the floor was covered thickly with fresh hay. The clean, sweet smell permeated the air. On a wall of the shed hung dozens of knives of various shapes and sizes used in the cleaning and skinning of game. A large table, darkly stained, stood in the middle of the room. There was a smoke-darkened fireplace of native stone against the wall where the skinning knives hung.

"For our winter trysts, darling." Cavenal gestured to the fireplace. "I'll come first and build a good fire. No one need ever know. I think we can trust Ezekiel and Abraham implicitly."

He took her in his arms and kissed her deeply, moving his mouth from her lips to her throat rising from the frilly blouse. She clung to him, a tide of heat rising in her, engulfing her. She moved her mouth to his face with hot, hurried kisses, her passion growing. George began slowly removing her riding jacket. Then with expert swiftness he unbuttoned her blouse.

Chapter 14

Earlier, when Louise and George Cavenal left, Lady Marguerite rose and said, "Come, Gina, dear. We won't lunch until three. George should be back by then. And we have time for a nice long nap."

Georgina followed her mother upstairs obediently, entering her room and closing the door gently behind her. She knew her mother would sleep heavily, once she disrobed and lay down. So she stood beside the door for an instant, before going swiftly to her armoire and pulling out her everyday riding habit. Donning it quickly, she pulled her riding hat from a hatbox and set it properly on her pale gold hair.

Then she tiptoed into the hall and paused before her mother's closed door. She leaned down, listening. All was quiet. Lady Marguerite was already slumbering.

At the stables, she routed out Ephraim and had him saddle up her favorite mare. In minutes, she was heading west. Ephraim was used to her short, unannounced rides. She never rode more than a mile from home and was usually back within the hour.

She put the mare into a gallop, riding sidesaddle easily. In a short time, the game shed could be seen among the trees. At some distance from it, she dismounted and looped the mare's reins over the limb of a low bush. There was good grass around the area and the mare began cropping it. Georgina, her polished boots gleaming, picked her way to the cabin.

She went to the place where mud that chinked the logs had long ago fallen out and put her eyes to the opening. Ah, it was just as she expected. They were there, naked and writhing together on the hay on the near side of the blood-stained table.

Among her other talents, Georgina was an accomplished voyeur. She had discovered the pleasures of peeping at people in intimate moments when she happened to witness her mother and father years ago, as a very young child. She had watched her brother with Sophie, when he got her pregnant with the near-white little Sammie—only George and Georgina knew the overseer, Olen Jensen, had been, as he insisted, innocent of fathering the child.

And she had watched him with Nonny Jenkins, so only she and George knew why Nonny had elected to stay with the Cavenals after her indenture was long over. He didn't bring Nonny here often now, and he had become quite rough with her when he did. But Nonny, caught in the thrall of his charm and her love for him, took it all and hoped for more.

Georgina thought of Nonny now with contempt as she watched George and Louise coupling on the hay. She was contemptuous of Louise as well. She knew her brother's ungovernable lusts and she loved him because of them. It was from them she drew her satisfaction. She licked her lips with pleasure.

She watched until the lovers, spent, lay naked on the hay and spoke of dressing. Then swiftly she retraced her steps to the mare and, mounting, galloped home. She was there a good hour before George and Louise rode in. She watched from her bedroom window as George summoned the waiting Ezekiel and saw the two, Louise and her servant, leaving from the rear of the compound. A small secret smile tucked the corners of her curved mouth as she watched her tall, handsome brother return to the house.

Louise, riding home, savored thoughts of the interlude with Cavenal. When they were dressing, he had told her of his dreams of power in the Republic. He had talked of Mason Regrett, quoting Regrett's statements about traitorous neighbors.

"I hate to buy horses from that blackguard. I ought to go to Galveston to buy. Everyone in that Senate Chamber knew his close neighbors were Richard Daventry—and George Cavenal. I have plans to wipe out that insult."

"How?"

"You'll see. In the next few days, we'll be rid of the Regretts."

"You won't do anything dangerous?" she asked anxiously.

He kissed her swiftly. "Only a little dangerous, my love. You'll know about it soon enough."

"I couldn't bear it if anything happened to you, Cav. I—I love you!"

As she and Ezekiel rode along silently, she reflected on his words. She had actually told him she loved him. And she knew that for the first time in her life, she actually meant the words.

She straightened in the saddle. He had implied he loved her a dozen times. And he had said more than once, "Ah, love, if you were only free!" Marriage was implied in that as well. The thought of it filled her with heady happiness.

By the time they reached the Daventry compound, Louise was at ease with herself. She was already looking forward to

the next time she and Cavenal would be together in the
game shed on the Guadalupe River.

Louise, however, was far from Cavenal's thoughts as soon
as they parted. The next five days he thought of her inter-
mittently, and with the pleasure he always felt when he had
satisfied his desires with a new conquest. This one had an
extra fillip however, for Richard Daventry, besides being his
friend, was an eminently honorable man. Cavenal made no
effort to stem the pleasure of knowing he had cuckolded
such a man.

But at the end of the fifth day, he was ready to put into
action his plans for revenging himself on Regrett. Cavenal
had a useful store of knowledge from his stint in Her Majes-
ty's 5th Cavalry Regiment in India. He had learned, among
many other things, how to wind cloth about a rough stick,
dip it in oil, and hurl it on roofs and at the base of buildings. This was what he had in mind for the Regretts. He
would burn them out. He and Abraham. He hadn't approached the big black, but he had already decided on a
means of persuasion in the event that he balked at the job.
Abraham, like Richard, was an honorable man, and
Cavenal knew it. He expected and got an argument.

When he approached him in the east field where he was
working with the other men to remove weeds from the rows
of cotton, he sketched his plans briefly. Abraham demurred.
His brow furrowed.

"Mister Cav, it ain't right to burn out the Regretts. They
ain't done nothin' but sell you good hossflesh."

"Regrett is standing in the way of expansion for the republic. Worse, he's insulted me before the Senate of the
United States. He's a bloody blackguard, Abraham. Come,
let's go over to the water stand."

Cavenal turned his mount toward a small cluster of trees
under which was kept a large bucket of water and a dipper

for the workers. He swung down from his horse as Abraham dipped up water and drank. George Cavenal was a tall man, over six feet, but Abraham had him bested by five inches. Cavenal admired his slave's powerfully muscled build, and knew that with those arms, he would be able to hurl the torches to the roofs of the Regrett buildings with ease.

He thought fleetingly of Sophie, and the blame that cost Olen Jensen his overseer's job, and was satisfied. He could have his cinnamon-colored mistress whenever he wanted her. He felt no responsibility for the child he had sired. Yes, buying Abraham Johnson to replace Jensen had been a good move.

"Abraham," he said firmly. "It's no more than the Regretts deserve." He thought of the Regretts' barely concealed contempt for him when he came to their ranch to buy horses, and his anger fed on itself. "Those two brothers need to be run out of this part of the country. All you'll have to do is ride with me at about two tomorrow morning, and we'll have it done handily."

Abraham again removed his hat and wiped his face. He did not want to do this. The Regretts were good white men. They had no slaves. Didn't believe in it. Paid all their workers good wages. All the slaves on the Cavenal place knew this, and respected both the Regretts and Daventry for their refusal to countenance slavery. Always Mason and Julien Regrett had treated him as another human being—not a piece of property.

"I ain't the best man for this job, Mister Cav," Abraham said stubbornly. "I ain't no good at settin' fires."

"Nonsense! I'll have the torches all ready. All you have to do is light them and throw them on the roofs of the stables and the main house. I'll be with you. We'll do it together."

"You mean you goin' to burn all that fine hossflesh?"

Abraham's jaw dropped with real distress. "You can't—we can't do that!"

"It's the only way to get them out of the country. It'll bankrupt them."

Abraham shook his head vigorously. "I can't burn no helpless hosses, Mister Cav."

Cavenal was silent a long minute before he pulled his trump card. "I know you fancy Mrs. Daventry's maid, Tina."

Abraham looked at him, startled. At the sound of her name, emotion exploded in him. He had loved the girl with the magnificent tumble of curling mahogany hair from the moment he first saw her. He looked down at the dipper in his hand to hide his feelings.

"It might interest you to know," Cavenal lied smoothly, "that I've talked about buying Tina from Mrs. Daventry for you to marry."

Abraham's head lifted, his dark face alight with hope.

"And she has agreed. If you do this for me, I'll buy Tina for you, Abraham."

The big man was silent. Every nerve in his body cried out for Tina, but the iron code of honor he lived by was a wall within him. Cavenal sensed it.

"This is an order as well, Abraham. You will have to do as I tell you. If you refuse, I'll have you beaten publicly, before all the slaves on this place, and make you a field hand again. You have no choice." Then his voice softened persuasively once more. "You won't have to do much. Just throw the torches on the building roofs. I'll throw the ones at the base—and Tina will be yours the next day."

"You'll really buy her?"

"I swear it," Cavenal said solemnly. In casual conversation, Louise had mentioned she would never sell her slaves. But he had no compunctions about using Tina as bait. He could always make the excuse that Louise had changed her mind.

"We'll meet in the main stable at two in the morning, dip the torches I've made in oil and be on our way. It shouldn't take more than an hour's ride there, and an hour's ride back. We can set the fire and be gone before they even awaken—be home and safe in our beds. And Tina will be yours."

Abraham said nothing. Foreboding filled him. Reluctantly, he nodded his acquiescence. "I'll be there, Mister Cav."

That night at the supper table, George was hard put to keep his mind on conversation with his mother and sister. It was especially hard because his mother was off on one of her litanies against Texas.

"I really feel seven years in this—savage wilderness is quite enough. It will *never* become anything like our homes in England, George—even if I live long enough to see it civilized."

"Ah, my lady mother, but it will! There's every possibility Texas will become an empire in the New World—a land richer in resources than Canada, and like Canada, have ties to the mother country."

"I really don't see how you can say that and believe it, my son. All these Texas people *want* to become part of the United States. They're all like those arrogant and overbearing Regretts."

"There are many more than we who see a future empire here," George said confidently. The coming events of the night filled him with exhilaration and a strong sense of power over the future. "And who knows about the Regretts? Something could happen to cut off their constant agitation for statehood. Give us a bit more time, dears."

"Time! Seven years of time!"

"When I leave this land," George said buoyantly, "I'll see that as much money comes in from it as comes to us now from our estates in England. And think of the triumph of our return with a fortune made here!"

Cavenal made a pretense of retiring when his mother and sister ascended the stairs. After changing into his oldest and most worn clothes, he lay on the bed, his mind teeming with plans. He had been unable to bring himself to don the bulky, worn boots he had secured from Abraham. It would be dark and his fine boots were so comfortable. He could ride like a centaur in those boots, so he pulled them on.

He waited until nearly two, peering out the window and congratulating himself on having chosen a moonless night. The sky was thickly starred, but clouds were blowing in from the gulf on a strong wind. Good, he thought. Wind would whip the flames to a crackling fury, and the stables and house would be gone before the Regretts could rouse their workers. He stretched lazily. He had never felt better. This would be a good night's work. Mason Regrett's contemptuous insults would be wiped out in less than an hour if the wind held.

When he went to the stables, Abraham was not there, and he knew a moment of anger. He'd beat the man senseless if he failed to show up! He dipped the thickly wrapped torches in oil, and put them, dripping, into the two saddlebags on either side of his stallion. As he was dipping the torches for Abraham, the big black man came silently into the stable.

"You're late!" he hissed.

"I'm sorry, Mister Cav. I—I ain't sure this here's right."

"Don't be a fool, Abraham. Here are your torches—six of them. Put them in your saddlebags after you've saddled up. Be quiet about it. We'll light one when we get there, and light the rest from each other as we throw them."

Abraham had never had any respect for Cavenal, sensing

that he was an amoral man. He knew about his sexual exploits, which were common gossip among the slaves. Ephraim, Sophie's husband, hated him enough to kill, but his fellow workers had dissuaded him for fear they would all hang. This errand tonight solidified Abraham's hatred of him. But the thought of Tina blotted out all reason. He kept his mind on Tina as he did Cavenal's bidding, and the two men slipped silently out of the stable. They closed the door without a sound from its well-oiled hinges.

Yes, Abraham thought, his chest tight, he would do this to make Tina his, no matter how heavily it would rest on his conscience.

No lights gleamed from cabins or house windows as the two men made their way through the back gate. Once in the open, Cavenal spurred his horse to a gallop, with Abraham close beside him. The wind was rising, and looking up, Cavenal could see the sky was now heavily overcast.

The two men did not talk. Abraham was silent because he knew what he was doing was wrong, and he was trying desperately to weigh it against his love for Tina and his desire to make her his wife.

Cavenal was silent with tension. Even with the strong south wind from the gulf, he took out his handkerchief and wiped his damp neck and face. This cursed climate! No matter. In another three or four years he could take his mother and sister home, leaving great estates in Texas. He'd buy more slaves, secure overseers and caretakers. Most of all, his many friends and acquaintances in England would look at him with respect and awe reserved for men of enterprise—successful enterprise.

When at last they arrived on the little rise above the Regrett ranch buildings, not a light could be seen. Under the clouded sky, the barns, stables, cabins, and houses could barely be discerned. The two men reined in their horses and sat a moment.

"I want the stables fired first, Abraham. Understand? Then the house last—so they won't waken until it's too late. I want those blooded horses to die. *That's* where most of his income is." He chuckled softly. "We'll take him completely by surprise!"

His words were punctuated with a distant roll of thunder, and far to the south, lightning flickered among the heavy clouds.

"Come on! We want to get it started before the rain blows in. Damn! I hadn't thought of a gulf storm. But we've plenty of time. It's a long way off." The wind blew his words to Abraham, who didn't answer.

They descended slowly to the stables. Dismounting, Cavenal made quick work of lighting three of the torches. As he handed two to Abraham, another distant flash of lightning flickered over the barns.

"We'd better work fast. That storm's blowing in from the south faster than I thought, Abraham. Here—on two stable roofs. I'll hit the base with mine."

Abraham took the lighted torches and hurled them high on the roof of two stables. One smoldered, the other caught rapidly. Lighting one on another, they threw them from roof to base where they burned brightly. The sudden sound of crackling shingles could be heard, and horses in the stable began to whinny frantically.

"We've got all three—now make it to the house, Abraham!" Cavenal said, low-voiced. "And then we'll bloody well get out of here!"

They had but one torch left, which Abraham threw forcefully to the roof of the long, low adobe brick ranch house. It rolled to the edge, hung there and caught suddenly in the wind, the flames snapping orange and red. The dry wooden shingles caught immediately. Every building was afire now, and Cavenal paused to watch the destruction.

The horses were frantic, smelling smoke, hearing the

crackle of fire, and were lunging in their stalls. The rooftops of the stables were ablaze.

Lightning was near now and more frequent in the heavily overcast sky. The first of the lashing summer storms rolled in from the Gulf of Mexico.

Julien, who had worked hard that day, and had drunk Watkins corn liquor equally hard that night, rose from his bed for a drink of water to quench his parched throat. He heard the rolling thunder, and saw the flashes of lightning through the windows as he made his way to the kitchen. The night had been hot, and Julien was sweating slightly as he lifted the dipper and drank from the bucket Mamacita had left on the table for the men. He could hear the wind rising and the rain coming as he went to the back door.

The lightning suddenly illuminated the back of the house as he stepped outside to let the wind cool him. He looked across the broad sweep of land between the house and the first barn.

Shock and fear wiped out his grogginess as he saw the roofs of the barns flaming. His eyes swept from the barns to the house, and he saw two figures on horseback ride by. One hurled a lighted torch.

Flames from the barns reflected brightly on the polished boots of the foremost rider before they vanished among trees surrounding the Regrett place.

English riding boots! The vanished figure on horseback reappeared behind Julien's narrowed eyes, and he remembered the hat pulled low, the shapeless shirt and breeches. It had to be Richard Daventry! Fury boiled afresh in Julien as he ran to the suspended bell that hung for dinner call at the back of the house. Feverishly he began pulling the rope. The bell clanged wildly over the roar of the coming storm.

Now the panicked horses could be heard dimly, neighs of frantic fear piercing all other sounds.

"Mase! Mase!" Julien roared as he sped away toward the stables, now burning at both base and roof. He did not look back as his brother followed at a dead run.

The men who worked the ranch spilled forth from their cabins, followed by their wives and children, crying out with anger and alarm. Joe Herrera and Renaldo Flores split up, and each ran to the second and third barns, darting in through thick smoke and the hungry flames.

Mase Regrett caught up with his brother outside the first barn, and they entered together. They did not speak, and fought to breathe as they ran to the last stalls, one man on each side, unlatching the gates and attempting to steer the maddened animals out.

As the men reached the wide barn doors, they hit each horse on the rump, sending it racing into the corral.

As Mase and Julien worked the first barn, Tony Martinez, Joe Herrera, Renaldo Flores, Young Miguel along with several other men, worked at the remaining two. The wind had risen to a howl, whipping the orange flames into frenzied tongues of fire. Inevitably, the men, staggering, coughing, choking on black smoke, were forced from the barns. The screams of the horses that remained in the barns tore at the Regretts and their men.

Young Miguel, swearing loudly, turned to reenter the second burning barn, but Mason Regrett stopped him.

"No, Miguel—it's too dangerous. There's no more we can do—"

The women were running up now with buckets of water sloshing in their hands, their nightclothes whipping around their bodies. They could not get near the barns and they turned their frightened faces toward the roof of the main house, which had caught at last from the final torch thrown.

"Come on—bring the water," Mase called, running toward the house. His voice was cut off by a vivid flash of lightning, followed by a roaring crash of thunder. At that instant, the house and barns were deluged in torrents of rain. Sheets of water from the gulf storm poured healing waves over the fires.

Those who had come to fight it stood silently in the flood, letting it pour over them gratefully. They did not flinch as lightning played over them, and thunder followed immediately.

Mase turned a wet, smoke-grimed face to his brother. Each man was still in his underclothing. "Could it be the Bosquezes finally got up nerve enough—"

"It was that goddamned son of a bitch Daventry!"

"Daventry?" Mase's jaw fell. "He may be a son of a bitch, but he's not a barn burner who'd murder fine horseflesh."

"Did you get to Slyboots?" Julien asked harshly.

"No!" Mase, still stunned by his brother's accusation, turned involuntarily back toward the first stable. It was steaming blackly in the gloom. The horses still inside made no sound now. "I thought you got to her in time," he added, his voice sickened.

"I thought you'd gotten her."

"We left three in the first barn—the two sorrel geldings and Slyboots."

"Well—" Julien said vengefully. "Daventry won't get his money back on that one. I wish we could make the bastard rebuild for us."

"How can you be sure it was Daventry?" Knowing the man, Mase could not conceive of him perpetrating such a tragedy.

"Hell, Mase, I *saw* the lousy weasel! I'd know those boots of his anywhere. Nobody but Daventry wears those English boots of his the way he does. I've told you before, I think the bastard wears them to bed!"

"You saw him—alone?" Mase asked. The men and women around them were listening acutely now.

"No. He had someone with him. I don't know who, but he was bigger than Daventry. Probably Big Miguel."

Young Miguel drew in his breath sharply.

"No, Señor Julien." Velma Flores, Renaldo's wife, spoke up indignantly. She had been an orphan, and the Puentes had raised her on the Daventry place, before she fell in love and married Renaldo. "Big Miguel would never do such a thing. I do not think Señor Richard would do such a thing—"

"Velma, *I saw the man!*"

"Jus' the same, I tell you Big Miguel would never burn horses."

"No," Miguel said softly, "mi padre loves horses."

"Daventry hates us," Julien said ruthlessly. "He hates us enough to try to burn us out—and he had *someone* with him!"

"Thanks be to God, he did not succeed—whoever he was," Twyla said uneasily.

"Thanks to the storm," Julien responded bitterly. "I'm for going over and facing the son of a bitch—telling him I saw him—face him and his new wife, and his hotheaded daughter, and tell them all we saw him. Damned low barn-burner! Horse killer!"

Mase felt his wrath congeal and turn over slowly, hotly, like the living coals that lay hissing in the rain about the half-burned barns.

"We'll round up what we can of our horses," he said slowly. "Then, by God, we'll do just that—ride over to his place and face him with it."

It was nearly dawn before the smoke-blackened men and women of the Regrett ranch finished their work. Clad in the dirty breeches and shirts which they had put on to round up their stock, Mason and Julien rode directly to the Daventry compound.

Roosters in the chicken pens around the cabins of the workers were announcing dawn as the two rode up to the back fence. They opened the gate and entered slowly. Men were up and fragrant odors of breakfast bacon and coffee hung in the cool air.

Josey came to the back door in time to see the two grimy men hitch their horses to the back rail.

"Law me! Mister Mase, is that you—an' Mister Julien?"

"Yes," Mase replied tersely. "We want to talk to Richard Daventry, Josey."

"He ain' up yet," she began hesitantly, aware suddenly of the tension in the two soot-darkened faces before her. Feenie peered around her shoulder and gasped in surprise. Josey added, "Reckon you two might come into the kitchen an' have a mornin' cup of coffee? 'Pears to me you could both use it."

"I reckon we might come in, Josey—but we'll forgo the coffee and I think you might wake Daventry. It's important," Mase said grimly. "I think you might even find he's *still* up."

Josey's face furrowed with puzzlement and she said shortly, "Feenie, go knock on Mister Richard's door an' tell him Mister Mase an' Mister Julien is here."

In less than two minutes Feenie was back. "He say he's gettin' dressed to come to breakfast anyways an' will be here in a minute."

When Richard, fully dressed, strode into the kitchen, Josey and Feenie went into the foyer hall discreetly, but not so far that they could not hear the men.

"What brings you both to my house?" Richard asked frostily.

"You ought to know," Mase said laconically, looking at Richard's English boots that reached to the knee. They looked a little worn, not so highly polished.

"I don't know what you mean," Richard said.

"I think you do," Julien said, his voice thick with rage. "And it might interest you to know Slyboots, our prize mare you bought for Monty, died in the fire you and your partner set last night."

Beneath his tan Richard blanched. "Fire? What do you mean, I set a fire at your place?"

"Burned all three barns," Mase said quietly, "but your torch on the house roof was put out by the rain, and there's enough of the barns to rebuild, thanks to the rain."

"You mean you think I set fire to your stables and house?" Coming into the foyer, Abby, Monty, and Louise caught these last words and their faces showed their incredulity.

Chapter 15

"*I* know *you set fire to our place*," Julien said harshly. "I saw you riding away with your partner. Lightning flashed—it reflected on those damned English boots of yours. It outlined that black, flat-brimmed hat of yours. I got a clear glimpse of your partner. He was big enough. I'd know Big Miguel anywhere!"

"You didn't see *me*, nor did you see Big Miguel," Richard lashed out. "What Englishman—what kind of man *with any honor* would burn helpless horses? Regrett, you know damned well every Englishman loves horses second only to his wife."

Abby's face was white, but Monty's was suffused with color as her anger mounted with her father's. Only Louise, in a peach silk peignoir, was unperturbed. Her mind was clicking swiftly over George Cavenal's recent words to her. *This, then, was what he had meant about the Regretts!*

"So you say." Julien was sarcastic and his fists were knotted. "But I *saw* you. I'll swear to it."

"I did not leave this house last night. Men like you have made other enemies besides me!" Richard's color had returned with a rush and his gray eyes were flat as steel. He turned to see his wife beside him, her small white hand reaching for his arm. "Louise can tell you I never left our bed last night, can't you, Louise?"

But Louise's mind was racing. George Cavenal had said to her, *I have plans to wipe out that insult . . . only a little dangerous, love!* She must protect her lover! She looked up at her husband in wide-eyed innocence.

"Darling," she said hesitantly, "I sleep so soundly. I—I really can't *swear*—whether you left or not. Oh, darling"—her eyes filled with helpless tears—"I can't say—you wouldn't want me to lie!"

Richard looked at her piercingly. "You really sleep that soundly, Louise?"

Faith had joined the group by now, fully dressed, as were Abby and Monty. She was a quiet shadow, the gray net tight on her bright hair.

"I—I'm sorry, Richard darling! I can never *lie!* I wish with all my heart I could say you certainly didn't leave our bed. But I wouldn't be truthful." She fought down a sob.

Mason Regrett's eyes on her held contempt. Even Julien looked at her with disfavor, but his conviction regarding Richard Daventry's guilt grew.

"I can say he never left this house." Faith stepped forward and spoke clearly. "Miss Abby can tell you I don't sleep well." She paused and all eyes were on her pale, resolute face. "Last night, when I couldn't sleep, I lit a lamp and came down to the library. I read from one in the morning until five. I could see the staircase through the open library door from my chair. *No one* came down it." Her voice was low and carried irrefutable truth. "No one went up it before me."

Remembering Faith's pale face as she came from the British Embassy library those months ago, Mase knew this girl would not lie.

"That settles it, Julien," Mase said abruptly. "We can't prove he did it."

"But I saw the man!"

"You didn't see his face. It could've been any one of the renegades in this country—even Indians."

"Wearing English boots?" Julien asked his brother scornfully.

"Indians steal everything. Boots would be no exception."

Julien turned with his brother to go, but he looked back over his shoulder. "You did it, Daventry, because we're for annexation! And you won't get away with it. You also killed your daughter's mare. Slyboots didn't get out!"

Monty's hand went to her mouth. Slyboots! She had come to love that little mare! But she made no sound as the two men stalked to the kitchen door, opened it and were gone. The smell of burnt cloth, soot, and smoke hung in the air after the door closed. Then she turned furiously on Louise.

"Even if you slept like the dead, you could have lied! You *know* Pa didn't do it!"

"But you wouldn't want me to lie, Richard darling?" Louise wailed. Her tear-filled eyes beseeched her husband.

Richard looked at her, his eyes cool and reflective. "No," he said slowly, "I wouldn't want you to lie. But I'm damned glad Faith was able to tell the truth, too." His eyes went to the girl. Her face reddened as he moved to her and leaned down to kiss her cheek lightly. "Thanks for standing by me, my dear." He was still shaken by the horror of knowing fine horses had died and a man's home was very nearly destroyed. It was inconceivable to him.

Feenie and Josey came back into the kitchen from the foyer. Josey muttered angrily, "I bet you it's them Bosquez brothers—two of 'em anyways."

"She's probably right, Richard," Abby said calmly. "They've 'requisitioned' everything under the sun from all the families in this area. The boots could have been stolen from George Cavenal, the Arterbury men, or the Bedfords too for that matter."

"An' Miss Abby," Josey said feelingly, "them Bosquezes is just mean enough to burn good hossflesh to get back at the Regretts." She paused and added, "I got breakfast all ready."

As they walked into the dining room, Monty drew up beside Louise.

"I think you're an expert liar, Louise," she whispered. Rage blotted out reason and she no longer cared whether she angered this woman or not.

Louise made no reply and she restrained a small smile of triumph, but her gaze touched Faith and grew baleful beneath thick lashes.

Over breakfast, Monty was silent, though the others spoke of the fire and conjectured about the identity of the marauders who had wreaked such havoc. Faith, sitting beside Monty, reached for her hand under the white tablecloth and squeezed it.

"I know how you loved that beautiful little mare—how you fed her apples and sugar when you went to see her at the Regretts', Monty," she whispered.

Monty looked at her swiftly through eyes that had filled despite her efforts to restrain tears. She was amazed at Faith's insight and her hand tightened on the fingers entwined in hers.

"And you know Pa would never set fire to a stable," Monty whispered back. Faith nodded quickly.

"I'd know it even if I hadn't been where I could see the stairs."

"Thank God you were. Though nothing can convince Julien. He hates my father."

"I know—I could tell—"

"What are you two whispering about, Faith?" Louise asked sharply.

"She's merely sympathizing with me on the loss of my mare," Monty said tartly, tears vanishing.

"She can answer for herself." Louise frowned at Faith.

Monty looked at her father, to see that he was observing Louise himself and there was a new, faintly discernible reserve in his eyes.

"Monty was very fond of—what was her name, Monty? Slyboots?" Faith met her cousin's sharp eyes steadily but respectfully. "I know it's a great loss to her."

"I'm sure it is," Louise replied, mollified. "We're all terribly sorry about it, Montrose."

"Thank you," Monty said with heavy irony.

The following morning after breakfast, Monty sought Faith out in her room where she sat reading, as usual.

"Faith, how would you like to take a ride with me this morning? Josey's fixed a picnic lunch and we can ride as far as a mile from home without an escort. The Navidad River winds through the south end of Pa's cotton crop."

"Oh!" Faith's breath was quick and the book slid to her lap. Her face fell. "Monty, I—I told you—I don't know how to ride horseback."

"But Louise rides so well—"

"She's never let me learn," Faith said slowly, "because she says I was—I *am* so awkward. She says I could never handle a horse. I might take a bad fall."

"Of all the poppycock!" Monty replied explosively. "You are *not* awkward, Faith! You'd make a marvelous rider and I propose to teach you. And not on that silly sidesaddle. I'll teach you to ride astride, like a real rider!"

"But Louise! She—she'll be angry—angrier than ever with you, Monty!"

"Who cares? She doesn't like me and I certainly don't like her. I don't care how angry I make her. Anyway, she's gone off with Ezekiel and I think she's going to spend the day with the Cavenals again." Monty's eyes twinkled, narrowing. "And that means she won't be back before three-thirty or four. We'll be back before then."

"I—haven't a riding habit." The book was forgotten on the table nearby and Faith's hazel eyes shone, flecks of mischievous green in them.

"You don't need one. Come on to my room. I'm going to outfit you in pants and a shirt—and you can wear my old boots. But that hair net has to go, Faith! We'll tie your hair back with a ribbon and it'll fit better under the hat I have for you."

Like a pair of truants, the two made their way to Monty's room. There, Faith, who was as tall and slender as Monty, fit snugly into the extra pants and shirt. Even the boots were a fit.

Monty was pleased. She liked Faith tremendously and had from the moment she met her. Besides, it was very pleasant to be doing something which would frustrate Louise. Faith echoed this.

"Louise is going to be *angry* with me." She looked at herself in Monty's mirror. She filled the pants tightly and the shirt was taut across full, provocative breasts. "She—she really doesn't want me to learn to ride."

"And why not?" Monty asked impudently. "She knows you'll probably be better at it than she is—and you look just wonderful in those pants. Much more beautiful than *she* would. I think Louise is jealous of you."

"Jealous of *me?*" Faith was shocked.

"Why else would she keep you in those gray dresses and that awful gray hair net. Sure—she's jealous, and more than that, Faith, she's *mean* and you know it."

"Oh, Monty! You shouldn't say that. If she becomes angry enough with me, she can send me back to Charleston."

"She cannot! I'll bet you my father would never permit such a thing—not if you didn't want to go."

Faith's face paled. "She could, Monty. She'd find a way to do it, and your father is so—so in love with her." Faith's eyes were frightened now and there was sadness in them as well.

"Now don't lose your spunk, Faith. Let's go!"

Later, at the stables, with their lunch in a saddlebag behind Monty's saddle on Warlock, the two girls were stifling laughter as Monty spoke to Carlos.

"Carlos, we're going to put Faith on Mandy." Then to Faith, she explained, "She's our oldest, slowest critter—so there's no need for you to worry. All you have to do is sit there and I'll tell you what to do with your knees and hands."

Before they reached the banks of the Navidad, Faith had shown a natural talent for riding. She responded to Monty's instructions swiftly and surely. The old mare, recognizing her rider's growing expertise, responded well to each movement. As they rode, they talked of the books Faith had read, for Monty was well acquainted with all of them. By the time they finished the sandwiches and cookies Josey had prepared for them, a deep and understanding friendship had solidified. They talked beside the whispering river.

"I was only six when my . . . father died and I came to live with Louise and her father. Louise was sixteen and I—I looked up to her then. She sort of took over with me, and I've always had to do just as she says or she can hold back Father's money—or—well, Louise has a bad temper, and sometimes she would . . . punish me severely."

"You mean she'd *strike* you?"

"When—she—felt she had to." Faith looked away.

"Great Caesar's ghost!" Monty burst out, much like her father. "How dare she hit you!"

"She said she did it for good reasons—to train me."

"I'll bet!"

"Oh, Monty, this has been so wonderful! You can't know how much this day has meant to me!"

"It's only a beginning," Monty vowed. "We'll go again tomorrow."

They stayed longer than they had intended and rode into the Daventry compound only minutes before Louise and Ezekiel returned from the Cavenals'.

Louise was mounted on one of Monty's favorite geldings, and when she drew up before the two girls in the stable, she looked them over swiftly.

"You two look disgusting," she said, but her face was suffused with an evanescent glow. She looked satiated and relaxed and, to Monty's surprise, there was no real venom in the words. "Faith, you go upstairs and get out of Montrose's ridiculous male clothing at once."

"Yes, Louise," Faith said meekly, but Monty spoke up.

"We'll have to curry our mounts, Louise," she said firmly.

"Very well. After that."

Dismounting, Louise left the gelding in Ezekiel's care and walked to the house alone.

"You see?" Monty said. "She just wants to be bossy. I don't care if she did catch us. We'll do it again tomorrow anyway."

And the two girls did ride out the following day and for four days after that. Though Louise saw them twice more on separate days, she said nothing. Monty was beginning to savor her triumph. Her father appeared as much in love with Louise as ever. Yet Monty, knowing him well, recognized the faint reserve that had entered his eyes and was encouraged. Too, he hadn't told her she must wear dresses at supper each night, as Faith did in obeisance to Louise's tyranny.

Once, Richard came in from his fields at the same time Monty and Faith returned from a ride, and he saw Faith clad in the tight pants and shirt. His eyes widened slightly at the voluptuousness of the girl. But they immediately filled with affection.

"You girls look very fetching, pants and all." He grinned, eyes twinkling. "You look especially beautiful, Faith. But I'm sure Louise will disapprove of your following Monty's example in pants and boots, my dear." Still he laughed indulgently as he said it, and Monty was even more encouraged.

Faith flushed to the roots of her fair hair and her murmured "Thank you, Richard" held a wealth of concealed emotion.

During the five days Monty spent teaching Faith to ride and shoot—in pants and shirts—Louise said no more. She went twice to visit the Cavenals while Richard rode his acres with Big Miguel, staying until nearly three in the afternoon. But she always managed to be home and waiting when Richard came in. Both Monty and Faith had avoided Louise whenever it was possible, but Faith remained her usual subdued self with her cousin.

Monty had begun to think that Louise had accepted the changes that had swept through her cousin. The lack of the eternal net on Faith's hair let it frame her face in such a way that the girl's ethereal beauty was accentuated. The days in the saddle and the reflection of the sun under the broad-brimmed hat Monty had given her put golden color in her face.

But Monty was wrong. Louise was only waiting for her chance to strike, and that chance came after supper on the fifth night. Louise had spent the morning with Lady Marguerite and Georgina, and she was full of their talk of England, and the fact that eventually the Cavenals would return to their home there. They were gathered in the parlor, Richard having brandy and the ladies enjoying coffee.

Richard was speaking of the events that took place in Washington City, and as usual Louise managed to bring the conversation around to herself.

"But the most important event of all was when you met me, wasn't it, darling Richard?" she asked coquettishly.

He looked at his wife with the same faint reserve that had been born in his eyes the morning she could not, or would not, tell the Regretts that he had not left her bed. Still, his big hand covered her small white one where it lay on his arm as they sat side by side on the sofa.

"Yes, my dear. You were most important." His eyes, despite the reserve, were caressing as they lingered over her high breasts and narrow waist in the pale blue batiste summer dress. Monty was watching, and she felt the sharp visceral twist that came when her father looked with desire on Louise.

Feenie came in the door with the steaming coffeepot and asked, "More coffee, Miss Abby? Miz Daventry?"

Abby nodded, but Louise didn't answer. She simply stroked Richard's hand. It was Richard who turned to Feenie and smiled.

"You can fetch me another small brandy, Feenie, too. A last cup of coffee all around?" he asked of Faith and Monty.

"Not for me," Monty said abruptly, impatient to get away from Louise's presence.

"Why not, daughter? You usually drink two after dinner." Richard looked mildly surprised at his daughter's short, almost angry refusal.

"Not tonight," she replied briefly, aware that Louise was scrutinizing her intently, more intently than at any other time during the past week.

"You can see how it is with Montrose, Richard darling," Louise said with tender concern, "how like an angry boy she reacts? I didn't mean to mention it tonight, my darling, but I do feel time is short for teaching Montrose to become a lady."

"She knows how to be a lady," Richard replied shortly.

"It's just right now she doesn't want to be one." His glance at Monty was sharp and disapproving.

"I've tried so hard," Louise said sadly. "Ever since the day I came. And everyone else here, by contrast, has been so kind to me—not at all like Montrose."

"You mean to tell me my daughter hasn't been kind to you, Louise?" Richard's color, like Monty's, was rising with temper.

Louise shook her head mournfully. "And really, Richard darling, Montrose is so—beautifully developed—and those male outfits she wears are terribly revealing. They expose her, ah, body to the eyes of all the men on this place. I've seen them, Richard, staring." She caught her breath and blushed. "And worse, she's persuaded my dear little cousin to wear them! In the last five days they've ridden everywhere looking like little wantons—and Faith has always been the soul of decorum." She hesitated, then said again, "I've felt all along you'd want Montrose to behave more . . . more modestly."

"I certainly expect her to behave modestly—whether in pants or a dress, Louise."

"I have a number of dresses. I'd be glad to give—"

By now, Monty was in a towering rage. "Nothing you have would fit me!" she shouted. "I'm taller than you are! Besides, I have plenty of dresses of my own, and you know it!"

Louise's eyes filled readily with glistening tears, and she put a hand to her trembling lips. "You see how it's been for me," she said tearfully. "Montrose has taken a most monstrous dislike to me and I've tried so hard to win her!"

Richard put an arm about his weeping wife and his face was stern. Monty felt he was reprimanding her with his quick glance.

Feenie stood spellbound at the foyer door, coffeepot in hand, during the exchange, and Faith's golden face was paling. She wore a dress of soft gray, with little white cuffs and matching collar. The gray net was carefully in place. She had said only that afternoon, *No, Monty, you know I don't dare wear these pants and this shirt at supper! Louise would surely punish me in some way.* The girls had argued briefly over it, but Faith had been obdurate. Now Louise was preparing to punish them both.

"Feenie," Richard said shortly, "fetch my brandy, please." Feenie started in surprise.

"I think I'll have a little brandy in my coffee as well, Feenie," Abby put in, and the young girl fled like a shadow.

"I think we should forget this thing for tonight," Richard said firmly.

"But we can't, Richard darling," Louise said, her voice growing more troubled. "I—I didn't want to tell you, Richard—but I *must.*" She paused, and the silence was heavy in the room. "It was at the embassy ball last February, when I left you to get my handkerchief, darling. I found Montrose in a passionate embrace with Mason Regrett in the library." Her voice lowered.

Monty drew a sharply audible breath, but Louise continued, lifting her head bravely as she spoke.

"It was most compromising, Richard darling. She was kissing him with such—such abandon! She was . . . she was making love to him— Oh, I was so embarrassed!"

Monty cried, "That's not true!"

"My God, Monty!" Richard Daventry burst out. "Mason Regrett? What in heaven's name were you thinking of?"

"That's not the way it happened, Pa!" Monty leaped to her feet and turned on Louise with blazing eyes. "What a liar you are! You *know* I wasn't making love to Mase! He— You've been after me from the moment you came to this house, Louise. You haven't ever given me a chance—" And with the words, Monty swung her arm in a wide arc to emphasize her point. She had completely forgotten the recent addition of the delicate Dresden figurine to the table beside her, and her gesture swept it to the floor, where it splintered into fragments.

"Oh, Pa!" Monty exclaimed, stunned. "Pa, I'm sorry! I didn't see—I forgot Louise had put it there. I'm so sorry!"

Chapter 16

In the brief silence, Louise drew a deep breath. "There!" she cried, "you see what you've done in your wildness?" Then realizing the words sounded too accusing, she put both hands to her cheeks in an old childish gesture of surprise and sorrow, and she began to cry.

Monty, overwhelmed by the disaster she had created, and by the fact that her secret kiss had been revealed to her father, stood in pale, stricken silence as Louise's tears shone in the lamplight, rolling down her smooth cheeks. The woman dabbed at them futilely as she knelt to the floor.

She began picking up the larger shards, placing each one in the handkerchief she had pulled from her waist, murmuring, "The beautiful, beautiful little French lady is broken. Oh, Richard darling, it's all my fault! I should never, ever have brought it out of the china cabinet."

"Louise"—surprisingly it was Faith who spoke, but her voice trembled—"it's hardly worth making Monty feel so guilty. It was obviously an accident and—and I'm sure the —the kiss was, too."

Richard was silent, his accusing eyes on his daughter.

Louise shot her cousin a venomous glance from beneath

her lashes as she continued tenderly gathering the pieces of Dresden.

Monty swallowed and started to apologize again, but words stuck in her throat. She wheeled and fled through the foyer and up the long staircase to her room.

"Monty didn't mean to do it, Louise." Abby's voice was even. "She's very like her father in many ways."

"Perhaps—perhaps I shouldn't have said anything about Mason Regrett," Louise remarked with sudden anxiety as she placed the pieces of broken Dresden in her handkerchief on the little table. Then, virtuously, she added, "But I really felt you should know, Richard. It's all the more reason I should teach her to conduct herself like a lady."

"I'll go up and have a talk with that young lady." Richard's voice was grim. "She'll have to curb that temper of hers—and a few other things as well. Mother"—he looked around at Abigail—"you're right. She's just a little too much like me."

"You might watch *your* temper in this case, Richard," Abby retorted. Her own eyes on her son were slate-hard.

"Darling," Louise said swiftly, laying both hands on Richard's broad shoulders as he rose from his chair, "let me go up to her. It's I who should apologize for bringing the figurine out of its safe place. It was wrong of me—but you had said I was like your little French lady, and I'm afraid I wanted her where *you* could see her."

"No, Louise. I must have a talk with my daughter. This incident with Regrett worries me deeply, and I intend to have it out with her. I cannot believe she has come to love that—cad. And I'll tell her she must obey your wishes in the matter of clothes and behavior."

"But Richard darling, we women can speak to each other about matters of the heart better than men can. I'll talk to her about Mason Regrett, and then I must apologize about the figurine." She wiped her eyes and smiled mistily, adding, "You can tell her she must behave after I've smoothed the troubled waters somewhat."

"You're very gentle and kind-hearted, my dear," Richard said, catching his mother's warning glance, and frowning back at her as Louise pressed her body to his with quick urgency. She excited him, despite her failure to corroborate his statement the night of the fire. He tried to reconcile his mixed feelings. After all, his wife conducted herself with every grace that a woman could bring to a marriage, and she was more than satisfactory in bed. Now, he reassured himself, her refusal to lie was another admirable characteristic. But it only worried him more, for it lent credence to the story of Regrett and Monty in the library. After all, Monty was a grown woman now.

Observing his exquisite wife, he did not see the look Faith Warren gave her cooing cousin, nor the grim set to Abby's mouth as Louise rustled out of the room, her skirts whispering about her dainty feet. Her slippers made only a faint brushing sound on the polished pecan wood floors.

She took the steps quickly, the heat of her fury rising with each one. Reaching Monty's door, she flung it open and swept in, closing it firmly behind her. She leaned against it, eyes glittering as she looked at Monty, who was lying prone across the bed.

Monty rolled over to sit up in surprise when she saw who had entered her room.

"Listen to me, you—you little slut—" Louise hissed. "You're not going to ride high around here any longer! You may have *been* Richard's favorite, but you aren't now. *I am.* And I'm going to make your life so miserable you'll be glad to be in skirts and sit in your room with a book! No more showing off—showing off your figure to every man you see!" She made no effort to hide her vindictiveness. *"I* know you broke that piece of Dresden because it looked like me— because *I* liked it!"

"You're jealous!" Monty rose to her feet, the realization sweeping away her guilt. "You hate me because my father loves me. And you hate the men looking at me—even though they think nothing of my wearing boy's clothes because I always have—"

"Don't talk back to me like an equal! Your father is going to see that you obey my wishes. Those were his very words, before he sent me up here to tell you so. *He'll* see that you do just as I say, just as I wish. And what I wish is for you to be as inconspicuous as a shadow on the wall!"

"And you're jealous because Mason Regrett kissed me—wants me." A note of wonder touched Monty's voice. "And I know you made Young Miguel fall in love with you. God only knows what you've done to him!" Monty drew a deep breath, her voice lowered. "I'll wager my father won't be fooled much longer. You're going to let something slip and he'll see what a—what a— My God, there *must* be a name for women like you!"

Louise walked slowly toward her. The fact that she was small and delicately boned did not decrease the air of powerful menace about her.

"You'll do as I say from now on—or I'll persuade Richard to ship you off to a finishing school, and there won't be any horses to ride there, Montrose Daventry!"

Louise's hand flew up, swift as a striking snake, and cracked across Monty's mouth and cheek. Monty reeled backward, stunned by the viciousness that distorted the woman's face. In the shocked silence between them, the white marks left by Louise's hand faded and reddened painfully.

"Get out of my room, Louise," Monty said huskily. Beneath the blow to her face she had blanched. She was at least four inches taller than the diminutive blond woman, and she took two steps forward to stand over her.

"I'm bigger than you are, Louise, and stronger. If I hit

you, I'll leave a mark you'll have to explain to my father. Not that you couldn't, but you wouldn't like a black eye, either."

Louise laughed contemptuously and turned away. Unable to resist one last taunt, she smiled over her shoulder. "Don't expect any sympathy from Richard. He'll believe *me*. If you don't behave as I say, I'll tell him you threatened me when I came up to sympathize with you, and it won't be a lie!" She closed the door softly behind her.

Monty sank back on the bed. Louise's slap had cleared her mind like a cold, sharp wind. She thought coldly and planned coldly.

She would leave. Long before morning, she would be gone. She got to her feet and methodically began preparations for her journey. First she took her pistol from the bureau drawer, and checked it carefully. Monty was a crack shot, as good as Abigail. She was equally good with a rifle.

Then she began packing her clothing, three pairs of pants, three shirts, camisoles, chemises, and stockings. Abigail had taught her years ago to cut small fresh twigs, fray the ends, and brush her teeth thoroughly each day. That she could do as she made the day-and-a-half-long trip to the Arterburys'.

Brushing her long bright hair, she plaited it into one thick braid and let it hang down her back. She added comb and brush, and two more pairs of stockings to her clothing. Then she rolled it up in a neat bundle, which she would tie to the back of her saddle. She put her worn felt hat beside it.

She would leave long before anyone could see her go. She knew she was disobeying Richard's edict that she have an escort on so long a journey, but rebellion melted any fear. She was well aware of the dangers of traveling over seventy-five miles alone, but compared to the prospect of staying on in the face of Louise's threats, it seemed easy.

Seating herself at the small Winthrop desk, she put an oil

lamp on top of it and took out a sheet of paper. Picking up the quill, she dipped it into the small inkwell and began to write.

> Dear Pa and Abby,
>
> I've gone to visit the Arterburys. Amy asked me to come the last time we were together. I'll be gone a week or two. Don't worry, I'm taking my pistol and rifle.
>
> Love, Monty

She sat a moment, pen poised. Yes, her father would be furious when he found she had left without Big Miguel beside her. But she would not tolerate another day in the house with Louise. And after two weeks with the Arterburys, well, in that length of time, she could come up with a plan of action. The thought of being shipped east to a finishing school frightened her most. Abby had spoken of that once, but then finding Monty an apt pupil, she had taught her at home instead.

Anyway, none of it mattered, she thought—none of it— only that she be gone in the morning.

Fully dressed and feverish with impatience, she lay down on her bed to wait. She did not sleep, for Louise's threats rang through her like warning bells.

It could have been no more than four in the morning when she tiptoed from her room. She carried her new boots in one hand and her roll of clothing in the other.

The darkness was a warm tide flowing about her as she took the stairs in stockinged feet. She knew every step like the palm of her hand. In the dimness of the kitchen, she saw a white bowl of cold rolls on the table, left over from last night's supper. She ate one and put three in a neckerchief. Picking up her bundle and boots, she slipped silently from the kitchen to the granite stoop out back.

There, she sat down and pulled on the butter-soft new boots. Her throat grew tight remembering how her father had swung her around when he first saw her—and kissed her cheek after giving her his present. She had been so sure then that he would set Louise straight. Instead, he had sided with his new wife. And worse, now there was the kiss with Mase Regrett at the ball in Washington—a further wedge between them.

Resolutely, she picked up her bundle and headed for the stables. The waning moon had long since set, and the sky shed only starlight. She was a shadow among other shadows as she entered the stable.

In minutes she was mounted on Warlock, baggage tied neatly behind her, and on her way. She had determined to take the road that led to Houston City until she reached the turnoff on the old and less-used Indian trace. There was less likelihood of meeting anyone on the winding, tree-shaded trace during the long ride to the Arterburys. They were farther north and east than the Daventrys, and only a stone's throw from the Brazos River. In two hours she would reach the old Indian trace where she planned to branch over. The trace was thickly shaded nearly all the way to the Colorado River by heavy stands of live oaks, interspersed with cottonwoods and native pecans.

When Monty reached the worn path where she could turn off the main road, she knew she was approximately twenty miles from home. By now, the sun was brassy hot in the blue bowl of the sky, and she was relieved to edge Warlock down the slight incline and into the trees that arched over the old trace.

As she headed north, squirrels chattered angrily at her approach and a deer darted away. She frowned, noting there were recent prints of hooves in the dark soft loam of the trace ahead of her. She hadn't expected that. It would be less than a mile now until she reached one of the many small springs along this ancient path.

Then she could refill her canteen, and Warlock could slake his own thirst. Reaching down, she patted the animal on his gleaming black neck and murmured reassuringly to him. She took off her hat and wiped the back of her neck, then her forehead, with the scarf that had been tied at her throat. When they reached the spring, she decided, she and Warlock would not only make good use of the water, but she would eat, and let the horse graze for half an hour.

As the trace twisted and turned in its devious course, Monty was alert to what she might meet around the next bend. She was not prepared when she rounded a curve for the glint of sunlight on metal as she looked ahead.

Her heartbeat quickened as the glint continued to move forward until it was lost in the shade. Not only was someone with two horses ahead of her, but there were travelers coming toward her. She urged Warlock to a canter, but he was impatient with thirst and more than six hours of travel.

She strained to look ahead once more and the trees parted on the winding trace, opening a sunny space, and she could see them plainly.

It was four Mexican soldiers only a short distance ahead now. They were moving in a fast trot, single file, and through the open space, the leader spotted her.

"Damn!" she muttered. Why would four Mexican soldiers be on the trace instead of the more traveled road? There was no turning around or trying to outrun them. She would have to stand her ground and face them down. She drew her pistol, stopping Warlock, and waited.

Less than fifty yards beyond Monty Daventry, with one side of his leather saddlebags filled with reports for Sam Houston, Mason Regrett turned his horses off the trace toward a bubbling spring. He did not want to hurry Coffee, nor tire the packhorse loaded with his supplies for camping out indefinitely.

He had taken the little-used trace for the same reason Monty had chosen it, and he had been traveling since three in the morning. As they approached the spring, both Coffee and the packhorse made snorting, thirsty sounds, and Regrett slid from the saddle. He led them both to the spring and waited while each drank, before stooping to bathe his own hot face and fill his canteen. A mile back, he had eaten, and let the horses graze.

After allowing the horses another leisurely drink, he checked the baggage straps on the packhorse, adjusted the saddle on Coffee, and was about to mount.

When the faint sounds of clinking spurs and Spanish curses reached him, he mounted quickly and caught the bridle on the packhorse, urging the horses silently to take cover. From a heavy stand of brush on his side of the trace and away from the spring, he had a narrow view of the worn path, and what he saw did not surprise him.

It was Captain Felipe Bosquez, a packhorse, and his two brothers, Lorenz and Hernando Bosquez. There was one other soldier he did not know. Coffee saw them and, from the pressure of Regrett's knees, knew silence was expected of him. The packhorse, intelligent and observing, followed suit.

There was no plunder tied to the saddles of the four and Mase wondered what could have brought them in this southwesterly direction, away from the plantations and farms they usually sought?

Suddenly he saw Monty Daventry ride into view on Warlock, holding a pistol in her hand. She faced Bosquez, who stared at her in amazement. There was a moment of silence.

Regrett, behind the brush, was directly across from them. He could hear the horse Captain Bosquez rode snort at the approach of Warlock. Monty said nothing. She merely looked at Bosquez squarely over her pistol.

"It is the Señorita Daventry—*alone*—and such a long way from home. What brings you here, señorita?" Felipe Bosquez asked with a gallant bow from the waist.

"I'm on my way to the Arterburys'." Monty's words were clipped. "And if you and your men will ride on by, I'll water my horse at the spring over there."

"Why do you hold your pistolo on me an' my brothers, señorita? You know we do ladies no harm."

"Like you did the Arterburys no harm?" Monty asked. "Did you bow to him before you shot and killed Jim Arterbury?"

Captain Bosquez flushed darkly under his swarthy skin, his hairy black brows drawing together sharply. "The señorita has a bad way with words. I shot in self-defense—you think I stand and get killed myself, when I am only doing my duty?"

"Your duty!" Monty was scornful. "Stealing what you're too lazy to grow or make yourselves!"

"The señorita is make these ugly accusations because she knows we do not harm ladies."

"Then go on your way, Captain."

"You would not shoot me, Señorita Daventry," he replied, smiling now. His brothers and their companion had begun to edge their horses toward her.

"Get back!" Monty warned. "I *will* shoot you—"

Hernando suddenly spurred his horse forward, but Monty whirled and snapped off a shot. It grazed the fleshy part of his arm, and he let out an explosive oath, dropping his reins and clapping his hand to his arm. But his brother, Lorenz, taking full advantage of the action, was on Monty in a flash, wrenching the pistol from her hand, yanking her rifle from the saddle holster. He did not attempt to take hold of her;

he simply caught Warlock's reins as he flung her weapons to the ground.

Monty shouted, "You'll pay for this! My father will send a whole posse after you, and they'll kill you!"

"Your padre *will* pay this, señorita," Bosquez said coolly now. "For we will retrace our steps and take you to Matagorda as our prisoner. I can handle my business there as well as San Antonio. You will sail from Matagorda to Vera Cruz and from there you will go to Mexico City, an' your padre will pay plenty *dinero* to get you back."

Monty's eyes widened. He was taking her prisoner like so many Texans before her. She would be locked up in Mexico City for months—maybe years! But she did not let her fear show on her face.

"You'll be caught before you can ever reach Matagorda." The words were bravely said, but they were empty.

"I think not. Lorenz," Bosquez took a rawhide thong from a bundle of them hanging from his saddle, "tie her hands behind her back."

At that, Regrett kneed Coffee through the brush, his rifle trained on the four men.

Chapter 17

"*Never mind,* Lorenz," Regrett said. "You won't need to tie her hands. I'm ordering all of you to move on. And I won't hit an arm. I'll kill you."

The four men stared at him in astonishment. Monty felt a great rush of relief. The soldiers stood frozen under the rifle Regrett held so steadily. For a moment, no one moved. Then Captain Bosquez spoke up in Spanish.

"This is none of your affair, Señor Regrett. You know well we have not requisitioned from your ranch in many months—"

"I sure do. That's because we shoot to kill," Regrett answered in English.

"This girl. She is nothing to you. Let us take her and be on our way."

"Not on your life, Bosquez. You and your brothers line up over there—and you too whatever your name is. Monty, come over here to me."

Lorenz let go of Warlock's bridle and Monty seized it, putting her heels in his flanks and riding the few feet to Regrett.

As she did so, the fourth rider suddenly drew his pistol. Regrett saw the movement, and before the man could fire a shot, he swung his rifle and fired simultaneously. Regrett's shot blew the man from his saddle and he fell heavily.

The shot stirred the Bosquez brothers to action. They drew their pistols and rode forward. Before Regrett could fire his pistol or reload his rifle they were upon him. Lorenz and Hernando jammed their pistols into Regrett's chest and stomach and Felipe Bosquez seized Monty. Swiftly, he began tying her hands behind her despite her frantic struggles.

"One move and you are a dead man, Señor Regrett," Hernando said in English. The three brothers were proficient in English, though the two younger ones had heavy accents.

Monty freed a hand momentarily and raked her nails across Felipe Bosquez's face, drawing blood.

He swore gustily in Spanish and seized her hand. Then he drew the rawhide thong about both wrists with furious tightness. Monty cried out in pain.

"Bosquez!" Mase shouted. "You harm the girl and there'll be hell to pay. Her father's a former Englishman, and England will hear of your treatment."

Bosquez sullenly loosened the thong a fraction and Monty spoke sharply. "You'll have to loosen it more than that, or my hands will be cut off."

"You deserve it," Bosquez muttered. "If I loosen it more, you may scratch again, you little cat." Then to his brothers he said, "Bind Regrett, and tightly. I'll check on Dominguez."

"No use to check on him," Lorenz, the youngest, said in Spanish. "He is dead."

"Then we'll bury him here," Felipe Bosquez replied. "In fact, we can let Señor Regrett dig his grave here beside the trace." He spat, then reaching into his uniform pocket, put a fresh piece of tobacco into his mouth.

"You mean we can't tie him yet?" Hernando asked uneasily.

"Well?" Felipe looked at his younger brother with a trace of contempt. "You have your guns. Keep him well covered. All we need is a little excuse to kill him instead of take him prisoner."

Though their conversation was conducted in Spanish, both Regrett and Monty understood them well enough.

"I do not like this man—tied or untied. He kills too quickly," Lorenz grumbled.

"I would kill him now," Felipe said, spitting again. "But he killed in self-defense. Too bad Dominguez wasn't fast enough to get off a shot. Besides, Regrett will bring a good ransom. He owns many cattle and horses, and he has friends, I am told, in high places."

Prodded by Hernando's gun, Regrett dismounted and he looked at Felipe with level black eyes.

"I'm surprised," he said evenly, "that your sense of honor observes the rule of self-defense."

Bosquez's swarthy cheeks reddened. "Didn't they tell you I shot the Arterbury man in self-defense?" He scowled. "A man cannot be punished for defending himself." He dismounted and pulled a short spade from the packhorse behind him. He threw it at Regrett. "Dominguez was a good man, but slow. Still, we shall miss him. Dig there, señor." He pointed to a loamy spot a yard or two from the trace.

"And remember," Hernando said in English, "we watch you with our guns ready."

Regrett started to dig, and without compunction, Felipe Bosquez began going through the supplies on Regrett's packhorse and his saddlebags.

"Ah," he said with a triumphant grin, "you carry reports to the evil Sam Houston." He rifled through them, coming to the last—the report of the Mexican-Texan truce, and the promise not to annex to any country for ninety days, that Monty had learned of from Captain Charles Elliot. He laughed shortly.

"These are no good anymore, señor. None of them." He crumpled all the carefully written reports in his hand and threw them to the ground.

"You'd better read that last one again." Regrett looked up at him impassively. "You've violated the truce by taking us prisoner—and you will pay for it when you reach your superiors."

Bosquez's eyes creased in a canny smile. "You are a fool, Señor Regrett. The Texans have already rejected this so-called truce, for they are bent on becoming part of the United States."

"You don't know that."

"Don't I?" He patted his breast pocket. "Why do you think we are headed for Matagorda? Why do you think I travel with only my brothers and Dominguez? Why do you think I send my troops back to Mier?"

"I guess you'll tell me—in time," Regrett answered, burying the spade and lifting it out filled with soft earth.

"I'm glad to tell you now," Bosquez said boastfully. "I intercepted a courier out of San Antonio de Bexar. He fought back and he too is buried by the road. I carry his secret dispatch addressed to your Presidente Jones. The Texans will not accept the truce. Why, even now, this dispatch reveals that the Presidente Polk of the United States is sending troops to Texas—to a place near our Rio Grande, in fact." He paused, then added slowly, "War between us is inevitable. I will be commended for capturing you and the señorita."

"So that's why you aren't out plundering!" Monty burst out.

" 'Requisitioning,' señorita." He bowed to her once more from the saddle. "When I have delivered this captured dispatch"—again he patted his pocket—"I and my brothers will rejoin my men and we fight these invading Americans when they reach Texas."

Both Regrett and Monty were silent, surprised by Bosquez's revelation that American troops were actually on their way to Texas, even though annexation was not yet a fact. Despite his astonishment, Regrett was still seething over the loss of his painstaking reports for General Sam. As his foot on the spade pushed it deep into the damp earth, he reflected on Bosquez's veracity. The man could well be lying.

But if Captain Bosquez was telling the truth and President Polk was sending troops to insure the border, it meant annexation was going to be a reality. His heart lifted with hope.

When they had unceremoniously buried Dominguez, it was well past noon. Felipe Bosquez had taken all Monty's and Regrett's weapons and packed them securely behind the baggage on his packhorse.

Monty complained of hunger as he did this, and she insisted that Warlock be allowed to drink from the nearby spring before they rode on. Lorenz, at his older brother's command, loosened the rawhide around her wrists. Then he led her horse to the spring, while she untied the neckerchief from behind her saddle and began eating the cold rolls.

In another twenty minutes, they were on the trace once more. Hernando rode behind Monty and Mase, his rifle across his saddle, two pistols in his belt. Lorenz rode beside them some of the time, dropping back every so often to his other brother's side while Felipe Bosquez was at the head of the entourage. They rode in silence for a while. Then Monty spoke with low bitterness.

"You could've remained hidden behind those trees and escaped, Mase. I didn't ask you to do anything so foolhardy as try to rescue me."

"And I haven't asked you why you were damn-fool enough to be so far along the trace alone."

Captain Bosquez turned in his saddle and favored them both with a grin. "I can guess why Señor Regrett tried to get you away from us, señorita, and I think you can, too. But *why* are you on the trace alone—which I know your padre has forbidden—and with clothes and food so well packed?"

"That's none of your business, Bosquez," she retorted in Spanish, "nor of Señor Regrett's."

"I've a good idea what you're doing, Monty," Regrett said cynically. "You're running away from that beautiful, chancy new stepmother of yours again. It's becoming a habit with you."

"What do you mean by that? You've said it before—chancy?"

"Just that." He shrugged. "She likes men—and I use the plural."

"Then you ought to understand why I had to leave. You wouldn't believe the things she said to me last night . . ." She trailed off.

"I think you ought to face up to the fact you've a step-mother. Running away isn't the way to do it."

She turned on him angrily. "She struck me—she hates me!"

"Which doesn't alter the fact that running away isn't the way to settle it."

"I was only going to the Arterburys for a couple of weeks," Monty retorted. "I was going back home eventually. Besides, my father sides with her on everything."

Regrett grinned at her. "So Papa siding with Louise is what sent you flying off unescorted on this ill-fated trip of yours."

Monty reddened and said stormily, "Like I said, you certainly didn't have to interfere and—"

"Silence! Not so much quarreling, señorita!" Bosquez scowled at her over his shoulder. "We have solved your problem with your new stepmother," he said impatiently.

"And we have solved Señor Regrett's problem of reports to that devil Houston. They blow with the wind across our land, and you both go to Mexico City."

"You're going in the wrong direction for Mexico City, Bosquez," Regrett responded.

"It does not matter if you know. We have friends in Matagorda. We will put you and this dispatch on a vessel for Vera Cruz. From there, they will take you and it to Mexico City. You are as good as there, amiga, amigo."

"You'll never take me to Mexico City. My father will come after me when he finds I'm not at the Arterburys'." Brave words. How long would it be before her father found she was not at the Arterburys'?

"Chiquita," Bosquez said familiarly, "you *are* going to Mexico City. You may even learn to like it there—a pretty chiquita like you, with hair like fire."

Regrett smiled at her sardonically.

They rode for hours and little was said. Toward sundown they approached the Colorado River. They could hear the cooling sounds of water as it flowed between heavily wooded banks.

"Soon we'll come on old Señor Watkins's cabin and I'll requisition some of his chickens for our supper tonight," Felipe Bosquez said.

"Watkins is a lot more famous," Regrett drawled, "for his corn liquor." He and Julien had often ridden to Watkins's cabin to buy it, and Mase was very familiar with this area.

"We know that, señor." Hernando grinned. "And we'll requisition some of that, too."

All at once Felipe Bosquez held up his hand, motioning those behind him to a halt as he peered through the trees. Monty glimpsed the rough log cabin. Behind it, smoke was drifting lazily into the air. The sound of the flowing river beside them was louder now. Trees were thicker and provided some coolness despite the hot sun still above the horizon.

Monty caught a glimpse of several acres of green cornstalks around the cabin. Her eyes widened as she realized there was a man at the river's edge, filling a bucket. She did not know it, but Watkins's sharp old eyes had spotted the riders before Felipe ordered Lorenz to keep the prisoners out of sight.

"That's old man Watkins, himself," Regrett said to Monty, his voice low as he edged Coffee nearer to Warlock. "That's his still—smoking out back."

Felipe turned on his captives. "You will stay back here with Lorenz, while Hernando and I requisition supplies."

"Don't forget the whiskey," Lorenz admonished.

Felipe grinned at his brother, as he and Hernando slapped their horses' rumps with gathered reins. The horses bolted from the woods, thundering down to ford the river in a splashing run.

Watkins looked at them in alarm. He had expected customers. Seeing they were Mexican soldiers, he dropped the bucket and, with a whoop, started on a run for his cabin. He was too late, for the Bosquezes were on him, one on each side, guns in hand. They caught him without weapons. He slowed to a stop and began haranguing his captors, his gray beard wagging comically.

"Señor Watkins, we will not harm you," Felipe said, cutting in on his protests. "We will requisition a few supplies only."

"I ain't got nothin' for th' likes o' you thievin' crooks! Robbers ye are! If the Texas Rangers run onter you, they'll skin you alive!"

"Bah!" Felipe spat angrily. "Your rangers can never catch us. We are too smart for them—"

"They just been here," Watkins lied, his eyes squinting as he noted Hernando's quick, frightened looks about the place. The rangers were not to be treated lightly, and both Hernando and Felipe knew it well.

Suddenly, in the door of the cabin, a woman of ample proportions appeared with a rifle at her shoulder. Her hair was jet-black and pulled smoothly to a thick loop at the back of her neck. Her bronze face revealed her Indian heritage and her black eyes were unafraid. She did not hesitate, and the rifle cracked loudly, the bullet whistling with vicious closeness to Felipe's ear.

"Put down your gun, señora," Felipe called roughly, "or we kill your man, here and now!" Watkins was pinned between their two horses and Felipe had his pistol trained on him.

Slowly the woman lowered her rifle, and the three men approached the cabin.

"Señora," Felipe said, "we want only a few of your chickens and some of the bread you bake."

"And a jug or two of your tequila, made with the corn you grow." Hernando grinned at Watkins as he slid from his saddle, carefully holding his pistol on the man.

Felipe pushed the elderly man into the cabin along with his wife and motioned them to sit on the bed in the corner. "I will guard them while you get the supplies, Hernando. Get anything fit to eat."

In less than twenty minutes, Hernando had secured six squawking chickens and tied them to his saddle. He had, despite Watkins's and his wife's protests, secured a flour sack filled with four freshly baked loaves of bread, and half the jerky in the Watkins pantry. He took another flour sack, putting in four pottery jugs of Watkins's prime whiskey. He and Felipe took the precaution of confiscating the rifle and two pistols in the house.

As they left, Hernando said, "We make a packhorse now out of Dominguez's horse, eh brother? It is good we have it, though I miss Dominguez. I think you should have killed Regrett for that."

"Dominguez drew on him first." Felipe shrugged as they forded the river. He was an unscrupulous man in many ways, but he clung to the shred of honor that self-defense implied. It kept many murders from troubling his mind. Besides, he would receive a portion of the ransom paid for these two he had captured.

Watkins and his wife stood in the cabin door, watching them as they rode away. The old man's keen eyes were on the stand of trees where the others waited for them.

"Nola," he said slowly to his squaw wife, "that's Mase Regrett on Coffee over there. An' I caught a good squint at the redheaded girl on the black stallion. I'll bet you this summer's corn crop that's Daventry's daughter. Bosquez bragged he'd took two prisoners, and they're the two they's goin' ter send to Mexico City fer ransom."

As soon as Felipe and Hernando reached the three waiting, they melted into the woods, but Watkins determined they were following the river south.

"I ain't goin' to stand by an' see it happen." He paused, drawing a long breath. "I'm goin' to strike out fer Regrett's an' tell Julien—then I'll stop by that high-nosed Daventry's an' tell him—an' I'm leavin' right now. If Julien an' Daventry ride hard with their men, they may be able to catch 'em afore they get to th' coast."

After their confrontation, Louise had returned to the parlor, and assured the others that Monty was comforted and all was well. It always exhilarated her to best an opponent, and she relished her triumph over Monty.

Later, in the bedroom with Richard, her exhilaration became the old familiar craving. Cavenal was in her thoughts as she grew warm, and the slippery moisture came on her, but Richard was *here* and he was an expert lover—though his did not compare with the exotic and strange delights Cavenal brought her. Too, she was not ready to dispense with Richard yet. Cavenal must make a stronger commitment to her. He had implied it, of course, but she wanted to hear him say he would marry her if she were free.

When Richard closed their bedroom door, she was fully aroused. Always before, she had waited demurely until Richard made the first sexual overture, but tonight, triumphant and less cautious, she undressed quickly, draping her clothes hurriedly over a chair. Then she reclined on the bed, naked, waiting for Richard to turn and see her.

Deep in his own thoughts concerning Monty's outburst, and her open rebellion against his new wife, he slowly undressed. The thought of that, plus the disturbing confirmation that there was something between Mason Regrett and his willful daughter, put him on edge. He had suspected it, when Monty defended the man in Washington. He went to the washstand, poured water into the bowl, and washed his face and hands. He should have gone up to her room to see her—to set the whole affair to rights himself, he reflected. He would have felt better for it.

He stepped away after toweling his hands and face, and Louise called softly to him.

"Richard . . ."

He looked the length of the room to see her reclining, provocative body naked on the big bed. Last night they had made love, and it had been deeply satisfying, a meshing of body and spirit, he told himself. Now he knew Louise expected it tonight as well, but his preoccupation with thoughts of Monty's defiance cooled his ardor. He walked to the bed, and as he did so, Louise rolled on her side, lowering the lamp on the table beside it.

He eased his lithe body down on the bed beside her.

"I need you tonight, my darling Richard. I want to feel you need me—love me—"

"You mean I didn't convince you last night?" he asked lightly. He was a man who preferred to be the pursuer. Her urgency tonight irritated him slightly.

He looked at her in the dim light. Her perfectly shaped body beside him was an enticement, and so was the hot avid light in her eyes.

"I'm still thinking of Monty. She should have come back down after you talked—had that final cup of coffee, to show things were right again."

Hiding annoyance, she said plaintively, "Don't think of Monty, love. Think of *me!*" No man had ever been able to resist her when she set out to excite him. She was confident that Richard would not.

She began kissing his body with smooth skill, her mouth traveling over him, slowly approaching his lips. As she kissed him, she caressed him with practiced fingers that left no senses untouched. She stroked him deftly, and his body responded.

As she joined passionately with him, she put from her mind the realization that Richard Daventry was not the weak man Randolph Lynchley had been. Ridding herself of Daventry might be more difficult. There would be a way, she thought as a gust of passion shook her, wiping out thought as her tide of desire peaked.

As Richard reached his climax, he looked down into Louise's flushed face. In that instant, she looked to him like any of the girls he had had in Rebecca's house in Victoria. *I could be any man with her,* he thought with sudden revulsion.

The revelation so startled him that he rolled off her still-pulsating body. His voice husky, he said, "Turn out the lamp, Louise."

When Richard and Louise descended the stairs the next morning, Louise had not yet dressed for the day. Instead, she wore a heavy silk crepe peignoir of coral, lavishly trimmed with ecru lace, and a matching nightgown beneath it. Her golden curls were tied up with a coral satin ribbon. She was well aware of the picture she made as they seated themselves with Abby and Faith.

Feenie, trying hard not to stare, quickly poured steaming coffee from the polished silver pot for each of them. Richard sipped from his cup and eyed his wife speculatively. His thought last night had shaken him.

"You look lovely this morning, my dear," he said, trying to forget it.

"That's because you're with me now, darling Richard!"

"Where is Monty, Abby?" Richard asked abruptly. He had long ago adopted Monty's name for his mother.

"I expect she may be sleeping late, Richard. Or perhaps she's already gone out with the horses after an early breakfast with Feenie and Josey in the kitchen."

Richard turned to Feenie, who lingered in the dining room doorway, pot still in hand. "Did she eat earlier, Feenie?" When the girl shook her head, he said, "Then run upstairs and wake her. Tell her I want her at the breakfast table." His frown deepened.

Feenie handed the ornate silver pot to her mother, who had come up behind her.

"Yes, sir." The light patter of her feet sounded as she entered the foyer and took the stairs rapidly.

"Abby, I discussed Monty with Louise this morning, and Louise agreed that Monty should be allowed to wear her breeches when working with the horses." He put his cup down and his eyes twinkled at Faith. "And you may ride with her in yours, Faith. But you both must wear dresses at dinner."

"Which Faith does already," Abby said, her voice chill.

"That way," Louise said complacently, ignoring Abby, "Montrose can acquire ladylike manners and deportment by degrees."

"Ah. I see." Abby's eyes were cold.

Feenie could be heard skittering down the stairs. She approached Richard's side, breathing hard.

"Mister Richard, Monty's bed ain't been slept in, and this here was pinned to her pillow," she said hurriedly, handing Monty's note to him. He scanned it quickly.

"It's Monty—she's gone to the Arterburys' for a week or two. *Alone!*" Amazement and fear were heavy in his deep voice. "She *knows* better than to try to make that long trip alone—with Indians and renegade Mexican soldiers taking everything and *everyone* in sight!"

He crumpled the note in his fist. Shoving his chair back, he stood up and looked at his wife intently over his half-finished breakfast, ignoring her smile.

"Where are you going, Richard darling?"

"Just what did you say to Monty when you went up to her room last night, Louise?"

"Why, I told you, darling. The main points, anyway. I told her how sorry I was for putting the figurine on the table—that neither you nor I blamed her for it, and I promised to speak to you about letting her wear what she wanted when riding or working with the horses." Louise was about to cry. "Why, we even embraced when I left her! Don't you believe me, darling?" she added, piteously.

His eyes were penetrating as he said evenly, "I learned with the Regretts the morning after their fire that you can never lie, Louise." His big hands were flexing at his sides. "But *something* has sent my daughter off in a temper. And I'll be damned if it wasn't something you said, or something she thought. She won't have gotten too far—and I'm going after her. It would be like her to take the trace, because it's less traveled, even though it's farther."

"She's never spent two weeks with either the Bedfords or the Arterbury girls," Abby said worriedly.

"And she won't stay two weeks this time. I'm leaving

now! Get Josey to fix a sack of provisions. LeRoy can saddle up Nate and Beau. I can't pull Big Miguel off his duties right now, but I'll take LeRoy with me."

"Richard!" Louise said indignantly. "You mean you're going to leave me to go after Montrose? You know she's all right—let LeRoy and Ezekiel go after her!"

"Yes, my dear, I'm going after her. You'll be quite all right for the short time I'm gone. We'll be back from the Arterburys' as soon as I can."

Fury filled Louise. That brat! That spoiled brat, coming first with Richard! Even as she frowned, Richard was leaving the dining room on his way to the stables.

There, Richard found only Carlos, who was currying Beau. Hastily he told the boy of Monty's departure alone in the dark hours.

"If your brother were here, I'd take him with me instead of LeRoy. Young Miguel's a much better shot."

At the sound of his brother's name, Carlos's young face contorted with grief and anger. Words erupted involuntarily.

"Is all the Señora's fault that he is gone! Mi madre, she cry all the time. Mi padre is sad—because they don't know—" Realization of what he was saying struck the boy. His face whitened. He had sworn on the blessed Virgin Mary to respect his brother's confidence.

Richard, his hand lifted to take the saddle from its hook, froze. He stood perfectly still.

"What did you say, Carlos?"

"Is nothing, Señor Richard. Is nothing, I swear!" he said hastily, and sweat sprang out on his forehead. "I—I know nothing. It is just that I am frighten for Monty, Señor Richard!"

Richard let out his breath. "Go fetch LeRoy for me, then. Tell him we're going to the Arterburys' to bring Monty back, and he is to bring his rifle and pistol."

He began to saddle the powerful gelding Nate as the boy ran out the stable door.

Is all the Señora's fault that he is gone! The words tolled like a bell behind Richard's worry over his daughter. What was there between Louise and Young Miguel that had sent him away from his family and this place Richard knew he loved so well?

What had Monty said? *I'll bet I know why he left.* Her eyes had fallen under his sharp question. Now this. His mouth tightened as he took the reins to his horse. Evidence was mounting that Louise had much to explain.

Chapter 18

Watkins rode all night and at dawn arrived at the Regrett ranch, where the barns were in the process of being rebuilt. His horse was heaving with exhaustion, his legs buckling under him, after being forced to gallop over forty miles when he reached Regrett's corrals. He had taken the well-traveled road and made good time. Now it took him only minutes to outline the events of yesterday afternoon to Julien.

"I know it was Mase an' I recognized Coffee," he finished. "An' I've seen that redhead of Daventry's here at the ranch—an' at the Arterburys', too. They buy my liquor instead of sendin' off for it from England like Daventry does. Don't you reckon we ought to stop an' tell Daventry?"

"I guess so," Julien said grudgingly. "He has as much right to know as I have. She's his only daughter, and much better than her pa, anyway. He'll want to go with us, of course. I guess I can endure him until we catch the Bosquezes."

As word spread over the ranch that Mase had been captured by the Bosquezes, men crowded around the nearly rebuilt stables, all wanting to ride with Julien. Young Miguel was the most persuasive.

"Señor Julien, I owe Señor Mase and I owe Señor Richard for many things. Besides, I ride fast—an' you know how good I am with guns!" His smile broadened as Julien nodded agreement.

Julien supplied Watkins with a fresh horse, a big gelding that would eat up miles on the road. He also supplied him with a fine rifle and a pistol from the Regrett arsenal. By the time the sun was well over the horizon, all three men were on their way to the Daventry place.

When they reached the compound, Richard and LeRoy were just readying themselves to leave. Julien rode up to them, his face truculent.

"Watkins here came to me with word that Monty and Mase have been captured by the Bosquezes," he said bluntly.

Richard whitened under his heavy tan as he looked at the wiry old man, who returned his stare defiantly.

"I seen 'em on t'other side of the Colorado, Mister Daventry, when two of them Bosquezes come by an' stole chickens an' liquor an' food off me. I know it was your daughter," he said flatly.

"We're leaving now to try to catch them," Julien said, his voice hard, "and blow the Bosquezes out of their saddles."

"That Felipe Bosquez," Watkins put in, "bragged he had two captives an' was goin' to send 'em to Mexico City an' hold 'em fer ransom. But if we ride fast today, I think we can catch 'em afore they git too fur along."

"Do you mean to tell me my daughter was captured in company with Mason Regrett?" Richard's nostrils flared.

"That ain't the way it sounded to me," Watkins said firmly. "While his brother was raidin' my supplies, ol' Felipe talked like they was ridin' separate when he captured 'em."

Julien added curtly, "My brother left here at three yesterday morning, *alone*. He was on his way to see General Sam with his reports." Sardonically, he said, "I thought you'd want to go along with us, Daventry."

"I certainly do. Monty left a note that she was going to the Arterburys' for two weeks and that she was going alone. I was preparing to go bring her home—"

"And Mase said he was going to take the old Indian trace," Julien interrupted. "She must've taken it, too."

"Evidently," Richard replied grimly. "We'll be five—all of us together—enough to take the three Bosquezes when we catch them." He sent a searching look at Young Miguel. "I'm glad you're going, Miguel—I was wishing you were still with us this morning, because of your sharp eye and good aim."

The young man reddened and he forced himself to meet Richard's penetrating eyes. "I would not stay behind when I could be of help—to you, Señor Richard—and Señor Mase."

With provisions strapped to their saddles, rifles in holsters, and pistols at their waists, the five men rode to the front of the Daventry house. There, Richard dismounted and spoke curtly.

"Wait while I tell the women of these developments. It won't take long."

After the Bosquezes and their captives left the Watkins cabin, they rode south along the river. It surprised Monty when Regrett began talking to their captors in a half-mocking, half-friendly way. Once she caught his eye, and her brow lifted questioningly, but there was a warning in his black eyes and she said nothing.

As evening came on and the woods grew darker, Felipe sought a campsite, finally choosing a large stand of ancient live oaks not far from the river. Hunger was plaguing Monty, for her meager provisions earlier had not been satisfying.

Lorenz untied her and Regrett. "You can go wash up at the river," he said, "but I will be with you." Dusk had fallen but it was still and hot. No cooling breeze stirred the trees. "And you will not go far to relieve yourselves. I'll be in sight of you all the time."

Monty had almost become used to that during the afternoon, but she envied Regrett, who performed his necessities without a qualm, even asking on occasion to do so.

She felt cooler after washing her arms and face in the river. She had even taken off her beautiful new boots and washed her feet. Mase had stripped off his shirt. A sharp thrill jolted her at the sight of the broad, muscled chest. Did he ever think of those wonderful moments they shared the night he came home escorting Louise to Texas? No, he was probably remembering the moment in the stable when they had parted so coldly, and all because she had admitted Abby's revelation. As she washed her feet, Lorenz spoke impudently.

"You can take a whole bath, señorita. I will watch to see you without your boy clothes on."

She made no response as she air-dried her feet, but Regrett, washing beside her, muttered under his breath, "Bastard!" And she knew that despite his banter with their captors, he seethed with anger.

At the campsite, Felipe and Hernando had built a good fire within a small cairn of rocks. They had plucked and cleaned all six of the chickens and the birds were strung over it, small saplings running through them.

"Aren't you going to give us a drink of that good corn whiskey before dinner?" Regrett asked with a laugh. His eyes sought the sacks from Watkins's cabin. One looked empty—the other held stolen food. Where had the robbers put that whiskey?

"We won't tie you up again until after we eat, but Hernando will keep his pistol handy," Felipe said, ignoring his suggestion, as the two seated themselves across from the fire.

"A needless precaution. We're too hungry to try to run, Captain." Regrett smiled.

"You look ready to run, señor."

"But I'm not." Not yet, Regrett thought. Then he asked again, "Aren't you men ready for some of Watkins's fine liquor?"

"You'll get none of it," Lorenz said angrily. "You do not deserve any special treatment—after killing our good comrade Dominguez. My brothers and I will drink some of it."

"What's the good of just some?" Regrett asked reasonably. "We'll be tied up—and you can celebrate."

"We will celebrate when you both are on the boat to Vera Cruz."

"Two prisoners are not too much to celebrate, I agree— pretty poor pickings, Captain," Regrett joked.

Felipe shot him a dark, cunning glance. "I have plenty to celebrate. You forget the dispatch I took from the courier!"

Lorenz came up to the fire with fresh wood, some of which he slipped under coals beneath the chickens. He turned on his brother.

"Now!" The word was explosive. "Maybe you'll let us have some of Watkins's tequila."

"Get the cups, Hernando," Felipe said, "and we'll have some."

"Except Señor Regrett and the señorita," Lorenz said vindictively as Hernando moved with alacrity to take cups from their gear.

So, as the chickens slowly browned, sending out mouthwatering fragrances in the air, the three brothers each had a cup of corn liquor.

Talk grew louder and Regrett joined in, speaking of the merits of one horse versus another. With an offhand, casual air, he spoke of breeding stock, and what he and Julien were doing with the blooded animals they ordered sent from England.

Felipe laughed coarsely, and said, "When I get you to Matagorda, Regrett, I will take your Coffee and the señorita's stallion. I know good horses when I see them. These horses are too good for gringos such as you."

It seemed an eternity to Monty as she sat listening to the men laughing and talking, though she was silently thankful for the relief of her chafed wrists. She noted that Hernando and Lorenz prevailed on the older Bosquez to have more of the liquor.

By the time they removed the roasted chickens from the spit, the brothers were well liquored. And further, they refilled the cups as they took the chickens and began to tear them apart and eat.

Regrett took Monty's chicken from Lorenz's hand and tore it into pieces she could handle. She was so hungry she ate too fast at first, but when Regrett handed her a cup of coffee, she slowed so she was able to enjoy the succulent, smoke-flavored meat. She and Regrett were the only ones to drink coffee.

Finally, Regrett said with deep asperity, "I think you're a selfish swine, Felipe—not to give the girl and me a drink of that fine whiskey. It would make us sleep better. God knows," he added arrogantly, "we'll sleep poorly enough on these thin blankets you've allowed us."

"That wildcat doesn't deserve to sleep better—I still suffer from her scratches. It is enough that we untie her hands and let her wash and eat. As for you—ha! It will be a long time before you taste of Señor Watkins's whiskey again."

The sixth and last chicken was taken from the spit by Lorenz, and he and Hernando quarreled good-naturedly over who got the bigger half. Once again, the jug was passed around.

"You're a fool, Captain," Regrett said suddenly, "believing there will be war. You will find yourself in deep trouble when you arrive in Matagorda with us as prisoners—I don't believe the truce between our countries has failed. Your friends will condemn you."

"You lie, Regrett." Felipe glared at him over the rim of his tin cup. "I have positive proof of the coming war—"

"That's what you *say,* Captain! I think you lie! I've seen no proof of it."

"I have it here—here!" He patted the medals on his chest. "I have something our commander, Avrillago, will like even more than receiving two such wealthy prisoners."

Lorenz held his cup to his lips with one hand and with the other, he fingered a knife at his belt. Monty could not be sure what Regrett was trying to accomplish, but sweat broke out on her upper lip, and she edged farther back from the fire.

"I say you're risking your reputation in taking us prisoners," Regrett said with certainty. "I say President Jones has signed the peace treaty between Texas and Mexico!"

Felipe Bosquez stared at Regrett, his eyes glistening like black marbles in the firelight. Lorenz got to his feet, and bringing the jug, poured more whiskey in his older brother's cup. He spoke thickly.

"Why not kill them now, brother, and have done with it? I will do it—quietly, with my knife."

"No," Felipe said angrily. "No murders. I kill in self-defense."

"But it is self-defense," Lorenz replied, pulling out the knife and polishing it on his breeches. "They would kill us quickly enough if they could."

"Your brother proves my point," Regrett said with contempt. "You have no proof. You are merely a pack of thieves, not soldiers at all."

Monty's heart was beating wildly, and she reached over to

pinch Regrett's arm fiercely in an effort to shut him up. He would surely get them killed!

Felipe gave the youngest brother a shove as he rose to his feet. "Put your knife away, muchacho. These two will bring a fine ransom, and we will get our share of it. And I will show this ugly gringo my proof, but we will bind them first."

"Pour me another," Hernando said, handing his cup to Lorenz and getting thongs ready to bind their prisoners' hands once more. He approached Regrett first, who turned around readily, holding his hands behind him. Hernando fumbled a little in winding the rawhide about his wrists, but jerked it tight with an expert twist.

Then he turned to Monty, twisting the leather thong tight about her lacerated wrists. She gave a cry of pain.

"Hurts, does it?" he growled at her. "You deserve it, gringo boy-woman."

Monty was crying silently for she knew her wrists were bleeding under the cruel bite of rawhide. Felipe observed her without sympathy.

"Check their feet, Hernando—see they are bound tightly as well. We have enjoyed our liquor tonight, and we will sleep soundly—and we do not want them trying to get away."

Hernando did as he was bid, and Monty and Regrett were trussed as helplessly as the bound chickens stolen from Watkins. Then Felipe strode to Regrett and pulled him upright.

"Here," he said, pulling a thin leather packet from the inner pocket of his coat. "I hold it so you can see."

"I can't read *that* in this light! It looks like nothing but a piece of paper—with a scrawl on it."

"Look! Look!" Felipe held it closer, so that Regrett could see that it was addressed to the President of Texas, Anson Jones, but he snatched it back. "We were making a profitable sortie among good farms around San Antonio, when I intercepted the courier from the rangers—a man named Jack Hays, who signed this letter to your President Jones!"

"I saw nothing but a scrawl." Regrett laughed. "I think you imagine the whole thing."

"It contains the news that Americans are being sent from the United States—even the numbers of battalions. These Americans are coming to Texas to fight Mexico! This news is so important to my country, we will carry it now to Captain Pancingo in Matagorda. It will go on the same vessel with you, to Vera Cruz!"

Regrett shook his head in disbelief. "I think you make this long trip away from your duties for a message that means nothing. I think you lie about its importance."

Felipe Bosquez's face was suffused with rage. He raised his hand slowly and struck Regrett across the face with all his strength. It rocked Regrett, and he reeled back.

"Oh, Mase—don't argue with him!" Monty cried out suddenly, real terror in her voice. "He might kill us—"

"I think you're trying to impress the señorita with these lies," Regrett interrupted mockingly. "It's easy enough to strike a man who's tied, and who isn't impressed with your fancies."

The red faded from Bosquez's face and he laughed. "I do not need to boast to the señorita. I tell you the name of the American general who brings American soldiers to Texas— General Zachary Taylor."

Regrett was silent. He had met Taylor when he was in Washington. The man was a rough sort, not even clad in the uniform to which he was entitled, and he was what the Americans called a Whig. But he was highly regarded among the military. If the Bosquez brothers would get a little more of Watkins's liquor in them before they lay down to sleep . . .

"You believe me now, gringo?"

"I think you know some important American names and that's all, Bosquez." But he did believe him, and he knew he must get that letter from Bosquez and deliver it to Anson Jones. The news it contained was vital to Texas.

Felipe shrugged. "I cannot make you believe, gringo—but I can make big trouble for you—and I am doing that. Here, Lorenz, pour me a nightcap."

"I will have one with you, brother."

The three brothers filled their cups, and sat around the fire drinking.

"Aren't you going to give us those blankets, Captain?" Monty asked in a small voice.

"Why should I? You and Regrett think me a liar and a fool. Sleep on the ground, señorita." He turned his back to her. The three brothers began talking to each other, their Spanish so rapid and colloquial, Regrett and Monty had a hard time keeping track of the topics they covered: women, horses, liquor, past conquests and triumphs. More importantly, they discussed triumphs yet to come.

The fire died to coals before the brothers spread out their bedrolls and blankets. Before lying down, Felipe examined their bonds again. He reeled slightly as he did so, but grunted his satisfaction as he went back to his bedroll and lay down upon it. He did not seem as drunk as the other two, but he had matched them, drink for drink, and for that reason, Mason Regrett's hopes rose.

In a little while, all three were sleeping deeply. The two younger brothers snored, but Felipe Bosquez's breathing was quiet and deep.

After an hour, Regrett turned to Monty, who lay two feet away from him. "Are you awake?" he whispered.

"Of course."

"Then roll over and inch down to my right boot—my knife's in there. Pull it out."

Excitement and hope surged in her. Struggling against the

tight thongs binding her booted feet, she began to hitch herself down the length of Regrett. He turned his bound heels to her, and she backed up to his legs. For a panicky moment, she couldn't remember which was his right leg from the position she held. But she recovered and bent her elbows, bringing her tied wrists up to his leg. His twill breeches covered the top of the boot, and she wrestled with the obstinate material to hitch it over the boot.

At last, straining against the rawhide on her wrists, she stretched one hand inside the boot as far as the thong would permit. It was far enough. Thank God! she thought, as her fingers closed on the bone haft, and she got a purchase on it. It was not easy to pull loose from its tight holster within the boot. Slowly she worked it out and up to the top.

Regrett was silent, neither urging her on, nor commenting on her success as she pulled the knife out. It fell from her fingers, striking a rock with a small nicking sound. Frantically she felt for it, found it, and clung to it tightly.

"You have it?" Regrett whispered.

"Yes."

"Turn around and give it to me. I'll cut your hands free, and then you can cut mine."

When Regrett got his hands on the knife, Monty backed up to him, and he felt for her hands carefully. Locating the rawhide thongs, he began cutting them. The knife was fairly long and sharp as a razor. Tough as the leather thong was, in an instant her hands and feet were free.

She took no time to ease her painful wrists but, with the knife, cut Regrett's bonds swiftly.

She handed him the knife, and he whispered, "Take off your boots—carry them. They're drunk enough, but we can't risk any sound." She was free in an instant.

Together, boots in hand, they moved silently to the horses. The Bosquezes had unloaded all the gear near the animals, but Regrett began systematically cutting all the horses' bridles except for Coffee's and Warlock's.

Then he stooped quickly to the gear piled nearby. "Look for your guns," he whispered, "—and your roll of clothes."

They went through the gear as fast as they could, taking what they could carry with them, scattering what they could not. Their guns were near a packhorse. The dead Dominguez's guns were there as well, and Regrett also took them.

"Now put on your boots, Monty," Regrett commanded as he pulled on his own.

Silently, they swung their own saddles up on their mounts, and in a matter of minutes were ready to leave.

The two had their pistols thrust in their belts, and their rifles in the saddle holsters. Regrett thrust Dominguez's firearms into his bedroll.

"I'm going to get that packet out of Felipe Bosquez's pocket."

"Oh, no, Mase," Monty whispered in dismay. "Let's go while we can!"

"No." His voice was hard. "That's something that must reach Anson Jones, and as soon as possible. I saw enough of it to know it's imperative that he receive it. I think Bosquez is just drunk enough for me to get away with it." He paused, then ordered swiftly, "You hold the horses here." He looked at the three sleeping men. "Here," he added, "tie all these cut reins on my saddle—so they won't have them to mend. Now cover me, Monty—I'm going after that packet."

Her heart was in her throat as she looped the reins around his pommel, and took her pistol to watch him quietly make his way to the sleeping Felipe.

Sweat broke out on Regrett's face and back, as he slipped his hand into the sleeping captain's coat. Felipe's eyes opened slowly as Regrett eased the packet out. Then they widened, and he gave a hoarse cry, reaching for the gun beside him. But Regrett, with a kick, sent it spinning into the darkness.

As Felipe struggled to sit up, Regrett doubled his right fist and lashed at Felipe's jaw. Flesh and bone connected in a crushing impact, Felipe's head snapped back, and he sank down without a sound.

But the damage had been done, and both Lorenz and Hernando lurched to their feet, pistols in hand.

From the dark, Monty's pistol cracked out, and with a scream of pain, Lorenz clutched his groin, falling to the ground. Hernando wheeled unsteadily, getting off one shot, which whistled past Regrett's head.

It coincided with Regrett's own pistol shot, which knocked Hernando to the ground.

Regrett sprinted to the horses Monty held. "Let's get the hell out of here before the captain gets his wits back."

They swung into their saddles, and gave the horses their heads. Progress was slowed by thick trees, but both stallions seemed at home in the darkness about them, and moved in a swift, dodging canter. When they were well away, Regrett spoke.

"Let's cut across the Colorado and get back on the trace. We'll make better time," he said, heading Coffee to the east. "We'll need to find a shallow spot so we can ford it. I want to stop by Watkins's for supplies," he added as they heard the soft rushing sound of water.

They angled their horses along the bank where the ground was uneven.

"Thanks," Regrett said abruptly, "for getting Lorenz before he could get me."

"Did I kill him—do you think?" she asked in a small, troubled voice.

He laughed shortly. "No, but you hit him where it'll do the most good." He paused, then said, "Damn, I wish we could've taken the packhorses and all their gear." He untied the cut reins from his pommel, hurling them into the river.

"Why didn't we?"

"Slow us down too much. We've a long way to go. The letter I took off Bosquez is much more important than my reports to General Sam. Here—I see a few stones above water down yonder. It looks pretty shallow—current not too swift." He swung the reins, and Coffee splashed into the shallow edge of the clear, flowing water.

Monty followed and found it grew swifter and deeper as they reached the center.

Regrett, ahead of her, urged her to hurry. "It's getting shallower," he called. "We've almost made it."

In another five minutes they were pulling out on the far bank. The horses were dripping, and so were Monty's boots. With difficulty she leaned over and slipped them off, one at a time, to empty them, then pulled them back on her soaked, stockinged feet. Her momentary dismay vanished as she spoke anxiously.

"Do you think they'll come after us?"

He laughed shortly. "I think the captain is nursing his jaw, a hangover, and both of his wounded brothers. He's got his hands full, but he's a determined devil, and anything's possible."

They rode a few yards from the river's edge, and the trees thickened about them once more. Only the muffled footfalls of their horses and creaking of leather saddles could be heard. They were not able to travel fast, for the horses were tired from the long ride yesterday and had had little rest. The abrupt hoot of an owl and upward rush of wings drew an exclamation from Monty.

"Monty, it would be hours before Bosquez could tend to his brothers and leave them to follow us," Regrett said reassuringly. "Besides, he knows we're armed, and he'll think twice before he comes alone."

They traveled slowly but steadily on the dark trace, a deep narrow track that cut through the trees. Just before dawn, they spotted Watkins's cabin. Monty drew a breath of relief. That meant miles were between them and their former captors. Her chafed wrists were painful reminders of their ordeal, and she slipped her fingers over the pistol in her belt, then the rifle in her saddle holster, with renewed relief.

Smoke trailed thinly from the cabin chimney in the pre-dawn hour, blowing away in a south wind from the gulf.

"I'll go in and tell Watkins what's happened to us—get some supplies from him. You take Warlock and Coffee to the river. I know they're thirsty and tired. Watkins will have some feed for them, and we'll give them an hour's rest."

When Monty returned to the cabin with their mounts, she found Regrett talking to Nola.

"I'll pay for these supplies, Nola. The Bosquezes took what gold I carried, but you and Watkins know I'm good for it." Then he turned and said, "Monty, Watkins took off for my place—and yours—as soon as we were out of sight, to tell Julien and your father we'd been taken by the Bosquezes. He's there by now, but we can't wait until they get here. As I told you, it's vital that this letter reach Anson Jones—we're going on to Washington-on-the-Brazos."

Nola had a flour sack full of bread, dried fruit, and bacon. Regrett was wrapping a dozen eggs carefully to put into his saddlebags. "We'll have to shoot game as we go along, because the Bosquezes took nearly all his dried meat, and Watkins took the rest."

"*We?* Aren't you going to take me home first?"

Regrett looked at her in astonishment. "Home? Nearly fifty miles there and back—and lose two days? My God, Monty, don't you realize that this letter contains the news that American troops are on their way to Texas? Jones has to have it as soon as possible—I can't take you home!"

"You mean I'll have to go with you to Washington-on-the-Brazos?" Her brows drew together and her face flushed with anger.

"Certainly—it'll only be for a few days more—and—" his eyes were mocking, "you'll be safe *in every way,* I swear it."

He was throwing up to her the request she had made of him the last time they started to make love. The memory of herself sitting naked and repentant on the hay rose up along with increasing fury.

"But I'll slow you down—a woman on the trail!"

"Not you, Monty. You're as good as any man in the saddle."

"You'll take me home, Mason Regrett, or I'll ride from here alone. I know my way!"

"You won't do that if I have to tie you on Warlock! Are you such a fool that you've already forgotten the Bosquezes? They aren't the only renegades in this part of the country."

"All right! I'll stay here with Nola, until they come!"

"No, no, little one! Ol' Felipe will get friends to come up from Matagorda. He say to my man they come by here later, to see if your pa try to follow an' help you an' Mister Regrett!"

"You mean more Mexicans could come here?" Monty asked in disbelief.

"I know they will, little one. I will tell them my man, he gone to San Antone for more jugs for his whiskey. I often do this. They no bother me after stealing a jug or two of our whiskey. But you—oh, little one—you have money an' you are beautiful! They take you."

Monty felt her flesh crawl at the thought, and Regrett's next words were mocking.

"It won't take more than eight or ten days to get to Washington-on-the-Brazos, deliver the letter, and get you safely back with your father and stepmother."

She was silent. There was nothing to do but accompany Regrett on his errand. She sent him a sooty glance from under her lashes. *You're as good as any man in the saddle.* But she wasn't a man! She squared her shoulders. Eight or ten days with him—alone most of the time. That would be a real test of her determination to give no quarter to this man.

After letting the horses rest a full hour, Monty and Regrett struck out up the trace on the long ride to Washington-on-the-Brazos, and Monty's anger did not dissipate as they cantered forward in the dewy morning.

Chapter 19

Richard strode into the house and informed the women of Monty's capture by the Bosquezes. His look at Louise where they gathered in the foyer was distant.

"Now you know why I never let women leave here without an escort, Louise."

"But Richard! I'm sure Captain Bosquez will free her!" Louise protested, unable to hide her insensitivity. "He was so polite—bowing to all of us ladies when they were here requisitioning supplies."

"Louise"—it was Abby's measured voice—"he means to take her to jail in Mexico City—hold her for ransom. Those jails are barbaric—Monty could die before we are able to ransom her."

"I don't see why you have to go," Louise said stubbornly. "Young Miguel, LeRoy, and the others should be enough." But she was angrily thinking it served the little slut right, running off in the middle of the night. With any luck, she could remain for years in a Mexican jail. "I don't suppose you'll agree to that, darling Richard," she added, trying to sound resigned. "How long will you be gone?"

"Until I find her."

"You know well enough I'll be half-sick with worry while

you're gone—and I suppose you've forgotten all about the social the Cavenals are having for the two of us this weekend?" She sounded aggrieved, and came to put her arms about his neck, and kiss his mouth lingeringly, but he reached up and removed her arms.

"That's too damned bad about the Cavenals' social," he said roughly. "And your concern for Monty is touching, Louise."

"My concern is for *you,*" she said reproachfully, "just as yours should be for me, and what I want. I've been looking forward to that social for weeks!"

Richard looked at the white, stricken Abby. "Don't worry, Abby," he said, "I'll bring her back if it's humanly possible."

Faith stepped forward impulsively, her pale features set. "Richard, please let me go with you! Monty's taught me to ride and shoot—I could help!"

Richard's smile was grim. "No, Faith. We have men to do that—but thanks for wanting to help."

"Oh, I can't bear it!" Faith fought back tears. She did not cry easily like Louise. Crying made Faith's nose and eyes red. And when she did cry, as she wanted to now, with great wrenching sobs, it left her drained. She was aware of Louise's contemptuous stare.

"Good-bye, my son. Be careful," Abby said as he left.

Silence fell.

Then Louise wheeled about. "I certainly don't intend to mope around here until they come back with her, as I'm sure they will. I'm going to visit Lady Marguerite and Georgina, and apologize for Richard's absence! Ezekiel will accompany me as usual." Then under her breath she muttered, "Imagine having to cancel the lovely social—"

The other women looked at her silently as she turned to the slender black girls who served her. "Tina, come—I'll give you my pink silk blouse with the lace jabot. I want you to press it, for I'm going to wear my pale blue faille riding habit. And Merzella, you can come wash my hair and arrange it afterward."

Abby turned to Faith as Louise mounted the stairs. "Come, Faith, dear. I want you to see the box of new books that came for Richard last week. We must all keep our minds busy until Monty is returned safely."

Abby was also keenly aware of this innocent young girl's worshipful eyes on her son. She was weighed down by strong foreboding as she led the way to the library.

Louise, as she entered the big bedroom, tried not to think about the fact that her triumph over Monty had suddenly become a disaster. Richard himself had looked at her with doubt. Lady Abigail and that little mouse, Faith, had seemed to form a silent alliance against her. She would have a talk with Faith!

And today, she wanted to look especially desirable, for she felt that Cavenal was coming closer to a declaration. When he made it, she could dispense with Richard Daventry. This time she would tell him she wanted a divorce. It wouldn't be wise to lose two husbands to self-inflicted wounds. She turned from the thought, summoning up the image of Cavenal in her mind.

But erotic daydreams of George Cavenal eluded her as Merzella combed and arranged the faintly damp, naturally curling ringlets. Later, as Louise fought down impatience, Tina's quavering voice interrupted.

"Miss Louise"—the girl's eyes were round with fright— "I ain't never got used to the iron here. It ain't got no special place to heat an' it gets too hot—"

"What are you saying, Tina? For heaven's sake, don't ramble so stupidly!"

The girl held out the pink blouse. A large, brown-ringed hole was visible in the delicate material. "I—I just stopped a minute to get some biscuits out of the oven fer Feenie an'—" Tina's voice broke.

For a long moment, Louise stared silently at the ruined blouse. Then suddenly all her frustrations rose up. She got to her feet and turned on the girl.

"You little slut! You know that was my favorite riding waist, and you've ruined it! This, on top of cold water in my tub last night, makes *twice* you've been careless—unforgivably careless!"

Violence, always lurking under Louise's pretty manners, burst out. She strode to Tina, and slapped the slender black girl with all her strength. Tina dropped the blouse, putting her hands to her throbbing cheek.

Louise picked up the blouse, flinging it at Tina, her voice low and threatening. "One more careless mistake, Tina, and I'll punish you. It'll be worse than any whipping I ever gave you." Her smile became cruel. "I know you have eyes for Lord Cavenal's man, Abraham—and you can be sure nothing will come of it. *I'll see to that!* Now I give you fair warning. One more mistake, my girl, just—one—more."

Louise enjoyed the hour it took her and Ezekiel to canter to the Cavenals'. It had rained briefly the night before, and all the foliage, the rolling acres of cotton, and Three Points Lake had a fresh, crisp look about them, even though the June day was heating rapidly.

She arrived just in time for morning tea. Both the Cavenal ladies were cordial.

"Georgina and I have been busily planning the social we're going to have for you and Richard this weekend." Lady Marguerite smiled, passing pastries to Louise.

"Oh, Lady Marguerite," Louise replied, "I must tell you —Richard's gone off—and I don't know where to—or when he'll be back. Could we have the social later?"

"Dear me." Lady Marguerite was distressed. "You don't know where or why he's gone, my dear?"

Louise made a face. "It's that headstrong daughter of his! She took it on herself to run off in the dead of night without an escort. An old man named Watkins rode up to the house with Julien Regrett, and told him she's been captured, along with Mason Regrett, by those Bosquezes, and Richard flew into a tantrum. He's gone with Julien Regrett and some of their men to catch them, and bring them back."

"How dreadful!" Lady Marguerite and Georgina chorused. Then Lady Marguerite added, "But the Mexican soldiers do often kidnap citizens with wealthy families and hold them for ransom for months."

"That's Richard's cry. He's a perfect fool about that willful girl! There's no telling how long they'll be gone."

"No matter," Lady Marguerite said soothingly. "The social can be postponed. We'll have it one day toward the end of July. Everyone will be ready for a party by then!"

"Have some clotted cream on your scones," Georgina said, smiling, as she extended the bowl of cream with a spoon in it.

As Louise was finishing the first of her scones, George joined them. She looked up at the tall, fair man, impressed anew by his fascinating golden eyes.

She could scarcely control her impatience as the four of them finished a leisurely tea, and George offered to take her once more on a ride about the Cavenal acres.

As always, they went to the game shed on the Guadalupe River.

Later, as she and Ezekiel rode away, Louise hummed lightly to herself, savouring the memory of Cav's words spoken a mere hour earlier. *My darling, if only you weren't married, we could be together always.* She had asked him if he meant it, sure that he would mention marriage if only she were free, and he had smothered her mouth with kisses.

It was practically a proposal of marriage, she told herself. He surely meant they would be married. She knew it! Richard, his love for his brat Montrose, the cold Lady Abigail, none of them mattered! Faith had not mattered for a long time.

There was a soft, southerly afternoon breeze that cooled her as she alternately trotted and cantered the gelding. Trees on either side of the narrow road gave shade often enough to compensate for open spaces under a hot June sun, while birds made a chorus of music. At last, the tall redbrick house, the stables, and smaller cabins could be seen through the heavily leaved trees that surrounded the Daventry compound.

Richard, Julien, and Watkins, followed closely by Young Miguel and LeRoy, pounded down the dirt road without speaking. They had gone at least five miles before Richard spoke to Julien.

"It's damned strange your brother would be on the trace the same time as Monty."

Julien turned his tight dark face to him. "You can forget any idea they were together, Daventry. Mase was in a hurry, and on government business. The last person he'd ride with is Monty."

"Still pushing hard for annexation, eh? After nine years of rebuffs, you boys ought to give up."

"The Regretts aren't quitters, Daventry. You should know that by now. *We couldn't even be burned out!*"

"By God, I wouldn't be a party to burning any man's horses or stables! Are you accusing me again?"

"Not *again.* Once was enough."

"Now, you boys is a team here!" Watkins rode up beside them, short gray beard wagging. "It ain't goin' to help Miss Monty or Mase, if you two squabble 'fore we can ketch up to 'em."

"We'd better not talk politics then," Julien said darkly.

"Or throw unfounded accusations around," Richard added, his eyes steely.

"You calling me a liar?" Julien's temper flared.

"About that fire you are!" Richard shot back.

Watkins dropped back then, pushing his gelding between the two men. "Here! Here! I tell you, you boys ain't got no call to quarrel. Ain't you worrit 'nough 'bout Miss Monty an' your brother, Julien?" The wiry old man was genuinely distressed.

"Do not quarrel, señors," Young Miguel said placatingly from behind. "We know Señor Richard does not burn horses, and we know Señor Julien is a truthful man."

"And for your information, Watkins," Richard said sharply, "I intend to find my daughter. I'll kill *any* man who's harmed her."

"In which case, Mase can certainly go on to Washington-on-the-Brazos," Julien said flatly.

Richard was silent, but his hand strayed to the butt of the gun thrust in his belt.

It was fully ten in the morning when they reached the cutoff to the trace. "We better folly th' trace, 'cause they was on it when they come by my place," Watkins had said. Richard looked at the ground hopefully. Monty might have left a sign. Automatically, Daventry rode ahead, taking the lead.

Julien scowled, but fell in behind him as the five men strung out in single file along the narrow trace. Watkins brought up the rear, and LeRoy rode ahead of Watkins. The three men had tacitly made a joint effort to keep themselves between Richard and Julien. Now LeRoy nervously moved his horse forward, as he saw the distance between the two men narrowing.

He found no way to put himself between Daventry and Julien, for the trace was cut deeply and would permit horses single file only. An occasional branch had to be pushed aside, but the leafy ground beneath them looked well traveled.

They stopped beside a spring at two in the afternoon, to rest the horses and eat. Grass grew tall and thick in the patches of sunlight and their horses grazed as they rested. By three, the five were trotting swiftly down the trail once more.

They talked little, and a steady trot, alternating with a canter, found them well on the way to the Colorado River. Richard spoke to Julien for the first time since their angry exchange.

"Why was it necessary for your brother to ride to the capital? Wouldn't a letter have sufficed?" Richard's uneasiness over Monty's proximity to the man he so disliked had grown as the hours passed, especially when he recollected Louise's assertion that she had seen them kissing at the embassy in Washington. Had Louise's observation been completely true? He did not know.

Julien answered without hesitation. "There's no love lost between President Jones and General Sam. For some reason, Jones seems to suspect Houston's motives, and Mase didn't trust a letter that would have to be mailed from Victoria." His lips turned down sardonically. "You know how fine our mail service is, since we're an independent republic!"

"And with such fine men as Houston having been our president," Richard said derisively. "It's the way the republic's governed that's kept the mail from being delivered properly."

"And you think England could do a better job governing us?"

"That's false and you know it! I've never advocated England governing us. You know well enough I gave up my English citizenship when I became Texan."

"Mister Richard, we're comin' to Brushy Creek. Look!" LeRoy cut in quickly. "That means we ain't too far from Mister Watkins now."

They crossed two more creeks, and a tributary of the San Bernard River. At the latter, they stopped to let the horses rest and to refill their canteens. The day was hot now, and the sky was filling with great, darkening thunderheads, but there were no cooling rains in the bluish flat bottoms of these clouds.

By late afternoon, they reached the winding Colorado River. There had been little or no conversation between the men since the most recent sharp words between Julien and Richard. Even Young Miguel, who had tried briefly to converse with Watkins, was now silent. His young face was drawn and sad.

They followed the trace along the river as the sun lowered redly behind them. Then they saw the Watkins cabin through thick trees along the riverbanks. A lazy curl of white smoke was rising from the chimney. All five of the men were hungry again, and a current of edginess ran among them.

Daventry was still at the head of the short column. Eager to reach the cabin, his big, dun-colored animal broke into a gallop. The others followed, and Julien drew up beside him as the trace widened at the river. They forded the shallow crossing and stopped before the cabin.

Watkins shouted, "Ho, Nola gal!" and she appeared in the door. She did not smile but her black eyes shone as she wiped her hands on her floursack apron.

Daventry and Julien swung down from their mounts simultaneously.

"Ain't seen nothin' o' th' Bosquezes, have you, Nola gal?" Watkins asked as he dismounted with the others.

"Seen 'em come an' seen 'em go," Nola said succinctly. The men stiffened.

"You mean they come back today?" Watkins asked.

"They all come back. Miss Monty an' Mister Mase come first late last night, an' leave at dawn after buyin' some food an' supplies from me." Nola paused, and Richard frowned.

"Did they head back to my place?" Richard asked.

"No, they headin' fer Washin'ton-on-th'-Brazos, an' this mornin' ol' Felipe Bosquez an' Colonel Delgado come here from Buckeye, lookin' fer 'em. I tell 'em they go back home all right." Nola still did not smile, but her black eyes twinkled. "Miss Monty, she fuss big with Mister Mase—she want ter go home. But he got a letter off ol' Felipe that's heap important ter th' President, an' Mister Mase ain't got time ter take her home afore he get it ter 'em in Washin'ton-on-the-Brazos."

"Good God, woman," Daventry burst out as he stood beside his horse. "Are you telling me they escaped capture, and Regrett wouldn't take my daughter home?"

A shutter fell over Nola's eyes and she shrugged silently, as she looked at the dismounted men standing outside the cabin.

"That ain't no way ter talk ter her, Mister Daventry," Watkins reproached. "Lemme ask her what happened. Now honey," he began coaxingly, "how come Miss Monty an' Mase was loose an' runnin' from th' Bosquezes?"

"Mister Mase, he beat up ol' Felipe," she said sullenly. "An' Miss Monty shot Lorenz an' Mr. Mase shot Hernando. They come here fer food late last night."

"Honey, tell us agin about Felipe an' Colonel Delgado."

"They come thinkin' they'd ketch Miss Monty an' Mister Mase agin—but they give up when I told 'em they was nigh back home by then. So's they turned around an' went back ter frien's outside o' Buckeye. Ol' Felipe's brothers is there, nursin' theyselves."

"An' why didn't Mase take her home agin, Nola, honey?"

"I tol' you. He say he knock ol' Felipe out an' got a letter off 'im —an' it's got ter be took ter th' President as fast as he could git it there."

"What time'd they leave, Nola?"

" 'Bout dawn, I said. They're a long ways toward Washin'ton-on-the-Brazos by now."

"Goddamn that son of a bitch Regrett!" Daventry swore, flushing to the roots of his dark hair. All the men were around the front door now, where the heavyset Nola stood framed, her round bronze face impassive.

At Daventry's outburst, Julien's face paled, and his glance at Daventry was dark lightning in the late dusk, but he said nothing.

"Did Regrett force her on her horse? Did he use force to —to take her with him?" Daventry's white-hot eyes pinned Nola.

"No, he didn't," she said flatly, her brow as low as Daventry's. "She went along with him easy like when she seen he meant it—'bout the letter."

Watkins was observing Daventry with eyes that held no warmth. This man had his liquor imported from England and spurned Watkins's corn liquor. And Watkins was proud of his liquor.

"Wasn't Mase gonna take Miss Monty home after he delivered the letter, Nola, honey?"

" 'Course he was. That's why she went with him. Good thing she did"—Nola shot a surly glance at Daventry— " 'cause ol' Felipe would'a got her agin if she'd stayed here, or started back down th' trace alone."

"By God, Regrett should have taken her home!" Daventry's voice rose. "I'd rather the Mexicans have her than know she's on the road with that man alone."

"What the hell do you mean, Daventry?" Julien's jaw tightened and a muscle along it quivered.

"I mean just what I said. She's a mere child—a perfect

target for that hot-blooded bounder. I'll kill him when I catch them!"

Julien uncoiled like a spring, his face white with rage. Young Miguel's eyes went swiftly back and forth between the two.

"You're accusing my brother of forcing Monty to yield to his attentions—of him *taking* her?"

"Damn right I am—"

"You're a low-down barn burner, Daventry," Julien said clearly. "My brother is as honorable as any man that lives. He'd never force your daughter to do anything she didn't *want* to do!"

"You're implying my daughter would *let* him take her?" Daventry's eyes grew colder, his mouth tight. "That's a lie! You two bloody Frenchmen are old hands at seduction, and I've heard stories—you don't confine it to Rebecca's house in Victoria!"

Color rushed back into Julien's face under the heavy tan, and his black eyes filled with fury. He waited no longer. With a swift, practiced movement, one of the pistols was out of his belt and leveled at Daventry.

Young Miguel was swifter, as he flung himself in front of Daventry. "No, no, Señor Julien—" His words were cut off by the roar of Julien's pistol, and the shot struck home over Miguel's heart. The boy sank at Richard's feet as Julien pulled the second pistol from his belt.

But Richard had drawn his own, and their shots rang out simultaneously. Julien, struck in the heart, as Miguel had been, staggered, dropping both pistols to the ground. Richard reeled back as he took Julien's second shot in his shoulder.

For an instant, the tableau was frozen in the hot, still twilight, until Julien slowly collapsed, blood staining the blue shirt over his left breast. Richard moved at last, his hand going to his left shoulder where blood was welling rapidly.

Slowly he sank to his knees, and slipped his right arm under Miguel's head, raising it slightly. The boy's breath was ragged, his eyes fastened on his friend since childhood.

"Señor—Señor Richard—" His voice was breathy and his eyes imploring. "Señor Richard. The Señora—I'm so sorry —forgive me—" A cough cut his words off, and a bloody froth appeared at the corner of his mouth. A shudder passed through him. Richard could feel it as he registered Young Miguel's words.

He looked across at Julien, cradled in Watkins's arms. The old man was shouting something at Nola, but all Richard could hear was *Señor Richard. The Señora—I'm so sorry— forgive me*—and Carlos's echoed corollary, *Is all the Señora's fault*—

Adultery with the young boy. Richard was certain now. He felt his own heart pumping out his blood in warm, aching spurts. Miguel's eyes were on Richard still, but they no longer saw him.

A slow, sick realization came to Richard that the boy was dead. Julien across from them was dead. And all because of him. Yet from the beginning it had been inevitable. There was nothing he could have done to stop it.

LeRoy was bending over him, trying to pull him upright by his unwounded arm.

"Mister Richard—your shoulder looks bad!" The black man reached a cautious hand to Richard's bleeding left shoulder, his eyes showing his distress at the sight of the widening red stain on the white shirt.

Watkins rose from Julien's side as Nola rushed back out of the cabin, one hand filled with bandages, a bowl of water in the other.

"Ain't no use, Nola, honey. He's gone." He looked across at Daventry, bright old eyes hostile now. "Well—you done it, Mister Daventry," he said heavily. "You killed Mase Regrett's brother an' I reckon you *will* have to kill Mase when you find him now."

"Julien was going to kill me. And he killed Young Miguel," Richard said coldly.

"Reckon you brung it on, Mister Daventry. Mase'll figure it that way."

"Cheer up, Watkins," Richard said ironically, feeling weakness seep through him and a blurring of his eyes. Blood was pumping with heavier gushes from his left shoulder now. He could feel it running in a hot stream down his arm. "Julien may have killed me after all."

A slow wave of blackness, like the descending night about them, enveloped him, and despite LeRoy's grasping hands, he slid to the ground.

Chapter 20

Watkins's cabin on the trace was miles behind Regrett and Monty as evening drew on. Regrett picked their way carefully through the trees in a northerly direction. He knew they were not far from the river the Spanish had romantically named River of the Arms of God, shortened to the Brazos, by both Mexican and Texan alike.

Monty was more saddle-weary than she had ever been in her life. Still she refused to voice a complaint, though she'd had no sleep the last twenty-four hours. Unless Mase planned to travel all night again, he was going to have to stop soon and make camp. Their noon meal had been scant and unsatisfactory.

Monty sent him a rebellious glance. She envied the ease with which he sat his saddle. *Mason Regrett's a rough customer, but he knows his horses and, by God, the man knows how to ride them.* Richard Daventry had said that to his daughter years ago, and the words came back to her now as she observed her companion. She rode beside and a little behind him, and their journey thus far had been a remarkably silent one. Even their brief capture by the Bosquezes, and subsequent escape together, had not broken down the barrier between them.

Suddenly both horses threw up their heads, and a low whicker came from Coffee.

"What is it?" Monty asked, alarmed.

"The horses smell water. We're finally nearing the Brazos."

"Do you plan to camp for the night there?" she asked tiredly.

Regrett shot her a swift glance. She looked ready to drop in the saddle. Frustration made him short with her.

"Yes." He wanted to take her into his arms, comfort her and make love to her, but he had sworn she would be safe from any overtures by him. Now that she was his responsibility—no matter how reluctant each of them was about it —his vow took on iron meaning.

Regrett reflected silently on the hostility between the brothers and Richard Daventry. But that wasn't the only reason why he couldn't make love to Monty as he had beside Three Points Lake.

No, Regrett reflected, it was because he *respected* her. She was responsible for that herself. He had realized it, when she begged for protection in the Regrett stables that day. He winced, remembering.

And the feeling went deeper than respect, but he was not prepared to face that. In fact, when it attempted to surface in his mind, it made him angry, not only with himself, but with Monty. Let her be tired, damn it! She had gotten herself into this scrape—and he would get her out of it, but not before he delivered the Hays dispatch.

Now the horses had quickened their pace. The cooling sound of rushing water could be heard over the murmuring sounds of the forest, and the ever-present burring of cicadas. Monty strained to see through the trees. As the horses topped a little rise, she glimpsed the Brazos, wide and filled with swirling currents, full to its brushy banks. Spring rains had been plentiful this year, and the river was swollen with them.

"You'll be glad to know we don't have to cross it. Washington is on the west side," Regrett told her.

She was too tired to answer.

"We'll stop and make camp here." He reined Coffee to a halt and dismounted. "Come on," he added impatiently, "get down and I'll take them both to the river for a drink."

Monty looked at him. She wasn't sure she could get off Warlock without falling. Pride held her stiffly in the saddle.

Regrett recognized her fatigue in the dimming light, and looping Coffee's reins over a low, brushy tree limb, came to her without a word. He reached his arms up, and she leaned into them. For a brief, blessed moment, she felt his strength, the hardness of his long body as he lifted her to the ground. Her knees buckled, and he caught her against him before she was able to straighten.

"Sit down," he said gruffly, releasing her slowly. "Rest while I take them down to the river."

She took off her dusty felt hat, and sat down gratefully, leaning back against a rough oak trunk. It was some time before he returned, and by then, a little strength had flowed into her. She became aware of how dust-grimed and gritty she was. Sweaty, too, she thought, wrinkling her nose. She had worn these same clothes for two days, and suddenly she was vastly uncomfortable.

She was still sitting there when he finished hobbling the horses and readying the campsite.

"I need a bath and a change of clothes," she said wearily, shifting her long slender legs, and gingerly touching her raw wrists.

"There's a rock off the bank where I watered the horses that breaks the current some." He looked at her sharply. "Think you're up to bathing and washing your clothes without being swept away?"

"Certainly!"

"I don't know," he muttered, tossing her roll of clothing to her. "Maybe you ought to wait until morning—after you've had some rest."

"I'll rest a lot better after a bath."

"I'll have to stand watch." He handed her his bar of rough soap.

"You can't do that," she said flatly. "I won't have you watching me undress—and bathe."

"I won't watch you undress," he retorted. "I'll stand by while you're in the water. I can't take the chance of your drowning."

"I'm not *that* tired!"

"This is ridiculous, Monty." His laugh was explosive. "We've seen each other naked before—and more than once."

She clutched her clothing and soap to her breast. "You'll never see me naked again! I'll give up bathing before I let you see me do it!"

He shrugged. "The sun's about to set. If you don't take your bath while there's still daylight, I won't let you take one."

She turned, looking westward at the blood-colored sunset, and said, "You stay right here then, Mason Regrett!"

He knew she could swim like a fish, having learned in Three Points Lake, but he also knew the currents in the flooding Brazos were treacherous. He waited until she was out of sight, then put down his armload of firewood and followed her.

Monty's head could be seen above the outcropping rock where he had watered the horses. There was a small crescent of wet sand around it.

In another moment he saw the splash, then she appeared a little beyond the rock, her rounded, white shoulders visible above the water. It must be shallower there than he realized. He was relieved, and made a mental note of it for his own bath later.

He saw she had loosed her long, heavy braids and begun soaping her head first, scrubbing the lathered hair vigorously. For a long, heart-stopping moment, she disappeared beneath clear green water over which evening shadows were lengthening.

Just as he was about to rip off his boots and run forward, she came up dripping, only to disappear from view again behind the rock and then reappear, her hands full of her soiled clothing.

He watched patiently while she scrubbed herself and her clothes. He did not move until he saw her shoulders and head above the rock, over which she flung her washed garments. He could tell by the movements of her head and shoulders that she was dressing.

He was totally unprepared for the sudden impact of his longing to see her bare body, the round, firm little buttocks, the challenging upthrust bosoms, and the kissable little hollow at the base of her throat. He realized as he began to sweat that he had forgotten none of those passionately sweet moments they had shared by the lake. His temper rose with frustration, as he realized desire and fury are two sides of the same coin.

Rising abruptly, he made his way silently back to the campsite. It was going to be hell, having her so near, and being unable to assuage his mounting thirst for her.

His terrible desire to seize her damp cool body, strip it bare, and cover it with kisses was still on him, when she walked up where he was laying limbs ready for the fire.

"I thought you'd have the fire going by now!" she accused. She was clad in a clean denim shirt and dark blue pants. She carried her washed clothing in one hand, and her fine leather boots in the other. Only her feet were bare.

"I watched you in the river," he said, his voice muffled with rage at himself.

"Damn you!" she said with equal rage.

"Don't worry," he replied grimly. "I didn't see anything but your head, you little prude."

"Don't call me names!" She flung her clean, wet clothes over a nearby low-hanging limb.

"They won't dry there by morning."

"Then just where should I put them?"

"On sticks I'll put around the fire as soon as I get it going." He blew on the spark as he struck flint. Dried leaves and twigs caught, and it flared up.

"I hope we'll have something more than coffee and bread tonight. There are those eggs and cornmeal—and bacon Nola Watkins gave us," she said.

"Gave? I'm going to pay for them."

"Pardon me! That you *bought!* Can't we take time to fix them?"

He didn't answer, and Monty retreated into angry silence.

Later, Regrett mixed cornmeal, eggs, and water, making corncakes in a small tin bowl. As he sliced bacon from the side Nola had provided, Monty fixed coffee, and in a short time they ate together hungrily.

Monty's temper improved slightly as her hunger abated. When they finished, he picked up the utensils.

"I'll go to the river and wash them up," he told her. "And I'm going to take a quick bath too, so don't look for me to return in a hurry." He kicked his bedroll toward her, adding, "You can sleep on that. I'll use the extra blanket." He caught up his clean clothes along with the stacked utensils and started to leave.

"Don't you think I should watch *you?* We know the current's strong." The question was heavy with sarcasm.

"I'd enjoy that." His smile was malicious. Then, as she quickly turned away, he instructed, "Keep the fire going,

Monty. Bobcats and wolves thrive along with deer in Brazos country."

She had the fire blazing brightly when he returned, and he hung his own washed garments beside hers on the sticks he had placed at intervals close to the heat. She watched him without comment.

"Good night," he said, and lay down with his back to her, putting his weapons near to hand.

Though he was less than three feet away, silence between them stretched the distance achingly. Abruptly, Monty had to fight tears as she turned her back to his.

They were on the trail once more after a predawn breakfast. Just before they stopped at noon, Regrett pulled his worn felt hat a little lower, and spoke to her for the first time in over an hour.

"This time tomorrow, we ought to be in Washington-on-the-Brazos."

"Is it a big town?" she asked, anxious to keep him talking. He had not even glanced at her since he inquired about her wrists shortly before breakfast.

"Not too big. About four or five hundred people would be a good guess. It's grown some in the last nine years."

"Doesn't sound like a good place to keep as the capital—"

"I know your father wants it moved to Austin again," he said, favoring her with a cynical smile. "Personally, I think it's one of the few things he's right about."

"Why don't you tell him so?" she challenged. "You two might get along better if you talked about what you agree on, instead of your differences."

"The one big difference between us makes that impossible." He shrugged, and pulled the reins on Coffee. "We'll stop now. The horses need water and rest."

* * *

The June sun bore down hotly upon them as they neared
the capital of Texas. When the town came into sight, Monty
understood fully the reason why her father and Regrett
wanted the capital moved back to Austin. Its isolation from
other settlements and the roughness of the terrain made it a
poor capital for the republic. Even Harrisburg, the city that
now bore the name of Houston, would be better.

In a brief nine years, many changes had taken place in
Washington-on-the-Brazos. Since 1836, it had grown from a
small, struggling settlement of some eighteen log cabins to a
sprawling little city seething with the excitement of its own
importance.

Located on the west bank of the Brazos River, the town
was in a grove of post oaks, trees that thrived all over south
Texas. The houses and cabins were on a bluff, out of sight of
the river from which the town drew part of its name.

The noise assaulted Monty's ears long before the trail met
dusty Ferry Street, which cut through the heart of town. It
astonished her.

"It's so noisy!" She spoke involuntarily.

"That's mostly from the saloons and gambling houses.
They're open day and night."

"I'm surprised they'd allow such places in the capital,"
Monty said primly.

Regrett burst into laughter. "They allow anything you can
name and can pay for, Monty. There are promoters, gam-
blers, thieves—worse, politicians, here in the capital—anyone with an axe to grind."

As they rode down Ferry Street, Monty looked at signs
proclaiming Lawyer—All Claims, and three signs that read
Doctor in Practice. A land office and three general stores
could be seen on Austin Street. Several dogs were sleeping
in drowsy peacefulness on this street, despite the rowdiness
of saloons and gambling houses beyond them.

On the far side of Austin Street, half a dozen chickens pecked determinedly at the ground around two large log houses. Men were everywhere, either lounging outside the various stores and saloons, or coming from them. Some wore the dusty buckskin of plainsmen and trappers, some, black broadcloth that spoke of more civilized occupations. Others were clad in a mixture of both.

Monty's eye was caught by two women coming from one of the general stores on Austin. Their cheeks were unnaturally pink, their lips red, and they were laughing at the men they passed.

She could hear coarse approval from admiring males. "Hey! How about later, Irene?" and, "You're a beauty, Nan!"

The women responded with broader smiles, swaying their full and gaily printed skirts provocatively, as they turned and went into a structure that looked fairly new. White paint on the milled lumber was not weathered.

"What is that place—where those ladies went?" she asked Regrett.

"They aren't exactly what Miss Abby would call 'ladies,' and you don't need to know what kind of house that is."

Monty looked back down the road at it, fascinated. *Rebecca's house in Victoria.* She and Feenie had talked about it, and she had overheard her father and Cav laughingly refer to it years ago. Now instinct told her this house must be like Rebecca's. She looked back at it as long as she could see it.

"We'll go to Independence Hall and the President's office," Regrett told her.

Monty kicked her booted heels against Warlock's sides. She had no desire to remain alone in this maelstrom of humanity.

"Where's Independence Hall?" she asked.

"On Main Street, naturally. It's that old log barracks down yonder."

Monty looked at the weather-beaten structure. It was not very impressive. There was a much smaller, newer structure beside it. But both buildings boasted windows that had neither curtains nor glass in them. Men were coming and going. Beside the door of the smaller building, a man sat whittling in a chair.

"That's the new building they put up for the President's office." Regrett pointed to the smaller structure. "Come on," he urged impatiently.

They drew up before the man in the chair. A large plug of tobacco bulged in his left cheek, and his hat was pulled low against the brilliant noon sun.

"Wait for me here, Monty. I won't be long."

Then, "I want to see the President," Regrett said to the man.

"I guess you're another one of them complainin' about th' treaty." He spat, and put his knife and the piece of wood on the window frame beside his chair. "Gimme your name."

"Mason Regrett."

"I'll tell him you're here. Guess you got another petition against th' treaty with Mexico."

Regrett did not correct him as he went through the open door. Voices could be heard through the uncurtained windows.

The man came back. "Go on in," he said, resuming his seat. "There's two more of 'em in there now."

Regrett stepped up to the door and entered. The one room contained a battered but sturdy desk, and Anson Jones sat behind it. He lifted dark, sunken eyes to Regrett. The desk was littered with papers. Two men occupied two of the six cowhide and oak chairs in the room. One had a sheaf of papers in his hand. Both men wore blue cotton shirts, sleeves rolled to the elbow.

"I'm Mason Regrett, President Jones."

Jones's ringed eyes narrowed. "I remember you, Regrett. Houston brought you to a meeting here two years ago." He reached across the desk to shake Regrett's hand.

"I didn't know if you'd remember."

"I never forget a face."

"A handy talent," Regrett replied laconically. "I have a dispatch here for you from Jack Hays of the Texas Rangers in Bexar. I took it off Felipe Bosquez three nights ago when I and another prisoner escaped from him." He put the flat leather case containing the dispatch on the desk.

Jones took out the letter, scanning it swiftly.

"By God! Hays has been to Fort Jessup in Louisiana and conferred with General Zachary Taylor! He says American troops are already on their way to Texas, and Hays is organizing a regiment of Texans to join him!" Jones's eyes shone with astonishment and pleasure. The two seated men, who had been silent, exploded in oaths of pleasure.

"Doesn't this conflict with the peace treaty you signed with Mexico, which was sponsored by the British?" Mase's smile was wintry. Jones looked at him from under his brows.

"That treaty's been rejected by the Legislature," he said tersely. "Why were you a prisoner of Bosquez?" The two men behind him were talking to each other in low, excited voices.

Regrett shrugged. "He captured me and my neighbor's daughter on the old Indian trace. I was on my way here with messages for General Houston. She was on her way to visit friends. Bosquez was taking us to Matagorda to ship out for Vera Cruz—from there to Mexico City, where we'd be held for ransom or exchange."

"What about the courier Bosquez took this dispatch from?"

"Bosquez said he killed him. In self-defense." Regrett's lips turned down cynically.

"That's a hell of a lie, I'll wager," Jones muttered. "I appreciate this, Regrett. It'll alter our plans—knowing American troops, and how many, are on the way. I'm calling a convention to vote on joining the Union and to write our constitution—July fourth."

"Here?" Regrett asked alertly.

"No, Austin. We're moving the capital to Austin again."

"Good! That's a meeting I don't want to miss! Where is General Houston?"

Jones's eyes grew cold. "Haven't you heard? Sam Houston and his family have gone to Tennessee to see Andrew Jackson. The Old Chief is dying."

"Damn!" The oath escaped Regrett. "I'm sorry to hear that!"

"You can make your reports to me."

"Bosquez destroyed my reports. They were summaries of what happened in Washington City last winter and spring, when I was there making a speech for annexation."

"Then you need not worry any further," Jones said, lifting his shoulders and letting them fall. "Now that the Americans have voted to take us in, our efforts must be directed toward getting the most advantageous terms for our entry into the Union."

"I'm sure you'll see to that, Mr. President," Regrett said blandly.

Surprisingly, two spots of color appeared in Jones's hollow cheeks. "I will, despite what some may think," he said firmly, his eyes going to the two men who were now observing Regrett and Jones silently. "These gentlemen are from the Nacogdoches area, and they've brought petitions against the peace treaty. I've been able to tell them it's already rejected and annexation will be approved. What remains are the conditions offered us and what we choose to accept. Then a constitution can be framed."

"And we're mighty glad of it," the bearded man put in

quickly, "but gladder to hear the message you brought, Regrett."

"Actually," Jones said, his eyes suddenly veiled and secretive, "that treaty the British Captain Elliot brought was nothing more than another maneuver of mine to solidify the Texas desire to enter the Union. I've been working for statehood a long time—and at last, my efforts have borne fruit."

Regrett hid his surprise. "Glad of it," he said noncommittally. There was something about Anson Jones that made Regrett uneasy. Not just his claiming credit for the annexation, which Sam Houston, with Andrew Jackson's help, had brought to this moment of fruition. But something else made Regrett distrust him.

"Mr. President, I must get my neighbor's daughter back to her home. I didn't take time to do that, considering the importance of getting this letter to you."

"You were right to bring it first. I'll tell the news to those legislators who are not in town. They'll be elated—as I am. I've worked so long for statehood, and God knows how intransigent the Mexican government has been. I know war's inevitable after annexation. It's a great satisfaction now to know the United States Army, under General Taylor, is already coming to our aid." Once more he reached across the desk and shook hands with Regrett.

As he went out, Regrett replaced his hat and nodded to the man who sat beside the door. What was there about Anson Jones, he reflected, that made him uncomfortable? His eyes? A sense of doom pervaded the man. Regrett shook his head. He had accomplished what had driven him to Washington-on-the-Brazos, but he was saddened by the news that Old Hickory, Andrew Jackson, the man who had so inspired Texas, as well as the United States, was about to die.

Monty was still astride Warlock. She waited with Coffee under the shade of a scrubby post oak.

"Well," he said to her, "the letter is where it can do the most good. We can leave now. But I've credit in this town. I want to go to Wharton's Emporium and buy supplies for the ride home. I need another bedroll and we need food. Wharton's is on Austin Street, where most of the saloons are—stick close to me."

As they turned into Austin Street, Monty remarked, "I wonder what all those men gambling and drinking use for money?" They rode past two saloons. The places were all flourishing, and people they saw looked at them without curiosity. Newcomers to Washington-on-the-Brazos were no novelty.

"Gold," Regrett answered briefly, "and some U.S. green-backs. Texas currency's been worth little or nothing—too long. Another good argument for joining the Union—a sta-bilized currency."

It was nearly four in the afternoon when Regrett and Monty left the town behind them. Wharton and Regrett had talked at length about the convention Anson Jones had called for three weeks hence in Austin, on July fourth.

Now, as the two big horses cantered along the narrow trail beside the Brazos River, Monty spoke tentatively.

"I think my father would like to attend that meeting in Austin."

"What for?" Regrett asked roughly. "He won't have any friends there."

"You smart aleck! Pa knows Anson Jones."

"And Jones is good company for him."

"Just because you don't like Jones!"

"Houston got him elected. And now he hasn't any use for Houston."

"He's not the only one who hasn't any use for Sam Hous-ton."

"I know that. The general has a few enemies, and if a

man is known by the enemies he makes, as well as by his friends, all of them do him credit."

"You are undoubtedly the most arrogant man I ever knew!"

"That's not saying much. How many men do you know?"

Monty flushed angrily, subsiding into silence. She sat Warlock stiffly, and refused to meet Regrett's eyes. Silently she cursed him for the fire he set burning in her. She bit her lip on angry words that rose in her, and they rode in silence for two hours, until suddenly Coffee blew through his nose with an unexpectedly sharp snort.

Instantly Regrett knew they were being followed. Coffee's reaction had always been thus when Indians approached. Coffee could smell an Indian as well as he could smell water, or sense an approaching storm. Many Indians in this part of the country were friendly, but there was always the chance that some of the fiercer tribes had ventured this far south. Regrett said nothing to Monty about it.

They'd have to stop for the night soon, he reflected. He must find a place that offered as much protection as possible. There would be no sleep for him tonight. He admitted to himself that Monty was a good traveling companion. She had not once complained about the pace he set, nor the hours they rode. And certainly he couldn't fault her for the heat that rose in him each time he looked at her.

"What's the matter with Coffee?" she asked finally, as the big stallion snorted for the third time, shaking his head and mane.

"He's tired and thirsty," Regrett said evasively. "We'll stop soon and make camp by the river."

They entered a tall stand of pines a half hour later, and he reined Coffee to the right, so they would be nearer to the river. The trail had long ago dwindled to nothing, and they were merely following the course of the Brazos.

They trotted no more than a mile along the river before

Regrett pulled up on a bluff. There were several boulders, massive rocks worn smooth by centuries of wind and rain, that circled one side of a flat, grassy spot. The descent to the river on the other side was almost precipitous.

"We'll make camp for the night here, Monty."

In response she slipped from her saddle, took her roll of clothing and the new bedroll he had bought for her at Wharton's.

"I'll unsaddle the horses," he said curtly as she reached under Warlock's belly for the cinch. "You can lay the fire ready."

Later, as they finished up jerky and dried fruit with a second cup of coffee, she looked at him levelly. "How many days before I reach home?"

He gazed at the horses, grazing on a thick crop of grama grass that grew just beyond the pines.

"About three, if we aren't interrupted." His eyes went to the final strip of red sky that could be seen from the west. He knew the Indians were just beyond the trees, waiting for dark. Coffee kept raising his head, looking to the west.

"And what could interrupt us?"

"I might break a leg." He smiled at her.

"Or I might. Why do you and Coffee keep looking at those pines behind us?"

"Just curious."

"I think you're lying. Some*thing* or some*one* is following us."

Chapter 21

When Richard Daventry regained consciousness, he looked over into LeRoy's anxious eyes where he sat in one of Watkins's handmade chairs. An oil lamp burned on the rough square table in the room.

"How long have I—what time is it, LeRoy?"

"Nigh onto mornin', Mister Richard. You been out nigh all night.

"How bad is my wound?"

Watkins came to the bed and looked down at him sourly. "You took Julien's shot in your left shoulder. Nola an' me got the bullet out, but you lost a powerful lot of blood afore Nola could bandage you tight enough."

That would account for his head feeling light and the extreme weakness in his limbs.

"Thanks, Watkins," he said dryly, lifting his head slightly, to see his chest and shoulder were tightly bound. His left arm was looped up in a sling, his shirt and breeches were off, and a rough unbleached-muslin sheet covered him to the waist.

Nola came to the bed, and motioned the two men away.

"You take some soup now, Mister Daventry. You lose plenty blood. You get yer strength back with this. I put potion I make from special herbs on yer shoulder—mus' be change twice a day. I show LeRoy how. But you stay here so I see blood stop afore you ride. Now eat."

Daventry took the broth Nola spooned him. Watkins and LeRoy sat to one side observing. The two were drinking coffee, and Watkins had lit a stubby black cigar. After a moment, Daventry spoke.

"What have you done with Young Miguel and Julien?"

"Wrapped 'em in tarpaulins an' buried 'em in the back section of my land, beyond th' cornfields," Watkins said tersely. "Mase is goin' ter be fightin' mad when—"

"But we couldn't take 'em home, Mister Watkins," LeRoy cut in. "It's June—so hot—an' you know they'd—"

"Sure, I know," Watkins interrupted. "But Mase Regrett set great store by his brother. He's like to come gunnin' fer you, Mister Daventry."

"I'll be ready for him," Richard said grimly, swallowing the hot broth Nola spooned up. "It was all so useless . . ." He paused, then groaned. "God, I hate to face Dorita and Big Miguel without their son." Then with more strength in his voice, he said, "Julien meant to kill me, Watkins, and you know it. If it hadn't been for Young Miguel, he would have!"

"You pervoked him," Watkins said grudgingly. "An' it ain't right. Them two youngsters dyin'."

"Julien Regrett was a hotheaded fool! I didn't *want* to kill him—and I'd have given my life to save Young Miguel."

"I know," Watkins said glumly. "An' I'll swear to it that Julien drew first, if I have to. An' I guess I'll have to—to Mase when he comes to fetch his brother's body home, an' his horses."

"You mean he'll come take Julien's body back to his ranch?" Daventry was incredulous. Nola held the spoon inexorably to his mouth and he gulped it angrily.

"You don't know how th' Regrett brothers was by each

other. They was all that was left of their family." Watkins's sharp old eyes were unfriendly.

"I'm sorry about that. If I could've winged him—"

"I know that," was the heavy reply. "But it ain't goin' to make no difference to Mase."

"I'll tell him Julien aimed to kill you, Mister Richard," LeRoy said, frowning at Watkins. "Ain't no man worth his salt gonna stand by and let hisself get kilt."

"We ought to go home now," Richard said shortly, finishing the broth and feeling some strength in his muscles. He raised himself on an elbow.

"No, you rest tonight, an' if blood stop, you start tomorrow afternoon. If it not stop, you stay another day." Nola shrugged as she moved away with the empty bowl.

Daventry lay back down. He was dizzy from the slight exertion. "Goddamn," he swore quietly. "I can't go looking for Monty now—and who knows what will happen to her with . . . Regrett." He turned his crisp dark head to one side in silent despair.

"Mister Mase knows Monty from a long time back, Mister Richard," LeRoy said quietly, leaning over him. "He ain' goin' to let nothin' hurt her. You gotta believe that, 'cause you done had a narrow 'scape an' we got to get you back home where—where Miss Abby can tend you."

After three long, tedious days on the trace with frequent stops along the way, Richard Daventry and LeRoy Beane were in sight of the Daventry house. During their frequent stops, LeRoy had carefully bathed and reapplied Nola's potions to Richard's shoulder. And there had been times when the pain was so intense, and his strength so weakened, that Richard feared he might not make it home.

His remorse over killing Julien was deep and bitter. He felt himself to blame for Young Miguel's death as well. He dreaded having to tell Big Miguel and Dorita their eldest son had lost his life saving Richard's own. He had nearly been killed by Julien even so, because of the younger Regrett's hatred of him, and this knowledge now stiffened Richard's spine. He would survive, and when Mase Regrett brought Monty home—and he *must* bring her home eventually— Richard would keep his gun handy, and face him as he had faced his brother.

It was late afternoon when they reached the house. LeRoy dismounted and helped Richard slide from his horse. His legs almost refused to support him, and he leaned heavily on LeRoy as they mounted the granite steps to the big red-brick house.

Abby appeared in the doorway almost immediately. "I thought I heard riders coming—" She broke off at the sight of her only son leaning in LeRoy's long arms. "Oh, dear God! Your shoulder and arm— Oh, Richard! What has happened?"

"I'll tell you everything, Abby, but I want LeRoy to get me upstairs before he sees to our horses."

"Yes, yes!" As she hurried ahead of them, she asked fearfully, "Where is Monty?"

"I said I'd tell you everything—" Richard began wearily.

"I know, I know," Abby cut in distractedly as they reached the top of the stairs. "I'll wait—"

Once in Richard's and Louise's large bedroom, she hastened to turn down the spread and top sheet of the big four-poster bed. As LeRoy and Abby helped him back upon the pillows, he looked at the worried black man.

"Thanks for everything you've done for me, LeRoy. I'll see your kindness is repaid."

"Ain't no more'n you'd have done for me, Mister Richard," LeRoy told him. "Reckon I'll tend to Nate an' ol' Beau —see they're rubbed down an' fed." Then with a look of deep sympathy, he offered, "Want me to tell Dorita an' Big Miguel how it happened?"

"When they see you without him—you'll have to. But tell them to come up here and see me. I'll explain it—or I'll try to explain how brave their son was, and—the sacrifice he—made for me."

As LeRoy disappeared into the hall, Richard looked up at his mother. He did not try to hide the anguish he felt as he began to tell her what had happened.

As he talked, Faith drew up silently in the doorway. Behind her, Feenie and Josey appeared.

"And there was nothing I could do then—but fire back at him," Richard concluded, his voice thick with sorrow.

Abby saw pain etched on his face, and he sighed deeply as she helped him remove his bloodstained shirt. She had never seen her son wounded or sick in his life. For all of his thirty-six years, he had been well and strong. Even the childhood diseases had passed him by, and he had grown tall and handsome. Now her heart ached with pity, for his face was drawn, and he appeared thinner.

He looked at the women standing in the open doorway. "You heard most of it," he said to them as the trio entered his room slowly.

"It wasn't your fault, Richard," Faith said swiftly. Her face was white beneath the golden tan and her hazel eyes were enormous. Her usual timidity was lost in the rush of relief that came with seeing him.

"Thanks for your vote of confidence, Faith," he said with a faint smile.

"Would you like me to fetch you a cup a' hot coffee, Mister Richard?" Feenie asked.

"I would. And Josey, you can bring the brandy, if you will."

The two disappeared into the hall, and Faith came to stand near the bed. "I know something of nursing," she said, timidity once more in her soft voice. "I—Louise arranged for me to work in the Sisters of Mercy Hospital in

Charleston last year when I—when our income was so low."

"By the way, where is my wife?" Richard interrupted.

Abby evaded his eyes. "She and Ezekiel rode over to the Cavenals' about ten-thirty this morning."

"My God! That's over six hours ago!"

"She's done it every day since you left," Abby said impersonally. "She always returns looking fit and happy. She says she stays for tea with Marguerite and Gina."

Richard's eyes flattened. "I've learned more about my wife in the few weeks since I returned, than I did during all our time together in Washington."

Abby did not reply, and Faith would not meet his eyes.

Feenie and Josey entered, bearing steaming coffee and brandy on a tray. Richard was propped up on pillows as they served him. With his right hand, he poured a generous dollop of brandy into the coffee, handing the decanter back to Josey.

He sipped the liquid, and his eyes clung to Faith.

"Faith," he said gently, "I'll have need of your nursing, though my mother is good at it as well. Between the two of you, I should recover immediately."

Faith's cheeks grew pink with pleasure, and she said haltingly, "I—I owe you all so much for allowing me to be part of your family, I can never repay you."

"Nola did a very good job on you, Richard." Abby was determinedly cheerful. "We must continue her successful prescription." She added, thoughtfully, "I expect Louise will be . . . devastated to find you wounded when she returns this afternoon. You'll have a bevy of nurses with the three of us."

Richard set his empty cup down on the table by his bed and lay back on the pillows.

"I can wait," he said.

Abby looked at her son sharply. Was he beginning to

realize what kind of woman he had married? Her heart was heavy with worry and foreboding. Already disaster had struck, for here was her son, dangerously wounded. And where was her beloved granddaughter? Could Mase protect her? Infection might cost Richard his life yet—and what was endangering Monty's? She desperately turned the thoughts away.

As for Richard, he was remembering his parting from Louise, when he had left to find Monty nearly a week ago. She had shown no more concern than if a pet gelding had strayed, and she had implied the fault was all Monty's. Her greatest sorrow was that the Cavenals' planned social would have to be put off.

"Shall I get the fresh cloths and soap and water to change his bandages now, Miss Abby?" Faith asked, as Feenie and Josey left the room.

"Yes—and I'll get my bag of emollients to dress the wound. I notice it's still bleeding through the bandage, Richard."

"That started again on the way home, Abby. Nola had succeeded in stopping it before I left—I had hoped it was sufficiently healed to ride."

A light, hurrying footstep came to them from the stairs and then the hall. Faith turned swiftly to leave, remarking in a low voice, "I'll be back with fresh bandages later, Miss Abby."

Louise swept into the room carrying her riding hat and jacket. She was radiant, and especially beautiful in her slight disarray.

"Richard darling!" she cried, coming to the bed and kissing his lips warmly. "What's all this about you being shot by Julien Regrett?"

Abby slipped past her, and Louise did not bother to acknowledge her as she spoke again to her silent and sharply observant husband.

"What in heaven's name did you do—to provoke him into shooting you? Is it a bad wound? Dear me! So much blood! So he and Young Miguel were killed. What a terrible thing to happen!"

She dropped her hat and jacket on the bed, and posed herself seductively on the chair Abby had left. Her hair was becomingly tossed as if she had ridden her horse at a fast clip.

"Where have you been, Louise?"

Her mind raced. She had hated to kiss her husband so soon after another glorious day in George Cavenal's arms. Further, she was repelled by the sight of blood on his bandaged shoulder.

"Just taking tea with Lady Marguerite and Gina—and riding. With Ezekiel, of course."

Slowly, she began to unbutton the silky shirtwaist covering her breasts. She knew well enough how to stir a man—even a man as distastefully wounded as Richard, she told herself, and a smile tipped the corners of her red lips. No, she wasn't ready to dispense with Richard Daventry yet. She must have Cavenal's proposal before giving up the safety and respectability that being Mrs. Richard Daventry afforded.

"It's so warm in here, darling." She rose and removed her garment. "And I've found the most beautiful place. You must ride there with me when you're well again. It's a little tributary of the Guadalupe River that runs near the Cavenals'. The willows grow so thickly there, and the breeze is so cool." She came and leaned over him, breasts against him, as she kissed his unresponsive lips again. What was the matter with him?

"Oh," she said low and sadly, "I've brooded so, since I said those foolish things—I mean, we had that misunderstanding when you left. I've been beside myself! I *must* apologize for what I said about Montrose to you."

She slipped out of her riding skirt and flung it over a chair. "You do forgive me, don't you? It was just that I was so worried about the whole terrible thing—" She slipped into a pale blue dress and began looping buttons on the basque. Her eyes beseeched him then, tears shining at the corners of her lashes.

He said nothing.

"The servants told me she's still with Regrett—on their way to Washington-on-the-Brazos, or somewhere," she went on. Why wasn't he responding? "And they gave me a sketchy story about your quarrel with Julien Regrett. Aren't you going to tell me a word about it, darling?"

He turned his head away, astonished by the revulsion that swept him. "I think not. I'm quite tired by my travel, and I've lost a good deal of blood, as you can see. Abby is coming in to tend me shortly." He paused, adding coolly, "It appears you've had Faith learn about nursing in a hospital in Charleston. I expect she'll help."

"Of course, darling! I'm so thoughtless!" She was taken aback by the unexpected coldness she felt in this man who had been so infatuated with her.

"And I'm going to move into the north bedroom," he said evenly. "I toss in the night, and I wouldn't want to disturb you."

"My darling! You are so thoughtful!" She was vastly relieved. She had thought fleetingly of lying beside this bloodied man, and was faintly nauseated by the prospect. So he did care about her after all! "But I shall hate having to sleep without you—still. I've missed you so much." She gave him a merry little smile and shook her finger playfully at him. "But it's only until that shoulder heals. Then we'll make up for lost time."

Under his sudden scrutiny, she ran her little pink tongue around her lips invitingly.

"Will we?"

"Of course, Richard. But I know you'll be more comfortable in a bed to yourself. Your bandages look so—so—"
—she repressed a shudder—"cumbersome, and I know you'll need care."

Now she could enjoy her freedom to dream at night of becoming Lady Louise Cavenal without having to make love to Daventry. Not that it was a chore, she reflected as she brushed out her long, curling hair. Richard was an expert lover, and could fire her blood with his expertise. But Cavenal's lovemaking was so much more exotic, so different, and so strangely erotic, she had developed a consuming lust for it. All her previous experiences paled beside Cavenal's knowledge and practice of the carnal delights.

Richard's eyes were closed now, and she looked at him with sudden, undisguised dislike. Yes, she would, with Lady Marguerite and Gina, persuade Cav to return to England, and his ancestral estates. She would enjoy the marvelous and wickedly sensuous nights with him the rest of her life.

She looked up as Abby and Faith entered with bandages and medicines, and smiled at them.

"I must go tell Tina I want her to heat water for my bath tonight," she said, smiling, and left the room quickly. "I'll sleep in the north bedroom tonight—Richard says he'll move to that room tomorrow."

The following morning, Richard Daventry developed a fever. Abby and Faith had once again changed his bandages, and cleaned the wound. Abby succeeded in spooning a poached egg into him, and he had drunk a half cup of coffee.

Later, in the kitchen, as Abby was preparing a potion of witch hazel and laying out fresh bandages for later in the day, Louise approached her.

"Lady Abigail, Richard looks so flushed and his eyes are so heavy," she said with concern. "I'm worried—and I'm such poor help in a sickroom. Especially with someone I love dearly."

Abby looked at her. "Faith and I will take care of him, Louise. It's not good to have too many nurses for a patient with fever."

"Oh, that relieves me so! When I looked in at him a few minutes ago, I could swear he didn't know me." It would be so convenient, she thought, if he died, and she were left a wealthy widow. Instinct told her Cavenal would welcome a wealthy wife.

"I don't think his fever is that high, Louise. I'm sure he knew you."

"Well, he looked at me so . . . coldly, as if I were a stranger. Oh, Lady Abigail, the sight of blood nauseates me and so do wounds! I feel quite faint! I really need to get out into the fresh air. If Richard were himself, I'm sure he'd tell me to take my ride today."

"I'm sure he would, Louise." Abby's eyes were veiled.

"I'll be too worried about my darling Richard to really enjoy it." She sent Abby a pensive and concerned glance from under gold-tipped lashes, but Abby was intent on the poultice. And at that moment, Faith entered the kitchen.

She carried a bowl of water, which she emptied into the broad drainpipe.

"I've bathed him with cool water, Miss Abby," the girl said, glancing apprehensively at Louise. "You know, at the Sisters of Mercy Hospital in Charleston, the nuns used to tell me that fever was the body's way of fighting infection—it can be a good sign."

"Yes, I've heard that. As long as it doesn't get too high—and I think we can keep it down. Why don't you fix a tall, cold glass of tea and take it to him now, Faith?"

Louise's eyes were slits as she watched Faith fix the tea. She registered the glow about the young girl, the look in her eyes as she spoke of Richard. Louise had begun to suspect long ago that Faith was too taken with Richard Daventry. Besides, in the last few weeks, Louise's dislike of her had grown into downright loathing. She certainly wouldn't be taking Faith with her to England when she was Lady Louise. Something had to be done—and right away—about this lovesick little rabbit.

"I don't imagine Faith's too much help to you," Louise said coolly. "She didn't seem to learn much at the hospital in Charleston. You're kind to let her try."

"On the contrary. Faith is as knowledgeable as I. I couldn't get along without her," Abby said succinctly.

"Oh? I think you're just being charitable, Lady Abigail. I'll go get on my riding habit, and I'll have Tina tell Ezekiel to saddle our horses." Louise turned, then wheeled about, adding, "Faith, I want to see you in my room when you've done as Lady Abigail asks." She left the kitchen then, and Faith would not look up from the glass of tea she was stirring. Her face was pale.

"Faith, Louise is mistaken. You are of great help, and I'm thankful that I have you here to help me." Abigail's voice was crisply British and convincing, but Faith still did not look up.

"Thank you." The words were muffled.

Louise's gladness at being relieved of nursing Richard was tempered by her renewed anger at Faith. She would rid herself of Faith, and soon, too.

She wished fleetingly that she might meet George in their trysting place again. But he had told her gently that their rides there every day would surely arouse suspicion when Richard returned. If only Julien Regrett's shot had been lower, she would be rid of the barrier that stood between her and marriage to George Cavenal! Ah, well, she thought, entering the big bedroom, things had a way of turning out well for Louise Lynchley Daventry, and so would this.

Anyway, she could take tea today with Gina and Lady Marguerite—and she would at least get to see Cav.

With Tina's help, she donned the freshly cleaned creamy riding habit, and as she put the finishing touches on her coiffure under the saucy little hat, Faith came quietly into the room.

"Louise," Faith said, "Lady Marguerite and her son and daughter are downstairs. They have come to see Richard. Ezekiel told Abraham last night, and Abraham told Mr. Cavenal."

"Oh, my God!" Louise's decision to tell Faith she must leave for Charleston flew out of her mind. She hastily took off her hat. "I must go down and greet them! Who would've thought they would ride over so quickly—"

When Louise and Faith entered the parlor, Abby was arranging for tea to be served.

"But we'd like to see Richard first, if we may. I've brought him one of our Emma's famous baked custards. So strengthening you know, Abigail." Lady Marguerite extended the covered bowl.

"How kind of you, Marguerite! Feenie, put it in the springhouse for me. He can have it at noon."

"We came as soon as we heard." Cav's clipped voice was solicitous. "Abraham said Ezekiel was terribly worried about him. As we all are, Miss Abby." His eyes went to Louise, and there was a delicious mischief in them, well hidden.

Louise assumed a look of grave concern. "I'm terribly distressed about it—that dreadful Julien Regrett."

"We knew you wouldn't want to leave him today, my dear," Lady Marguerite said kindly, "so we came to extend our sympathy."

"So good of you, Lady Marguerite!" Louise replied, her voice husky. "Would you all like to come up and express your concern and good wishes to him?"

Abby's eyes held irony as they all trooped upstairs to the north bedroom, into which Richard had just been moved. The effort had tired him. But he looked at them, smiling ruefully as he shook hands with Cavenal.

"I'm glad you gave that bloody blackguard, Julien Regrett, what he deserved, Richard!" Cav said fervently. "He's been telling everyone he's seen that you and Big Miguel burned their place."

"Julien and I have had no use for each other for a long time—long before the fire took place." Richard's voice was husky, his lids heavy from a dose of laudanum Abby had administered earlier. "But he died still believing I did it."

"Of course you didn't, no matter what people believe," Cav soothed. "I'm sure it was Indians—or Mexican soldiers. The English boots, like those you wear, could have been stolen easily enough."

Lady Marguerite came forward and put her cool lips to his forehead, murmuring, "You must get well. We will have our social for you and Louise as soon as you're strong enough, my dear Richard."

"We'll certainly be back to bring you more of Emma's delicacies as you recover, Mr. Daventry." Gina smiled, her large, white-rimmed eyes shining sympathetically.

When they were gone Louise, having been put in a position where she could not leave the Daventry place all day, was in a fine temper. She went back to her room, and sent Tina to bring Faith to her. She was filled with frustration.

When Faith entered the room, Louise said coolly, "You may leave, Tina. And close the door behind you."

As soon as the slender black girl was gone, she turned on Faith. Without preamble, she said, "I know you're in love with my husband. I know you have been since the beginning."

"Oh, Louise, I love him only for treating me like a member of the family—and he's so sick now!" Faith burst out, fear tightening her throat. "I'm so glad you've decided to stay with him today—surely you'll stay until he's recovered from his wound?"

"You'd like me to believe you're merely grateful, but I know *desire,* you little rabbit, and it's in your eyes even when you speak of him." She laughed shortly. "Well, it'll do you no good. Richard loves me and he always will."

"I know it," Faith said humbly. "I only want to help . . . him."

"Playing the ministering angel, eh? Think it'll make him turn to you? That only happens in those silly books you read. What a fool you are!"

"No, no, Louise! I only want him to get well. Please stay with him while he's so sick. He needs you!"

"No," Louise said firmly. "I loathe sick people. And I'm going to solve the problem of your love for Richard—as well as getting rid of the responsibility you are to me."

Faith was silent, her eyes wide with fear.

"I'm going to send you back to Charleston, you little rabbit."

"And when—will that—be?"

"Less than two weeks, I imagine. I'll send you to Galveston with Ezekiel. He can put you on the steamer for Charleston." She'd had this girl underfoot for so many years and all because of her father's will. It would be good to be rid of her at last.

"How—how will you pay for my—"

"You know Father said I was to handle the money so you wouldn't squander it."

"But the mail from Texas is so erratic. Would you mail it?"

Louise pursed her lips, and looked back in the mirror at her reflection with pleasure. "I'll give you a letter to old Driscoll, the lawyer who handled Father's will. I'll tell him to give it to you each month—as long as it lasts. I've told you time and again you'd better find employment. You could use some of that education Father paid for, to tutor children. Or you could even be a lady's maid to some wealthy woman."

"I—"

"Come along now," Louise interrupted, walking from the room into the hall. "You have two weeks to play nurse to Richard. Run down and make yourself useful to Lady Abigail. I'm going to ride for an hour—Ezekiel's waiting."

Faith followed her into the hall, and stood watching as she walked gracefully to the north bedroom and entered without knocking.

Richard looked up at his wife with fever-bright, heavy-lidded eyes.

"Darling Richard! I'm such a poor nurse, and it hurts me so to see you with such a wound! Lady Abigail said you'd want me to take the air today, even so. Still, I know I won't enjoy it. I'll worry about you every minute!"

He said nothing and she hurried on. "Lady Abigail says you'd want me to go on and ride for an hour or so. It would make me ill to—to try and dress such a dreadful wound."

Still he did not speak and she leaned over, brushing his hot cheek with her warm, moist lips, and smoothing back his thick, curling hair. "Now darling, you must get well." She smiled with tender sympathy, adding, "I know you don't feel like talking, so I'll leave and you can rest."

What a sullen beast he was, she thought angrily as she left the room. Get well, indeed! Nothing would be better than complications of his wound and his eventual death. She thought once more of that pleasant prospect as she passed the kitchen, and went out the back to the stables, where Ezekiel waited with two saddled horses.

In the kitchen, Abby saw Louise pass by, clad in the cream riding habit. She turned to Faith, who had just come in and stood nearby, her head bowed, lashes dark fans against pale gold cheeks.

"I'm glad you don't share your cousin's queasiness with illness, Faith, dear."

The girl looked up swiftly. "I hope I'm of some help. *I want so to be of help!*" There was desperate intensity in her voice and in the big haunted eyes.

"Then take this second glass of tea to Richard for me. We must get him to drink as much liquid as we can. And I'd like you to bathe his hands and face with cool water." Abby looked after her reflectively as Faith walked quickly from the kitchen, glass and towels in hand.

In his room, Faith saw the man lying with eyes closed. His finely etched, aristocratic features were sharper and flushed with fever. He heard the rustle of her skirts as she came to him and his lids lifted slowly.

She looked into cloudy gray eyes, and her heart caught painfully. In two weeks she must leave, and she would never see those eyes or that face again. It was too terrible to contemplate, and her own eyes stung with hot tears.

"Miss Abby wants you to drink another glass of tea, Richard." She handed him the glass, and he propped himself up to take it with his right hand. He drank it all, never taking his eyes from her face.

"I'm to bathe your hands and face with cool water. It might lower the fever," she said, going to the washstand and pouring fresh water into the bowl.

He lay back, and she took a cloth and washed his hands, then his face. As she was drying his face, she leaned over him tenderly, her eyes filled with love and compassion. Richard did not recognize that, but he knew her ripe lips were warm and inviting, and lightheaded with fever, he raised his right arm. With surprising strength he brought her face to his.

His lips crushed her mouth in a passionate, fevered kiss

and she responded passionately, returning the kiss with love born of desperation. For an interminable and bitterly sweet moment they were fused, and Faith realized she would love this man all her lonely life. He let her go and groaned aloud.

"My God, Faith—forgive me! You're so young—and so sweet! I took terrible advantage of you."

"Don't blame yourself, Richard. You're very—nearly delirious." She swallowed painfully. "I know you didn't mean it, so don't worry."

She folded the towel and hung it on the washstand as she struggled to control her breath, and the dizzying excitement he had stirred.

"I'm so sorry—"

"I tell you, there's no need to worry. I understand perfectly. You're very ill and not accountable for such an action."

"You're so young—" he whispered, turning his head away.

Not that young, she thought clearly. Not so young that she did not know she loved him with an intensity that took her breath away when she thought of him—which was all too often.

"Try to sleep now, Richard. Miss Abby and I must put a new poultice on your wound in the afternoon. If you could sleep until then, your fever might abate."

His face was turned away, and he made no response as she quietly left the room.

After three days, Daventry's temperature was down, and he was feeling well enough to dress in the afternoon and sit in the large easy chair in the north bedroom. Louise had come in frequently, staying only a few minutes each time, her eyes drawn unwillingly to the bandaged shoulder, which no longer showed any blood. The bullet hole had closed and it was only a matter of time before Daventry's strength fully returned.

Faith and Abby brought his trays to him, and his appetite was growing. Once Louise brought his supper, and he looked at her speculatively.

"I hope you and Ezekiel are taking your rides, Louise."

"Yes. It's the only thing that brings me any peace of mind, Richard darling. When I think of your narrow escape, I worry so, I stay awake half the night."

"I think you can give up worrying. I'll be on my feet in a couple of days," he said impersonally.

The following day, two hours after Louise, dressed in a dark blue silk riding habit, had left, Faith took Daventry's noon meal up to him. Now that his fever was gone, he had reverted to his usual kindly and affectionate attitude toward the young girl.

Richard loves me, Faith, and if he knew the truth about you, he'd boot you out of his house before I could make arrangements for your transportation! Louise had uttered this only yesterday as Faith had been preparing fresh bandages for Richard's wound.

These words rang in Faith's ears as she entered his room with the tray of smoking food at noon. To her surprise, Daventry was not in his dressing gown, but fully clothed as he lay, half sitting, his back against pillows on the bed. He looked up, smiling.

"Ah, Faith—I thought I could come downstairs before you brought up my tray."

"You must really feel better. I'm so glad!"

"With you and Abby nursing me so carefully, it would be impossible for me not to heal quickly."

"You're teasing—a sure sign you're better." She laughed, putting the tray down on the lamp table beside the bed. "Miss Abby says we can start looking for Monty any day now—even though Washington-on-the-Brazos is so far away."

"I know," he said. "I've thought about it more than I should." Then with determined cheerfulness, he continued, "I'd say let's take that tray down so I could eat at the table, but I want to talk to you, Faith."

She had turned to go, but halted, apprehension rising like a sickness in her. If he knew—if Louise had said anything— Did he suspect?

"Sit down," he said quietly, "and don't look so frightened! I won't bite. Do you mind telling me exactly how old you are, Faith?"

"No," she said miserably, certain now that he suspected her origins. "I'm eighteen." She remained standing.

"Why is it that a young woman as beautiful as you—with as much as you have to offer, remains with her cousin? And why do you insist, as Louise says you do, on such unbecoming clothes?" He was blunt, and Faith's misery deepened.

"I'm dependent on my—on Louise. I have no income— and she chooses my clothes, because she pays for them."

"I suspected as much," he said grimly. "And you seem uncommonly afraid of her. Why is that?" His eyes were penetrating, and she looked away from him.

"I'm—not—afraid of her. You mustn't ask me such questions—Richard." Her eyes met his, and she knew her love for him lay unconcealed in their hazel depths. His scrutiny grew sharper, and driven by the knowledge she would never see the man again after she returned to Charleston, she whispered, "It doesn't matter anyway. I'll be leaving here in a few more days, now that you're almost well."

"Leaving?" He was astounded. "Where are you going?"

"I'm returning to Charleston. Louise will have Ezekiel take me to Galveston and I'll board the steam packet. I'll find . . . work in Charleston. I have a good education, and I can teach young children for families who can afford it."

"Be a governess? Do you *want* to leave us, Faith?"

"No!" The word burst out involuntarily. "I mean, yes! I *must* leave."

"Who says you must leave?"

"I—Louise and she's right. I'm just a charity case with you—one you don't need. Don't press me, Richard." Her voice broke on his name.

"I say you stay," he said, his voice cold and hard. "I'll take you to Victoria or San Antonio myself and you'll pick out your own clothes. I'll pay for them, not Louise."

"But you can't!" There was panic in her voice. "Louise will never—I mean, Louise won't—" She faltered. The truth goaded her unmercifully. She owed him the truth for his many kindnesses, for the compassion in his eyes as he regarded her.

"I don't want to tell you," she whispered, "but I feel I must."

"Tell me? Tell me what?"

Her voice lowered. "I—I'm not Louise's cousin. I am her half-sister. My mother was our father's mistress. When she died, our father took me in. I've had to lie about it so long . . ." She trailed off, her eyes fixed by his piercing ones. She saw his face go white as stunned realization flooded him. "Now you know why I must leave when Louise tells me. You wouldn't want a bastard in your house. Father's will made me Louise's responsibility, and she has been good to keep my secret all these years."

"Faith—"

"Don't say anything," she cut in resolutely as she turned. At the door she paused, sending a fleeting, haunted glance over her shoulder. "I must do as my—as Louise says. It will be better for all of us."

She closed the door softly behind her.

Chapter 22

"You're right," Regrett said to Monty. "We are being followed. Coffee's been signaling it all afternoon."

"By whom?"

"Maybe Indians." He shrugged.

Monty reached for her rifle and pistol, putting them near at hand. She remembered Indians coming to the Daventry place when she was no more than ten. That had been before Sam Houston made treaties with the tribes. They were the last of the fiercer tribes to molest that section. Her father, his workers, and even women in the house had used guns to stand them off, but it had been touch and go for a while.

"You scared?"

She looked at him squarely. "Certainly. Aren't you?"

"Better take it easy with the guns. We may be able to parley our way out when they come."

His own pistol was thrust in his belt and his rifle was beside him. "We'll go about our business as usual, Monty. I'll keep the fire going."

"Aren't we going to take cover?"

He laughed shortly. "Where? These rocks were the best I could do—and I'm sure there are more than one Indian."

"What makes you so sure?"

"Coffee."

An uneasy silence dropped over them. Regrett picked up the pot and cups. Theirs had been a cold supper. Plates and skillet were still in his pack.

"I'll go with you. We'll wash them together," she said quickly.

They took the steep incline that was before them and washed the few utensils in silence.

When they returned, Monty spread out her new bedroll and looked at her companion where he sat at ease, his back against a rock. He had replenished the fire and it flared brightly.

"Aren't you going to put down your bedroll—business as usual?" she asked.

"No. I'll wait a while. Lie down and sleep if you can."

"If I can! I'd laugh at that if I didn't know what Indians can do."

"I speak Cherokee. I ought to be able to parley with them."

"If they give you time."

"I'll take that chance, Monty. Now lie down. At least pretend to be asleep."

She sat down on the bedroll, and did not remove her prized boots. She put her hat beside her guns, and loosened her two heavy braids, running fingers through them until the hair fell curling to her waist. Apprehensively, her eyes went to the thick pines beyond the river's edge and their half-circle of boulders.

She made no attempt to sleep or even rest. Every nerve in her body was attuned to the tension in Regrett's, even as he casually threw additional limbs on the fire.

In less than an hour they came. But before they stepped into the circle of firelight, the wind carried a powerful stench to Regrett and Monty. It was the alligator grease and animal fats the Tawakonis rubbed over their bodies to ward off mosquitoes and ticks.

Suddenly their bronzed bodies, strangely tattooed, gleamed in the light of the fire. There were three of them. They wore stained buckskin breeches and each had a knife at his waist. One carried a bow and a quiver of arrows over his shoulder. Their long black hair was braided and feathered. The one in front, who appeared to be the leader, wore a necklace of animal teeth. They had no firearms but their ebony eyes were full of danger, and the aroma surrounding them was overpowering.

Lying on the bedroll, Monty closed her eyes swiftly and pretended sleep as Regrett spoke quietly to them in Cherokee.

"Greetings, brothers. What is your tribe and why do you wait for nightfall to visit? We are friends and would do you no harm."

The one in front appeared older, his hawk nose sharp, and it lifted arrogantly. "I am Running Deer. We are Tawakonis—not Cherokee, but we speak their words."

"What brings you here, Running Deer?"

"We were hunting and were attacked by Apaches. And we were separated from our brothers. Black Eagle has been riding behind Silver Water." Now it could be seen that two dappled ponies waited in the shadows behind them.

Regrett knew immediately what they wanted but he spoke formally. "I am sorry for your trouble, Tawakoni warriors. Would you take food with me?"

"No. We want the big black horse for Black Eagle."

"I cannot give you the black horse. He belongs to the young maiden who sleeps now. He was given to her by her father."

Before Regrett could move, one of the younger Indians stepped quickly to Monty, who was feigning sleep. Reaching down, he seized her long bright hair in one hand and pulled her half upright.

Her eyes flew wide open and her lips parted on a silent scream.

"Don't make a sound, Monty," Regrett said calmly. "Just stand, if you can—quietly."

She swallowed the sound that pushed up in her throat, and stood up. The young Indian shook her hair and said, "I am Silver Water. I watched this hair all day. It would be a worthy addition to my tepee."

The other two moved swiftly forward and seized their guns. Regrett did not move. He knew he could shoot one of them, but the other two would surely kill both of them, for their knives were drawn.

"I take sticks that shoot fire," Running Deer said as the one he called Black Eagle began rummaging through their packs. Silver Water dropped Monty's hair and joined Black Eagle in his search through their packs. Running Deer, holding rifles and pistols, squatted over Regrett's saddle-bags.

"Do you know the great white brother of the Cherokee, Sam Houston?" Regrett asked quietly.

The three ceased ransacking the packs and looked up at him, their obsidian eyes sharp. Their faces were impassive as they rose to their feet and stood before him silently. Running Deer finally spoke.

"We know and honor the Raven—the great white warrior who made a treaty with our tribes."

"Good," Regrett replied. "Then in his name I give as a gift the maiden's horse. You would not take more from a true friend of the Raven, would you?"

"No. We would accept a gift and leave you in peace," Running Deer said slowly. "How do we know you are a friend of the Raven?"

"I fought with him against the Mexicans."

"What sign have you to prove he is your friend?" Running Deer's eyes grew cunning.

Regrett did not hesitate. He stooped to his saddlebag and pulled forth a Cherokee arrowhead with a hole in the center. Through the hole was a narrow leather thong. It was meant to be worn about the neck.

"I have this Cherokee sign from the Raven's guide. It was given to me by the Raven after the fight at San Jacinto. I carry it always in friendship with my Indian brothers." He extended it to Running Deer.

All three Indians examined it carefully. They talked with each other rapidly before Running Deer turned and handed the arrowhead back to Regrett.

"You speak true. This is a Cherokee warrior arrow. We will take the black horse and leave you. Here, keep your sticks that shoot fire." Running Deer pushed the rifles and pistols toward Regrett with his moccasined foot.

"Here is the bridle for the black horse." Regrett handed Black Eagle the reins and bridle. "You want the saddle?"

"No," Black Eagle said contemptuously. "Saddles are for the weak."

In less than two minutes, the Indians melted into the night. Warlock's whicker came to them as he was led away by his new owner.

Both Monty and Regrett stood silently until they could hear no more sounds. Then Monty expelled her breath in a loud sigh. She was trembling, and wanted desperately to fling herself into Regrett's arms.

"I thought they were going to kill us," she said, trying to keep her voice from shaking.

"They might well have, if I'd given them any more resistance about Warlock."

"I didn't understand a word you said, but that arrowhead seemed to carry a lot of weight. Why, in the name of heaven, would you carry an arrowhead on a rawhide strip?"

"I never travel without the hard evidence of my friendship with General Sam and his Indian guide. I carry it for the purpose it just served."

"Where *did* you get it?"

"General Sam's Cherokee guide took a fancy to me when I was just seventeen—gave it to me a few months after the battle at San Jacinto. You don't think it's the first time I've used it?"

"No." She remembered the practiced ease with which Regrett had drawn the talisman from his saddlebag. "I just thank God you had it."

"Now we can both get some sleep."

"Maybe you can, but I won't sleep a wink! And my beautiful Warlock *gone!* Suppose they come back for our clothes and food?"

"They might as well have taken it. We're going to have to get rid of most of it. Coffee can't carry both of us and heavy baggage, too."

She was dismayed. "I need my comb! And clothes and—"

"Your comb and one change of clothes. That's all. We have to take the dry supplies, and skillet, if we want to eat. I can shoot game on the way. Why, Monty, you're shaking—"

His voice was tender, and the tone of it was more than she could withstand. Tears filled her eyes, and she blinked furiously to stop them. But Regrett saw the tears, and he was suddenly victim of his own desires. He came to her, and put his arms about her.

She melted against him and a shuddering sigh came from her. Putting her own arms about him, she pulled herself close in his grasp as fire slipped through her.

"Mase . . ." she murmured. "Hold me tight. I was so scared . . ."

He stroked her hair, and his hand slipped down along

her spine, to cup her bottom and pull her against him. She felt him, then, rock hard. He laid his cheek on top of her head, and she tilted her face up for his kiss.

Then his big body stiffened abruptly, and he put her from him with a fierce, rough gesture. "I said you'd be safe from me—now get to that bedroll and get some sleep. I can't play nursemaid to a crying child the rest of the way to the Daventry place."

She recoiled. "Don't worry. I won't cry again!"

They awakened early. Dawn was crimson in the eastern sky, when Regrett fried two eggs with bacon and corncakes. Monty had gone to the river and washed her hands and face. The silence between them was filled with unspoken hostility.

"We'll have to leave the rest of the eggs and the sack of cornmeal, along with most of our clothes, and one of the bedrolls," he said impassively over the meal. "And your saddle, of course. You'll have to ride behind me."

"Don't worry. I'll get along."

By noon, she was stiff and miserable, her back, shoulders, and legs aching with the effort of balancing herself without touching Regrett. His silence was unnerving as well, for she wondered what he was thinking. Certainly not of her, she thought angrily.

In that she was wrong, for Regrett was acutely conscious of the slender, curved figure that refused to yield itself to the gait of the horse, or touch its rider. Too, he thought, Richard Daventry, with his cold hatred of the Regretts, would be filled with fury when he saw his daughter riding home on Coffee with his owner.

After Julien had blown off at him for shooting the mare with the broken ankle, Richard had said, "I'll buy my beef and my horses from you two hotheaded fools because I want the best. But by God, that's all the dealing I'll have with you!" His patrician nostrils had flared with rage when he said it, and it had taken all Regrett's powers of persuasion to keep Julien from pulling a gun and riding after the man. It was always touch and go when Daventry came to buy horses or cattle, if Julien was there.

A little after noon, he pulled up, reining Coffee nearer to the river, and stopped in a grove of shady live oaks. A cooling breeze was blowing off the river, and Coffee whinnied thirstily. Regrett swung out of the saddle, and held his arms up to Monty.

"Come on. Time to let Coffee take a breather."

She looked down at him disdainfully. "Thanks, but I can dismount easily enough." This was a lie, for as she swung her leg over the side of Coffee, she misjudged the distance, and her legs, overtired from clamping Coffee's backside so tightly, gave under her, and she fell heavily to the ground.

Regrett came around the horse, and picked her up silently. "I can see you need to take lessons in how to ride double." He smiled at her grimly.

"I know how to ride double. It's the company I have to ride with that keeps me from doing it the easy way."

"I advise you to do it the easy way, or you'll be sick before I can get you home. Come—we'll have a cold meal except for hot coffee. I'm going to unsaddle my horse. He can graze for an hour and a half."

"We'll never get home at that rate!"

"If you think I'm going to kill my horse to get you home to Daventry, you're a fool," he said brutally. "If it takes a week, I won't push Coffee."

She said nothing as she began to gather firewood from under the surrounding trees. The day was barely half over, and she was hot and dusty, each muscle in her body silently complaining.

By the time they were ready to ride once more, the sun was at its zenith, and there was no breeze. The coffee they drank made her hotter. She had bathed her arms, face, and even her feet in the river, but that had done little to cool her.

"There's bound to be a break in the weather soon." He spoke for the first time since their stop. "It's too hot for June."

She continued to sit stiffly as the horse cantered through trees into an open space where the sun beat down upon them. Perspiring under the hat, she reached up and let her braids fall from under it and put it back on her head.

"Monty, sulking won't make me hurry Coffee."

"I'm not sulking! Whatever I say, it's the wrong thing."

"What you're doing is the wrong thing. For God's sake, relax!"

Suddenly her arms went out and she leaned into his back and shoulders. He was unprepared for the shock of her firm breasts hot against him.

"Now who's tensed up?" she asked mockingly. When he did not answer, she laughed softly, leaning closer.

They rode thus for over an hour, with Regrett cursing himself for opening his mouth. They didn't talk when he stopped once more to water the stallion, but each of them bathed their face and arms. Regrett had rolled up his sleeves as high as he could on his muscled arms.

Remounting, Monty resumed her position with perverse pleasure. It was a form of sweet torment for both of them. The inevitable desire that resulted from such close contact ached in each, like the steady beat of a tom-tom. By the time they stopped to make camp, well before dark, both were short-tempered and yet passion simmered just under their skin.

Once the fire was started, Monty spoke, and her tone was short as she took her clean breeches, shirt, and under-clothing from the small pack.

"I'm going to the river to bathe." They had left their single towel with the other supplies miles behind them. "I'll wash my clothes—and it'll take a while—and I *don't* need a lookout!"

With a jaunty air, because she knew Regrett was watching as he bent over the firewood, she sauntered off among the scrub that hugged the riverbank.

Once out of sight, she drooped slightly. It was good that Regrett stopped early, for she had been stimulated unendurably. The close proximity to him, the movements of the horse that kept friction between their bodies, left her frustrated, hungry not only for food but for the feel of his arms about her.

At the river's edge, Monty saw that the scorching June sun had lowered the water. It still coursed swift and clear, eddying near narrow little beaches that had formed along the sides as the river dropped.

She had finished her bath when a sudden swift current swept her feet from under her, carrying her downriver a few yards. Catching herself, she put her feet down quickly. They encountered the submerged branches of a long-dead tree, and she floundered as she tried to move back upstream.

She kicked hard, knowing those sunken limbs that clawed at her were near the surface of the river. She did not know they extended deeply to the trunk, which lay unmoving on the riverbed.

Thrashing about, her right ankle was suddenly jammed into the closely woven branches. As if moved by some inimical hand, they closed over her foot and ankle. A series of violent pulls did not free her. Fear touched her briefly as she fought to stay above the swift current.

Drawing a deep breath, she plunged underwater and attempted to free her ankle with both hands. Her strength was not enough. Sputtering, she rose to the surface.

Again she strained every muscle in her right thigh, trying desperately to free herself from the wedge among the limbs.

Diving once more, seizing the ankle with both hands, she twisted it fiercely against the narrow web that imprisoned it.

It was useless.

As she rose to the surface, she saw dusk was beginning to fall and panic gripped her. Regrett was far back on the bank among the trees. Could he hear her?

Drawing a quick breath, she screamed his name. She had been swept out far enough so that her free foot had nothing on which to stand. The clutching branches might catch it, and with both feet caught, she would surely drown in seconds.

She screamed again, "Mase! Help me—Mase!"

It seemed an eternity before she saw him on the bank, swiftly pulling off his boots. At a run, he hit the water, only yards from her.

She was terrified by now and her struggles were weakening imperceptibly. Her eyes on him were imploring.

"Foot—caught in branches—underwater—" She coughed as her mouth filled with water.

Reaching her, he dived below. She felt his hand travel down her thigh to the foot that was caught. Then miraculously, the tight wedge loosened under his two hands as they pulled the branches apart, and she drew her foot up. Weak with relief, she paddled against the current with no result.

Regrett surfaced, caught her around her waist, and began swimming strongly back upriver where the narrow beach would afford them footing to the shore.

"I can swim," she protested feebly.

"Be still. Relax. We'll be there in a minute."

Once he was knee-deep, he scooped her into his arms, and strode back up from the river. Shaken and unresisting, she clung to him as he carried her through the trees to the fire, where he put her on her feet. She was trembling and swayed toward him. He caught her once more and held her for a long minute.

"Can you stand now, Monty?"

She nodded, not heeding her nakedness, only shocked and relieved to find herself safe. Regrett turned and caught up the blanket he had spread nearby, and put it around her. His breath was short and his face still white.

"Submerged trees are always a river danger in this country," he said angrily.

She shook her head, still trembling. He caught her in his arms once more, then seated himself before the fire, holding her blanket-wrapped body close.

Slowly, slowly, held fast against the warmth of him, her cold trembling ceased, and strength edged itself into her limbs once more. He did not speak, but his arms were strong, and from them she drew additional strength. Abruptly, desire threaded her warming blood and her heartbeat stepped up.

She looked up into his firelit face to find he was watching her closely. His firm lips were clearly defined. Without thought, she lifted her bare arms from the blanket to encircle his neck and swiftly brought her mouth to his.

"Monty." The word was a groan as he lifted her tighter to him, and bent his mouth to hers again. It was a long, thirsty kiss. The hours he had spent wanting this were in the quick heat of his lips. He lowered her to the ground without breaking the kiss and she leaned her naked body into his, her arms slipping down around his broad chest.

Hostility, differences between them, Richard Daventry's certain rage, were all swept away by the passion that was building. It mounted steadily as his tongue parted her lips further. Drenched as they were, their wetness seemed to conduct sensation like electricity, shocking and intensifying the current of desire that flowed in a tide between them.

"Mase," she whispered huskily, "take off these wet clothes . . ."

He turned swiftly, caught up the tarpaulin, and spread it wide before the fire. He began to unbutton his shirt, and she lay white and beckoning in the lowering dusk.

He stooped, and caught her to his own body. This time, he laid her gently on the tarpaulin, still cradling her in his arms, and bent his mouth to hers once more. Her passionate response sent fire through him.

"Mase—Mase!" she murmured huskily. "I've wanted you so long. I think I've wanted you since that day you rode up to our house with that horse and those longhorns for Pa."

His head lifted briefly. "Your father," he said with husky bitterness, "will kill me for this—but by God, it'll be worth it. Monty, Monty, you're so sweet—"

The words were lost as his lips traveled over her clean, damp skin, reaching places untouched before, seeming to draw the very heart from her breast. His tongue explored her navel, sending tremors through her. With sudden instinctive sensuality, she slid her fingers over the flat rough planes of his face, down to the mat of thick, springy dark hair covering his chest. Slipping them over the smoothly muscled shoulders, she drew him up to her again, putting her mouth on his.

Lifting his head at last, he murmured, "My God, Monty, how did you know to make love like this?"

"But you showed me, Mase! Oh, Mase—I must say it—*I love you!*" Wonderingly, she said, "Why, I must have loved you for years—even when I thought I hated you most."

He said with sudden possessiveness, "And I've loved you, wanted you, even when I knew I shouldn't."

Monty's laugh was throaty. She was remembering all the talks she'd had with Abby over the years. Abby had said to her once, dreamily—as if remembering long-ago sweetness, "The line between love and hate is no thicker than a single hair." All Monty's disagreements with Regrett, the ramrod pride between them, was nothing but the reverse side of a deep and lasting love. Lasting, Monty thought with faint uneasiness, because she knew she would never love again. Not like this. Not ever.

He pressed her hips against his with a rough and urgent hand, and her thighs parted of their own volition. A sharp thrill knifed through her at the touch of him between her legs, as he slowly drew out the pleasure that came with penetration. He did not rush her. Instead, his hands caressed her, his mouth finding the little pulse that beat in her throat and kissing it insistently. Then finding her lips, he put his mouth over them once more, his hard-fleshed hand tenderly stroking her hip, loin, and the crescent of curly, red-gold hair between them.

She could see his mouth in her mind—the clearly defined curve she had looked at so often over the years, and always with fascination. Now she knew why—at last. His breath was clean and warm, mingling with hers as their movements grew more passionate.

Then suddenly, for a brief moment that might have been eternity, she was one with heaven and earth, and all its secrets were hers to explore in the delirium that shook both of them. She lay still as the waves that beat through her slowly receded and Regrett held her close in his arms.

At last she murmured, "I can't believe anyone ever loved like this before." His husky laughter was genuine, and she said, slightly offended, "I don't know why you laugh! I'm serious when I say I love you."

"I laughed because you're so young, Monty, that you still wonder about love."

"I don't do any wondering about my love for you. It's real!"

He sat up suddenly. Darkness had fallen, and the moon cast patterns of light through the trees. Cicadas sounded their somnolent serenade to the summer night, and the echo of rushing water reached them where they lay before the fire.

"Why are you so . . . silent?" she asked, apprehension stirring. She sat up beside him, putting out a hand to stroke the broad muscles that ridged his shoulders and neck.

He looked at her from under brooding black brows. "I just told you I love you, Monty—"

"I know." She leaned to him, her left breast pushing its rosy nipple against his arm. "And I told you I'd loved you for years!" She laid her cheek against his shoulder. "Don't you believe me?"

"Of course," he said, his lips against her hair. "Aren't you hungry, Monty?"

"Starved!"

He rose to his feet to put more wood on the fire.

Later, after they had eaten the last two potatoes, they went to the river. Wading into it, they let the cool water rush about their waists and legs.

A breeze was rising from the south where the gulf pounded the sandy shore, as the two lay once more on the blanket-covered tarpaulin before the fire. The flames were rose-red embers now, and even the cicadas slumbered.

It came to Monty slowly as she lay in his arms, listening to his even breathing. What had been in his voice when he had said, "I just told you I loved you, Monty"? Doubt. There had been doubt in his voice. Even in his warm embrace, she was suddenly cold.

Shivering, she pressed her body to his, so they touched throughout their length. He felt the unexpected shiver, for he was not asleep, and he drew her closer.

"What is it?" he whispered huskily. "You're not afraid?"

"No. I was thinking."

"What could make you shiver—just thinking?" Amusement threaded the deep voice that rumbled against her cheek.

"You—*not* loving me."

He sat up, pulling her with him. "But I told you I loved you," he said gently, taking her chin in his hand and looking at her.

Her face was shadowed, for the embers glowed only faintly. Reaching to the pile of firewood he had placed nearby, he threw several branches on the dying fire. It licked up suddenly, casting brightness over them.

She looked away from him, unable to face the penetrating eyes.

"You sounded . . . unsure," she murmured.

"I am unsure."

"Then you only said 'I love you' because you thought I expected it—just to *make* love to me?"

"No. I meant it," he replied grimly.

"Then why do you sound so . . . disappointed?"

"That's not disappointment. That's worry, Monty. And if you think ahead for just a minute, you'll give some thought to worrying, too."

"What do you mean?"

"My God—you are a child! Have you thought of what love means?"

"Of course! It means—it means—" She floundered and stopped. He caught one of her hands in both his big hard ones.

"It means I don't want you just tonight. It means I want you always. It means marriage, Monty, and your father will never agree to that."

Her breath left her in a small gasp. He was right. Richard Daventry would forbid her even to see Regrett, if he knew she wanted to marry him. He hated everything the brothers stood for, and he had for years, despite his purchases of horses and cattle. She lifted her chin.

"I don't care," she said defiantly. "We'll tell him the minute we get home—"

"And when we get to Daventry, and tell him we've been on the road together alone for nearly two weeks, then hit him with marriage, what do you think he'll do?"

She hesitated, then said, "He'll just have to accept it."

"And he just may shoot me on the spot!" Mase replied.

"Pa would never do such a thing! Why, he's the kindest, gentlest, most wonderful man in the world—except for you." She was laughing now. Her father had never denied her anything she *really* wanted. He would not deny her now.

Monty slept that night in Regrett's arms. It was well past sunup when they woke. Over their meager breakfast of coffee, and the last of the bread he had bought from Wharton's in Washington-on-the-Brazos, her voice was light and merry.

"You just wait and see! Pa's going to welcome you as the son he's never had!"

But Regrett's smile was wintry. He had good reason to doubt Monty's happy assumption. He was older, and he knew the man whose cold gray eyes had looked into his with unconcealed violence when they met in Washington.

He did not confide his doubts to his slender and smiling companion, as they took up their journey that sunny morning.

June would end in a few days, and July, with its hot, fragrant wind, was waiting to stroke the heavily leaved trees about them as they rode south.

Chapter 23

Regrett put Coffee *in a walk,* for they had left the trace and were on the road that ran past Daventry property. It was mid-afternoon and a breeze was rising. The trees whispered with it.

Monty, her cheek against his broad back, lifted her head and sighed, her happiness tinctured faintly by anxiety.

"I feel I've been gone such a long time—that so much has happened, and I feel so *changed.* Older and wiser." She laughed, adding, "And now I have to face being under the same roof with that—woman Pa married. And I can't tell him what she said and did, the night I ran away. He's in love with her."

"You ought to level with your father."

"He won't believe me."

"Don't be too sure of that. I doubt you've lied to him too often."

"I've never lied to him!"

"Then don't start now." *She had better start now!* If Daventry suspected she had slept in Regrett's arms these warm June nights, he would surely call him out. As he shrugged silently, Monty echoed his thoughts.

"I'd better not tell Pa *all* about us. I won't lie—I just won't *tell* some of it."

"I'd sure hate to be shot before I can marry you." His laugh was dry. "And Monty, I think you're going to have one hell of a time getting Daventry to agree to a wedding."

"Pa's never been mean! And when he knows how much I love you, Mase—"

"It might be better to let him get over the fact we've been traveling alone together night and day, before you pull a wedding on him."

"I won't wait!" Monty had never waited for anything in her life. "We'll tell him the minute we get there."

"Not the very minute." Regrett paused. "At least give him a chance to see you're all right, or he may throw me out before I can draw a breath."

They drew up to the Daventry gate. In a rising breeze, the single starred flag on its tall, slender pole in front of the house was moving lazily. As always, it lifted Monty's heart, and now it eased her apprehension. Everything was going to be all right.

"We'll tie Coffee to the hitching rail," she said hastily, "and go right in!"

In seconds, Monty flung open the door and ran through the big foyer to the parlor. She stopped so abruptly, Regrett almost ran into her.

Abby was sitting in a rocker beside her son. Daventry was reclining on the large sofa. The bandages and sling on his shoulder and arm were startlingly white.

"Pa! Abby! Oh, Pa, what's happened to you?"

"Monty!" Abby cried. "You're home—thank God!"

"Monty, don't worry. I'm all right—" Daventry was up from the sofa in an instant, and had his right arm about her as Abby caught her hands. "Regrett." He nodded over her shoulder by way of greeting, then he said, "Monty, you—"

"Pa," she said, cutting him off quickly, "I'd be on my way

to prison in Mexico now, if it hadn't been for Mase Regrett. He had a knife in his boot—cut us loose and we shot the Bosquez brothers—"

"I thank him for that, but the bounder took you off with him to Washington-on-the-Brazos." Daventry's voice was rough. "Why the hell didn't you bring her home first, Regrett?"

"It would've meant a four-day delay, Daventry," Regrett said evenly, "and I couldn't afford the time."

"Couldn't afford the time! That's what Watkins's woman babbled. What was so goddamned important you couldn't bring my daughter home?"

"I'd taken a letter off Bosquez from Ranger Captain Jack Hays, in San Antonio de Bexar. In it, he told Anson Jones that American troops under General Zachary Taylor are already on their way to Texas both by land and sea, to defend us from Mexico. Bosquez had taken it from a courier he intercepted and killed. It'll alter Jones's plans—we'll be able to fit our plans with those of the United States."

"So the American President is sending troops down here —damned officious!"

"It's just a matter of time. Jones has called a convention to meet in Austin on July fourth, to draft a constitution for Texas—to be presented at the time we're annexed."

"By heaven, I'll be at that convention! So will George Cavenal and the Arterburys. We're still an independent republic!"

"Oh, Pa—don't argue politics with Mase now! I'm home safe and you haven't told us what happened to your shoulder and arm."

"Monty, when we heard you'd been captured by the Bosquezes, Julien Regrett and I, and some of the men, set out after you." He said grimly, "We were at Watkins's cabin and learned from Nola you'd gone on to Washington-on-the-Brazos. It was there—I was shot."

"Pa! Who shot you?"

"Julien Regrett. He fired twice." Daventry's face darkened and sorrow was in his voice. "The first shot, Young Miguel took for me—it killed him. The second one I took in my left shoulder." He paused and looked directly at Regrett. "I had to defend myself. I shot him—just once."

Regrett stared at him, his brows drawing together fiercely. "Are you saying my brother, Julien, is responsible for your wound?"

"He meant to kill me, or I'd never have drawn my pistol."

"You shot my brother?"

"My God, Regrett, I didn't want to!"

"Where is Julien now?"

"Watkins and LeRoy buried him and Young Miguel beyond his cornfield." Breaking the silence that followed his words, he added, "I never killed a man in my life, Regrett! I tried to wing him—"

"You killed my brother?"

"I tell you I didn't want to! I had no choice. Ask Watkins and his wife. It was just outside their cabin and they saw it all. Hell, Regrett, I might have died right there from loss of blood, if Nola Watkins hadn't treated my wound—"

"And we could have lost him even so, Mase," Abby put in hurriedly, "for he ran such a fever—and was so sick when he first came home."

Stunned, Mase asked, "Why would Julien shoot you—without cause?"

"I didn't say it was without cause, Regrett." Despite his resolve, Daventry sounded defensive.

"Then what did you *do* to make him shoot you?"

"It was what I said." Richard stiffened. "A perfectly natural remark for a distraught father to make. It doesn't matter what it was now."

"The hell it doesn't! *What did you say to my brother?*"

"I don't mind saying it again. It's the truth. I said I'd as soon see my daughter in the hands of the Bosquezes as with you on the trail alone."

"Oh, Pa!"

"Richard! You didn't tell me that!" Abby's voice was anguished.

"I meant it then. I mean it now."

Regrett's eyes narrowed further, bitterness and grief glittering in them. He was silent, every muscle taut.

"I swear to you I didn't mean to kill him, Regrett. Watkins said you'd likely come to fetch his body home." Richard dredged the words up from the depths of his pride. "I—we would have done that, but I was sorely wounded, and we couldn't manage it."

"Watkins was right. I'll fetch Julien—and I'll fetch Young Miguel so his parents can give him a decent burial, as well." Regrett did not look at Monty, and she felt coldness seep into her bones. Hatred was a living thing in the room. Her heart beat heavily as sorrow filled her. Julien, with his merry eyes and his funny way of playing with words, was gone—Young Miguel was gone. And all because of something her father *said*.

She put her hand to Regrett's sleeve, but he shook her off without looking down into her pleading face.

"And you're not even sorry," he said, his fierce eyes on Daventry. "You can have your daughter—and without your thanks. I'll bury Julien on his own land. And if you come to the convention in Austin, you'd better keep the hell out of my way!"

He turned, violence in the movement, and strode swiftly to the door. Monty ran after him, catching his arm.

"Mase, wait! I—I love you!"

He turned his griefstricken face to her, and he said in a choking voice, "So 'he's the kindest, gentlest, most understanding man in the world,' eh?" He twisted his arm away and in long strides went to his horse. He vaulted into the saddle, and the thunder of hooves broke the stillness.

In the terrible seconds after his departure, Monty buried her face in her hands. Looking up, she saw Faith's stricken face where she stood in the foyer. Josey and Feenie were in the shadows back of the stairs, Josey's hand to her mouth. Monty ran past them back into the parlor.

"Pa!" she cried. "I love Mase Regrett—I'm going to marry him!"

Her father stared at her in silent shock. "I can't believe you've come to love a—scoundrel—like Regrett—I won't believe it!" he said. There was a long pause and his face softened. "You don't really love him, little girl. You're just a baby still. And I've thanked him for bringing you home— we owe the man nothing more." His voice grew heavy. "I will never permit you to marry him."

"But I do—I *do* love him!"

Daventry shook his head, and his voice was gentler. "Come sit down beside me, daughter, and tell us you're all right. Abby and I—all of us—have been so terribly worried."

Faith came slowly into the room and seated herself in a chair next to Abby. Relief, combined with sadness, filled Abby's eyes as she looked at father and daughter together on the big sofa.

"I'm all right, Pa," Monty said, her voice whispery, and she began to cry at last. "Oh, Pa, why did you have to kill Julien?"

He put out his right arm and drew her head to his broad chest. "Monty, you know well enough that I didn't want to kill him. But murder was in his eyes. Would you have me stand and be killed by a hot-tempered boy who took offense at every word I ever uttered?" He put his hand under her chin to look into teary eyes.

"No, Pa. I wouldn't want you . . . to be killed. I love you, Pa, but I love Mase, too. I want to marry him!"

"You don't mean that, Monty," he said quietly. "Give yourself a few days to regain your perspective. You're merely grateful to him for saving you from the Bosquezes."

"You need a good hot bath, darling," Abby said, pulling Monty up and into her own arms. "She's going to feel differently after a night's sleep in her own bed, Richard. Ah, my little Monty," she murmured against Monty's cheek. "We've been so worried. Faith and I have ached with it, while nursing your father these two weeks."

Faith came over and caught one of Monty's hands in hers. "You'll never know how hard I've prayed for you, Monty," she said thickly, "or how glad I am that you're safely home."

"I've missed you, Faith." Monty smiled tremulously.

None of them seemed to realize her heart was breaking with love for Mason Regrett—or care. For the first time in her life, she had come up against a problem she could not solve with tears, or coaxing. Her father's face held grief when she cried her love for Mase, but he was as unyielding as the gray granite steps leading to the house.

She pulled from Abby's arms and turned to go, but her father spoke again, his voice kind.

"Monty, don't go up just yet." His hand caught hers to pull her back beside him. "Sit down and tell your grandmother—and Faith—and me why you did such a foolish thing."

"Foolish thing?" she asked, seating herself once more. Her mind was still focused on Regrett and the chasm that was now deep between them.

"Yes—leaving in the night to go to the Arterburys' with no escort," Richard said.

"It doesn't matter," she said dully. Mase was gone, gone! "You'd never believe me, anyway."

Daventry's eyes hardened. "Try me."

"Where is Louise?" Monty asked, anxiety stirring again.

"She's at the Cavenals'," Daventry said, his voice as hard as his eyes. "She'll be back about four-thirty, as usual. Now what did she say to you the night you left?"

"I can't tell you, Pa." She shook her head positively. "You love Louise, and it would only make you angrier at me." Her face was so woebegone, Abby stretched out a comforting hand. She and Faith seated themselves once more.

"Did Louise say something to make you run away?" His words were rough with resentment, but not at her. Monty looked at him in surprise.

What had Mase said? *You ought to level with your father.*

She looked at Abby, then Faith. "If I tell you, you won't think I'm lying, Pa?" she asked cautiously. "Abby—Faith?"

"Try me," her father repeated.

"She—called me a—slut and a spoiled brat. And she struck me—hard—across my face." She grew more hesitant.

"Go on," Richard said.

"She swore she'd persuade you to send me to a finishing school back east, if I didn't wear dresses every day, Pa! She also said I'd broken the Dresden figure on purpose, because it looked like *her*—" Monty broke off, then burst out, "I can't say these things about your *wife!* She's always so sweet and—and good around you. Pa, I'm not just making this up!" For the first time, Regrett left her thoughts, and her quarrel with Louise took precedence. "You wouldn't believe the look in her eyes—the things she said."

"I believe you, Monty."

"What?" She looked at him uncomprehendingly, then at Abby's closed, unreadable face. "You believe me?" Astonishment sharpened the look she turned on her father.

Richard Daventry's face was like stone. "Of course I believe you. You've never lied about important things—and this is important."

"But—you love her and—"

"Monty, Abby's taught you the meaning of the word 'infatuation'?"

"Uh . . . yes." Regrett's strong face, his black dancing eyes and white smile rose up in her mind. But that wasn't infatuation! She *loved* him, and loved him for years!

"Louise has taught me the meaning of infatuation, Monty."

"Oh, Pa!" She looked into his disillusioned eyes, and her arms went about his shoulders swiftly. "I'm so sorry—"

"I'm the one who's sorry. I'm married to her. I'm saddled with her now, but by God, I'll do something about that! I can promise you she'll never strike you again, Monty—and you will wear whatever you like, when you like." With a lightning glance at the other girl, he said, "And so will you, Faith."

Faith's eyes filled with sudden tears, and abruptly the girl rose from her chair and fled, her quick running steps tapping on the foyer floor to the staircase.

"Did I speak too roughly to her?" Daventry asked Abby.

"No," was her swift reply. "I think you relieved her so greatly it overcame her. After all, she's done Louise's bidding for twelve long years."

"She'll do it no more," he said. "I'll have a talk with Louise this evening—and believe me, things will change in the Daventry household."

It was nearly five before Louise returned from the Cavenals', her face luminous and beautiful, the curved mouth extraordinarily full and red.

She came into the parlor where Abby and Richard sat. She was smiling and joyous.

"Oh, Richard darling—Lady Abigail! LeRoy told me. Montrose is safely home! How wonderful for all of us! Life can return to normal at last. Where is she?"

"She's had a bath and an early supper, and she's retired. It was a long, hard ride for her," Richard said.

"I'm glad. I'm sure she'll be quite herself tomorrow." She hesitated before asking, "Did you—I'm sure you saw Mason Regrett and told him about his brother. Did he take it well?"

"No."

"Oh, dear. I know you told him it wasn't your fault! Did he make trouble?"

"He was griefstricken," Abby said quietly.

"And he said I'd better keep out of his way at the convention on July fourth," Richard added dryly. "He need not worry. Tom Arterbury can stand in for me. I've decided I cannot leave my household again—for any length of time— for any reason."

"Cav said today—over tea—that Arthur Bedford came by yesterday and told him about that convention," Louise said casually. "In fact, he's promised his mother and Gina that if Texas votes for annexation, he'll return to England with them. Would you do that, Richard?"

"Not on your life. I won't like it, but I've put down roots here, and I'll stay, no matter what takes place."

"Dinner will be served in half an hour, Louise," Abby said coolly. "I know you'll want to wash up after your long ride."

Louise dimpled. "You're so thoughtful, Lady Abigail. I'll run right up and do so. Where is Faith?"

"In her room, I expect," Abby replied.

"With another book, I'm sure. I wish she were more social."

"She's a wonderful girl," Richard said flatly. "And she's as social as she's been allowed to be."

Louise looked at him, first puzzled, then sharp-eyed. What had that girl said to Richard? She'd have a talk with her tonight. Maybe she shouldn't wait to bundle her off to Charleston. And what did he mean when he said he couldn't leave his household again, for any length of time—or for any reason?

"I'll run up and change," she said sweetly, "and join you for supper in half an hour. Oh, Lady Abigail, will you have Merzella and Tina put on water for my bath tonight?"

After supper with Louise, Faith, and Abby, Richard left them, going into the small office that had become a retreat for him through the years—a place conducive to facing and solving problems.

A stiff dollop of brandy was on the desk. He had poured it for himself before he sat down. Louise had become more than a problem. She was an unbearable burden and a menace. His determination to rid himself of her grew. What a fool he had been, thinking she was like his adored Elizabeth! There was not a doubt in his mind that Monty had spoken the truth about her confrontation with Louise the night she ran away. And Miguel's words haunted him: *The Señora—forgive me, Señor Richard.* The memory was a sickness in the pit of his stomach.

He sat sipping the brandy as he waited for the house to grow quiet. He would go to their bedroom—*her* bedroom for the time being—and face her with his decision.

He slipped his arm from the sling. It was really no longer necessary. He had worn it the last two days merely to satisfy his mother and Faith. Faith! She was another casualty of Louise's headlong, amoral behavior, and he would set the woman straight on that, as well. His mind veered guiltily away from the kiss he had shared with Faith—she was so young. Too young.

It was well after ten when he finally took the stairs and made his way to the bedroom. Light showed under the door. He knew it was her custom to brush the long golden curls a hundred times each night. He did not pause, but opened the door without knocking.

As he had surmised, she sat before the dressing table, brush in hand. She was clad in the peach peignoir with a matching gown beneath it. She turned, eyes widening and lips parting in a welcoming smile.

"Richard darling," she breathed, "you've come at last. Your arm has healed—you're well enough"—she paused, her lids dropping seductively—"to make love to me again." Rising quickly, she went to him, arms outstretched.

"Spare me the 'darling,' Louise." Reaching up, he pulled her arms from about his neck. "We can dispense with making love as well."

"But, my darling!" She drew back. "What's happened to make you so—so distant? You know how much I love you!" She reached for him once more, and he read disbelief in her face. He stepped away.

His lips twisted downward. "Yes. And how much you loved Young Miguel. Don't bother to deny it, my dear. He died *because* of you as well as *for* me, not that it will trouble your conscience."

"But I cared nothing for Miguel!"

"I'm sure of that."

"Then how can you blame me?" Her bewilderment was genuine. She turned away, slipping the peignoir from her shoulders to fling it across the foot of the bed. Lamplight shining through the translucent gown outlined her body. "Come to me, darling." She turned, eyes beseeching. "Let me put all those terrible thoughts out of your mind . . ." Once more she held out her arms to him.

He was filled with an almost irresistible urge to strike her and his fists doubled tightly at his sides. She saw the movement, and believed it to be passion and desire restrained. She smiled slowly, eyes dreamy now, and moved toward him.

Unable to control himself, he lifted his hard hand and

struck her face with the flat of it. She reeled back, falling across the bed.

Raising herself on her elbows, she looked at him, stunned. "But Richard darling! Miguel followed me about like a puppy! I never encouraged his—his attentions. I swear, he begged so hard—it meant nothing."

"It's not just Young Miguel, Louise. It's the way you've treated Faith all her life. The things you called my daughter —the lies you've told, *and continue to tell!*"

He was not to be seduced. She rose swiftly, confidence flooding her, with the realization that battle was joined.

"And what has Faith told you, Richard?" Unafraid, she stood close to him, her own fury rising unchecked. *"She's* the liar! She's been a whiner since she was six years old. I've stood it for years! But no more!" She drew a deep breath, triumph lighting her face as she said slowly, "You won't be so anxious to defend her when I tell you she's my father's bastard!"

"I know that," he said, smiling sardonically. "And she has had the strength to withstand you for twelve years. I admire her for it—*because of it!* Believe me, my dear Louise, I haven't the stomach for standing you that long."

She was stunned. Her face paled and the print of his hand showed clearly. George Cavenal had said he loved her, wanted her. He had said, *If only you weren't married, we could be together always!* That was as good as a proposal. She drew a deep breath and lashed back.

"I'm sending Faith back to Charleston. I won't wait another minute! I never dreamed you'd fancy yourself as her knight on a white charger. I suppose you feel very heroic defending her? I'll have Ezekiel drive her to Galveston tomorrow!"

"You will not. If anyone goes to Galveston tomorrow, it will be you, Louise—"

"You can't possibly mean that! I'm your *wife*. You'd better consider that before you try to take any such actions—"

"And as my loyal wife, what did you say to Monty the night she ran away?"

"I told her she was selfish and spoiled, which she certainly is!"

"And don't forget the important fact that you struck her —and threatened her." He laughed suddenly. "You're good at threatening, aren't you, Louise?"

Her eyes were slits. "I never threaten unless I can follow through with it. And I tell you now, Richard, I'm your wife, and I'll remain your wife until I decide to end our union, *or you'll regret it.*"

"You will not." His voice was quiet. "You're not fit to be my wife—"

Her control broke suddenly. "You're not fit to be *my* husband, Richard Daventry! How I laughed at you in Washington, telling me in the night you wanted a son—what a fool you are! I'll never bear a brat to be spoiled by you. You have no idea what my childhood was like—I had an abortion at fourteen and do you know who took me to that butcher? *My own father!*" Her voice broke on these words. "The old woman told me I could never have children—"

Richard remained unmoved. "Makes it nice for you," he said, his face set. "You can seduce the young—like Miguel —anytime you choose."

"Miguel meant nothing to me! I've found a man—*a man,* do you hear? One that satisfies *all* my needs, money, a title —*and* love! And when I'm rid of you, I intend to marry him!"

"Let me guess. George Cavenal." He laughed shortly. "Don't think I hold someone like you against Cav."

"You've talked to Cav—about me?" She was disbelieving.

"You flatter yourself, madam. You aren't important enough for us to discuss. In fact, Cav's been to Rebecca's house in Victoria a number of times since he met you, he's told me." He laughed again, adding, "But he's an Englishman and a gentleman and he'll never marry someone like you."

She reddened with fury. "He *will!* He's already said so."

He ignored her comment and asked, "And how many times through the years have you struck Faith?"

"I care nothing for Faith. My father took me when I was ten to the house he bought for his paramour and I saw that little bastard in her crib—and heard my father promise her mother he'd raise her as his own. And he did! Until the day he died, he favored her against me!"

"It appears you care nothing for any of my household, with the shining exception of yourself—"

White and shaking, she could no longer control her voice. It rose shrilly. "Get out! Get out of my bedroom!"

"My dear, I will divorce you if I have to take it before the Texas Legislature—and then I'll send you packing on the first steamer out of Galveston, but you'll not take Faith with you."

"Get out! I never loved you—I married you for money and to escape after the death of my husband—"

Richard's eyes narrowed. "And what about the death of your husband?"

Her eyes darkened and her face smoothed suddenly. "You know well enough. He left me nothing—all the Lynchley money went to that sour-faced mother and sister of his—isn't that enough?"

He turned and stepped to the door, closing it softly behind him.

Chapter 24

Richard stood a moment, his eyes adjusting to the darkness about him, and drew a deep breath. He grew very still as he caught a faint fragrance floating on the warm air. Flowers, he thought, gillyflowers, like those he had known long ago in England. The light suggestion of cinnamon was sweeter than honey.

It was then he became aware of someone nearby, standing so close he could feel a certain warmth. There was a crack in the door beyond, and in the faint light he saw that his companion was Faith Warren.

"I—I heard—part of it," she whispered. "I was going down to the library for a book—"

"You would've heard, had you been in your room with the door closed, Faith," he said ironically. "I hoped the household was asleep. I suspected it would be so with her." He turned to go.

A light touch caught his sleeve. "Richard . . ." It was the barest of whispers.

He stopped and turned, smiling quizzically. In the light from the partially opened door, he could see her luminous eyes. It shone on her long tumble of pale blond hair.

"Faith?"

He could see the rise and fall of sharply tilted breasts beneath a thin batiste gown, and the scent of gillyflowers was even more persuasive.

"What is it, Faith, dear?" All at once his breath quickened, and a slow, hot stirring began in his throat, seeping down to his loins. Involuntarily he reached out to her.

Without a word, she came to him, arms reaching upward, face lifted. Silently they melded together, his lips seeking and finding her soft, yielding mouth. For a long, heart-turning moment, their kiss warmed, growing hotly demanding before Richard could tear himself away.

"My God," he whispered hoarsely, "what am I doing?"

Without words, Faith took his hand and pulled him after her. When they were in her room, she closed the door, leaning against it, her eyes on his face.

"Forgive me, Faith—I—"

"There is nothing to forgive." There was a touch of ruthlessness in the girl's husky whisper. "It's *my* doing, Richard. Tomorrow she will send me away, and I will go—with you never knowing how much I have come to love you."

"Faith—"

"Hear me out, please, my love. All I want is just once to know your touch. Pretend, if you have to, but please let me love you. *Just once.*"

He pulled her roughly into his arms, kissing her swiftly, uncontrollably, her face, her closed lids, the base of her throat, and then again and again, her mouth.

Lifting her high in his arms, he carried her to the big, canopied bed, laid her upon it, and began undressing. All the rage and frustration, the fury and hatred, he had known before in Louise's presence coalesced in the torrent of fire that swept him now.

It burgeoned and grew as they clung together in the languorous June night. The faint, delicious scent of gillyflowers filled his lungs and mingled with the fragrance of June roses from Abby's garden below the open windows. The two meshed within him and bound him to Faith with ties stronger than steel.

Richard and Faith slept in each other's arms that night.

The following morning sunlight streamed into the dining room through the open windows where Louise sat at the foot of the breakfast table. Richard sat at the head, and Monty, Faith, and Abby were in their usual places.

Louise had just spoken lightly about a beautiful horse Cavenal had bought for his sister this year from the Regretts. Smiling archly at Richard, she asked him to look at one for her. It was obvious she intended to ignore their altercation of last night.

"I'll have Big Miguel choose one for you," Richard said coldly. "I'm not ready to take another bullet from a Regrett. Besides, Big Miguel—like his son Young Miguel—is a better judge of horseflesh than of women. I'll tell him to get a mare, one that Monty can ride when you're gone, Louise."

"I don't think I care to share one with Monty," Louise replied coolly.

"And I certainly don't intend to share a horse with Louise, Pa!"

"I meant at a later date, Monty. Louise is thinking of going to Charleston, aren't you, Louise?"

"No," Louise said a touch violently. "I've changed my mind, Richard darling. I'm going to let Faith go in my place. Aunt Florence will be very glad to have her help. She's been poorly for some time now."

"I didn't realize you had relatives still in Charleston, Louise," Abby remarked, brows lifted.

"Yes. It's my father's older sister. She's rather a recluse, but well-to-do. Faith wants to go help her, don't you, Faith?"

"If I must," Faith said in a low voice.

"I think not, Faith," Richard said slowly, his voice growing colder. "Monty needs your companionship very much now. Besides, Abby and I have grown far too fond of you to let you go care for an old aunt. I'm sure if she's well-to-do, she can hire a companion."

"Aunt Florence has asked particularly for Faith."

"When?" Abby asked innocently. "I didn't know you'd received any letters, Louise."

"Not by letter. She asked me before we left, but Faith wanted so very much to travel with me, I indulged her." Louise was regretful but firm. "We've talked it over, haven't we, Faith dear? And she's ready to go now." Louise paused, then added, "You can be packed by tomorrow morning, Faith, and Ezekiel and LeRoy can drive you to Galveston."

Richard looked down the length of the table at his wife. "I won't permit it, Louise."

Color flooded Faith's face, and Monty looked in astonishment from her father to his wife. Abby sipped her coffee tranquilly, then spoke.

"Feenie, dear." The young girl's face appeared around the doorway immediately. She had obviously been listening. "Fetch some hot coffee and refill the cream pitcher, will you, please?"

"I can't understand you, Richard darling." Louise's honeyed voice had a sharp edge to it. "Really, Aunt Florence needs her!"

"Aunt Florence will have to do without Faith. I forbid her to leave."

There was a tense, momentary silence. "Very well, Richard." Coaxingly, she tried, "But you—you really should attend the convention at Austin." The words were thick, and her face mottled. "The Bedfords, Arterburys, and Cav will be there. They'll need you."

"And let you run my household in my absence, my dear wife?" Richard laughed derisively. "Not a chance, Louise.

You'll not be ordering my daughter or Faith about during a convenient absence by me. Nor bullying your servants or mine."

Louise shoved her chair back violently and rose, leaving her breakfast half finished. "I don't know what's got into you, Richard darling," she said with forced sweetness, "but I certainly don't have to sit here and listen to it!" She flung herself out the door into the foyer. Her footsteps could be heard on the stairs.

Faith and Abby stared down at their plates silently. A look of wonder brightened Faith's golden face. Monty was scrutinizing her father's hard features with the impudence of an indulged, only child.

"Pa, I didn't know you had it in you! Yes, I did, too. But I thought she had you so fooled—"

"Louise," he said deliberately, "has all the instincts of one of my boar hogs in heat."

"Richard!" Abby murmured, staring at her son. "No gentleman would say such a—"

"Louise has erased some of my gentlemanly manners, Mother dear. Allow me this moment of truth. None of you need fear Louise's edicts again—I'll be here to restrain her."

"Are— Will you allow her to ride each day—to the Cavenals'?" Abby asked, restraining an uncharacteristic grin.

"Of course. The more often she goes, the better." His eyes were on Faith, but Monty could not read what lay in their gray depths.

That afternoon, Louise rode as usual to the Cavenal house, where she had tea with Lady Marguerite and Gina. And as usual, Cavenal joined them later.

As they finished, he said with impersonal courtesy, "I'm sure you'd like to ride over to the Guadalupe with me for our usual outing, wouldn't you, Louise?"

"Indeed I would, Cav! I always enjoy riding over this beautiful estate of yours."

"You're quite a horsewoman, Louise." Lady Marguerite smiled, and Georgina put down her napkin with a little laugh.

"I do love to ride. Why not go with us, Gina?" Louise asked, knowing that Georgina always refused.

"Not I, dear Louise. I'm for a good long nap."

Cav grinned at his sister knowingly. "Yes, Gina's a great one for naps."

As soon as they were out of sight of the house, Louise turned to Cav with sudden passion. "Cav darling—Richard's becoming impossible! I can scarcely stand him any longer. Today he forbade Faith to leave for Charleston, and we had planned for her to go stay with Aunt Florence, who needs her."

"Aunt Florence?"

"I never told you about her. My father's older sister. She's becoming quite helpless and really needs Faith."

"That's unkind of Richard. I've always thought him a very reasonable man."

"He's not! Since the deaths of Young Miguel and that Julien Regrett, he's been an absolute beast. I think he's taking his feelings of guilt out on me."

"Well, he was, in a way, responsible for both deaths."

"Yes, he was," she said righteously. "But to take it out on me—"

"That *is* unkind. Perhaps it's just that his wound is bothering him—and you did say Faith was nursing him? Perhaps he feels she doesn't want to go."

"Of course she doesn't want to go! But she feels it's her duty—and it is."

They dismounted at the game shed, and Cav held his

arms up to her. She slipped down into them and tipped her face up for his rapacious kisses.

As they disrobed, he grinned at her mischievously. *"Is there an Aunt Florence, love?"*

She burst out laughing, pushing her breasts against his bare chest. "No. But I want to be rid of that little mouse. She's been a bother to me for twelve years. And there's no place for her in *our* lives, Cav darling, is there?"

"True enough," he replied easily, and began stroking her rounded thighs.

Later, she roused in his arms, utterly spent and relaxed. He lay beside her, easy and satiated. Now was the perfect time.

"I must tell you, darling Cav—"

"Tell me what? You sound very ominous."

"It is ominous. I've asked Richard for a divorce—and he says he'll give it to me. It probably means going to the Texas Legislature—God knows how hard it will be—but I'm sure he can do it."

Cav made no reply.

"Then too," she continued, "his wound *is* still bothering him. It could very well be the end of him."

"You mean, he could die of it?"

She nodded, smiling. "Other men have died of lesser wounds." Still smiling, she said, "But it would be a pity to be free of him that way!"

"I think Richard's hardier than you imagine, love. When I saw him last, he looked well on his way to recovery. Besides, it's convenient for me since he's blamed for the Regrett fire."

"But if something should happen to him," she said, "then I'd be free, and we could be together, as you've said, forever."

"That's true," he replied, beginning to dress. "The divorce seems the logical way—I hope." He looked at her sharply.

She slipped on her underclothing, and smiled at him over the dress she held up. "We can wait, can't we, darling Cav? The divorce may not take long at all."

"True, my dear. Meantime, I must leave for Austin. I want to be at that convention on July fourth. It means we can't be together the next few days, Louise."

"Oh." She was dismayed. "Do you still want to go to that tiresome meeting? Richard says he isn't going." She was petulant. "I think he's afraid the long ride might reopen his wound."

"That 'tiresome' meeting will settle a lot of things for the Cavenals', Louise." He smiled wryly.

"Such as?" She was keenly alert as she buttoned her basque.

"Such as packing up my lady mother and Gina, and going back to England. I'll not live under the flag of the United States."

"You'd go without me?"

He smiled again. "No, love, I wouldn't go without you."

Relief flooded her. *He had as good as asked her to marry him!*

"But go to Austin, I must," he went on, buttoning his shirt above his dark fitted pants, and stooping to pull on the polished leather boots. "There's an outside chance we might still remain a free republic."

"I can't see where it would make much difference."

"Louise, it would make all the difference. I would have to observe all the laws of the United States. Do you think I could create the empire I have in mind with their officials peering over my shoulder?"

"In Charleston, my first husband created quite a large estate—under their rules. Of course, it would be different here. I realize that."

"The officials in Washington can make any rules they like —including passing a law to tax. My incentive to stay here will be gone with the end of this republic." He picked up his wide-brimmed panama from the stained table, and set it on his fair head at a jaunty angle. "Come along, love. It's time you got back to Richard."

"A plague on Richard!"

"You must try to get along with him—after all, he's still your husband."

"I still bear his name. That's the only privilege he has as a husband," she said sulkily.

"No kisses?" he teased. "None of the fun—we have together?"

She took a quick step to him, flung her arms about his neck, and kissed his mouth quickly. "No one," she whispered against his lips. *"No one shares a love as deep as ours."* She turned and they went out the open door together.

It was the sound of wagon wheels three days later, coming around the side of the house and into the rear of the Daventry compound, that woke Monty in the early morning. Instinct told her it was Mase and his men bringing Young Miguel and Julien back for burial. Swiftly, her bare feet touched the smoothly polished floor, and she went to the first of three open south windows.

Voices were muffled, but she saw Mase's tall, lean body first. Renaldo Flores on the wagon box, and Tony Martinez on a gelding, were with him. Two long pine boxes, chinked with Colorado River mud, lay in the flat bed of the Regrett wagon. From out the doors of the cabins in the compound poured women and children. Men came from the barns, among them LeRoy and Big Miguel, who had not yet left on his rounds as foreman.

Tony and Renaldo, with Mase's help, removed one of the pine boxes, and laid it on the ground before the Puentes's big adobe house. Dorita, a black shawl over her head and shoulders, fell on her knees, clasping her hands together, elbows on the coffin. She bent her head to her hands. Angelita, Young Miguel's baby sister, who was not quite four years old, pulled at her mother, her high baby voice carrying on the wind that blew into Monty's window.

"Mamacita, what is the matter?"

Carlos came and caught her up in his arms, and carried her, as the rest of the Puentes and the other Mexican families gathered about the wagon.

In a moment, Monty saw her father stride out and join them. She could hear his deep voice.

"We'll have the services this afternoon, Dorita, Big Miguel—I'll conduct them myself. We're all very proud of Young Miguel. He'll be buried with honor."

Mase Regrett looked at Richard Daventry, and Monty could see his glittering black eyes.

"Young Miguel's arrangements are yours, Daventry," he said remotely. "I'm taking Julien on home with me—and *I'll* conduct his services this afternoon."

"Thank you for bringing Miguelito home to us," Richard said stiffly.

"Sí, sí," put in the weeping Dorita. "Gracias, gracias, Señor Mase, with all our hearts."

"Glad to do it for you and Big Miguel, Dorita," Mase said huskily. With that he, Renaldo, and Tony moved away through the compound. Carlos put down Angelita, and ran after them to open the south gate.

As Monty watched the small funeral cortege move away and become lost to view among thick trees, her eyes stung hotly.

It came home to her with heart-wrenching clarity that not only was one of her childhood playmates actually gone forever, but she might never be loved by Mason Regrett again. Everything in her body and mind rebelled at those two facts.

She turned from the window, and flung herself on the disheveled bed with a smothered sob. She could not bear it! Miguel was gone. That, she *must* accept, no matter how it tore her heart. But she could not—*would not*—accept the loss of Mase's love. There had to be a way—there had to be something she could do!

When she rose at last, and looked out again through eyes swollen by grief, she saw the pine box had disappeared, and none of the Puentes were to be seen among the people who went about their appointed chores. She saw LeRoy Beane and Santiago Espinosa with spades over their shoulders, as they went out the south gate, closing it behind them.

She knew they were going to the Daventry cemetery to prepare a place for Young Miguel. There would be two funerals today, she thought, as she began donning her fitted pants. At the thought of Julien's, with only Mase and his ranch people there to mourn him, she fought fresh tears. Mase wouldn't want *her* there—he looked on her father as a murderer. She went to the washstand and bathed her face repeatedly.

They gathered for breakfast in unaccustomed silence. Abby's usually serene face was somber, and Daventry's jaw was set. Faith slipped into her chair, her voice a low murmur.

"Louise said to explain that she's having breakfast in her room. Tina's bringing it to her."

"Isn't she feeling well?" Abby asked.

"She said she wanted to bathe this morning after breakfast, and before going to tea at the Cavenals'," Faith said. Catching her glance, Monty gave her a sardonic smile that matched her father's, and Faith colored faintly.

"She won't be going to the Cavenals' today," Richard Daventry said, "with or without a bath."

Feenie, pouring coffee, looked quickly at her mother, who

placed a steaming platter of scrambled eggs before Abby. "Maw," she whispered, "did you start Miz Daventry's water?"

"Merzella's tendin' to that," Josey said briefly. "I'll have hot biscuits an' jam here in a minute, Miss Abby."

The two had their heads together as they left the dining room.

"What time is the service for Young Miguel to be held, Richard?" Abby asked.

"At four," Richard said, meeting his mother's eyes. "And Faith, you might tell your . . . cousin that I expect everyone on Daventry land to attend."

"I will, Richard," Faith said, her color deepening.

"On second thought, I'll tell her myself, Faith," he said slowly. "I expect she'll have objections, and I want to handle them personally."

Chapter 25

At a quarter to four the entire population of the Daventry place had gathered at the cemetery at the southwestern corner beyond the compound. As Richard, Abby, Faith, and Monty prepared to join them, he paused at the door.

"I told Louise to be down here by three-thirty," he said, looking at the stairs behind them.

"I'll go see what's keeping her," Faith said hastily, but Richard caught her arm.

"No, I'll go." His long legs took the stairs two at a time while the women waited below.

In Louise's room, he found her sitting at the dressing table, brushing her long blond curls. She was clad in a pink dress with daring cleavage at her piquant bosom. It was entirely unsuitable for the occasion.

"Get downstairs," Richard said tersely. "We're waiting."

"I've decided I won't attend this unnecessary foolishness over that boy." She continued to brush her hair, but her eyes locked with his in the mirror.

"You will attend." He drew nearer.

"I will *not!* I won't have all the servants staring at me. I can't shed tears over that stupid boy."

He looked at her for a long moment. Then with quiet menace, he said, "None of them expects you to shed tears. If you think my people don't know about you and Young Miguel, you're a bigger fool than I suspected. They know. And they are going to have the satisfaction of seeing you show your respect for the boy."

"Respect! That ignorant boy deserves no respect."

"You underestimate him—and me, Louise. Now get up!" He reached out and caught her arm roughly. The brush clattered to the floor.

"I will not go!"

"You'll go," he said grimly, "if I have to drag you every step of the way." Then with a dry laugh, he added, "I think I'd enjoy that—and your humiliation would be complete." He jerked her forcefully to her feet.

"I hate you for this, Richard Daventry!"

"Don't worry. Tom Arterbury will take my request for a divorce to the Legislature in Austin when he leaves in two days. I've already written a formal statement, citing grounds in detail, and I'll give it to him when he stops by. Now stand up. We're going."

"But I'm not dressed for a funeral," she cried.

"You look every inch what you are. I think your dress is highly suitable." He pulled her along to the door. "Straighten up, madam, or I'll drag you there by the heels."

Realizing resistance was useless, Louise allowed herself to be propelled to the stairs and down them. She looked fiercely at the three women who waited below. The sun outside was scorching hot. Faith looked at her half-sister's defiant face, her frilly, ridiculous dress, and pity stirred her.

"I'll get you a bonnet, Louise," she said quietly and turned. She went to the hall tree and took a wide-brimmed straw hat belonging to Abby from one of the arms and handed it to Louise.

Without a word, Louise jammed it on her head, with her

long curling hair tumbling from beneath it. Abby handed Richard her Bible, and in silence the five of them walked the entire length of the compound and beyond, to the cemetery.

The trench LeRoy and Santiago had dug was wide and deep under the huge oaks that dotted the cemetery. Miguel's body was next to it in the sealed new pine box.

Richard waited until all were gathered near before he opened the Bible and began reading quietly in Spanish.

" 'To everything there is a season, and a time to every purpose under the heavens. A time to be born and a time to die—' "

As his voice rose and fell in the musical language, Dorita shook with sobs that she tried vainly to stem. Other women about her were weeping silently. Big Miguel stood stone-faced as he put an arm about his wife's shoulders.

Louise, in her revealing pink dress, stood restlessly, her impatience obvious. Her small feet shifted in their impractical, heeled slippers. She did not look at the pine box, nor the people about her. Her eyes were fixed on the road off to the side that led to George Cavenal's big house.

When Richard closed the Bible at last, he lifted his head and viewed the crowd about him. Still speaking in Spanish, he made his short eulogy.

"I owe Miguelito my life. Without his swift thought and action, it would be my body in this coffin instead of his. He was a fine young man—a credit to his parents—and loved by everyone for his kindness and regard for duty. It is with great sadness that I accept his sacrifice. It is a burden I will carry with me to the end of my days."

He fell silent then and nodded to Big Miguel, who turned and put a hand out to his youngest daughter. Over Angelita's slender brown arm was a cutting basket filled with roses from Abby's and Dorita's gardens.

She stepped forward and passed a rose to each woman

gathered around the gravesite. The sorrow of the occasion had not touched her and those present took comfort in her innocence.

She reached Abby, extending a dark red rose to her. Faith and Monty took theirs, eyes filled with tears.

Then the child extended a pale pink rose to Louise, who smiled brilliantly for the benefit of those around her as she reached for the flower.

But Richard was swifter than she. He leaned forward, taking the rose before Louise could touch it.

"I'll take the rose, Angelita," he said, leaving his wife's outstretched hand empty.

Louise paled with fury, and her chagrin was noticeable. She drew back her hand swiftly, and her eyes on her husband were venomous. The faces about her held knowledge, contempt, and not a trace of pity. She flushed with indignation.

After Angelita had passed all her roses among the women, the young men slowly lowered the casket while Richard recited the Lord's Prayer in Spanish. Then, along with the women, he tossed his rose among theirs on the lowered coffin.

Voices were low, and the people stood beside the open grave, as LeRoy and Santiago Espinosa began to shovel the mound of earth back into it. Louise turned sharply to walk away, but Richard's hand came out and caught her bare arm in a viselike grip. He held her there beside him until the last shovel of earth closed the grave. Dorita, her husband, and their many friends knelt, making the sign of the cross, before Richard released his wife's arm.

Only then did the five of them walk in silence back through the open gate to the house.

Louise wanted to shout at her husband and would have, but she did not know how much of their quarrel was known by Lady Abigail and his hoyden daughter. Even Faith had been unresponsive to her questions.

As Louise walked beside them in the broiling afternoon sun, she thought silently, *I can't leave him—not yet anyway. And this was the last day I could see Cav. God only knows how long he'll stay in Austin! But he'll be leaving tomorrow and now Richard will stay here. Damn him! Damn the whole Daventry household!*

"I'll take supper in my room, Richard darling," she said lightly. "All this has been very hard on me. After all, the boy rode escort for me for a few days, and I'm terribly grieved over his death."

He did not answer, but turned instead to Abby. "Abby, have Feenie and Josey take two of the smoked turkeys to the Puente house, and send a length of the silk I brought home from Washington to Dorita. Tell her it's for Angelita."

For the next two days, Monty fluctuated between hunger to see Mase and wanting to please her father. She knew Richard had come to grips with the fact that his marriage was a mistake, and she did not want to hurt him further. Yet she longed to mount Dolly and ride to the Regrett ranch, even though she knew Mase had left to attend the convention.

And too, Mase couldn't come and see her, even when he returned, she argued with herself. He knew how Richard Daventry felt, so it was up to Monty to heal the wound of Julien's death and show Mase that she loved him despite her father's disapproval.

The last night of June was stiflingly hot and Monty was restless. Even the sheets burned as she shifted, seeking a cooler spot in her bed. It was then she heard the first faint rumble of thunder.

When the storm broke over the big house, it somehow lifted the oppression that weighed on her. Sleep took her as rain beat a staccato tattoo against the windows and on the roof.

She woke early and, after dressing, went into the hall. Tom Arterbury and her father stood in the foyer and their voices drifted up the stairs. Arterbury was speaking of the meeting he was on his way to attend and the chances of stopping annexation.

"I never want to hear the word 'annexation' again," her father was saying bitterly.

She stood, her hand on the newel post, listening openly. She was sure Tom hadn't been there but a few minutes.

"You ought to be used to it by now, Richard."

"No," her father said with curbed passion. "I don't intend to get used to it. I don't intend to speak the word again."

"What will you do if Texas becomes a state?" Tom asked with a good-natured chuckle.

"Accept it and go on."

"You won't return to England—as George Cavenal has threatened?"

Her father laughed ironically. "No. I'm here to stay."

"Despite the fact that Julien's spread it over the countryside that you set fire to their place, old boy?"

"You know damn well I didn't do that, Tom."

"I know, Richard. Julien told me about the boots he thought he recognized, when Tim Bedford and I were over there buying horses and cattle a couple of weeks ago. I'll bet you a hundred in gold, it was the Bosquez brothers, boots and all."

"Cav suggested that, the time he and his mother and Gina came to see me after I came home. I appreciate your standing up for me."

"Still, I wish you'd come with me to Austin—though I know your wound was a bad one."

"That's not what's keeping me."

"Then why not come on with me?"

"Circumstances demand that I stay here, Tom. The envelope you're carrying to the Legislature for me contains my reasons."

"You think it'll sway the Legislature to vote against—"

"I hope it will sway the Legislature." Richard's smile was without humor.

"You place a good deal of faith in the written word." Tom laughed. "If all your efforts in Washington didn't stop the juggernaut of annexation, I doubt if writing them will do it." There was a hint of curiosity in the statement.

"My written request doesn't concern what this convention is trying to do, Tom."

The two men bade each other good-bye, and Richard stood at the front door, watching Arterbury trot away.

Monty, at the top of the stairs, was intensely curious. What had her father written about to the Legislature of the Republic of Texas? *The divorce!* He had certainly been quiet and aloof these last two days. More than that, Faith had been looking at him with curious intensity and her father had returned her glances quickly. Monty had seen something almost pleading in his eyes—and a kind of remorse. It was as if Faith and Richard shared a very personal secret.

Preoccupied with her own fierce desire to see Mason Regrett, Monty had not registered these things fully. Now she thought about them as she descended the stairs slowly.

Richard turned away from the door as Monty reached the bottom step. She heard the clink of bridle bits and the crunch of hooves on the graveled drive.

"Pa," she said tentatively, "how long do you think that meeting in Austin will last?"

He shrugged. "A week—maybe a month. Maybe longer."

They made their way to the dining room where the table was laid for breakfast.

"And all the men—they'll stay until it's over?" Her heart sank. Mase would be gone so long!

"The Legislature will."

"I mean the men like Tom Arterbury," she said doggedly, *and Mason Regrett,* "who aren't in the Legislature."

"No. I expect they'll come home as soon as the decision's made."

"Why would any of them stay after the decision's made?"

"Because if they vote to join the Union, the Legislature will have to write a constitution."

"A constitution?"

"Rights reserved to Texas under the laws of the American government." He paused, looking at her quizzically. "That could mean the difference between a good deal and a bad one. A lot rides on the rights reserved for Texas—the advantages we will receive if they vote to join." He looked down the foyer. "Ah, good morning, Abby—good morning, Faith."

"Then you look for Tom Arterbury to be back in about a week?" Monty returned tenaciously to the subject that interested her most. Mase would likely be back when Tom returned.

"Possibly two weeks. The vote should be over by then. If it's no, they'll all go home. If it's yes, the legislators will stay and hammer out a constitution."

A week dragged by and Richard rode his fields regularly with Big Miguel, but only part of the day. He stayed at the house until Louise left for the Cavenals', and he was always back before she returned. She had reverted to her customary blithe confidence since the funeral and chatted at the supper table about her rides with Georgina, and the graciousness of Lady Marguerite. She no longer tried to impose her will on Monty or Faith, but she had become increasingly ugly with her personal servants.

Abby was coolly polite to her, but Faith seemed as eager to please Louise as ever, and there was always a touch of fear in her voice when she spoke to her. This puzzled Monty, and she tried to win Faith's confidence when they took morning rides together that first week. But Faith, still fearful of her half-sister's violence, would not be drawn into confiding in Monty. Restless with her own problems, Monty gave up, and talked books, horses, and finally, what they would all do if annexation became a fact.

Toward the middle of July, Faith waited until the house was quiet. One hot, humid night, on bare silent feet, she slipped to Richard's north bedroom. Opening the door silently, she found him still fully dressed, reading. He rose at once, putting the book aside, and came to take her in his arms.

Tightness filled his chest. He loved her. He had told her he loved her, and blamed himself for that dark, sensuous night in her bed.

"Faith," he whispered into her hair, "I've sworn to God that I would not touch you again until I'm free from Louise."

"But Richard, I love you! And who knows what Louise can do? You don't know her like I do. I'm still afraid of her."

"You should fear me more, Faith, for I've done you a great wrong! You're so young, you can't know the consequences of what I've done. I've written to the Legislature for a divorce and when I receive it—I'll be free to come to you. Until then, I swear again, I won't touch you!"

She cried then, and he held her in his arms. It was a bittersweet ache, feeling her warm, trembling shoulders and back under his hands. He held her until her sobs slowed, and she spoke huskily.

"Richard, Randy Lynchley was going to divorce her in Charleston—I heard him say it during a wild quarrel they had. And the next day, he was *dead.*" Faith did not lift her head from his shoulder as she talked. "They said it was an accident—but I think he shot himself rather than face the disgrace. You wouldn't do that, would you?"

He laughed and there was gentle irony in it. "I certainly wouldn't, my beloved. I have every intention of living to a ripe old age—and with you."

"But you don't know Louise," she repeated.

"I know her well enough."

Two days later, Monty decided to lay the groundwork for a visit to the Regrett ranch. She broached the subject to her father over after-dinner coffee. He was having brandy in his, and she knew he would be more approachable—though God knows he had been remote enough in the past ten days.

"Pa, I miss Warlock more every day," she began, and set her cup on a nearby table to lean forward earnestly. "And I had come to love Slyboots long before she died in . . . that fire. When can I pick out two others?"

"Whenever you like," he said casually. "I'll have Big Miguel go to the Regrett ranch and bring several for you to choose from."

"No. I want to go see them all, and make my choice."

He looked at her from under his brows, gray eyes darkening. "I suppose you can go—tomorrow. Regrett's still in Austin."

"Oh, I didn't mean now," Monty said offhandedly. "I meant in about a week."

He looked at her narrowly. "Then we'll talk about it in a week."

He was thinking, *She wants to see the man. I'll be damned if I let her do it! She seems the same, she looks the same—yet I swear something must have happened to her during those days on the road alone with Regrett.*

But Monty was on her guard after this. She did not mention it again.

Mid-afternoon of July twenty-seventh, a weary but jubilant Tom Arterbury rode up to the Daventry house. Abby welcomed him, and sent Carlos Puente posthaste to the fields to bring Richard back to the house. There was immediate excitement in the compound, as Carlos, on his way to the stables, shouted of the arrival of the visitor from Austin.

Monty ran from the stables with a currycomb still in her hands. Faith, hearing Abby's excited voice, came down from her room. Feenie and Josey stood in the back of the foyer, smiling as Abby led Arterbury into the parlor.

Louise was, as usual, at the Cavenals'.

"Would you like brandy, or whiskey and water, Tom?" Abby asked as he pulled off his hat and sank down in a big, tall-backed chair.

"I believe I'd prefer a big glass of cold tea, Miss Abby, if you have it," he responded, leaning back gratefully into the softness of the chair.

"Oh, Mr. Arterbury," Monty cried, following Faith into the room, "has *everyone* come home from Austin?"

"Bless you, no, Monty. The Legislature will be there until they finish writing the constitution—and it may take weeks. But George Cavenal, Mason Regrett, and I left after its terms were pretty well settled."

"Did—did—" Faith began timidly. "Did Texas agree to annexation?"

"We did—and a good thing it is, too."

Disappointment was in Faith's eyes. Monty herself was exasperated—this would be a blow to her father's hopes. But Tom Arterbury said Mason Regrett had come home!

Abby sent Feenie and her mother to get cold tea and serve their guest, while Monty tried to phrase her questions casually.

"So Cav has come home too—and did he say he would stay in Texas?"

"No, miss, he said he would not. He was in a fine state over our acceptance into the Union. None of the generous terms that have been laid out could appease him." Arterbury pulled a pipe from his shirt pocket, and taking out a small leather pouch of tobacco, tamped it into the bowl.

"Feenie," Abby said to the young girl as she appeared with glasses of tea on a tray. "Bring a coal from the kitchen fireplace for Mr. Arterbury's pipe." Feenie placed the tray on the table before her and hurried out.

"I suppose Mason Regrett crowed all the way home—or did you all ride together?" Monty asked innocently.

"We did. I left them where the road branches to their places. And surprisingly, Mase was quiet enough. He listened to Cav rant most of the way home without comment. They took their separate roads where I left them."

Abby sighed deeply. "So it's all over at last," she said slowly.

"Yes and I for one, thank God that it is." Arterbury took a deep draft of cold tea as Feenie appeared with a live coal between the kitchen tongs. He lit his pipe silently. At that moment, Richard came striding into the room. Arterbury rose swiftly, taking the hand Richard extended, and clapped his friend on the shoulder.

"Carlos couldn't tell me a thing, except that you were here, Tom. Now tell me everything."

With that, Arterbury launched into details of the some-times stormy, sometimes majestic meeting of the Legislature in the small settlement of Austin. He told Richard and his women that emissaries from the United States agreed that Texas alone, among all the states in the Union, was to be allowed to keep her public lands. Regular postal service would begin as soon as the state constitution could be written. A stable currency would be established. A homestead law would be included in the terms and taxes would be delayed until the state was financially solvent.

Furthermore, the Texas boundary would be the Rio Grande River, and the United States would provide military protection from Mexico and the Indians. In fact, it was well known that American soldiers were already stationed in Texas.

"Oh, by the way," Arterbury said offhandedly, "I delivered your letter to a man they said was chairman for legal matters. He read it, and told me your request would have to be tabled until the state constitution was completed. But you'll hear from them after it's written."

Monty noted her father's guarded face, and Arterbury's concealed sympathy and curiosity.

When Arterbury finally took his departure, Richard had recovered from his initial dismay. He was able to laugh wryly, as he and the women stood by the door.

"Maybe it's a good thing," he said, unconvinced. "If the terms are as generous as you say, Tom, perhaps we can all live with it."

Arterbury mounted, then turned and waved when he took the long, dusty road. July heat shimmered between them, and a dry wind rustled the oaks around the house. It fanned out the flag at the top of the tall pine pole to the right of the stoop.

Richard looked up at the bright colors, bearing the single white star, his face sad.

"You can live under two flags, my son," Abby said quietly. She put her hand out to his arm. Her quick touch was gentle. "I'll make one with stars and stripes—I know it well —but your flag of Texas can fly below it as long as Daventrys live on this land."

Chapter 26

Louise had breakfast served in her room the follow-ing morning, as usual, while she prepared for her customary ride to the Cavenals'. Monty, on her way downstairs as Tina brought the tray up, scarcely noticed.

All through breakfast, she concentrated single-mindedly on how to approach her father with the fact that she was going to ride to the Regrett ranch this morning. She would use the horses as a reason, she decided, but go she would. Nothing short of physical restraint could keep her from it.

"You're very quiet, Monty," Abby said, smiling at her across the table. "A penny for your thoughts."

"They aren't worth it, Abby," she said, flushing. "As usual, I was thinking about horses—and wishing I had an-other stallion as well as a mare. I don't suppose I'll find any as beautiful as Warlock or Slyboots."

"But you will, Monty," Faith said with an encouraging smile.

Richard's eyes went to the girl, and Monty could not read the strange expression in them, nor could she recognize the banked fires that lay behind them.

"Pa, could I talk to you later?"

He looked at her warily. "We're finished now—come into my office with me."

Abby turned to Faith. "Come upstairs with me, Faith. You tell me you can sew." Her eyes twinkled. "I'll give you a chance to show me how well. I have red, white, and blue cloth in abundance, and I propose to make a new flag."

Monty heard this as she followed her father to the small room. They went through the foyer and took the door into the office, where Richard remained standing as he leaned against the desk. His eyes on her were speculative.

"Pa," she blurted out, "I want to go pick out my horses today."

"You mean you want to see Regrett."

"Why would you say that? I *told* you days ago I meant to go there, and you said I could."

"Did I?"

"Of course you did!"

"But Regrett wasn't there, then."

Monty bit her lip, then took up her argument. "It's better that he is. After all, it's him we'll be buying from!"

"I won't have you seeing the man, Monty. He's accused me falsely of trying to burn him out. He's insulted us time and again. His brother tried to kill me. Regrett's a black-guard."

"You think you're *always so right!*" she blazed. "You were wrong about Louise—and now you've half admitted you were wrong about annexation! Doesn't it occur to you that you could be wrong about Regrett?"

"Monty"—his voice was low and reasoning—"you know what I've said is true. You know nothing of his life in Louisiana before settling here. He has no family—"

"No, he hasn't, now that you shot his brother!"

"You know I didn't want to do that. And it's made Mason Regrett more bitter toward us than ever." Richard's voice grew harsher. "He won't welcome you, because you're my daughter—a Daventry. I saw his eyes as he flung out of here that day—and there was no love in them!"

Monty's restraint broke abruptly and words boiled out. "I told you that awful day we came home, Mason Regrett was going to ask your permission for me to marry him! I love him, and that's why I'm going to ride over there today. *Nothing can stop me!*"

Richard Daventry straightened up, white and silent, but Monty, her emotions raw, saw him only as an obstacle to her happiness.

"LeRoy can take me over there, but I tell you now, Pa, I mean to marry him no matter what you think of him—if we have to run away together to do it!"

"Monty"—her father's voice was husky—"wait! Promise me you won't marry him hastily! Give yourself time—don't rush into it."

As she turned on her heel and ran from the room, Richard looked after her, his mind suddenly clearing through the smoke of fury and fear for his daughter's future.

I suspected Mason Regrett of doing to my little girl the thing I did to Faith—destroying her innocence in one night. Monty is right. I've been wrong about so many things.

In the dark coolness of the stables, Monty ran her hand across her damp forehead. This day was going to be a scorcher and she'd forgotten her hat! Well, she'd just take one of those hanging in the stables for the hands. The horses snuffled and whickered as she moved about. From the wall near the tack room, where shears and currycombs for grooming the horses hung, she pulled a small straw hat from a hook. Jamming it over her bright hair, she opened the gate to Dolly's stall.

"Come on, old girl. We're going to see Mase!" She swung the saddle from the top rail of the stall, slinging it easily over the horse's back.

"Monty—my Feenie just tol' me your pa say—"

"I know what he told her, LeRoy," she cut in, smiling innocently at him as he came past the tack room. "I'm going to Mase Regrett's to look at horses. You saddle Johnsy and we'll go."

LeRoy's eyes were inscrutable as he got the big gelding from his stall. He knew Monty had left trouble with her pa, and she was heading for trouble with Mase Regrett. But he made no further comment.

The burring of cicadas in the big oaks grew loud as they neared Three Points Lake. Then, as they trotted close to the Regrett ranch house, Monty glimpsed men working on the stables. She looked more closely. They were almost finished! The one that had been least damaged by fire appeared as it always had. She glanced upward. It couldn't be more than ten in the morning.

"Reckon Mister Mase'll be out with his herd by now," LeRoy said suddenly, corroborating her unspoken thought.

"We'll stop at the big house and ask Mamacita," she said, hiding annoyance. LeRoy was on her father's side all the way.

"An' if he ain't comin' in till dark?"

"I'll look at the horses. Someone's bound to be at the stables, and can show me which ones he's ready to sell."

"Well—that's what you tol' your pa you was comin' for."

"That's right."

Silence fell between them again as they rode up to the fence around the house and yards. LeRoy got off his gelding silently, opening the gate for Monty to ride through. After he secured his horse, he closed it, and they rode up to the back of the house.

"Mamacita!" Monty called. Curtains belled at the broad windows as a strong south breeze poured through the big adobe brick house. The back door was suddenly thrown wide open and Twyla Salazar's ample figure appeared, followed by Velma Flores.

"Monty, niña! Come into this house—how long has it been?"

"Come in, LeRoy," echoed Velma. "We get you some cold tea."

Monty and LeRoy dismounted swiftly and followed the two inside.

"I want to see the horses," Monty said. Then coming directly to the point, she inquired, "Where is Mase, Mamacita?"

As they all entered the kitchen, Twyla Salazar answered. "He an' my Andrew out to the corral. They breakin' some year-old stallions to saddle. I think maybe he ready to come in for some col' tea, too. Velma, you go tell Señor Mase Monty's here." She handed tall pewter mugs of tea to the visitors.

"No," Monty said swiftly. "I came to buy horses, Velma. I'll go to the corral myself."

Since the main corral was attached to the center stable, her chances of getting to see Mase alone were much better there. They could go into the stable and talk. That prodded the memory of the last time she was there, lying naked on the pile of hay at the end of the stalls, and she felt her face heat up. Today, it would be different. Today, she would tell him that she loved him—and her father's objections meant nothing to her any longer.

She gulped the last of her tea, and handed the empty mug back to Velma.

"You in a big hurry, Monty," Twyla said shrewdly.

"I want to buy a stallion and a mare. Did Mase . . . tell you Warlock was—stolen by Indians?"

"He tol' us," was the brief reply. "An' he tol' us about your padre shooting his brother. Is a bad thing, Monty.

Señor Mase, he ver' angry—he have deep sadness about Señor Julien."

"I know. I'm going to try to make it up to him."

"Can't nothin' bring back Señor Julien," Velma said uneasily. "Señor Mase, he say he have nothin' more to do with Señor Richard, ever." Her dark brown eyes fell under Monty's sharp blue glance.

"Did he say he'd have nothing more to do with *me?*"

Both Twyla and Velma were silent.

"Then he *did* say he'd have nothing more to do with me."

"No . . ." Velma said slowly. "He say he'll have nothin' more to do with the *Daventrys.*"

"Surely he'll sell us horses?"

"Sure he will, Monty," Twyla said soothingly, shooting a sharp glance at Velma. "You go to the stables an' ask him."

Later, as she drew near the corral, she could hear the shouts of men. She saw that two of the vaqueros sat on the fence watching the violently arching horse in the center of the corral. Mason Regrett's free arm beat the air and he held the reins hard against the pommel of his saddle as the stallion attempted to unseat him. Intent on his effort to subdue the big animal, he did not see Monty's slender figure nearing the enclosure.

The horse slowed an instant and Mase swept off his hat and began to fan it near the animal's head. The horse leaped high and came down stiff-legged. It was a bone-jarring stop, but Mase Regrett leaned into it gracefully and clapped the hat back on his head as the gyrations of the horse began anew.

"Hello, Andy," Monty greeted the vaquero seated on the fence above her. He and Renaldo Flores turned swiftly.

"Monty!"

"You surprise us, señorita," Renaldo said.

"I see Mase is busy. I want to talk to him. I want to buy horses to replace Warlock and Slyboots."

"Ah, yes. Is so sad—Slyboots," Andrew said uncomfortably.

"An' Warlock, too," Renaldo added.

"How much longer—" she began.

"Is almost over," Andrew said quickly. "This one, he is ver' stubborn, but he grow tired now, I think."

The horse under Mase was obviously tiring. He arched his back again and came down on his forefeet, then on his hind legs, almost in a sitting position. Mase fanned his hat about the stallion's head once more.

Monty climbed on the fence and watched for the next ten minutes, as the stallion's efforts to dislodge his rider grew less and less vigorous. When finally he began to walk around the corral, the two men beside Monty began to cheer and she added her voice to theirs. It was then that Mase's head swung in her direction. Her eyes were bright as blue fire.

His brows drew down, and he put his hat back on his dark head as Andrew approached and took the reins from his hands.

"I take him now, Señor Mase, an' ride him a mile or two —get him used to me in the saddle."

"Fine, Andy. I see I have company." His tone said clearly, *unwelcome company.*

For the first time, doubt assailed Monty. She smiled at him as their eyes held and he walked toward her. He removed his hat once more and dusted it against his tightly fitted pants.

"I didn't expect to see any of the Daventrys again," he said impersonally, as he drew up before Monty where she sat on the top rail.

"I want to talk to you," she said forthrightly.

"You mean you want to buy horses and beef from me?"

"Of course, Mase! Help me down."

Renaldo had followed Andrew and the two were leading the heaving stallion out the gate and into the fenced yard.

"You got up there. Can't you get down?"

"Yes, I can!" This wasn't at all the way she had intended to greet him! "Can't we go in out of the sun to talk?"

"Where do you suggest?"

"Why, the stable, the tack room—anywhere we can be alone."

"You haven't forgotten the last time you were in this stable?" he asked mockingly.

"No, I haven't! And that's one of the reasons I want to talk to you." She slipped down from the fence into the corral and started walking ahead of him toward the big stable. He followed without speaking. Once inside, seeing they were alone but for the horses, she pulled off the old straw hat, letting her bright hair tumble down.

"Mase, I came as soon as I could. You *knew* I would! I'm so sorry about Julien—it's terrible! And Pa's sorry, too. I know how you must feel!" The words burst from her. She had planned to be loving. She *would* be loving!

"I don't think you can, Monty." His voice was strange, hollow—somehow. His dark eyes were filled with pain as he registered her beauty and his own torment. "You still have your family intact. I have . . . no one."

"But you have *me*, Mase!"

He was silent. The stable loomed big, cool, and dark about them. Scents of horses, hay, mash, and leather harnesses filled her lungs. It was all so familiar, so reassuring to her, yet a coldness crept along her veins as she looked up into his eyes. They were icy; no answering spark lingered behind their blackness.

"Do I have you?" He laughed shortly. The rebuff in his words was like a blow to her. Tears burned her eyes, and she blinked furiously. "So we have each other—with the shambles of our families around our feet. Could—would you begin a life with me, with that on your conscience?"

"On my conscience?" Pride and anger surged up, and she wiped away the trace of tears. "I didn't—I *don't* feel that way about us, about our families. You make it sound as if it were our fault!"

"Well, isn't it? Whose fault would you say it was, *if not ours?* You ran away from your stepmother, outside the patrol limits and alone—got yourself captured. And I—" He laughed without a trace of humor. "I had to be your protector. Naturally, my brother and your father would come in search of us. Both of them hot-tempered men. And what did they quarrel about? *You and me!*"

Monty was speechless at the logic of his reasoning. Her heart grew leaden in her. Suddenly he struck the side of the tack room wall with the flat of his palm and groaned.

"Hell yes, it was our fault. *Nobody's but yours and mine!* All of it our fault! And I had to bury my brother because of us."

"What you really mean is it's *my* fault, don't you?" she blazed. "If I'd just stayed home and let my stepmother ruin my life—*none* of it would've happened!" Blind with tears and rage, she turned away from him, moving toward the door. She stumbled slightly, caught herself and said over her shoulder, "I'll leave you then—you with your guilty conscience." *And me with mine,* she thought with despair.

In two swift strides, Mase was beside her. He caught her roughly to him. She fought him then, with all the fierceness of her hurt and anger, until he pinned her against the tack room wall, and put his lips on hers.

At first, his kiss was hungry. Suddenly, Monty could no longer stem her own passion, but joined with him, and he kissed her with all the pain and longing for the brother he had lost, with all the knowledge that she could never be his now. He smelled of heat, sunlight, and all the fragrances dear to her, and her yielding body melted to his as her arms locked themselves about his shoulders. The terrible sweetness of their love, and their loss, was in the fusion of their kiss. They stood for an interminable moment, before he put her from him.

"That's for good-bye, Monty." His voice was husky. "The break between your father and me can never be mended. There was a chance, before he killed my brother—but not now."

Monty swayed, dizzy with desire, and disappointment. His words cut into her like a knife. She swung on her heel, and strode from the stables. Blindly, she climbed the corral fence and walked back to the house, where she found LeRoy still talking with Mamacita and Velma, who were making sandwiches to take to those at the corral later. The three looked at her in surprise.

"You finish picking your horses so quick, Monty?" Twyla asked.

"No. I didn't look at the horses—I'll do that another day. Come on, LeRoy, we have to get home."

"You come back tomorrow?" Velma asked tactfully.

"No."

"But you *will* come back?" Twyla's question was hopeful.

"Maybe. But not soon. Thanks for the tea."

The two women were silent as LeRoy and Monty mounted their horses and trotted to the rear gate.

Chapter 27

Louise, returning from the Cavenals' with Ezekiel beside her, was filled with dissatisfaction, bordering on anger. She had made love with Cav in the game shed, and it had been as satisfying as ever, perhaps more so because he had been in Austin so long. But he had spoken vaguely of returning to England. He had mentioned no date of departure. Again she told him she loved him, that she would go with him—let the divorce from Richard come later.

"He says the Legislature will take action on it as soon as the—the constitution for Texas is written," she told him. "I can go with you, darling Cav—I *will* go with you! I won't stay a minute longer with Richard than I have to!"

"Wait three days—we won't meet—and I'll send Abraham with a message about the time for leaving, love."

Now, as she and Ezekiel rode down the sun-dappled road, she reminded herself of the triumphant moment, weeks ago, when he had said, again, *My darling, if only you weren't married, we could be together always.* And he *had* vowed he wouldn't go without her.

As the Daventry compound came into view, she thought fretfully that she certainly wasn't anxious to go into the house. It was late enough for Richard to be there—and his haughty mother was always around. Lady Abigail was the only person Louise had ever met who could make her feel inadequate and shallow, damn her!

They rode to the stable. Ezekiel stopped outside, but Louise rode her horse into the dark opening where the stalls were. She halted the mare and looked with disbelief at the two who were embracing at the end of the stalls.

Abraham Johnson from Cavenal's and her own Tina Moses!
Tina's magnificent tumble of mahogany hair hung down her back, and their kiss was so impassioned, their bodies so tightly meshed, they did not hear the horse's hooves in the soft and finely broken sand of the stable floor. They did not look up.

Louise sat on her mount, staring. All her frustration and irritation rose up like bile in her throat at the sight of Cav's slave making love to hers. Fury choked her.

Feeling a presence besides themselves and the horses, the lovers suddenly separated, and Tina's wide eyes swung to the mounted woman. Her mouth formed a small O. Abraham drew himself up, and his gaze at Louise was level.

"You keep your dirty hands off my maid, Abraham!" Louise said commandingly. "And Tina, you know what I promised you, if you made another mistake—well, my girl, you've made another mistake!"

"Miz Daventry, I aim to marry Tina. Mister Cav's promised to buy her. He tol' me you said you'd sell her to him." Abraham spoke with cold dignity.

"Liar! Cav never told you any such thing. I've told him I'll *never* sell any of my slaves! You get on your horse and get back to the Cavenals, and do it *now!*"

"Miz Daventry, Mister Cav promised me he'd buy her. He's just waitin' till he leaves for England, and then he plans to sell all of us, an' his place, to Mister Richard. Mister Richard says he's gonter free all of us."

"Liar, liar!" she shouted, her rage growing. Cav had told

her none of this! Richard to buy Cavenal's place? It was preposterous that he would make all those plans without telling her. She slid from her mare and threw her reins to Ezekiel, who had just brought his horse into the stable.

"I ain't lyin', Miz Daventry—"

"Get out! Get out! And Tina, you stay right here! I'll teach you to sneak around and make a fool of yourself over a man!"

"I'll go," Abraham said tightly, "but I'll be back—with Mister Cav."

They were silent as he walked past Louise and out into the sunlight where his horse was tethered. Hooves sounded as he put his horse into a trot toward the back gate.

"Ezekiel, hand me those shears on the wall there—and Tina, come here to me."

Silently, Ezekiel stepped to the wall where shears for grooming the horses' manes and tails were hung, and handed a pair to Louise.

"Come here, Tina," Louise said ominously. "Ezekiel, you hold her hands behind her."

Divining what was in the woman's mind, Tina began to cry. As Ezekiel took her hands, she pleaded, "Please, Miss Louise, don't cut off my hair—please!"

"Hold her tight, Zeke! Now missy, you've always been so vain about this mop, we'll see how you like it shorter!" She reached out and jerked a thick fall of it up to the shears. The shears, kept sharp for use, cut through easily and the long, shining strands fell to the sandy floor of the stable. As Louise seized another thick lock, Tina began to wail in earnest, her screams echoing through the barn and out into the compound.

Her sister, coming from Dorita Puente's house, heard them and ran to the barn, halting abruptly as she saw her screaming sister's hair falling in great thick strands to the sandy ground.

"Oh, Miss Louise, don't—" Merzella began, but Louise interrupted.

"She needs a lesson, and she's always been too vain about this hair, Merzella. Get back to the house!" Then, as she cut another abundant mass, she said viciously, "And I'll give you a touch of my quirt for good measure after I've cut it all, Tina. You *knew* I'd never let you marry that uppity Abraham! I've told you a hundred times, you and Merzella will never marry!"

Merzella turned and fled toward the house.

Ezekiel's contorted face was a study in hatred, but fear kept him holding Tina's hands. The girl had ceased to struggle, but she wept noisily until the last lock of hair fell and the ragged short bob made her head look small and somehow helpless. Tears streamed down her smooth brown face and her sobs were unabated.

"Now hand me my quirt, Ezekiel. A few licks will teach her to obey me!" As the man picked up her quirt from the ground where she had dropped it, she said, "You'll make no more mistakes like this, my girl." Lifting the quirt, she brought it down across the girl's shoulders and Tina cried out in agony.

At that instant, Richard Daventry, followed by the frantic Merzella, charged into the stables. Without a word, he seized the quirt and tore it from his wife's hands.

"What the hell do you think you're doing?" he asked, his voice low and threatening.

"I'm teaching this wench a lesson. I caught her making love to Abraham Johnson! The next thing you know, I'd have a pregnant maid on my hands—and I've always forbidden marriage for my maids!" Her fury was white-hot. "Give me my quirt at once—she needs convincing my word is law!"

"Your word is *not* law, Louise. And by law, your property became mine when we married." Richard's eyes were icy.

"That being the case, I hereby free all three of your slaves. Ezekiel—Tina and Merzella. I'll give you papers showing manumission within the hour, girls, Ezekiel."

"You can't do that!" Louise exploded, her rage taking on new dimensions. "They are *mine!* You cannot free them!"

"Under Texas law I can—and you can do nothing about it." He turned to the three disbelieving blacks. "You can either return to Charleston and make your own way in the world, or you are welcome to stay here as part of my household, with good wages."

Ezekiel was the first to gain his tongue. "Mister Richard, I thank you," he said fervently, "an' I'll stay with you at wages, like LeRoy—can you use me."

Tina was still weeping and could not speak. Merzella merely stared at Richard, mesmerized by the unexpected blessing he had bestowed on them. Louise was rigid, her face a beautiful mask of fury, before she turned and strode toward the house.

Over her shoulder she shouted, "You'll regret this, Richard Daventry!"

"I can't hardly believe it," Merzella murmured.

"Believe it," Richard said shortly, "because it's true. Now go back to the house, girls, and let Josey comfort Tina." He turned to Ezekiel. "Zeke, you'll take no more orders from Mrs. Daventry, but I would appreciate your accompanying her to the Cavenals' when she goes. I wouldn't want her death by Indians—or capture by renegades—on my conscience."

He turned to follow the two girls, but Ezekiel reached out a hand and caught his arm.

"Mister Richard, I—wait." His voice was thick and deep with emotion. "I got to tell you somethin' I ain't never told nobody before."

"What's that, Ezekiel?" he asked impatiently.

"I'm scairt to tell it, but I'm more scairt for you, iffen I don't."

Richard's eyes and mouth tightened. The man's voice was hesitant, tinged by a reservoir of long-held terrors.

"Frightened for me?" Richard asked.

"Yessir. I—I knows you an' Miss Louise done talked about a divorce—Josey tol' LeRoy an' he tol' me."

Richard's laugh was harsh. "More than talked. We're *going* to be divorced."

Ezekiel's forehead beneath the graying hair furrowed deeply. "That's what Mister Randy thought, too. But in Charleston, Miss Louise was mighty conscious of scandal. She ain't want a divorce even though she don't—love Mister Randy. That's how come she—she—"

"Come on, Ezekiel. Out with it, man."

"I'm scairt she'll do to you what she done to Mister Randy."

Richard looked at him silently, a dark thought pushing at the inner recesses of his mind. "What did she do to Randolph Lynchley, Ezekiel?" he asked softly, his attention riveted to the man.

"Well, sir, she swore she'd kill me do I tell—an' believe me, Mister Richard, she would. But the night after she an' Mister Randy quarrel over divorce, she come out to the stable early that mornin', where he's gettin' ready to mount his hunter. I's up in the loft gettin' ready to fork hay down for th' horses." Ezekiel's voice fell lower and Richard strained to hear. "She come with her reticule an' that li'l derringer she always carries an' she say, 'Is you 'termined to go through with this divorce when I ain't give you no cause to?' An' he laugh an' say, 'No cause to? You done slep' with ever friend I ever had—they can't face me no more. Hell, yes, I'm goin' to file termorrer.' But, Mister Richard, he ain't see no termorrers. She pull out that li'l gun an' she shoot him right in the head."

Blood drained from Richard's tanned face.

"Murder—" His voice was a whisper. "With all the rest, she's got murder on her hands, too."

"Yessir. Murder. She seen me then in th' loft an' tol' me to come down an' take Mister Randy's body across his huntin' hoss. She make me fire one shot from his gun an' ride him out in th' woods. After that, she tell ever'body he musta stumbled an' his gun went off. It were said to be an accident. An' she tol' me she'd kill me do I ever breathe a word of it." He paused, drawing a deep breath, his large, troubled eyes on the man before him. Then slowly, he finished, "I'm afeared she mought do the same to you, Mister Richard."

Daventry's face was still pale and he looked stunned. He muttered, "She cares nothing for scandal in a vast country like this. Besides, she has another man she wants to marry. She's wholly in favor of our divorcing."

"I know that, Mister Richard, but she's a unforgivin' woman. An' you done run counter to her by freein' us."

Richard's jaw tightened and color slowly returned to his face. "By God, that'll stick. You're a free man, Ezekiel. I'll prepare the papers of manumission right now."

He turned from Ezekiel and went back toward the house. He had not revealed how deeply troubled he really was. Only a few hours ago, Monty had returned from Regrett's, her face white and strained. She said nothing except that he no longer need worry about Mason Regrett in her life. He had tried to question her, but she was stubbornly evasive, merely saying, "You were right, Pa. About everything."

It had not satisfied him but he said no more and Monty had spent the balance of the afternoon in her room. This was completely alien to her character and it fueled his uneasiness.

Now as he reentered the house, he could hear Tina's

muted sobbing in the kitchen and Josey's soothing voice mingled with Abby's, Merzella's, and Feenie's.

He went directly to his office to write the papers of manumission and found Monty there, her face still colorless. But her eyes were a bright, furious blue.

"She ought to be whipped herself for what she did to poor little Tina, Pa!"

"I agree. I think I got there before she had time to do much damage with her quirt."

"She got in one good lick. Abby's in the kitchen with them now, putting some of her arnica on Tina's shoulders —but nothing can bring back her beautiful hair."

"Yes, it can. Time will do it. Why aren't you with them, Monty?"

"Because I knew you'd come here first and Louise gave me a message for you."

Richard's face grew harder. "I want no messages from her."

"That's what I told her," Monty said shortly. "But she said, 'You'll give him this one—because it's the last you'll ever give him from me.' "

His mouth tightened grimly. Did she plan to use her derringer after all? "What was her message?"

"She wants you to come to her bedroom. She wants to talk to you." Monty was brief. "She says you've freed her slaves. Is that right, Pa?"

"I intend to give them the papers to prove it as soon as I can write them out." He pushed back the chair to his desk and sat down as he took quill and paper from the drawer.

"Aren't you going to talk to her?"

"She can wait until I've done this," he replied, dipping the quill and writing rapidly.

Monty said no more. Her father carefully filled out the three sheets of paper, signing his name at the bottom slowly and legibly. His Spenserian penmanship was perfect. He handed the papers to Monty.

"Here, Monty, you may have the pleasure of giving these to Ezekiel, Merzella, and Tina."

"Pa—" Monty began huskily. "You're a good man. I— forgive me for what I said and thought before I—I went to Mase's."

"I probably deserved what you were thinking, Monty. I've been a blind fool about Louise." His smile was wintry.

"But not about Mase," she answered bitterly.

"Maybe—" he murmured, his eyes brooding. Then he said, "I'll go see Louise now."

Monty and he left the small office together, Monty heading for the kitchen and Richard taking the stairs two at a time. Reaching the landing, he strode to what had been his bedroom and flung open the door. Louise was seated before the mirror in a pale orchid dressing gown, her golden hair spilling about her shoulders.

"You could have knocked," she said coldly.

"You wanted to talk to me?" He ignored her comment.

"Yes. Just when did you buy the Cavenal place?"

"Two days ago. Abraham came with a note from Cav asking to see me on business. I rode over early and he offered to sell the whole place—every man and woman on it —for ten thousand pounds. Since I thought it worth it, I gave him my letter of credit on the Bank of England. I plan to free the slaves and give them each twenty acres to farm." He paused, then with a smile, he asked, "Didn't he tell you when you were with him this afternoon?"

"Not—yet." She had paled.

"And yet you say he wants to marry you?"

"He's said he's going to take me with him! And he's said it more than once." Confidence flooded her again as she glimpsed her perfect features in the mirror. "As soon as I'm free of you, I'll become Lady Louise Cavenal! You can send confirmation of our divorce to me in London."

"I'm surprised at Cav," he said thoughtfully. "Is that all you wished to discuss?"

"No! Cav's going to send word to me in three or four days to join him. I'm to move my things to their big house—be with them when they leave for England!" *She had told Cav that was her plan and he had agreed only this afternoon. That sneaking Abraham was to bring her word when Cav was ready.*

Richard shrugged indifferently and turned toward the open door. "The sooner the better." Relief was obvious in his movements.

Fury shook her. "And"—she slammed the hairbrush on the dressing table—"I intend to take my slaves with me!"

"You will not!" Each word was like a pistol shot.

"I will!"

"Tina and Merzella—and Ezekiel—are free. You can do nothing—with murder on your hands, Louise."

The silence drew out between them. Her golden lashes lay in half-circles on pale cheeks. She did not look up at him when she spoke at last. The words were a half-whisper.

"Ezekiel has told you some lies—"

"Don't bother to deny it. And if anything happens to Ezekiel before you're gone from here, I'll see you hang higher than Haman, madam, woman though you may be."

Her lashes flew up and pale blue eyes glittered. "Get out! I never want to see you or—"

"You mean you won't take meals with us before you depart, Mrs. Daventry?" His smile was mocking.

"—you or your cold, haughty mother or that—that little slut—"

"I'm not averse to striking you again, Louise."

"I never want to see any of you again—"

"Then when you receive word from Cav, let me know. I'll have Ezekiel drive you and your baggage to him in the carriage. After which, Ezekiel will return here, where he is employed. I suggest you *ask,* and very politely too, for your baths and your meals while you're here. Tina and Merzella don't have to do your bidding any longer."

"Damn you, Richard Daventry!" she said huskily. "I think what you've done is illegal. I'm going to ask Cav about it. He knows I won't part with my slaves!"

"You've already parted with your slaves, Louise," he said indifferently. "And if you have nothing more than a harangue to offer, I'll ask you to excuse me."

"Go on! Go on and get out! You'll never be in my bedroom again, you—you—"

"Oh, but I will. As soon as you leave, I'll take back my bedroom with great pleasure."

"With Faith in your bed, I presume," she said with sudden spite. His jaw tightened. She laughed triumphantly. "Oh, I know the little rabbit has loved you since she first laid eyes on you—and bastard that she is, she won't demand marriage of you! You can have all the pleasures with none of the responsibilities."

"I'll never touch Faith until I can marry her, Louise. And marry her I will, as soon as I'm free of you."

"So it's gone that far, has it? What a fool you are, Richard, to marry a bastard!" She shrugged elaborately and drawled, "You two deserve each other."

"I think we do. We're both honorable people—something you can't understand. I pity Cav. And I bid you good evening." His voice was like iron and she watched him go out the door. He closed it with quiet finality.

Chapter 28

For Louise, the next two days crawled by. She kept to her room, packing and repacking her portmanteaus. And despite her inborn confidence, uneasiness touched her. She received no notes from Cav, but reassured herself that he was busy arranging their leave-taking for England. If he had gone so far as to sell his land and slaves to Richard, the move was bound to be imminent.

No, love, I wouldn't leave without you. She smiled. Cavenal loved her.

She had Ezekiel fetch the trunk Young Miguel had put in the storage barn and she filled it with the frothy lingerie and ruffled dresses she had taken from it a few short months ago when she arrived at the Daventry place. A little more than three months, she thought, with disbelief. It seemed longer —yet she had been so glad when she arrived, to be away from Charleston and all the gossip. In this godforsaken country, gossip didn't matter!

Oh, if only Cav would send Abraham with a note telling her to come! But after all, they had kept their love secret so long. He must break it to his mother and sister gently, tell them the divorce was pending, make them understand. That would be easy for they were fond of her. She *knew* they would welcome her!

Tina and Merzella waited on her as before, but she had been forced to be polite to them. Their allegiance was to Daventry now, and though they said nothing, Louise was keenly aware of their hidden contempt.

She could take no satisfaction in having stripped Tina of the shining glory of her hair, for the short, uneven ends had made a halo of curls around her dark, piquant face and she was undeniably beautiful.

By nightfall of the third day, when no message had come from Cavenal, Louise's impatience was unbearable. After four hours of fretting and picking at the delicious meal Merzella had brought to her room earlier, Louise determined to take action.

The house was quiet and dark and it was well after ten o'clock. Still she waited another hour to be sure everyone was sleeping before she slipped, barefooted, into the hall. She was going downstairs to the library for paper, quill, and ink. She would write Cavenal a loving and eager note, dwelling at length on how she felt a prisoner in Richard's house. She would dispatch Ezekiel with it the first thing in the morning.

She took the long stairs to the foyer without a candle. When she saw light spilling through the open door to Richard's office, she paused. She heard Richard's voice, a deep rumble, and a light voice that answered. It had to be Monty! What were they conniving now? She had to know!

She moved stealthily through the foyer and hid beside the door. A strong breeze poured through the door from the open windows in the small room.

"—and Pa, I *had* to come down and tell you. You can send Big Miguel to pick out horses. I won't see Mase Regrett anymore. You were right about him. But I want the horses!"

"All right. We'll send him tomorrow, Monty. Regrett's a

hard man and, in time, what you think is love will leave you, my dear."

"Oh, Pa! There's someone at the window! Why, it's Abraham!"

Abraham! Louise thought angrily. *He should be bringing me a note from Cav! What is he doing creeping to the office window so late at night?*

"Abraham! Why didn't you come to the door? You know you're welcome here," Richard said kindly.

"Mister Richard, I been slippin' off at night often as I can, to meet my Tina, an' tonight she tol' me you freed her an' her sister an' Zekiel—"

"Yes, I did. And I understand it's your wish to be married. You have my congratulations."

"Lordy, when Tina tol' me you was buyin' Mister Cav's place an' gonna free us all an' give us each twenty acres to farm— Well, I had to come clear my conscience."

"Clear your conscience?" Monty asked curiously.

"First, I got to explain Mister Cav done promised he'd buy Tina for me. He tol' me a lie when he say Miz Daventry would sell him Tina. An' more, he say he'd beat me half to death if I don't do the turrible thing he say to do."

"Abraham, it can't be as bad as you make it sound." Richard's voice was amused.

"It's worse. I got to get this burden off my back, Mister Richard. You're too good a man to carry th' Regretts' accusin' you of tryin' to burn them out."

"Man." Richard's voice was sharp. "Speak up!"

"Mister Cav done plan that fire an' him an' me done it. I ain't want ter do it, but I thought he'd kill me sure if I didn't. An' there was Tina—an' me wantin' her so bad."

There was a long silence and Louise, by the door, cursed the big black under her breath. This would surely mean trouble before they could leave for England. She drew her orchid peignoir close about her despite the warm August wind coursing through the house. She'd tell Cav about Abraham's disloyalty!

"I'll be goddamned," Richard said at last, his voice rough. "And goddamn George Cavenal—he's a man without honor. *And I held him in such high regard!*"

Abraham said softly, "I'm guilty too, Mister Richard. Reckon you ain't gonna look kindly on me marryin' Tina now."

"You were forced into it, Abraham—and I'm more than shocked at Cavenal's crime. I'm outraged. Burning fine horses! That's as black a crime as murder—it *is* murder!" A deep current of fury ran through his words. "And by God, I won't stand by and let him get away with it. Tell me, Abraham, did he wear his English boots that night?"

"He sure did. He got six pairs o' them an' he don't never ride without 'em."

"Pa," Monty interrupted excitedly, "Mase has got to know this! He wasn't as sure as Julien, but he halfway thought you set that fire. Oh, Pa, I'm going to ride over to his place first thing in the morning and tell him!"

"You can do that, Monty," he said. "Regrett should know the truth." Richard paused. Then he said, "And I'll ride to Cavenal's. I'll demand return of the papers I signed, buying the place, and my letter of credit unless he apologizes and makes restitution to Regrett."

"Mister Richard, Mister Cav gonna be gone in two days. His momma say you gonna handle shippin' they furniture back to 'em in England. All them English servants is leavin' with 'em, too."

"That's true, but I'll do none of it now unless he clears it with Regrett. And tomorrow, I'll face him down. He stood by and let me be blamed for that fire. By God, he'll make it right with Regrett or I'll call him out!"

"Pa! You wouldn't kill him!"

"Julien Regrett might be alive today but for Cavenal's act of revenge. Hell, yes, I'll kill him if he doesn't pay Regrett."

Louise, listening, went cold. Richard meant what he said. She knew it.

"You gonna forgive me, Mister Richard—an' let me an' Tina marry?"

"You're an unwilling and innocent accomplice, Abraham. Say nothing when you get back to Cavenal's tonight—nothing! I want to face him myself."

Monty said quickly, "And Pa, you and Mase can—"

Louise waited no longer. She fled through the dimly lit foyer and took the stairs silently. She would write in her room on the back of her last note from Cavenal, which was locked in her jewelry box. She must warn Cav of Richard's wrathful threat. Ezekiel could be persuaded to take it to him immediately, even if she had to give the black man one of her prized gold coins.

She penned her note swiftly with the stubby quill at the washstand. "My darling, meet me at our trysting place at nine in the morning. I have terrible news about Richard. He is planning to take drastic action against you regarding the sale of your property to him. I will explain all when I see you in the morning. Oh, my love, we must make our move together now! I love you, Louise."

In the moon-drenched compound she roused Ezekiel in his cabin. With one of her precious pieces of gold and the folded note in his hand, he went quietly to the stables and mounted the gelding Beau. He rode out toward Cavenal's slightly before one in the morning.

Louise crept back upstairs and lay wide-eyed in her bed until the first faint streaks of dawn showed lighter against the bedroom windows.

Monty, in her bed, did not know Louise was staring into the darkness, as sleepless as she. Excitement mounted as she twisted restlessly. Would Mase forgive her father when he knew Julien had accused him wrongly—that his younger brother's death was more misunderstanding, more acciden- tal than intentional? By the time light in her window slowly revealed the room, she was in a fever to leave. She rose and dressed at dawn.

Downstairs, Feenie and her mother had stirred up coals in the kitchen fireplace and Josey had biscuits rolled and cut to bake. The coffeepot hung over the glowing embers.

"You're up too early, Monty," Josey reproved. "Breakfast ain't for an hour."

"I know, Josey, but I couldn't sleep. If the coffee's hot I'll have a cup."

Josey poured it and Monty sat in one of the kitchen chairs sipping it. How could she wait another hour? Her father had said last night that LeRoy could ride escort for her this morning. She couldn't go out and make him accompany her before he'd eaten. Besides, Mase might be breakfasting if she arrived too early, and she wanted to see him alone. So she sat, in a turmoil, drinking coffee until breakfast.

It was eight o'clock when Monty and LeRoy trotted out on the road. Unknown to her, Louise had left for the game shed a little before her, and for the first time, the woman, for secrecy, rode unescorted.

The ride to the Regrett place had never seemed so inter- minable. But when they arrived, they found Mase at the corral, astride a gleaming, pale tan stallion the exact color of Coffee. Mase was riding him around in the corral and he was nervous, throwing his head up restlessly, not quite re- signed to the saddle and the man on his back.

Mase, in his concentration, was unaware of Monty lean- ing on the fence. She waited silently. LeRoy, on Johnsy, had gone into the last stable to visit with Andrew.

When Mase looked up at last, his black eyes were wary and unwelcoming.

"You're here to choose horses, I suppose?" The question was cold.

"Yes—and there's something I have to tell you."

He dismounted, throwing the reins over a fence post.

"He looks like Coffee," Monty said, anxious to tell him what she knew, but not wanting to blurt it out at once.

"His name's Cream—Coffee's colt."

"He's beautiful. Is he for sale?"

"All my horses, except Coffee, are for sale. But Cream's too hard for a woman to handle. You'd do well to look at the mares."

"I've seen the mares and I want to buy Cream. He looks like a good replacement for my Warlock."

"His mouth is just as hard, too. Why don't you stay in your own league, Monty, instead of bucking for a man's job?" Casually, he questioned, "Is this what you came to tell me?"

"No. I came to tell you George Cavenal and Abraham set fire to your place. Abraham came and confessed to Pa last night." There! She saw him grow pale as his mouth tightened.

"The hell you say!"

"Pa's going to see Cav today. He'll make him pay you for your barns and horses—and apologize, or Pa will call him out."

Mase's face was set in lines of bitterness. "Cavenal would choose hell over apologizing to me. Besides, that won't bring Julien back."

"No," Monty said, "but it explains why he was so ready to shoot Pa. He always did think my father was the one who burned your place." Monty was defensive. Mase wasn't reacting the way she had hoped. She had visualized him taking her in his arms and kissing her on learning her father was proven innocent.

"Monty, I'm glad to know this, but it changes nothing."

His face was expressionless as anguish and grief for his brother fought with the powerful desire to reach over the fence and lift her into his arms. "Your father hates me—for my promotion of statehood, for the speech I made in Washington. He won't accept me as a friend, let alone as a son-in-law." His mouth twisted as he added, "You'll forget about me, Monty. You're young and time's on your side."

Monty felt the breath go out of her. It made no difference to Mase. He would never yield. Tears gathered behind her eyes but she blinked them away.

"Then you can sell me Cream. Let me ride him—try him out."

He vaulted over the fence and pushed up his hat as he stood before her. His shirt was open and Monty had difficulty looking away.

"You think I'd let you get on that wild buck?" he drawled. "The fact that I can't have you doesn't matter, Monty—I love you just the same. No, you can't ride Cream."

Without a word she flung herself against him, burying her face where the strong column of his throat met his shoulders. He smelled of the fresh clean fragrance of August heat and that wonderful, indefinable flavor that was his own skin.

"I love you," she said, the words muffled against him. Her hat had fallen to the ground behind her.

His arms closed about her involuntarily. Then, with one hand, he tipped her face upward. Tears clung to her lashes and her cheeks were wet.

"Did Richard Daventry say he'd let you marry me—that he'd accept me?"

"No," she blurted out, tears welling anew. "But I don't care. I'll run away with you. I'll never see—P-Pa again, if that's what you want!"

He stroked her hair gently. "I can't do that to you, Monty. I love you too much." His voice rumbled under her ear.

"After a while, you'd hate me for estranging you from your family—from Abby, from Richard." He sighed and pulled her arms from around his shoulders.

"Then you don't really love me after all!" she cried stormily.

He spread his hands before her. "I love you too much to ruin your life."

"That's a lie!" She turned to Dolly and fumbled for the reins. She swung herself up on the young mare. Driving her heels into the animal's sides furiously, she caused the startled Dolly to spring to life.

Mase might *say* he loved her, but all she could think of was the fact she had offered herself freely and been rejected. She bent low over Dolly's neck, urging her to a faster gallop as they approached the fence of crossed pine saplings. The little mare barely cleared the top of it, but Monty did not see the danger for the blur of tears. She couldn't go home and face Abby and Pa like this, she thought, refusing to look back or think ahead.

Reaching the woods around the lake, she did not slow despite the foam that flew back from Dolly's bit to strike her hands. She veered the mare toward Cavenal's at a driving gallop. She'd go to the Guadalupe, where the willows grew thickest and pine scrub was plentiful. No one would see her there and Dolly could rest when they reached Cavenal's old game shed. She'd let the mare have a long, cool drink at the river, and by then, the tears that racked her now would be dry. She'd think of something to tell Pa and Abby. But she'd never go back to Mase's again. *Never!*

The mare slowed at last and Monty let her slip to a trot. She was not on the road, but in the woods that Monty knew so well. She had been there many times and felt at home among the old trees. True, Big Miguel or LeRoy had always been with her then— Guilt struck her suddenly. She had come off without LeRoy! And she'd be hard to track in these woods.

She looked around carefully. There hadn't been Indians in these parts for months and as for Mexican soldiers— Where had Tom Arterbury said American troops were now based? Somewhere on the lower Rio Grande River—a long way from here, she assured herself. And Mexican soldiers would certainly be near them, not roaming these parts.

So she slowed Dolly to a quick walk and rubbed her hands across her wet face, first one and then the other. *I must look like a wild woman,* she thought. Thank God, there was no one to see her.

Dimly she heard the sound of water moving through brush and over stones. The Guadalupe. They weren't far from the game shed now. She looked up at the sky through the treetops—the sun was climbing with the promise of a searing August day. She and LeRoy and Big Miguel had taken shelter in the game shed twice during storms. And she had once gone there with LeRoy, who'd shot a brace of pheasants and wanted to clean them before going home.

Well, they'd use it again for it would belong to them, she thought—unless her father and Cavenal killed each other. She put the thought away from her determinedly. She tried, but could not imagine the immaculate, swaggering Cavenal paying Mase any money for the property he and poor Abraham had burned. She thought of the cruel death of Slyboots and shivered. She had never suspected how utterly cold and merciless Cav was!

Turning the horse toward the river, they entered thick scrub, then met a gentle slope to the water. Looking back she saw the nearby game shed. She froze as voices came to her through the open door.

And there were two—no *three* horses there! One was tethered at some distance from the other two, and slightly to the rear. Was that *Georgina* peeping between two logs at the south end of the game shed? It was! Monty's gaze darted back to the open door. She could see Louise and Cav—worse, she could hear them, too. She was interrupting a tryst—but what was Gina doing? Her pale green riding skirt was flung up over one arm and her face was white and tense. *She was watching them! So that was what was wrong with Georgina!* She lived through her brother!

Cav was kissing Louise expertly now, and his hands slipped down along her back to cup her small buttocks through thin folds of her sky-blue summer riding habit. She had put her reticule on the old bloodstained table where game was cleaned.

"Cav, darling, I thought you'd never get here! I've been waiting an hour!"

"I came as soon as I could get away. Now what's all this about Richard, my love?" His eyes ran over Louise's face and settled on her provocative bosom.

"Oh, my darling"—Louise's bell-like voice reflected her distress—"Richard's coming to see you today—perhaps right now—to demand his letter of credit and the bill of sale back, unless you apologize and repay Mason Regrett for burning his stables and setting fire to his house."

"The devil you say! Who told him?"

"I had no chance to prevent it," she said defensively. "That sneaking Abraham confessed the whole thing to him and Montrose last night. I overheard it all from where I—I was hiding in the foyer."

Cavenal reddened and swore lustily. "And how does he propose to force me to apologize or repay?" he queried.

"He said if you refused, he'd call you out! Oh, my love, I'm so afraid for you! Richard is a dangerous man—"

Monty looked around her desperately. If only she could ride away! She was hidden from view by the thick scrub but she dared not move or she would reveal her presence. Dolly had finished drinking noisily, but those at the game shed were too intensely involved to have noticed the sound. Louise had thrown her arms about Cavenal's neck once more.

He pulled them gently away and his hands went to adjust the white silk scarf tucked at the open neck of his shirt.

"Well, now—we can't have Richard rushing over here with gun in hand, can we?" His voice was easy, almost amused.

"No—we can't," Louise responded.

"We'll just have to move up our departure date. Instead of tomorrow morning, we'll leave now—before he comes. After all, Richard has signed both the letter of credit and bill of sale."

"Leave now?" Louise asked eagerly.

"Now. You will excuse me, my dear. I must hurry."

"Hurry?" She was bewildered. "Hurry where?"

"To the house. My lady mother and sister must be told."

"Oh, yes!" she cried, relieved. "Let's hurry! You've told them I'm coming with you, of course?"

"No, Louise, I haven't told them"—his voice grew soft, but it came distinctly to Monty—"because you are not joining us."

Louise appeared stunned. She was silent a moment, staring up at him. "But you said—you *said* you wouldn't leave without me! You said we'd be together forever—and that means marriage!"

"My dear." His voice lifted slightly with anger and his words were cold and brutal. "You yourself have said many things in the heat of lovemaking—and you know you never meant a word of them."

"But we love each other!" Louise cried. "You said you'd marry me when my divorce came through!"

"Think back," he replied coldly, "I never once mentioned marriage."

"But you *said* you wouldn't go without me," she repeated,

moving blindly to the stained table and putting out a hand to support herself.

His smile was whimsical as he shook his head.

"Then you mean it was a lie? That it's *all* been lies with you?"

"Not all, Louise." Impatience edged his words. "I enjoyed a great deal of it. In fact, up to this moment, it was a pleasurable romp."

"A pleasurable romp!" she shouted, her hand clenching spasmodically on the table.

Monty looked at Georgina where she stood like a statue at the log wall. Monty's eyes went despairingly to Dolly, who stood nibbling at the grassy edges back from the water. If she just dared to get on the mare and ride away—but she was certain they'd hear her. She wouldn't put it past Cavenal to ride her down!

"I really must leave you now, love," Cavenal was saying politely, "if I'm to get my lady mother and Gina to leave for Galveston within the hour. Not to mention our English servants."

"Leave for Galveston," Louise parroted. "But Richard—"

"Louise, you surely don't think I'd pay Mason Regrett for damages to his property after the insults he paid us in Washington? He richly deserved to be burned out and more." His aristocratic nostrils flared as he added, *"I will never apologize to that blackguard!"*

Louise backed away, reticule in hand now, as she looked at him silently. Despite his cold eyes and set face, she said piteously, "But I love you, Cav—and you love me—"

"Love you?" His eyes grew more remote and his mouth thinned. "My God, Louise—everything I've done with you, I've done with other women and enjoyed it more," he added cruelly. "Sophie or Nonnie, for that matter, are better lovers than you—or anything in between at Rebecca's in Victoria."

Louise recoiled from him and her shock echoed in Monty's silent gasp.

Monty shrank against the shrubs, wishing there were some escape, but she knew if she left now and Louise saw her—or worse, if Gina saw her— Dear God, Louise had caught up her reticule and the little derringer was in her hand!

But Cavenal was laughing. The day was growing warmer now and already the cicadas had begun their steady burring song, intensifying the heat. His deep musical voice traveled clearly.

"My dear Louise, you're a woman of much experience." His growing laughter was genuine. "Why the gun? You can't force me to take you—"

The report of the gun seemed incredibly loud and even the cicadas fell silent for an instant. Monty saw the red stain spread on Cavenal's left breast before he slowly crumpled. She smothered a scream as the gun fell from Louise's nerveless fingers. The woman stood, seemingly rooted to the spot.

Georgina did not smother her scream as she ran from the south side of the shed to the open door. It cut the summer stillness with sharp anguish. Pale hair had loosened about the white face and her large eyes were distended.

"You've killed him! My brother!" High and sharp, her voice was a keening on the hot wind. "He was the only one who understood me! I loved watching him with you—with Sophie—with Nonnie. We used to laugh about all of you when we talked!"

Involuntarily, Monty took a step forward and Louise backed away from the distraught girl. But Georgina did not halt her headlong rush. She looked down at her brother in passing as she lunged at the wall where the game shed knives hung.

Monty divined her intent and, without pausing, began running toward the shed. Though she was but seconds crossing the short distance between shrub and shed, Georgina still had time to drive the long sharp blade into Louise's frilly pink blouse twice.

Then Monty was on her, shouting, "No! No, Gina—" Even with Monty hanging on her uplifted arm, Georgina was still possessed of superhuman strength. She managed to drive the knife a third time before she fell on her knees beside her brother.

"George, George! You can't be dead!"

Monty looked down at the carnage about her with disbelief. Louise lay on the hard-packed dirt floor. Surprise was still on her pretty face, but the wide pale blue eyes stared vacantly. The front of her riding waist was living color and the haft of the skinning knife protruded between her breasts.

Georgina was cradling Cavenal's head against her bosom, sobbing. She rocked back and forth in a paroxysm of grief. Monty saw that blood from his breast was smearing the front of Gina's pale green riding habit. As with Louise, his gold eyes were wide and he wore a look of surprise.

"Monty! Monty—" The powerful male voice penetrated Monty's numbing shock and disbelief.

Chapter 29

*"**M**onty, where are you?"* Mase called again.

Turning, Monty saw that Dolly, untethered, had followed her to the game shed. Now she and the other horses whickered a welcome to Coffee and his rider.

Every remnant of her heartbroken rage at Mase was washed away in Monty's rush of relief. She ran to the door and called, "Mase—here at the game shed!" She had never been so glad to see anyone in her life as he rode up the short distance from the river.

"Damn it, Monty," he swore, trotting forward. "You know I had to get Coffee saddled—and by that time I didn't know which way you went. LeRoy and I have been tracking you for two miles." He was scowling furiously. "You know better than to ride off in these woods alone!" Behind him, emerging from the thick oaks, was a worried LeRoy on Johnsy.

"Mase! I'm so glad you're here—" Her voice trembled and broke. "I—I—something terrible has happened—"

At the horror in her eyes, his face tightened and he dismounted swiftly. She half turned in the door, hands outstretched.

Reaching her, he took in the scene at a glance. "Jesus! How did it happen, Monty?"

Monty swallowed hard and recounted what took place from the moment she became an unwilling witness to her final effort to stay Georgina's hand. The girl still sat on the floor, cradling her dead brother in her arms, crying softly. She was oblivious of those around her.

LeRoy had ridden up at a gallop and now he too dismounted and looked in the door.

"Lord God! Mister Mase—are they dead?"

"Yes," Mase said, briefly recapping what Monty had told him. "Monty says her father's probably at Cavenal's now, waiting to accuse him of trying to burn us out. We'll go there—we've got to get Georgina home—and tell Daventry and Lady Marguerite what happened. Meantime, LeRoy, you go back and bring a wagon to take Mrs. Daventry home— I'll tell Daventry and he'll meet you here."

As LeRoy put Johnsy into a hard gallop and thundered away, Monty asked, "What can—how can we tell poor Lady Marguerite?" She looked down at Georgina, who was still rocking her brother back and forth.

"She'll have to be told. Maybe Georgina—" He leaned over Georgina and spoke gently. "Gina, come. Let Monty and me take you home."

"I can't leave my brother." She looked up at him, eyes wide. "I can't leave my loved one."

"We'll send a wagon for him when we get you home," Mase told her quietly, taking her arm. She pulled away from him fiercely.

"Can't you see he's hurt? That stupid woman shot him— I saw it! You and Monty go fetch my mama. She'll know how to stop all this—" She looked down at her brother, then at her reddened waist with disbelief. "She'll know how to stop all this blood."

"George must stay here, Gina—"

"He cannot!" she retorted angrily. "Can't you see he's hurt?"

"He's more than hurt, Gina," Mase said softly, taking her arm again. She jerked it from his hand, still clinging to Cavenal's shoulders and head resting in her lap.

"You go fetch my mama. I won't leave George." She looked up at Mase, her pupils so widely dilated and black, the milky white that surrounded them was eerily pronounced.

Mase pushed back his hat and said, "We've got more than one problem here, Monty."

Monty bent her knees until her face was level with Gina's. Her voice was filled with compassion. "Gina, dear, Cav's dead. Lady Marguerite must be told what happened. Don't you think—as her daughter—you should be the one to tell her?"

Slowly Gina's hands unclasped his head and shoulders. She looked across into Monty's eyes. "I avenged him, didn't I, Monty?" She peered at Louise, whose eyes had glazed over. Blood was congealing on her breast around the haft of the long, slender skinning knife.

"Yes, Gina, you've evened the score with Louise. But your mother must be told of his death. Mase and I can't do that by ourselves."

"You'll have to," Gina said with naked honesty. "I can't."

"But you will come with us, won't you?" Monty pleaded. "We'll send Abraham with a wagon to bring Cav home. I promise."

Gina sighed deeply. Then, with tender hands, she moved Cavenal's head and shoulders to the smooth-packed floor and rose. As she did so, it could be seen that her brother's blood had stained her skirt as well.

"All right. Mama will want to leave this terrible country right away," she said reluctantly. "She won't wait the two days George had planned."

"I expect she won't," Mase responded, taking her elbow. As he helped her to her feet, Monty took her other arm.

When they arrived at the Cavenal place, bringing Cavenal's horse with them, they dismounted in the rear. Sophie's husband, Ephraim, took their mounts. His eyes went to Gina's bloodstained riding habit and grew wide.

"You fall an' hurt yourself, Miss Gina?"

"No—my brother's been shot."

Ephraim's jaw fell. "He—he all right, Miss Gina?"

"He's dead."

"Law me," he muttered. As the three went toward the rear entrance, he called out, "Miss Monty, your pa is here— he been awful anxious to see Mister Cav." He turned then, and ran toward the back fields where other workers could be seen.

Lady Marguerite and Richard Daventry were together in the parlor as the three entered the room. The smoothly coiffed Lady Marguerite blanched and half rose from her chair as her eyes fell on her bloodstained, disheveled daughter. Richard Daventry jumped to his feet.

"Daughter—what has happened to you?" Lady Marguerite asked, her slim hand at her throat as she fought for composure.

Gina looked at her and shook her head helplessly.

"Monty—" Daventry began, then fell silent as Mase spoke.

"Lady Marguerite, Daventry—we bring bad news." He began recounting the events by the Guadalupe River that had brought them to this moment. He concluded, "Monty tried to restrain Gina, but her grief was so great—nothing could have stayed her hand. I think she was trying to protect her brother."

He made no mention of Gina's shocking revelation about her brother's philandering and Monty sent him a grateful glance. There was no need to burden Lady Marguerite with that. She was certain that only Cav's death could have elicited that confession from Georgina. Now that the girl had recovered a semblance of sanity, Monty felt it likely that she would never refer to it again.

Lady Marguerite's face was white, but she was hardly more shocked than Richard Daventry. He took out his handkerchief and wiped his face.

"You're sure they—they both are dead?" he asked.

"Positive, Daventry," Mase replied.

"Richard." Lady Marguerite rose, her face rigidly controlled. "I know you were agitated when you arrived this morning. I've thought all along—I'm sure you came to see my son about this liaison with your wife, though you tried to spare me by waiting to face him alone. Now you cannot face him with it. I can only tell you that George could never resist a pretty face, God bless and rest him—but in his defense, I am compelled to tell you Louise pursued him relentlessly."

"I'm sure of that, Marguerite. And my business with him —under the circumstances—is certainly finished."

Monty looked at her father swiftly, loving and admiring him silently for his restraint. He was not going to tell this kindly woman of her son's greater dishonor. He was not going to tell her that Cav had been guilty of burning helpless horses, of destroying another man's property. If Cav had killed the two brothers in the fire, he would have rejoiced, Monty thought bitterly. And how pleased he must have been when her father was blamed!

Lady Marguerite had twice been protected from ugly truths by the two men Monty loved best. Yet those two were at sword point with each other. Her heart ached afresh with that knowledge, as Lady Marguerite lifted a pale face to them.

"I must send Abraham with a wagon to . . ."—she

paused and drew a deep breath—"to bring my son to me here. And they must construct a heavy, tight coffin, for I intend to take him with me to England and bury him there."

"Let me tell Abraham for you, Marguerite," Richard said swiftly. "When I leave here I must go to the game shed, since Regrett has sent LeRoy for a wagon to fetch Louise's body home."

"You are kind, Richard. Very kind to buy this property and all on it. I will arrange to leave tomorrow instead of waiting further, if you will tie up any loose ends for me?"

"I'll be glad to, Marguerite."

She bowed to them slightly. "I'm sure you will forgive me in view of my daughter's needs—and I must prepare to receive . . . my beloved son's body and come to terms with my loss."

Jarrett approached, his face heavily lined with sorrow, and she turned to him, her inborn refinement with her to the last.

"Jarrett, you can attend to our guests. A brandy, perhaps, before you leave on your sad chore, Richard? You, Monty— Mr. Regrett?" Her face was white and strained but her composure was unshaken.

Daventry shook his head. Monty and Mase murmured their refusal.

"Then, Jarrett," Lady Marguerite finished, squaring her straight shoulders, "you can see them safely on their way— after Richard has talked to Abraham and Ephraim." Her arm tightened around her dazed, slender daughter. "After that, Jarrett, you can see that Nonnie, Mavis, and Emma— all of us—are ready to leave by six in the morning."

When Monty went out with her father and Mase, they were met by a throng of workers from the fields, including Abraham and Ephraim. Word had quickly spread that Cavenal was dead. It took some time to answer their questions.

It was noon and the sun beat down hotly as Richard, Monty, and Mase mounted their horses and took the road that led to the Regrett and Daventry places. They soon passed the wagon Abraham drove with his companions in back to collect Cav's body. They had not yet come to the narrow turnoff that led to the Guadalupe, when Monty broke the long silence.

"I guess now Cav can never repay Mase—"

"I am responsible for that now," Richard cut in. "His death leaves me to make restitution."

"You owe me nothing, Daventry," Mase said stiffly.

"I owe you a great deal." When Richard said these words, Monty turned and looked at him with astonishment. She had never heard her father come near to making an apology to another man.

"Nothing that can be repaid," Mase said coolly.

"On the contrary. Even after I free Cav's slaves and give each of them twenty acres and livestock, there will be a great deal of land left. I propose to repay you with two thousand acres of Cavenal's land that abuts yours."

"You're wrong. I can't let you do that," Mase said flatly.

"I've been wrong about too damned many things," Daventry said bitterly. "I was wrong about annexation— Tom Arterbury made me aware of that when he told us of the terms under which Texas becomes a state. I was wrong to marry Louise. Only God knows how wrong I was to believe Cavenal an honorable friend." His eyes on Mase were piercing as he added, "Don't make me wrong again, Regrett—by not accepting land for the horses and buildings Cavenal destroyed."

There was a long silence. Monty's eyes searched her father's mobile face. It was a study in sorrow.

"When you put it like that," Mase said at last, "I'd be a scoundrel to refuse."

"I've thought you that for too long." Richard laughed dryly. "I must turn off here, Regrett, to meet the others at the game shed. I'll leave you to see my daughter home safely." He leaned with the reins and Nate turned onto the long narrow trail leading to the Guadalupe.

Abraham and his companions could be seen far behind them as Mase and Monty continued down the main road without speaking. Trees were thicker here and a slight breeze had sprung up. Monty, who had left her hat in her furious departure from Regrett's corral earlier, shook her heavy hair to let the breeze through it.

She wanted to look at Mase, but could not bring herself to do so, and the silence between them dragged out. Only the ever-present cicadas poured out their serenade to the heat of the day. Even the birds were quiet, and looking ahead, Monty could see the hazy summer day shimmering on the winding road.

They rode for nearly a mile without words. Her father hadn't apologized, but he had admitted he had been wrong about everything—including the most important, *Mason Regrett.* Monty felt she could no longer bear it. Suddenly she whirled to face him, only to find he had faced her simultaneously.

"Monty, I—"

"Mase, I—"

And their laughter rang over the country stillness, over the cicadas' steady burr. The joyous sound startled a covey of quail in the tall grass of a meadow beside them and the birds rushed upward in the somnolent summer air.

She looked into his black, gleaming eyes, drinking in the sight of the beloved face as he pushed Coffee up to Dolly, so close his long leg pressed hers. Leaning over, he plucked her from her saddle easily.

Holding her, he began to kiss her eager mouth.

She clung to him and the hot afternoon sun splashed them between the dusty-leaved trees, while the two horses walked slowly, side by side, until finally, Coffee came to a halt.

Dolly stopped, turned her head and looked at him curiously. But the two on his back were oblivious to everything except themselves and their future, which stretched out like the land about them—rich, beautiful, and theirs to build on together.

Epilogue

Monty and Mase Regrett were married in November, a month before Richard Daventry wed Faith Warren. And on the following February 19, 1846, all of them, including a smiling Abby, attended the ceremony of the transfer of the Republic of Texas' sovereignty to the United States.

Anson Jones, of the tormented eyes, presided over the occasion and made an impassioned speech, closing with the words, "The final act in this great drama is now performed. The Republic of Texas is no more."

In the silence that followed his words, the President of Texas lowered the flag of the republic. As it came down, the pole from which the flag flew broke in two. For a moment, before the banner of the Union was raised, the Lone Star flag shrouded the retiring President with curious prophecy.

True to their threat, Mexico went to war with the United States. It began a little more than two months later, on April 25, 1846. Mason Regrett and Richard Daventry, as well as their neighbors, the Arterburys and Bedfords, fought courageously in their newly acquired allegience to the United States. They returned home shortly after the peace treaty was signed in May of 1847.

Thirteen years after annexation, embittered by his failure

to convert Texas to the belief that he was annexation's un-recognized hero, and after two unsuccessful bids for the U.S. Senate, Anson Jones went to his room in the Old Capitol Hotel in Houston, took up his gun and put a bullet through his head. The sensitive brooding man wore the shroud of the Lone Star flag one last time.

But that flag still blows in the strong gulf-driven winds over Daventry and Regrett acres in south-central Texas.